PRAISE FOR THE *New York Times* AND *USA Today* BESTSELLING
THRONE OF GLASS SERIES

THE ASSASSIN'S BLADE

"Fans will delight in this gorgeous edition. . . . Action-packed and full of
insight into Celaena's character. . . . What a ride!" —*Booklist*

THRONE OF GLASS

A *Kirkus Reviews* Best Teen Book

A YALSA-ALA Best Fiction for Young Adults Book

★ "A thrilling read." —*Publishers Weekly*, starred review

"A must-read for lovers of epic fantasy and
fairy tales." —*USA Today*

"Fans of Tamora Pierce and George R.R. Martin,
pick up this book!" —*RT Book Reviews*, Top Pick

CROWN OF MIDNIGHT

★ "An epic fantasy readers will immerse themselves in
and never want to leave." —*Kirkus Reviews*, starred review

"A thrill ride of epic fantasy proportions." —*USA Today*

HEIR OF FIRE

"Celaena is as much an epic hero as Frodo or Jon Snow!"
—*New York Times* bestselling author Tamora Pierce

"Readers will devour Maas's latest entry. . . .
A must-purchase." —*SLJ*

CROWN
OF
MIDNIGHT

Books by Sarah J. Maas

The Throne of Glass series

The Assassin's Blade
Throne of Glass
Crown of Midnight
Heir of Fire
Queen of Shadows
Empire of Storms
Tower of Dawn
Kingdom of Ash

•

The Throne of Glass Coloring Book

A Court of Thorns and Roses series

A Court of Thorns and Roses
A Court of Mist and Fury
A Court of Wings and Ruin
A Court of Frost and Starlight

•

A Court of Thorns and Roses Coloring Book

CROWN OF MIDNIGHT

OF

MIDNIGHT

— A *Throne of Glass* NOVEL —

SARAH J. MAAS

BLOOMSBURY

NEW YORK LONDON OXFORD NEW DELHI SYDNEY

First published in the United States of America in August 2013
by Bloomsbury YA
Paperback edition published in September 2014
www.bloomsbury.com

Bloomsbury is a registered trademark of Bloomsbury Publishing Plc

For information about permission to reproduce selections from this book, write to
Permissions, Bloomsbury YA, 1385 Broadway, New York, New York 10018
Bloomsbury books may be purchased for business or promotional use. For information on bulk
purchases please contact Macmillan Corporate and Premium Sales Department at
specialmarkets@macmillan.com

The Library of Congress has cataloged the hardcover edition as follows:
Crown of midnight / by Sarah J. Maas.
pages   cm
Sequel to: Throne of glass.
Summary: As the royal assassin to an evil king, eighteen-year-old Celaena Sardothien
must decide what she will fight for: survival, love, or the future of a kingdom.
ISBN 978-1-61963-062-8 (hardcover) • ISBN 978-1-61963-063-5 (e-book)
[1. Fantasy. 2. Assassins—Fiction. 3. Kings, queens, rulers, etc.—Fiction.
4. Courts and courtiers—Fiction. 5. Love—Fiction.] I. Title.
PZ7.M111575Cr 2013   [Fic]—dc23   2013009063

ISBN 978-1-61963-064-2 (paperback)

Book design by Regina Flath
Typeset by Westchester Book Composition
Printed and bound in Great Britain by CPI Group (UK) Ltd, Croydon CRO 4YY
27 29 30 28

To be kept up-to-date about our authors and books, please visit www.bloomsbury.com/newsletters
and sign up for our newsletters, including news about Sarah J. Maas.

For Susan—
best friends until we're nothing but dust.
(And then some.)

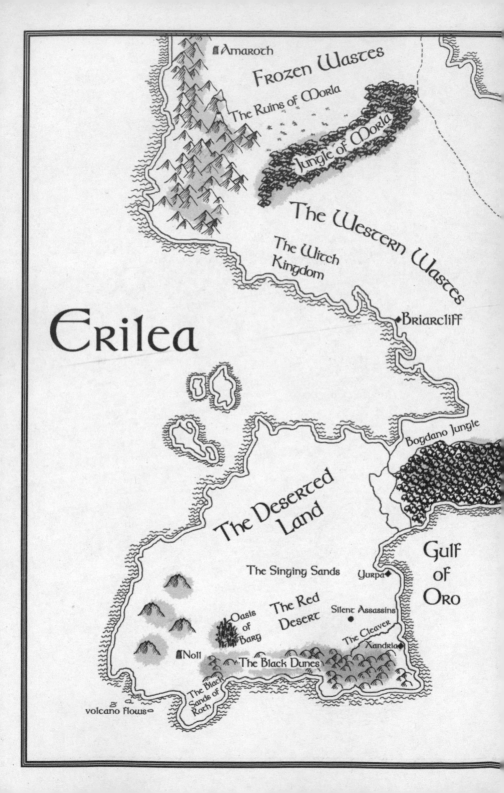

PART ONE

The King's Champion

CHAPTER 1

The shutters swinging in the storm winds were the only sign of her entry. No one had noticed her scaling the garden wall of the darkened manor house, and with the thunder and the gusting wind off the nearby sea, no one heard her as she shimmied up the drainpipe, swung onto the windowsill, and slithered into the second-floor hallway.

The King's Champion pressed herself into an alcove at the thud of approaching steps. Concealed beneath a black mask and hood, she willed herself to melt into the shadows, to become nothing more than a slip of darkness. A servant girl trudged past to the open window, grumbling as she latched it shut. Seconds later, she disappeared down the stairwell at the other end of the hall. The girl hadn't noticed the wet footprints on the floorboards.

Lightning flashed, illuminating the hallway. The assassin took a long breath, going over the plans she'd painstakingly memorized in the three days she'd been watching the manor house on the outskirts of

Bellhaven. Five doors on each side. Lord Nirall's bedroom was the third on the left.

She listened for the approach of any other servants, but the house remained hushed as the storm raged around them.

Silent and smooth as a wraith, she moved down the hall. Lord Nirall's bedroom door swung open with a slight groan. She waited until the next rumble of thunder before easing the door shut behind her.

Another flash of lightning illuminated two figures sleeping in the four-poster bed. Lord Nirall was no older than thirty-five, and his wife, dark haired and beautiful, slept soundly in his arms. What had they done to offend the king so gravely that he wanted them dead?

She crept to the edge of the bed. It wasn't her place to ask questions. Her job was to obey. Her freedom depended on it. With each step toward Lord Nirall, she ran through the plan again.

Her sword slid out of its sheath with barely a whine. She took a shuddering breath, bracing herself for what would come next.

Lord Nirall's eyes flew open just as the King's Champion raised her sword over his head.

CHAPTER 2

Celaena Sardothien stalked down the halls of the glass castle of Rifthold. The heavy sack clenched in her hand swung with each step, banging every so often into her knees. Despite the hooded black cloak that concealed much of her face, the guards didn't stop her as she strode toward the King of Adarlan's council chamber. They knew very well who she was—and what she did for the king. As the King's Champion, she outranked them. Actually, there were few in the castle she didn't outrank now. And fewer still who didn't fear her.

She approached the open glass doors, her cloak sweeping behind her. The guards posted on either side straightened as she gave them a nod before entering the council chamber. Her black boots were nearly silent against the red marble floor.

On the glass throne in the center of the room sat the King of Adarlan, his dark gaze locked on the sack dangling from her fingers. Just as she had the last three times, Celaena dropped to one knee before his throne and bowed her head.

Dorian Havilliard stood beside his father's throne—and she could feel his sapphire eyes fixed on her. At the foot of the dais, always between her and the royal family, stood Chaol Westfall, Captain of the Guard. She looked up at him from the shadows of her hood, taking in the lines of his face. For all the expression he showed, she might as well have been a stranger. But that was expected, and it was just part of the game they'd become so skilled at playing these past few months. Chaol might be her friend, might be someone she'd somehow come to trust, but he was still captain—still responsible for the royal lives in this room above all others. The king spoke.

"Rise."

Celaena kept her chin high as she stood and pulled off her hood.

The king waved a hand at her, the obsidian ring on his finger gleaming in the afternoon light. "Is it done?"

Celaena reached a gloved hand into the sack and tossed the severed head toward him. No one spoke as it bounced, a vulgar thudding of stiff and rotting flesh on marble. It rolled to a stop at the foot of the dais, milky eyes turned toward the ornate glass chandelier overhead.

Dorian straightened, glancing away from the head. Chaol just stared at her.

"He put up a fight," Celaena said.

The king leaned forward, examining the mauled face and the jagged cuts in the neck. "I can barely recognize him."

Celaena gave him a crooked smile, though her throat tightened. "I'm afraid severed heads don't travel well." She fished in her sack again, pulling out a hand. "Here's his seal ring." She tried not to focus too much on the decaying flesh she held, the reek that had worsened with each passing day. She extended the hand to Chaol, whose bronze eyes were distant as he took it from her and offered it to the king. The king's lip curled, but he pried the ring off the stiff finger. He tossed the hand at her feet as he examined the ring.

Beside his father, Dorian shifted. When she'd been dueling in the competition, he hadn't seemed to mind her history. What did he *expect* would happen when she became the King's Champion? Though she supposed severed limbs and heads would turn the stomachs of most people—even after living for a decade under Adarlan's rule. And Dorian, who had never seen battle, never witnessed the chained lines shuffling their way to the butchering blocks . . . Perhaps she should be impressed he hadn't vomited yet.

"What of his wife?" the king demanded, turning the ring over in his fingers again and again.

"Chained to what's left of her husband at the bottom of the sea," Celaena replied with a wicked grin, and removed the slender, pale hand from her sack. It bore a golden wedding band, engraved with the date of the marriage. She offered it to the king, but he shook his head. She didn't dare look at Dorian or Chaol as she put the woman's hand back in the thick canvas sack.

"Very well, then," the king murmured. She remained still as his eyes roved over her, the sack, the head. After a too-long moment, he spoke again. "There is a growing rebel movement here in Rifthold, a group of individuals who are willing to do anything to get me off the throne—and who are attempting to interfere with my plans. Your next assignment is to root out and dispatch them all before they become a true threat to my empire."

Celaena clenched the sack so tightly her fingers ached. Chaol and Dorian were staring at the king now, as if this were the first they were hearing of this, too.

She'd heard whispers of rebel forces before she'd gone to Endovier—she'd *met* fallen rebels in the salt mines. But to have an actual movement growing in the heart of the capital; to have *her* be the one to dispatch them one by one . . . And plans—what plans? What did the rebels know of the king's maneuverings? She shoved the questions down, down, down, until there was no possibility of his reading them on her face.

The king drummed his fingers on the arm of the throne, still playing with Nirall's ring in his other hand. "There are several people on my list of suspected traitors, but I will only give you one name at a time. This castle is crawling with spies."

Chaol stiffened at that, but the king waved his hand and the captain approached her, his face still blank as he extended a piece of paper to Celaena.

She avoided the urge to stare at Chaol's face as he gave her the letter, though his gloved fingers grazed hers before he let go. Keeping her features neutral, she looked at the paper. On it was a single name: *Archer Finn*.

It took every ounce of will and sense of self-preservation to keep her shock from showing. She knew Archer—had known him since she was thirteen and he'd come for lessons at the Assassins' Keep. He'd been several years older, already a highly sought-after courtesan . . . who was in need of some training on how to protect himself from his rather jealous clients. And their husbands.

He'd never minded her ridiculous girlhood crush on him. In fact, he'd let her test out flirting with him, and had usually turned her into a complete giggling mess. Of course, she hadn't seen him for several years—since before she went to Endovier—but she'd never thought him capable of something like this. He'd been handsome and kind and jovial, not a traitor to the crown so dangerous that the king would want him dead.

It was absurd. Whoever was giving the king his information was a damned idiot.

"Just him, or all his clients, too?" Celaena blurted.

The king gave her a slow smile. "You know Archer? I'm not surprised." A taunt—a challenge.

She just stared ahead, willing herself to calm, to breathe. "I used to.

He's an extraordinarily well-guarded man. I'll need time to get past his defenses." So carefully said, so casually phrased. What she really needed time for was to figure out how Archer had gotten tangled up in this mess—and whether the king was telling the truth. If Archer truly were a traitor and a rebel . . . well, she'd figure that out later.

"Then you have one month," the king said. "And if he's not buried by then, perhaps I shall reconsider your position, girl."

She nodded, submissive, yielding, gracious. "Thank you, Your Majesty."

"When you have dispatched Archer, I will give you the next name on the list."

She had avoided the politics of the kingdoms—especially their rebel forces—for so many years, and now she was in the thick of it. Wonderful.

"Be quick," the king warned. "Be discreet. Your payment for Nirall is already in your chambers."

Celaena nodded again and shoved the piece of paper into her pocket.

The king was staring at her. Celaena looked away but forced a corner of her mouth to twitch upward, to make her eyes glitter with the thrill of the hunt. At last, the king lifted his gaze to the ceiling. "Take that head and be gone." He pocketed Nirall's seal ring, and Celaena swallowed her twinge of disgust. A trophy.

She scooped up the head by its dark hair and grabbed the severed hand, stuffing them into the sack. With only a glance at Dorian, whose face had gone pale, she turned on her heel and left.

⁓

Dorian Havilliard stood in silence as the servants rearranged the chamber, dragging the giant oak table and ornate chairs into the center of the room. They had a council meeting in three minutes. He hardly heard as Chaol took his leave, saying he'd like to debrief Celaena further. His father grunted his approval.

Celaena had killed a man and his wife. And his father had ordered it. Dorian had barely been able to look at either of them. He thought he'd been able to convince his father to reevaluate his brutal policies after the massacre of those rebels in Eyllwe before Yulemas, but it seemed like it hadn't made any difference. And Celaena . . .

As soon as the servants finished arranging the table, Dorian slid into his usual seat at his father's right. The councilmen began trickling in, along with Duke Perrington, who went straight to the king and began murmuring to him, too soft for Dorian to hear.

Dorian didn't bother saying anything to anyone and just stared at the glass pitcher of water before him. Celaena hadn't seemed like herself just now.

Actually, for the two months since she'd been named the King's Champion, she'd been like this. Her lovely dresses and ornate clothes were gone, replaced by an unforgiving, close-cut black tunic and pants, her hair pulled back in a long braid that fell into the folds of that dark cloak she was always wearing. She was a beautiful wraith—and when she looked at him, it was like she didn't even know who he was.

Dorian glanced at the open doorway, through which she had vanished moments before.

If she could kill people like this, then manipulating him into believing she felt something for him would have been all too easy. Making an ally of him—making him *love* her enough to face his father on her behalf, to ensure that she was appointed Champion . . .

Dorian couldn't bring himself to finish the thought. He'd visit her—tomorrow, perhaps. Just to see if there was a chance he was wrong.

But he couldn't help wondering if he'd ever meant anything to Celaena at all.

Celaena strode quickly and quietly down hallways and stairwells, taking the now-familiar route to the castle sewer. It was the same waterway that flowed past her secret tunnel, though here it smelled far worse, thanks to the servants depositing refuse almost hourly.

Her steps, then a second pair—Chaol's—echoed in the long subterranean passage. But she didn't say anything until she stopped at the edge of the water, glancing at the several archways that opened on either side of the river. No one was here.

"So," she said without looking behind her, "are you going to say hello, or are you just going to follow me everywhere?" She turned to face him, the sack still dangling from her hand.

"Are you still acting like the King's Champion, or are you back to being Celaena?" In the torchlight, his bronze eyes glittered.

Of course Chaol would notice the difference; he noticed everything. She couldn't tell whether it pleased her or not. Especially when there was a slight bite to his words.

When she didn't reply, he asked, "How was Bellhaven?"

"The same as it always is." She knew precisely what he meant; he wanted to know how her mission had gone.

"He fought you?" He jerked his chin toward the sack in her hand.

She shrugged and turned back to the dark river. "It was nothing I couldn't handle." She tossed the sack into the sewer. They watched in silence as it bobbed, then slowly sank.

Chaol cleared his throat. She knew he hated this. When she'd gone on her first mission—to an estate up the coast in Meah—he'd paced so much before she left that she honestly thought he would ask her not to go. And when she'd returned, severed head in tow and rumors flying about Sir Carlin's murder, it had taken a week for him to even look her in the eye. But what had he expected?

"When will you begin your new mission?" he asked.

"Tomorrow. Or the day after. I need to rest," she added quickly when he frowned. "And besides, it'll only take me a day or two to figure out how guarded Archer is and sort out my approach. Hopefully I won't even need the month the king gave me." And hopefully Archer would have some answers about how he'd gotten on the king's list, and what *plans*, exactly, that the king had alluded to. Then she would figure out what to do with him.

Chaol stepped beside her, still staring at the filthy water, where the sack was undoubtedly now caught in the current and drifting out into the Avery River and the sea beyond. "I'd like to debrief you."

She raised an eyebrow. "Aren't you at least going to take me to dinner first?" His eyes narrowed, and she gave him a pout.

"It's not a joke. I want the details of what happened with Nirall."

She brushed him aside with a grin, wiping her gloves on her pants before heading back up the stairs.

Chaol grabbed her arm. "If Nirall fought back, then there might be witnesses who heard—"

"He didn't make any noise," Celaena snapped, shaking him off as she stormed up the steps. After two weeks of travel, she just wanted to *sleep*. Even the walk up to her rooms felt like a trek. "You don't need to *debrief* me, Chaol."

He stopped her again at a shadowy landing with a firm hand on her shoulder. "When you go away," he said, the distant torchlight illuminating the rugged planes of his face, "I have *no* idea what's happening to you. I don't know if you're hurt or rotting in a gutter somewhere. Yesterday I heard a rumor that they caught the killer responsible for Nirall's death." He brought his face close to hers, his voice hoarse. "Until you arrived today, I thought they meant *you*. I was about to go down there myself to find you."

Well, that would explain why she'd seen Chaol's horse being saddled at the stables when she arrived. She loosed a breath, her face suddenly warm. "Have a little more faith in me than that. I am the King's Champion, after all."

She didn't have time to brace herself as he pulled her against him, his arms wrapping tightly around her.

She didn't hesitate before twining her arms over his shoulders, breathing in the scent of him. He hadn't held her since the day she'd learned she had officially won the competition, though the memory of that embrace often drifted into her thoughts. And as she held him now, the craving for it never to stop roared through her.

His nose grazed the nape of her neck. "Gods above, you smell horrible," he muttered.

She hissed and shoved him, her face burning in earnest now. "Carrying around dead body parts for weeks isn't exactly conducive to smelling nice! And maybe if I'd been given time for a bath instead of being ordered to report *immediately* to the king, I might have—" She stopped herself at the sight of his grin and smacked his shoulder. "Idiot." Celaena linked arms with him, tugging him up the stairs. "Come on. Let's go to my rooms so you can debrief me like a proper gentleman."

Chaol snorted and nudged her with his elbow but didn't let go.

After a joyous Fleetfoot calmed down enough for Celaena to speak without being licked, Chaol squeezed every last detail from her and left her with the promise to return for dinner in a few hours. And after she let Philippa fuss over her in the bath and bemoan the state of her hair and nails, Celaena collapsed onto her bed.

Fleetfoot leapt up beside her, curling in close to her side. Stroking the dog's silky golden coat, Celaena stared at the ceiling, the exhaustion seeping out of her sore muscles.

The king had believed her.

And Chaol hadn't once doubted her story as he inquired about her mission. She couldn't quite decide if that made her feel smug, disappointed, or outright guilty. But the lies had rolled off her tongue. Nirall awoke right before she killed him, she had to slit his wife's throat to keep her from screaming, and the fight was a tad messier than she would have liked. She'd thrown in real details, too: the second-floor hall window, the storm, the servant with the candle . . . The best lies were always mixed with truth.

Celaena clutched the amulet on her chest. The Eye of Elena. She hadn't seen Elena since their last encounter in the tomb; hopefully, now that she was the King's Champion, the ancient queen's ghost would leave her alone. Still, in the months since Elena had given her the amulet for protection, Celaena had come to find its presence reassuring. The metal was always warm, as though it had a life of its own.

She squeezed it hard. If the king knew the truth about what she did—what she'd been doing these past two months . . .

She had embarked on the first mission intending to quickly dispatch the target. She'd prepared herself for the kill, told herself that Sir Carlin was nothing but a stranger and his life meant nothing to her. But when she got to his estate and witnessed the unusual kindness with which he treated his servants, when she saw him playing the lyre with a traveling minstrel he sheltered in his hall, when she realized whose agenda she was aiding . . . she couldn't do it. She tried to bully and coax and bribe herself into doing it. But she couldn't.

Still, she had to produce a murder scene—and a body.

She'd given Lord Nirall the same choice she'd given Sir Carlin: die right then, or fake his own death and flee—flee far, and never use his given name again. So far, of the four men she'd been assigned to dispatch, all had chosen escape.

It wasn't hard to get them to part with their seal rings or other token items. And it was even easier to get them to hand over their nightclothes so she could slash them in accordance with the wounds she would claim to have given them. Bodies were easy to acquire, too.

Sick-houses were always dumping fresh corpses. It was never

hard to find one that looked enough like her target—especially since the locations of the kills had been distant enough to give the flesh time to rot.

She didn't know who the head of Lord Nirall actually belonged to—only that he had similar hair, and when she inflicted a few slashes on his face and let the whole thing decompose a bit, it did the job. The hand had also come from that corpse. And the lady's hand . . . that had come from a young woman barely into her first bleeding, struck dead by a sickness that ten years ago a gifted healer could easily have cured. But with magic gone and those wise healers hanged or burned, people were dying in droves. Dying from stupid, once-curable illnesses. She rolled over to bury her face in Fleetfoot's soft coat.

Archer. How was she going to fake *his* death? He was so popular, and so recognizable. She still couldn't imagine him having a connection to whatever this underground movement was. But if he was on the king's list, then perhaps in the years since she'd seen him Archer had used his talents to become powerful.

Yet what information could the movement possibly have on the king's plans that would make it a true threat? The king had enslaved the entire continent—what more could he do?

There were other continents, of course. Other continents with wealthy kingdoms—like Wendlyn, that faraway land across the sea. It had held out against his naval attacks so far, but she'd heard next to nothing about that war since before she'd gone to Endovier.

And why would a rebel movement care about kingdoms on another continent when they had their own to worry about? So the plans had to be about *this* land, *this* continent.

She didn't want to know. She didn't want to know what the king was doing, what he imagined for the empire. She'd use this month to figure out what to do with Archer and pretend she'd never heard that horrible word: *plans*.

Celaena fought a shudder. She was playing a very, *very* lethal game. And now that her targets were people in Rifthold—now that it was *Archer* . . . She'd have to find a way to play it better. Because if the king ever learned the truth, if he found out what she was doing . . .

He'd destroy her.

CHAPTER
3

Celaena sprinted through the darkness of the secret passageway, her breathing ragged. She glanced over her shoulder to find Cain grinning at her, his eyes like burning coals.

No matter how fast she ran, his stalking gait easily kept him just behind her. After him flowed a wake of glowing green Wyrdmarks, their strange shapes and symbols illuminating the ancient blocks of stone. And behind Cain, its long nails scraping against the ground, lumbered the ridderak.

Celaena stumbled, but remained upright. Each step felt like she was wading through mud. She couldn't escape him. He would catch her eventually. And once the ridderak got hold of her . . . She didn't dare glance again at those too-big teeth that jutted out of its mouth or those fathomless eyes, gleaming with the desire to devour her bit by bit.

Cain chuckled, the sound grating on the stone walls. He was close now. Close enough that his fingers raked against the nape of her neck. He whispered her name, her true name, and she screamed as he—

Celaena awoke with a gasp, clutching the Eye of Elena. She scanned the room for denser shadows, for glowing Wyrdmarks, for signs that the secret door was open behind the tapestry that concealed it. But there was only the crackling of the dying fire.

Celaena sank back into her pillows. It was just a nightmare. Cain and the ridderak were gone, and Elena wouldn't bother her again. It was over.

Fleetfoot, sleeping under the many layers of blankets, put her head on Celaena's stomach. Celaena nestled down farther, wrapping her arms around the dog as she closed her eyes.

It was over.

In the chill mists of early morning, Celaena hurled a stick across the wide field of the game park. Fleetfoot took off through the pale grass like a bolt of golden lightning, so fast that Celaena let out a low, appreciative whistle. Beside her, Nehemia clicked her tongue, her eyes on the swift hound. With Nehemia so busy winning over Queen Georgina and gleaning information about the king's plans for Eyllwe, dawn was usually the only time they could see each other. Did the king know that the princess was one of the spies he'd mentioned? He couldn't, or else he'd never trust Celaena to be his Champion, not when their friendship was widely known.

"Why Archer Finn?" Nehemia mused in Eyllwe, keeping her voice low. Celaena had explained her latest mission, keeping the details brief.

Fleetfoot reached the stick and trotted back to them, her long tail wagging. Even though she wasn't yet fully grown, the dog was already abnormally large. Dorian had never said what breed, exactly, he suspected her mother had mated with. Given Fleetfoot's size, it could have been a wolfhound. Or an actual wolf.

Celaena shrugged at Nehemia's question, stuffing her hands into the fur-lined pockets of her cloak. "The king thinks . . . he thinks that Archer is a part of some secret movement against him. A movement here in Rifthold to get him off the throne."

"Surely no one would be that bold. The rebels hide out in the mountains and forests and places where the local people can conceal and support them—not here. Rifthold would be a death trap."

Celaena shrugged again just as Fleetfoot returned and demanded the stick be thrown again. "Apparently not. And apparently the king has a list of people whom he thinks are key players in this movement against him."

"And you're to . . . kill them all?" Nehemia's creamy brown face paled slightly.

"One by one," Celaena said, throwing the stick as far as she could into the misty field. Fleetfoot shot off, dried grass and the remnants of the last snowstorm crunching beneath her huge paws. "He'll only reveal one name at a time. A bit dramatic, if you ask me. But apparently they're interfering with his *plans*."

"What plans?" Nehemia said sharply.

Celaena frowned. "I was hoping you might know."

"I don't." There was a tense pause. "If you learn anything . . . ," Nehemia began.

"I'll see what I can do," Celaena lied. She wasn't even sure if she truly wanted to know what the king was up to—let alone *share* that information with anyone else. It was selfish, and stupid, perhaps, but she couldn't forget the warning the king had given the day he crowned her Champion: if she stepped out of line, if she betrayed him, he'd kill Chaol. And then Nehemia, and then the princess's family.

And all of this—every death she faked, every lie she told—put them at risk.

Nehemia shook her head but didn't reply. Whenever the princess or Chaol or even Dorian looked at her like that, it was almost too much to bear. But they had to believe the lies, too. For their own safety.

Nehemia began wringing her hands, and her eyes grew distant. Celaena had seen that expression often in the past month. "If you're fretting for my sake—"

"I'm not," Nehemia said. "You can take care of yourself."

"Then what is it?" Celaena's stomach clenched. If Nehemia talked more about the rebels, she didn't know how much of it she could take. Yes, she wanted to be free of the king—both as his Champion and as a child of a conquered nation—but she wanted nothing to do with whatever plots were brewing in Rifthold, and whatever desperate hope the rebels still savored. To stand against the king would be nothing but folly. They'd all be destroyed.

But Nehemia said, "Numbers in the Calaculla labor camp are swelling. Every day, more and more Eyllwe rebels arrive. Most consider it a miracle that they're *alive*. After the soldiers butchered those five hundred rebels . . . My people are afraid." Fleetfoot again returned, and it was Nehemia who took the stick from the dog's mouth and chucked it into the gray dawn. "But the conditions in Calaculla . . ."

She paused, probably recalling the three scars that raked down Celaena's back. A permanent reminder of the cruelty of the Salt Mines of Endovier—and a reminder that even though she was free, thousands of people still toiled and died there. Calaculla, the sister camp to Endovier, was rumored to be even worse.

"The king will not meet with me," Nehemia said, now toying with one of her fine, slender braids. "I have asked him three times to discuss the conditions in Calaculla, and each time he claims to be occupied. Apparently, he's too busy finding people for you to kill."

Celaena blushed at the harshness in Nehemia's tone. Fleetfoot returned again, but when Nehemia took the stick, the princess kept it in her hands.

"I must do something, Elentiya," Nehemia said, using the name she'd given her on the night Celaena admitted that she was an assassin. "I must find a way to help my people. When does gathering information become a stalemate? When do we act?"

Celaena swallowed hard. That word—"act"—scared her more than she'd like to admit. Worse than the word "plans." Fleetfoot sat at their feet, tail wagging as she waited for the stick to be thrown.

But when Celaena said nothing, when she promised nothing, just as she always did when Nehemia spoke about these things, the princess dropped the stick on the ground and quietly walked back to the castle.

Celaena waited until Nehemia's footsteps faded and let out a long breath. She was to meet Chaol for their morning run in a few minutes, but after that . . . after that, she was going into Rifthold. Let Archer wait until this afternoon.

After all, the king had given her a month, and despite her own questions for Archer, she wanted to get off the castle grounds for a bit. She had blood money to burn.

CHAPTER 4

Chaol Westfall sprinted through the game park, Celaena keeping pace beside him. The chill morning air was like shards of glass in his lungs; his breath clouded in front of him. They'd bundled up as best they could without weighing themselves down—mostly just layers of shirts and gloves—but even with sweat running down his body, Chaol was freezing.

Chaol knew Celaena was freezing, too—her nose was tipped with pink, color stood high on her cheeks, and her ears shone bright red. Noticing his stare, she flashed him a grin, those stunning turquoise eyes full of light. "Tired?" she teased. "I *knew* you weren't bothering to train while I was away."

He let out a breathy chuckle. "*You* certainly didn't train while you were on your mission. This is the second time this morning that I've had to slow my pace for you."

A blatant lie. She kept up with him easily now, nimble as a stag bounding through the woods. Sometimes he found it immensely hard not to watch her—to watch the way she moved.

"Keep telling yourself that," she said, and ran a little faster.

He increased his speed, not wanting her to leave him behind. Servants had cleared a path through the snow blanketing the game park, but the ground was still icy and treacherous underfoot.

He'd been realizing it more and more recently—how much he hated it when she left him behind. How he hated her setting off on those cursed missions and not contacting him for days or weeks. He didn't know how or when it had happened, but he'd somehow started caring whether she came back or not. And after all that they'd already endured together . . .

He'd killed Cain at the duel. Killed him to save her. Part of him didn't regret it; part of him would do it again in a heartbeat. But the other part still woke him up in the middle of the night, drenched in sweat that felt too much like Cain's blood.

She looked over at him. "What's wrong?"

He fought the rising guilt. "Keep your eyes on the path or you'll slip."

For once, she obeyed him. "You want to talk about it?"

Yes. No. If there were anyone who could understand the guilt and rage he grappled with when he thought about how he'd killed Cain, it would be her. "How often," he said in between breaths, "do you think about the people you've killed?"

She whipped her gaze to him, then slowed. He didn't feel like stopping, and might have kept running, but she grabbed his elbow and forced him to pause. Her lips formed a thin line. "If you think passing judgment on me before I've had breakfast is in *any* way a good idea—"

"No," he interrupted, panting hard. "No—I didn't mean it like . . ." He swallowed a few breaths. "I wasn't judging." If he could just get his damn breath back, he could explain what he'd meant.

Her eyes were as frozen as the park around him, but then she tilted her head to the side. "Is this about Cain?"

Hearing her speak the name made him clench his jaw, but he managed a nod.

The ice in her eyes melted completely. He hated the sympathy in her face, the understanding.

He was the Captain of the Guard—he was bound to have killed someone at some point. He'd already seen and done enough in the name of the king; he'd fought men, hurt them. So he shouldn't even be having these feelings, and especially shouldn't be telling *her*. There was a line between them, somewhere, and he was fairly certain that he'd been toeing it more and more these days.

"I'll never forget the people I've killed," she said. Her breath curled in the air between them. "Even the ones I killed to survive. I still see their faces, still remember the exact blow it took to kill them." She looked to the skeletal trees. "Some days, it feels like another person did those things. And most of those lives I'm *glad* I ended. No matter the cause, though, it—it still takes away a little piece of you each time. So I don't think I'll ever forget them."

Her gaze found his again, and he nodded.

"But, Chaol," she said, and tightened her grip on his arm, a grip he hadn't realized she'd still been holding, "what happened with Cain— that wasn't an assassination, or even a cold-blooded murder." He tried to step back, but she held firm. "What you did wasn't dishonorable— and I'm not just saying that because it was my life you were saving." She paused for a long moment. "You will never forget killing Cain," she said at last, and when her eyes met his, his heart pounded so hard he could feel it across his whole body. "But I will never forget what you did to save me, either."

The urge to lean into her warmth was staggering. He made himself step back, away from the grip of her hand, made himself nod again.

There *was* a line between them. The king might not think twice about their friendship, but crossing that final line could be deadly for both of them; it could make the king question his loyalty, his position, everything.

And if it ever came down to having to choose between his king and Celaena . . . He prayed to the Wyrd that he'd never be faced with that decision. Staying firmly on *this* side of the line was the logical choice. The honorable one, too, since Dorian . . . He'd seen the way Dorian still looked at her. He wouldn't betray his friend like that.

"Well," Chaol said with forced lightness, "I suppose having Adarlan's Assassin in my debt *could* be useful."

She gave him a bow. "At your service."

His smile was genuine this time.

"Come on, Captain," she said, starting into a slow jog. "I'm hungry, and I don't feel like freezing my ass off out here."

He chuckled under his breath, and they ran on through the park.

⟡

When they finished their run, Celaena's legs were wobbling, and her lungs were so raw from the cold and exertion that she thought they might be bleeding. They slowed to a brisk walk as they headed back to the toasty interior of the palace—and the giant breakfast that she was very much looking forward to devouring before going shopping.

They entered the castle gardens, weaving their way through the gravel paths and towering hedges. She kept her hands tucked under her arms. Even with the gloves, her fingers were frozen stiff. And her ears positively ached. Perhaps she'd start wearing a scarf over her head— even if Chaol would tease her mercilessly about it.

She glanced sideways at her companion, who had peeled off his outer layers of clothing to reveal the sweat-drenched shirt clinging to his body. They rounded a hedge, and Celaena rolled her eyes when she saw what waited on the path ahead.

Every morning, more and more ladies found excuses to be walking through the gardens just after dawn. At first, it had just been a few young women who'd taken one look at Chaol and his sweaty, clingy clothes and halted their walk. Celaena could have sworn their eyes had bulged out of their heads and their tongues had rolled onto the ground.

Then the next morning, they'd appeared along the path *again*—wearing even nicer dresses. The day after that, more girls showed up. And then several more. And now every direct route from the game park to the castle had at least one set of young women patrolling, waiting for him to walk by.

"Oh, please," Celaena hissed as they passed two women, who looked up from their fur muffs to bat their eyelashes at him. They must have awoken before dawn to be dressed so finely.

"What?" Chaol asked, his brows rising.

She didn't know whether he simply didn't notice, or he didn't want to say anything, but . . . "The gardens are rather busy for a winter morning," she said carefully.

He shrugged. "Some people go a little stir-crazy being cooped up inside all winter."

Or they just enjoy the sight of the Captain of the Guard and his muscles.

But all she said was, "Right," and then shut her mouth. No need to point it out if he was *that* oblivious. Especially when some of the ladies were exceptionally pretty.

"Are you going into Rifthold to spy on Archer today?" Chaol asked softly, when the path was mercifully clear of giggling, blushing girls.

She nodded. "I want to get a sense of his schedule, so I'll probably trail him."

"Why don't I help you?"

"Because I don't need your help." She knew he'd probably interpret it as arrogance—and it partially was—but . . . if he did get involved, then it would complicate things when it came time to smuggle Archer to safety. That is, after she got the truth out of him—and learned what plans the king had in mind.

"I know you don't need my help. I just thought you might want . . ." He trailed off, then shook his head, as if reprimanding himself. She found herself wanting to know what he'd been about to say, but it was best to let the topic drop.

They rounded another hedge, the castle interior so close she almost groaned at the thought of that delicious warmth, but then—

"Chaol." Dorian's voice cut through the crisp morning.

She *did* groan then, a barely audible sound. Chaol shot her a puzzled look before they turned to find Dorian striding toward them, a blond young man in tow. She'd never seen the youth, who was finely dressed and looked about Dorian's age, but Chaol stiffened.

The young man didn't seem like a threat, though she knew better than to underestimate anyone in a court like this. He wore only a dagger at his waist, and his pale face seemed rather jovial, despite the winter morning chill.

She found Dorian watching her with a half smile, an amused gleam in his eye that made her want to slap him. The prince then glanced at Chaol and chuckled. "And here I was, thinking that all the ladies were out so early for Roland and me. When all of them catch a vicious cold, I'll let their fathers know that you're to blame."

Chaol's cheeks colored ever so slightly. So he wasn't as ignorant of their morning audience as he'd led her to believe. "Lord Roland," he said tightly to Dorian's friend, and bowed.

The blond young man bowed back to Chaol. "Captain Westfall." His voice was pleasant enough, but something in it made her pause. It wasn't amusement or arrogance or anger . . . She couldn't put her finger on it.

"Allow me to introduce my cousin," Dorian said to her, clapping Roland on the shoulder. "Lord Roland Havilliard of Meah." He extended a hand to Celaena. "Roland, this is Lillian. She works for my father."

They still used her alias whenever she couldn't avoid running into members of the court, though most everyone knew to some degree that she was not in the palace for administrative nonsense or politics.

"My pleasure," Roland said, bowing at the waist. "Are you newly arrived to court? I don't think I've seen you in years past."

Just the way he spoke told her enough about his history with women. "I arrived this autumn," she said a bit too quietly.

Roland gave her a courtier's smile. "And what sort of work do you do for my uncle?"

Dorian shifted on his feet and Chaol went very still, but Celaena returned Roland's smile and said, "I bury the king's opponents where nobody will ever find them."

Roland, to her surprise, actually chuckled. She didn't dare look at Chaol, whom she was certain would give her a tongue-lashing for it later. "I'd heard about the King's Champion. I didn't think it would be someone so . . . lovely."

"What brings you to the castle, Roland?" the captain demanded. When Chaol looked at *her* like that, she usually found herself running in the other direction.

Roland smiled again. He smiled too much—and too smoothly. "His Majesty has offered me a position on his council." Chaol's eyes snapped to Dorian, who gave a shrug of confirmation. "I arrived last night, and I'm to start today."

Chaol smiled—if you could call it that. It was more a flash of teeth. Yes, she'd most *definitely* be running if Chaol looked at her like that.

Dorian understood the look, too, and gave a deliberate chuckle. But before the prince could speak, Roland studied Celaena further, a tad too intently. "Perhaps you and I shall get to work with each other, Lillian. Your position intrigues me."

She wouldn't mind working with him—but not in the way Roland meant. Her way would include a dagger, a shovel, and an unmarked grave.

As if he could read her thoughts, Chaol put a guiding hand on her back. "We're late for breakfast," he said, bowing his head to Dorian and Roland. "Congratulations on your appointment." He sounded like he'd swallowed rancid milk.

As she let Chaol lead her inside the castle, she realized she was in desperate need of a bath. But it had nothing to do with her sweaty clothes, and everything to do with the oily grin and roaming eyes of Roland Havilliard.

Dorian watched Celaena and Chaol disappear behind the hedges, the captain's hand still on the middle of her back. She did nothing to shake it off.

"An unexpected choice for your father to make, even with that competition," Roland mused beside him.

Dorian checked his irritation before replying. He'd never particularly liked his cousin, whom he'd seen at least twice a year while growing up.

Chaol positively hated Roland, and whenever he came up in conversation, it was usually accompanied by phrases like "conniving wretch" and "sniveling, spoiled ass." At least, that's what Chaol had been roaring three years ago, after the captain had punched Roland so hard in the face that the youth blacked out.

But Roland had deserved it. Deserved it enough that it hadn't interfered with Chaol's sterling reputation and later appointment to Captain of the Guard. If anything, it had improved Chaol's standing among the other guards and lesser nobles.

If Dorian worked up the nerve, he'd ask his father what he'd been thinking when he appointed Roland to the council. Meah was a small yet prosperous coastal city in Adarlan, but it held no real political power. It didn't even have a standing army, save for the city's sentries. Roland was his father's cousin's son; perhaps the king felt that they needed more Havilliard blood in the council room. Still—Roland was untried, and had always seemed more interested in girls than politics.

"Where did your father's Champion come from?" Roland asked, drawing Dorian's attention back to the present.

Dorian turned toward the castle, heading for a different entrance than the one Chaol and Celaena had used. He still remembered the way they'd looked when he'd walked in on them embracing in her rooms after the duel, two months ago.

"Lillian's story is hers to tell," Dorian lied. He just didn't feel like explaining the competition to his cousin. It was bad enough that his father had ordered him to take Roland on a walk this morning. The only bright spot had been seeing Celaena so obviously contemplate ways to bury the young lord.

"Is she for your father's personal use, or do the other councilmen also employ her?"

"You've been here for less than a day, and you already have enemies to dispatch, cousin?"

"We're Havilliards, cousin. We'll always have enemies that need dispatching."

Dorian frowned. It was true, though. "Her contract is exclusively with my father. But if you feel threatened, then I can have Captain Westfall assign a—"

"Oh, of course not. I was merely curious."

Roland was a pain in the ass, and too aware of the effect his looks and his Havilliard name had on women, but he was harmless. Wasn't he?

Dorian didn't know the answer—and he wasn't sure if he wanted to.

⌒

Her salary as King's Champion was considerable, and Celaena spent every last copper of it. Shoes, hats, tunics, dresses, jewelry, weapons, baubles for her hair, and books. Books and books and books. So many books that Philippa had to bring up another bookcase for her room.

When Celaena returned to her rooms that afternoon, lugging hat boxes, colorful bags full of perfume and sweets, and brown paper parcels with the books she absolutely *had* to read immediately, she nearly dropped it all at the sight of Dorian Havilliard sitting in her foyer.

"Gods above," he said, taking in all of her purchases.

He didn't know the half of it. This was just what she could carry. More had been ordered, and more would be delivered soon.

"Well," he said as she dumped the bags on the table, nearly toppling into a heap of tissue paper and ribbons, "at least you're not wearing that dreadful black today."

She shot him a glare over her shoulder as she straightened. Today she was wearing a lilac and ivory gown—a little bright for the end of winter, but worn in the hope that spring would soon come. Plus, dressing nicely guaranteed her the best service in whatever stores she visited. To her surprise, many of the shopkeepers remembered her from years ago—and had bought her lie about a long journey to the southern continent.

"And to what do I owe this pleasure?" She untied her white fur cloak—another gift to herself—and tossed it onto one of the chairs around the foyer table. "Didn't I already see you this morning in the garden?"

Dorian remained seated, that familiar, boyish grin on his face. "Aren't friends allowed to visit each other more than once a day?"

She stared down at him. Being friends with Dorian wasn't something she was certain she could actually *do*. Not when he would always have that gleam in his sapphire eyes—and not when he was the son of the man who gripped her fate in his hands. But in the two months since she'd ended whatever had been between them, she'd often found herself missing him. Not the kissing and flirting, but just *him*.

"What do you want, Dorian?"

A glimmer of ire flashed across his face, and he stood. She had to tip her head back to look at him. "You said you still wanted to be friends with me." His voice was low.

She closed her eyes for a moment. "I meant it."

"So be my friend," he said, his tone lifting. "Dine with me, play billiards with me. Tell me what books you're reading—or buying," he added with a wink in the direction of her parcels.

"Oh?" she asked, forcing herself to give him a half smile. "And you have so much time on your hands these days that you can spend hours with me again?"

"Well, I have my usual flock of ladies to attend to, but I can *always* make time for you."

She batted her eyelashes at him. "I'm truly honored." Actually, the thought of Dorian with other women made her want to shatter a window, but it wouldn't be fair to let him know that. She glanced at the clock on the small table beside a wall. "I actually need to go back into Rifthold right now," she said. It wasn't a lie. She still had a few hours of daylight left—enough time to survey Archer's elegant townhouse and start trailing him to get a sense of his usual whereabouts.

Dorian nodded, his smile fading.

Silence fell, interrupted only by the ticking of the clock on the table. She crossed her arms, remembering how he'd smelled, how his lips had tasted. But this distance between them, this horrible gap that spread every day . . . it was for the best.

Dorian took a step closer, exposing his palms to her. "Do you want me to fight for you? Is that it?"

"No," she said quietly. "I just want you to leave me alone."

His eyes flickered with the words left unsaid. Celaena stared at him, unmoving, until he silently left.

Alone in the foyer, Celaena clenched and unclenched her fists, suddenly disgusted with all of the pretty packages on the table.

CHAPTER 5

On a rooftop in a very fashionable and respectable part of Rifthold, Celaena crouched in the shadow of a chimney and frowned into the chill wind gusting off the Avery. She checked her pocket watch for the third time. Archer Finn's previous two appointments had only been an hour each. He'd been in the house across the street for almost two.

There was nothing interesting about the elegant, green-roofed town-house, and she hadn't learned anything about who lived there, other than the client's name—some Lady Balanchine. She had used the same trick she'd employed at the other two houses to gain that bit of information: she pretended to be a courier with a package for Lord So-and-So. And when the butler or housekeeper said that this was *not* Lord So-and-So's house, she'd feigned embarrassment, asked whose house it was, chatted up the servant a bit, and then went on her way.

Celaena adjusted the position of her legs and rolled her neck. The sun had nearly set, the temperature dropping with each passing minute.

Unless she could get into the houses themselves, she wasn't going to learn much else. And given the likelihood that Archer might actually be doing what he was paid to do, she was in no rush to go inside. Better to learn where he went, who he saw, and then take the next step.

It had been so long since she'd done something like this in Rifthold—since she'd crouched on the emerald rooftops and learned what she could about her prey. It was different than when the king had sent her off to Bellhaven or to some lord's estate. Here, now, in Rifthold, it felt like . . .

It felt like she'd never left. As if she might look over her shoulder and find Sam Cortland crouching behind her. As if she might return at the end of the night not to the glass castle, but to the Assassins' Keep on the other side of the city.

Celaena sighed, tucking her hands under her arms to keep her fingers warm and agile.

It had been over a year and a half since the night she'd lost her freedom; a year and a half since she'd lost Sam. And somewhere, in this city, were the answers to how it all had happened. If she dared to look, she knew she'd find them. And she knew it would destroy her again.

The front door of the townhouse opened, and Archer swaggered down the steps, right into his waiting carriage. She barely caught a glimpse of his golden-brown hair and fine clothes before he was whisked away.

Groaning, Celaena straightened from her crouch and hurried off the roof. Some harrowing climbing and a few jumps soon had her back on the cobbled streets.

She trailed Archer's carriage, slipping in and out of shadows as they made their way across the city, a slow journey thanks to traffic. While she might be in no hurry to seek out the truth behind her own capture and Sam's death, and while she was fairly certain the king had to be wrong about Archer, part of her wondered whether whatever truth she uncovered about this rebel movement and the king's plans would destroy her, too.

And not just destroy her—but also everything she'd grown to care about.

Savoring the warmth of the crackling fire, Celaena leaned her head against the back of the small couch and dangled her legs over the cushioned arm. The lines on the paper she held before her were beginning to blur, which was no surprise, given that it was well past eleven, and she'd been up before dawn.

Sprawled on the well-worn red carpet in front of her, Chaol's glass pen flickered with firelight as he scanned through documents and signed things and scribbled notes. Giving a little sigh through her nose, Celaena lowered the paper in her hands.

Unlike her spacious suite, Chaol's bedroom was one large chamber, furnished only with a table by the solitary window and the old couch set before the stone fireplace. A few tapestries hung on the gray stone walls, a towering oak armoire stood in one corner, and his four-poster bed was decorated with a rather old and faded crimson duvet. There was a bathing room attached—not as large as her own, but still spacious enough to accommodate its own pool and privy. He had only one small bookcase, filled and neatly arranged. In alphabetical order, if she knew Chaol at all. And it probably contained only his most beloved books— unlike Celaena's, which housed every title she got her hands on, whether she liked the book or not. Regardless of his unnaturally organized bookshelf, she liked it here; it was cozy.

She'd started coming here a few weeks ago, when thoughts of Elena and Cain and the secret passageways made her itch to get out of her own rooms. And even though he'd grumbled about her imposing on his privacy, Chaol hadn't turned her away or objected to her frequent after-dinner visits.

The scratching of Chaol's pen stopped. "Remind me again what you're working on."

She flopped onto her back as she waved the paper in the air above her. "Just information about Archer. Clients, favored haunts, his daily schedule."

Chaol's golden-brown eyes were molten in the firelight. "Why go to so much trouble to track him when you could just shoot him and be done with it? You said he was well-guarded, yet it seems like you tracked him easily today."

She scowled. Chaol was too smart for his own good. "Because, if the king actually has a group of people conspiring against him, then I should get as much information about them as I can before I kill Archer. Perhaps following Archer will reveal more conspirators—or at least clues to their whereabouts." It was the truth—and she'd followed Archer's ornate carriage through the streets of the capital today for that very reason.

But in the hours she'd spent trailing him, he'd gone only to a few appointments before returning to his townhouse.

"Right," Chaol said. "So you're just . . . memorizing that information now?"

"If you're suggesting that I have no reason to be here and should leave, then tell me to go."

"I'm just trying to figure out what's so boring that you dozed off ten minutes ago."

She propped herself on her elbows. "I did not!"

His brows rose. "I heard you snoring."

"You're a liar, Chaol Westfall." She threw her paper at him and plopped back on the couch. "I only closed my eyes for a minute."

He shook his head again and went back to work.

Celaena blushed. "I didn't really snore, did I?"

His face was utterly serious as he said, "Like a bear."

She thumped a fist on the couch cushion. He grinned. She huffed, then draped her arm off the sofa, picking at the threads of the ancient rug as she stared up at the stone ceiling. "Tell me why you hate Roland."

Chaol looked up. "I never said I hated him."

She just waited.

Chaol sighed. "I think it's fairly easy for you to see why I hate him."

"But was there any incident that—"

"There were *many* incidents, and I don't particularly feel like talking about any of them."

She swung her legs off the arm of the couch and sat up straight. "Testy, aren't you?"

She picked up another one of her documents, a map of the city that she'd marked up with the locations of Archer's clients. Most of them seemed to be in the posh district where the majority of Rifthold's elite lived. Archer's own townhouse was in that neighborhood, tucked into a quiet, respectable side street. She traced a nail along it, but paused when her eyes fell upon a street just a few blocks over.

She knew that street—and knew the house that sat on its corner. Whenever she ventured into Rifthold, she took care to never pass too close to it. Today had been no different; she'd even gone a few blocks out of her way to avoid walking by.

Not daring to look at Chaol, she asked, "Do you know who Rourke Farran is?"

The name made her sick with long-suppressed rage and grief, but she managed to say it. Because even if she didn't want the entire truth . . . there were some things she did need to know about her capture. Still needed to know, even after all this time.

She felt Chaol's attention on her. "The crime lord?"

She nodded, her eyes still on that street where so many things had gone so horribly wrong. "Have you ever dealt with him?"

"No," Chaol said. "But . . . that's because Farran is dead."

She lowered the paper. "Farran's dead?"

"Nine months ago. He and his three top men were all found murdered by . . ." Chaol chewed on his lip, searching for the name. "Wesley. A man named Wesley took them all out. He was . . ." Chaol cocked his head to the side. "He was Arobynn Hamel's personal guard." Her breath was tight in her chest. "Did you know him?"

"I thought I did," she said softly. For the years she'd spent with Arobynn, Wesley had been a silent, deadly presence, a man who had barely tolerated her, and had always made it clear that if she ever became a threat to his master, he'd kill her. But on the night that she'd been betrayed and captured, Wesley had tried to stop her. She'd thought that it was because Arobynn had ordered her locked in her rooms, that it had been a way to keep her from seeking retribution for Sam's death at Farran's hands; but . . .

"What happened to Wesley?" she asked. "Did Farran's men catch him?"

Chaol ran a hand through his hair, glancing down at the rug. "No. We found Wesley a day later—courtesy of Arobynn Hamel."

She felt the blood drain from her face, but dared to ask, "How?"

Chaol studied her closely, warily. "Wesley's body was impaled on the iron fence outside Rourke's house. There was . . . enough blood to suggest that Wesley was alive when they did it. They never confessed, but we got the sense that the servants in the household had also been instructed to *let* him stay there until he died.

"We thought it was an attempt to balance the blood feud—so that when the next crime lord ascended, they wouldn't view Arobynn and his assassins as enemies."

She stared at the carpet again. The night she'd broken out of the Assassins' Keep to hunt down Farran, Wesley had tried to stop her. He'd tried to tell her it was a trap.

Celaena shut down the thought before it reached its conclusion. That was a truth she'd have to take out and examine at another time, when she was alone, when she didn't have Archer and the rebel movement and all that nonsense to worry about. When she could try to understand why Arobynn Hamel might have betrayed her—and what she was going to do with that horrible knowledge. How much she'd make him suffer—and bleed for it.

After a few moments of silence, Chaol asked, "We never learned why Wesley went after Rourke Farran, though. Wesley was just a personal bodyguard. What did he have against Farran?"

Her eyes were burning, and she looked to the window, where the night sky was bathed in moonlight. "It was an act of revenge." She could still see Sam's twisted corpse, lying on that table in the room beneath the Assassins' Keep; still see Farran crouched in front of her, his hands roaming over her paralyzed body. She swallowed down the tightness in her throat. "Farran captured, tortured, and then murdered one of . . . one of my . . . companions. And then the next night, I went out to repay the favor. It didn't end so well for me."

A log shifted in the fire, breaking open and filling the room with a flash of light.

"That was the night you were captured?" Chaol asked. "But I thought you didn't know who had betrayed you."

"I still don't. Someone hired me and my companion to kill Farran, but it was all just a trap, and Farran was the bait."

Silence; then—"What was his name?"

She pushed her lips together, shoving away the memory of how he'd looked the last time she'd seen him, broken on that table. "Sam," she got out. "His name was Sam." She took an uneven breath. "I don't even know where they buried him. I don't even know who I would ask about it."

Chaol didn't reply, and she didn't know why she bothered talking, but the words just tumbled out. "I failed him," she said. "In every way that counted, I failed him."

Another long silence, then a sigh. "Not in one way," Chaol said. "I bet he would have wanted you to survive—to *live*. So you didn't fail him, not in that regard."

She had to look away in order to force her eyes to stop burning as she nodded.

After a moment, Chaol spoke again. "Her name was Lithaen. Three years ago, she worked for one of the ladies of the court. And Roland somehow found out and thought it would be amusing for me to discover him in bed with her. I know it's nothing like what you went through . . ."

She'd never known that he'd ever been interested in *anyone*, but . . . "Why did *she* do it?"

He shrugged, though his face was still bleak with the memory. "Because Roland is a Havilliard, and I'm just the Captain of the Guard. He even convinced her to go back to Meah with him—though I never learned what became of her."

"You loved her."

"I thought I did. And I thought she loved me." He shook his head, as if silently chiding himself. "Did Sam love you?"

Yes. More than anyone had ever loved her. He'd loved her enough to risk everything—to give up everything. He'd loved her so much that she still felt the echoes of it, even now. "Very much," she breathed.

The clock chimed eleven thirty, and Chaol shook his head, the tension falling from him. "I'm exhausted."

She stood, somehow having no clue how they'd wound up talking about the people who had meant so much to them. "Then I should go."

He got to his feet, his eyes so bright. "I'll walk you back to your room."

She lifted her chin. "I thought I didn't need to be escorted everywhere now."

"You don't," he said, walking to the door. "But it *is* something that friends tend to do."

"Would you walk Dorian back to his room?" She batted her eyelashes at him, striding through the door as he opened it for her. "Or is this a privilege that only your lady-friends receive?"

"*If* I had any lady-friends, I'd certainly extend the offer. I'm not sure you qualify as a lady, though."

"So chivalrous. No wonder those girls find excuses to be in the gardens every morning."

He snorted, and they fell silent as they walked through the quiet, dim halls of the castle, making their way back to her rooms on the other side. It was a trek, and often a cold one, since many of the halls were lined with windows that didn't keep out the winter chill.

When they reached the door to her rooms, he bid her a quick good night and began to walk away. Her fingers were around the brass door handle when she turned to him.

"For what it's worth, Chaol," she said. He faced her, his hands in his pockets. She gave him a slight smile. "If she picked Roland over you, that makes her the greatest fool who ever lived."

He stared at her for a long moment before he quietly said, "Thank you," and walked back to his room.

Celaena watched him go, watched those powerful muscles shifting in his back, visible even through his dark tunic, suddenly grateful that this Lithaen had long ago left the castle.

The midnight hour chimed through the castle, the off-kilter ringing of the wretched clock tower in the garden echoing through the dark, silent halls. Though Chaol had escorted her to her door, five minutes of pacing in her bedroom had sent her wandering again, heading for the library. She had mountains of unread books sitting in her rooms but didn't feel like reading any of them. She needed something to *do*. Something to take her mind off her discussion with Chaol and the memories she'd dragged into the open tonight.

Celaena wrapped her cloak tightly around her, glaring at the fierce winds whipping the snow outside the drafty windows. Hopefully there would be a few hearths lit in the library. If not, she'd grab a book that *did* interest her, run back to her room, and curl up with Fleetfoot in her toasty bed.

Celaena turned a corner, entering the dark, window-lined hallway that ran past the towering doors of the library, and froze.

With the chill tonight, it was no surprise to see someone completely concealed by a black cloak, hood drawn far over the face. But something about the figure standing between the open library doors made some ancient, primal part of her send a warning pulse so strong that she didn't take another step.

The person swiveled its head toward her, pausing as well.

Outside the hall windows, snow swirled, pressing against the glass.

It was just a person, she told herself as the figure now turned to face her fully. A person wearing a cloak darker than night, a hood so heavy it concealed every feature of the face inside.

It sniffed at her, a huffing, animal sound.

She didn't dare move.

It sniffed again, and took a step toward her. The way it *moved*, like smoke and shadow . . .

A faint warmth bloomed against her chest, then a pulsing blue light—

The Eye of Elena was glowing.

The thing halted, and Celaena stopped breathing.

It hissed, and then slithered a step back into the shadows beyond the library doors. The tiny blue gem in the center of her amulet glowed brighter, and Celaena blinked against the light.

When she opened her eyes, the amulet was dark, and the hooded creature was gone.

Not a trace, not even a sound of footsteps.

Celaena didn't go into the library. Oh, no. She just walked quickly back to her rooms with as much dignity as she could muster. Though she kept telling herself that she'd imagined it all, that it was some hallucination from too many hours awake, Celaena couldn't stop hearing that cursed word again and again.

Plans.

CHAPTER 6

The person outside the library probably had nothing to do with the king, Celaena told herself as she walked—still *not* sprinting—down the hall to her room. There were plenty of strange people in a castle this large, and even though she rarely saw another soul in the library, perhaps some people just . . . wished to go to the library alone. And unidentified. In a court where reading was so out of fashion, perhaps it was merely some courtier trying to hide a passionate love of books from his or her sneering friends.

Some animalistic, eerie courtier. Who had caused her amulet to glow.

Celaena entered her bedroom just as the lunar eclipse was beginning, and groaned. "Of course there's an eclipse," she grumbled, turning from the balcony doors and approaching the tapestry along the wall.

And even though she didn't want to, even though she'd hoped to never see Elena again . . . she needed answers.

Maybe the dead queen would laugh at her and tell her it was nothing. Gods above, she *hoped* Elena would say that. Because if she didn't . . .

Celaena shook her head and glanced at Fleetfoot. "Care to join me?" The dog, as if sensing what she was about to do, made a good show of turning circles on the bed and curling up with a huff. "I thought so."

In a matter of moments, Celaena shoved the large chest of drawers from its spot in front of the tapestry that hid the secret door, grabbed a candle, and began walking down, down, down the forgotten stairs to the landing far below.

The three stone archways greeted her. The one on the far left led to a passage that allowed for spying on the Great Hall. The one in the center led to the sewers and the concealed exit that might someday save her life. And the one on the right . . . that one led down to the ancient queen's forgotten tomb.

As she walked to the tomb, she didn't dare look at the landing where she'd discovered Cain summoning the ridderak from another world, even though the debris of the door the creature had shattered still littered the stairs. There were gouges in the stone wall where the ridderak had come crashing through, chasing her down to the tomb, until she'd just barely reached Damaris, sword of the long-dead King Gavin, in time to slay the monster.

Celaena glanced at her hand, where a ring of white scars punctured her palm and encircled her thumb. If Nehemia hadn't found her that night, the poison from the ridderak's bite would have killed her.

At last, she reached the door at the bottom of the spiral staircase and found herself staring at the skull-shaped bronze knocker in its center.

Perhaps this hadn't been a good idea. Perhaps the answers weren't worth it.

She should go back upstairs. Come to think of it, this could only be bad.

Elena had seemed satisfied that Celaena had obeyed her command to become the King's Champion, but if she showed up, then it would seem like she was *willing* to do another one of Elena's tasks. And the Wyrd knew that she had enough on her hands right now.

Even if that—that *thing* in the hall just now hadn't seemed friendly. The skull knocker seemed to smile at her, its hollow eyes boring into hers.

Gods above, she should just leave.

But her fingers were somehow reaching for the door handle, as if an invisible hand were guiding her—

"Aren't you going to knock?"

Celaena leapt back, a dagger already in her hand and angled to spill blood as she pressed herself into the wall. It was impossible—she had to have imagined it.

The skull knocker had spoken. Its mouth had moved up and down.

Yes, this was certainly, absolutely, undeniably *impossible*. Far more unlikely and incomprehensible than anything Elena had ever said or done.

Staring at her with gleaming metal eyes, the bronze skull clicked its tongue. It had a *tongue*.

Maybe she'd slipped on the stairs and smacked her head into the stones. That would make more sense than *this*. An endless, filthy stream of curses began flowing through her head, each more vulgar than the next, as she gaped at the knocker.

"Oh, don't be so pathetic," the skull huffed, its eyes narrowing. "I'm attached to this door. I cannot harm you."

"But you're"—she swallowed hard—"magic."

It was impossible—it *should* be impossible. Magic was gone, vanished from the land ten years ago, before it had even been outlawed by the king.

"Everything in this world is magic. Thank you ever so kindly for stating the obvious."

She calmed her reeling mind long enough to say, "But magic doesn't work anymore."

"New magic doesn't. But the king cannot erase old spells made with older powers—like the Wyrdmarks. Those ancient spells still hold; especially ones that imbue life."

"You're . . . alive?"

The knocker chuckled. "Alive? I'm made of bronze. I do not breathe, nor do I eat or drink. So, no, I am not alive. Nor am I dead, for that matter. I simply exist."

She stared at the small knocker. It was no larger than her fist.

"You should apologize," it said. "You have no idea how loud and tiresome you've been these past few months, with all your running down here and slaying foul beasties. I kept quiet until I thought you'd witnessed enough strange things that you could *accept* my existence. But apparently, I am to be disappointed."

Hands trembling, she sheathed her dagger and set down her candle. "I'm *so* glad you finally found me worth speaking to."

The bronze skull closed its eyes. The skull had eyelids. How had she not noticed it before? "Why should I speak to someone who doesn't have the courtesy to greet me, or even to knock?"

Celaena took a calming breath and looked at the door. The stones of the threshold still bore gouges from where the ridderak had passed through. "Is she in there?"

"Is *who* in there?" the skull said coyly.

"Elena—the queen."

"Of course she is. She's been in there for a thousand years." The skull's eyes seemed to glow.

"Don't mock me, or I'll peel you off this door and melt you down."

"Not even the strongest man in the world could peel me from this door. King Brannon himself put me here to watch over her tomb."

"You're that old?"

The skull huffed. "How insensitive of you to insult me about my age."

Celaena crossed her arms. Nonsense—magic always led to nonsense like this. "What's your name?"

"What is *your* name?"

"Celaena Sardothien," she ground out.

The skull barked a laugh. "Oh, that is too funny! The funniest thing I've heard in centuries!"

"Be quiet."

"My name is Mort, if you must know."

She picked up the candle. "Can I expect all of our encounters to be this pleasant?" She reached for the door handle.

"Aren't you even going to knock, after all that? You truly have no manners."

She used all of her self-control to avoid banging on his little face as she made three unnecessarily loud knocks on the wooden door.

Mort smirked as the door silently swung open. "Celaena Sardothien," he said to himself, and began laughing again. Celaena hissed in his direction and kicked the door shut.

The tomb was dim with foggy light, and Celaena approached the grate through which it poured, carried down from the surface by a silver-coated shaft. It was normally brighter in here, but the eclipse made the tomb increasingly murky.

She paused not too far from the threshold, set the candle on the floor, and found herself staring at—nothing.

Elena wasn't there.

"Hello?"

Mort chuckled from the other side of the door.

Celaena rolled her eyes and yanked the door back open. Of course Elena wouldn't actually *be* here when she had an important question. Of course she'd only have something like Mort to talk to. Of course, of course, of course.

"Is she coming tonight?" Celaena demanded.

"No," Mort said simply, as if she should have known already. "She nearly burnt herself out helping you these past few months."

"What? So she's . . . gone?"

"For the time being—until she regains her strength."

Celaena crossed her arms, taking yet another long, long breath. The chamber seemed the same as it had been the last time she was here. Two stone sarcophagi lay in the center, one depicting Gavin, Elena's husband and the first King of Adarlan, and the other Elena, both with eerily lifelike quality. Elena's silver hair spilled over the side of the coffin, disrupted only by the crown atop her head and the delicately pointed ears that marked her as half human, half Fae. Celaena's attention lingered on the words etched at Elena's feet: *Ah! Time's Rift!*

Brannon, Elena's Fae father—not to mention the first King of Terrasen—had carved the words into the sarcophagus himself.

The whole tomb was strange, actually. Stars had been carved into the floor, and trees and flowers adorned the arched ceiling. The walls were all etched with Wyrdmarks, the ancient symbols that could be used to access a power that still worked—a power that Nehemia and her family had long kept secret until Cain had somehow mastered it. If the king ever learned of their power, if he knew it could summon creatures as Cain had done, he could unleash endless evil upon Erilea. And his plans would become even more deadly.

"But Elena *did* tell me that if you deigned to come here again," Mort said, "she had a message for you."

Celaena had a feeling of standing in front of a cresting wave, waiting-waiting-waiting for it to break. It could wait—the message could wait, the oncoming burden could wait—for another moment or two of freedom. She walked to the back of the tomb, which had been piled with jewels and gold and trunks overflowing with treasure.

Before it all was displayed a suit of armor and Damaris, the legendary sword of Gavin. Its hilt was silvery gold and had little ornamentation save for a pommel in the shape of an eye. No jewel lay in the socket; it was only an empty ring of gold. Some legends claimed that when Gavin wielded Damaris, he would see only the truth, and that was why he had been crowned king. Or some nonsense like that.

Damaris's scabbard was decorated by a few Wyrdmarks. Everything seemed connected to those blasted symbols. Celaena scowled and examined the king's armor. It still bore scratches and indentations upon its golden front. From battles, no doubt. Perhaps even the fight with Erawan, the dark lord who had led an army of demons and the dead against the continent when the kingdoms had been little more than warring territories.

Elena had said that she was a warrior, too. But her armor was nowhere to be seen. Where had it gone? It was probably lying forgotten in a castle somewhere in the kingdoms.

Forgotten. The same way legend had reduced the fierce warrior-princess to nothing more than a damsel in a tower, whom Gavin had rescued.

"It's not over, is it?" Celaena asked Mort at last.

"No," Mort said, quieter than he'd been before. This was what Celaena had been dreading for weeks—for months.

The moonlight in the tomb was fading. Soon the eclipse would be complete, and the tomb would be dark, save for the candle.

"Let's hear her message," Celaena said, sighing.

Mort cleared his throat, and then said in a voice that sounded eerily like the queen's, "'If I could leave you in peace, I would. But you have lived your life aware that you will never escape certain burdens. Whether you like it or not, you are bound to the fate of this world. As the King's Champion, you are now in a position of power, and you can make a difference in the lives of many.'" Celaena's stomach turned over.

"Cain and the ridderak were just the beginning of the threat to Erilea," Mort said, the words echoing around the tomb. "There is a far deadlier power poised to devour the world."

"And I have to find it, I suppose?"

"Yes. There will be clues to lead you to it. Signs you must follow. Refusing to kill the king's targets is only the first and smallest step."

Celaena looked toward the ceiling, as if she could see through the tree-carved surface to the library far, far above. "I saw someone in the castle hallway tonight. Some*thing*. It made the amulet glow."

"Human?" Mort asked, sounding reluctantly intrigued.

"I don't know," Celaena admitted. "It didn't feel like it." She closed her eyes, taking a steadying breath. She'd been waiting for this for months. "It's all connected to the king, isn't it? All of these awful things? Even Elena's command—that's about finding whatever power *he* has, the threat he poses."

"You already know the answer to that."

Her heart thundered—with fear, with anger, she didn't know. "If she's so damn powerful and knows so much, then she can go find the king's source of power herself."

"It is *your* fate, and *your* responsibility."

"There is no such thing as fate," Celaena hissed.

"Says the girl who was saved from the ridderak because *some* force compelled her down here on Samhuinn, to see Damaris and learn it was here."

Celaena took a step closer to the door. "Says the girl who spent a year in Endovier. Says the girl who knows that the gods care no more for our lives than we care for an insect beneath our feet." She glared into Mort's gleaming face. "Come to think of it, I can't quite recall *why* I should bother helping Erilea, when the gods so clearly don't bother to help us, either."

"You don't mean that," he said.

Celaena gripped the hilt of her dagger. "I do. So tell Elena to find some other fool to impose upon."

"You *must* discover where the king's power comes from and what he plans to do—before it's too late."

Celaena snorted. "Don't you understand? It's already too late. It's been too late for *years* now. Where was Elena ten years ago, when there was a whole host of heroes that she could have had her pick of? Where were she and her ridiculous quests when the world truly needed them—when Terrasen's heroes were cut down or hunted and executed by Adarlan's armies? Where was she when the kingdoms fell, one by one, to the king?" Her eyes burned, but she shoved the pain down to that dark place where it dwelled inside of her. "The world is already in ruin, and I won't be set on some fool's errand."

Mort's eyes narrowed. Inside the tomb, the light had faded; the moon was almost fully covered now. "I am sorry for what you have lost," he said in a voice that was not quite his. "And I am sorry about your parents' deaths that night. It was—"

"Don't you *ever* talk about my parents," Celaena snarled, pointing a finger at his face. "I don't give a damn if you're magic or if you're Elena's lackey or if you're just some figment of my imagination. You talk about my parents again, and I'll hack this door to pieces. Understand?"

Mort just glowered at her. "You're that selfish? That cowardly? Why did you come down here tonight, Celaena? To help us all? Or just to help yourself? Elena told me about you—about your past."

"Shut your rutting face," she snapped, and stormed up the stairs.

CHAPTER 7

Celaena awoke before dawn with a pounding headache. It took one look at the mostly melted candle on her nightstand to know that her encounter in the tomb hadn't been some awful dream. Which meant that far beneath her room, there *was* a talking door knocker imbued with an ancient animation spell. And that Elena had yet again found a way to make her life infinitely more complicated.

Celaena groaned and buried her face in her pillow. She'd meant what she said last night. The world was beyond helping. Even if . . . even if she'd seen firsthand just how dangerous things could become—how much worse it could be. And that person in the hall . . .

She flipped onto her back, and Fleetfoot poked her cheek with a wet nose. Idly stroking the dog's head, Celaena stared up at the ceiling and the pale gray light seeping through the curtains.

She didn't want to admit it, but Mort was right. She'd gone to the tomb just to have Elena deal with the creature in the hallway—to be reassured that she wouldn't have to do anything.

My plans, the king had said. And if Elena was warning her to uncover them, to find the source of his power . . . then they had to be bad. Worse than the slaves in Calaculla and Endovier, worse than putting down more rebels.

She watched the ceiling for another few moments, until two things became clear.

The first was that if she *didn't* uncover this threat, it might be a fatal mistake. Elena had just said she had to *find* it. She hadn't said anything about destroying it. Nothing about facing the king. Which was a relief, Celaena supposed.

And the second was that she needed to speak with Archer—to get closer and start figuring out a way to fake his death. Because if he truly was a part of this movement that knew what the king was up to, then perhaps he could save her the trouble of spying on the king and piecing together whatever clues she could find. But once she took that step toward approaching Archer . . . Well, then everything would certainly become a lethal game.

So Celaena quickly bathed and then dressed in her finest, warmest clothes before calling for Chaol.

It was time for her to conveniently run into Archer Finn.

Thanks to the snow from the night before, some poor souls had been conscripted into shoveling Rifthold's most fashionable districts. Businesses stayed open year-round, and despite the slick sidewalks and slushy cobblestone streets, the capital city was just as vibrant that afternoon as it was at the height of summer.

Still, Celaena *wished* it were summer, since the wet streets soaked the hem of her ice-blue gown, and it was so cold that not even her white fur cloak could keep out the chill. As they walked down the crowded main avenue, she kept close to Chaol. He had been pestering her again to let him help with Archer, and inviting him along today was the most harmless thing she could do to get him off her back about it. She'd insisted he wear normal clothes instead of his captain's uniform.

To him, that meant showing up in a black tunic.

Thankfully, no one paid them much heed—not when there were so many people, and so many stores. Oh, how she *adored* this avenue, where all the fine things in the world were sold and bartered! Jewelers, hatters, clothiers, confectioneries, cobblers . . . Unsurprisingly, Chaol stomped right past every shop window, not even glancing at the delights displayed inside.

As usual, there was a crowd outside the Willows—the tea court where she knew Archer was having his lunch. He seemed to dine here every day with a few other male courtesans. Of course, it had *nothing* to do with the fact that most of Rifthold's elite patronesses also dined here.

She grabbed Chaol's arm as they drew near the tea court. "If you walk up looking like you're going to pummel someone," she crooned, linking her elbow through his, "then he'll certainly know something is amiss. And, again, *do not* say anything to him. Leave the talking and the charming to me."

Chaol raised his brows. "So I'm just here for decoration?"

"Be grateful I consider you a worthy accessory."

He grumbled something under his breath that she was fairly certain she would not want to hear, but still slowed his pace to a rather elegant walk.

Outside the arched stone-and-glass entrance to the tea court, fine carriages loitered in the street, people hopping in and out of them. They could have taken a carriage—*should* have taken a carriage, given how cold it was and the fact of her now-sodden gown. But she'd foolishly wanted to walk, to see the city on the arm of the Captain of the Guard, even if he spent the entire time looking like a threat was lurking around every corner and down every alley. Come to think of it, a carriage probably would have made a better entrance, too.

Entry to the Willows required a hard-to-attain membership; Celaena had taken her tea there several times while growing up, thanks to Arobynn Hamel's name. She could still recall the clink of porcelain, the hushed gossip, the mint-and-cream painted room, and the floor-to-ceiling windows that overlooked an exquisite garden.

"We're not going in there," Chaol said, and it wasn't exactly a question.

She gave him a feline grin. "You aren't afraid of a bunch of stuffy old ladies and giggling young women, are you?" He glared at her, and she patted his arm. "Weren't you listening when I explained my plan? We're just going to *pretend* that we're waiting for our table. So don't fret: you won't have to fight off all the mean little ladies clawing at you."

"The next time we train," he said as they eased through the throng of beautifully dressed women, "remind me to wallop you."

An elderly woman turned to glare at him, and Celaena gave her an apologetic and exasperated look, as if to say, *Men!* She then promptly dug her nails into Chaol's thick winter tunic and hissed, "This is the part where you shut your mouth and pretend to be a woolly-headed bit of decoration. Shouldn't be too hard for you."

His returning pinch told her that he was *really* going to make her sweat the next time they were in the training room. She grinned.

After finding a spot just below the steps that led up to the double doors, Celaena glanced at her pocket watch. Archer had begun dining at two, and usually the meal was over within ninety minutes, which meant he'd be leaving any second now. She made a good show of pretending to rummage through her small coin purse, and Chaol, mercifully, kept quiet, observing the crowd around them, as if these fancy women might attack them at any moment.

A few minutes passed, and her gloved hands grew numb as people continued walking into and out of the tea court, so often that no one bothered to notice that they were the only ones who *weren't* about to go in. But then the front doors opened, and Celaena caught a glimpse of bronze hair and a dazzling smile, and she moved.

Chaol played along with expert skill, escorting her up the steps, up, up, until—

"Oomph!" she cried, slamming into a broad, muscled shoulder. Chaol even pulled her to him, a supporting hand on her back to keep her from toppling down the stairs. She looked up through her lashes, and then—

A blink, two blinks.

The exquisite face gaping at her broke into a grin. *"Laena?"*

She'd planned to smile anyway, but when she heard his old pet name for her . . . "Archer!"

She felt Chaol stiffen slightly, but she didn't bother to glance at him. It was hard to look away from Archer, who had been and still was the most beautiful man she'd ever seen. Not handsome—*beautiful.* His skin glowed golden even in the height of winter, and his green eyes . . .

Gods above and Wyrd save me.

His mouth was a work of art, too, all sensual lines and softness that begged to be explored.

As if emerging from a daze, Archer suddenly shook his head. "We should get off the steps," he said, extending a broad hand to gesture to the street below them. "Unless you and your companion have a reservation—"

"Oh, we're a few minutes early, anyway," she said, letting go of Chaol's arm to walk back onto the street. Archer followed beside her, giving her a glance at his clothes—expertly tailored tunic and pants, knee-high boots, a heavy cloak. None of it *screamed* wealth, but she could tell it was all expensive. Unlike some of the flashier and softer male courtesans, Archer's appeal had always been more ruggedly masculine.

The broad, muscled shoulders and powerful frame; the knowing smile; even his beautiful face radiated a sense of maleness that had her struggling to remember what she'd planned to say.

Even Archer seemed to be searching for words as they faced each other on the street, a few steps away from the busy crowd.

"It's been a while," she began, smiling again. Chaol remained a step away, utterly silent. And unsmiling.

Archer stuffed his hands into his pockets. "I almost didn't recognize you. You were just a girl when I saw you last. You were . . . Gods above, you were thirteen, I think."

She couldn't help herself—she looked up at him from beneath lowered lashes and purred, "I'm not thirteen anymore."

Archer gave her a slow, sensual smile as he took her in from head to toe before saying, "It would certainly seem that way."

"You filled out a bit more, too," she said, returning the favor of surveying him.

Archer grinned. "Comes with the profession." He angled his head to the side, then flicked his magnificent eyes to Chaol, who now stood with his arms crossed. She still remembered how adept Archer had been at taking in details. It was probably part of the reason he'd become the top male courtesan in Rifthold. And a formidable opponent when Celaena was training at the Assassins' Keep.

She glanced at Chaol, who was too busy staring down Archer to notice her attention. "He knows everything," she told Archer. Some tension flowed out of Archer's shoulders, but the surprise and amusement were also wearing off, replaced by hesitant pity.

"How'd you get out?" Archer asked carefully—still not mentioning anything about her profession or Endovier, despite her reassurance that Chaol knew.

"I was let out. By the king. I work for him now."

Archer eyed Chaol again, and she took a step toward the courtesan. "He's a friend," she said softly. Was it suspicion or fear in his eyes? And was it merely because she worked for a tyrant that the world feared, or because he'd actually turned rebel and had something to hide? She kept herself as casual as possible, as unthreatening and relaxed as anyone might be upon encountering an old friend.

Archer asked, "Does Arobynn know you're back?"

That was not a question she'd prepared for, or wanted to hear. She shrugged. "He has eyes everywhere; I'd be surprised if he didn't know."

Archer nodded solemnly. "I'm sorry. I heard about Sam—and about what happened at Farran's house that night." He shook his head, closing his eyes. "I'm just—sorry."

Even though her heart twisted at his words, she nodded. "Thank you."

She put a hand on Chaol's arm, suddenly needing just to touch him, to make sure he was still there. Needing to stop talking about *this*, too, she sighed and pretended to look interested in the glass doors at the top of the steps.

"We should go inside," she lied. She gave Archer a smile. "I know I was a miserable little brat when you trained at the Keep, but . . . do you want to have dinner with me tomorrow? I have the night off."

"You certainly had your moments back then." Archer returned her smile and sketched a bow. "I'll have to move some appointments around, but I'd be delighted." He reached into his cloak and pulled out a cream-colored card, engraved with his name and address. "Just send word about where and when, and I'll be there."

Celaena had been quiet since Archer left, and Chaol hadn't tried to initiate conversation with her, though he was near bursting to say something.

He didn't even know where to start.

During the whole exchange, all he'd really been able to think about was how much he wanted to slam Archer's pretty face against the stone building.

Chaol wasn't a fool. He knew some of her smiles and blushing hadn't been acted. And though he had no claim on her—though making a claim would be the stupidest thing he could ever do—the thought of her being susceptible to Archer's charms made him want to have a little chat with the courtesan.

Rather than head back to the castle, she began walking through the wealthy district in the heart of the city, her steps unhurried. After nearly thirty minutes of silence, Chaol figured he'd cooled his temper enough to be civil. "*Laena?*" he demanded.

Slightly civil, at least.

The gold streaks in her turquoise eyes were bright in the afternoon sun. "Of all the things we said back there, *that* is what bothered you most?"

It did. Wyrd keep him, it bothered the hell out of him.

"When you said you knew him, I didn't realize you meant *that* well." He fought the strange, sudden temper that was honing itself again. Even if she'd been charmed by his looks, she was going to kill Archer, he had to remind himself.

"My history with Archer will allow me to get him to provide information about whatever this rebel movement is," she said, looking up at the fine houses they passed. The residential streets were tranquil despite the bustling city center only a few blocks down. "He's one of the few people who actually *likes* me, you know. Or he did years ago. It shouldn't be too hard to get some inkling of what this group might be planning against the king—or who the other members might be."

Part of him, he knew, should be ashamed for finding some relief in the fact that she was going to kill him. He was a better man than that—and he certainly wasn't the territorial type.

And the gods knew he had no claim on her. He'd seen the look on her face when Archer had mentioned Sam.

He'd heard of Sam Cortland's death in passing. He'd never known that Celaena and Sam had crossed paths, that Celaena had ever . . . ever *loved* that fiercely. On the night she was captured, she hadn't been out to collect cold coin for a contract—no, she'd gone into that house to get revenge for the sort of loss he couldn't begin to imagine.

They walked down the street, her side nearly pressed against his. He fought against the urge to lean into her, to tuck her in closer.

"Chaol?" she said after a few minutes.

"Hmm?"

"You know I absolutely *hate* it when he calls me Laena, don't you?"

A smile tugged at his lips, along with a flicker of relief. "So the next time I want to piss you off . . ."

"Don't you even think about it."

His smile spread, and the flicker of relief turned to something that punched him in the gut when she smiled back.

CHAPTER
8

She had planned to spend the rest of the day following Archer from a distance, but as they walked from the tea court, Chaol informed her that the king had ordered her to assist with guard duty at a state dinner that night. And though she could think of a thousand excuses to get out of it, any suspicious behavior on her part could draw the wrong sort of attention. If she was actually going to listen to Elena this time, she needed the king—she needed his entire *empire*—to think she was his obedient servant.

The state dinner was in the Great Hall, and it took all of Celaena's self-control to keep from sprinting to the long table in the center of the room and horking down the food right off the plates of the gathered councilmen and preening nobility. Roasted lamb rubbed with thyme and lavender, duck glazed with orange sauce, pheasant swimming in green-onion gravy . . . Truly, it wasn't fair.

Chaol had stationed her by a pillar near the glass patio doors.

Though she wasn't wearing the royal guards' black uniform with the gold embroidered wyvern across the chest, she blended in well enough in her dark clothes. At least she was so far away from it all that no one could hear her stomach grumbling.

Other tables had been set up, too—full of lesser nobility who had been invited to join, all impeccably dressed for the occasion. Most of the attention—of the guards, of the nobility—remained on the center table, where the king and queen sat with their innermost court. Duke Perrington, the hulking brute, also sat there, and Dorian and Roland were nearby, chatting with the precious, pampered men who made up the king's council. Men who had bled other kingdoms dry to pay for the clothes and jewels and gold in this room. Not that she was much better, in some regards.

Though she tried to avoid looking at the king, every time she did steal a glance at him, she wondered why he bothered attending these events when he could do away with this nonsense altogether. She gleaned nothing, though. And she didn't think for a moment that he'd be stupid enough to reveal anything about his true agenda in front of all these people.

Chaol stood at attention at the column nearest the king's chair, his eyes darting everywhere, always alert. He had his best men here tonight—all handpicked by him that afternoon. He didn't seem to realize that no one would be so suicidal as to attack the king and his court at such a public event. She'd tried explaining that, but Chaol had just glared at her and told her not to cause trouble.

As if *she'd* be that suicidal.

The meal ended with the king standing up and bidding his guests farewell, the auburn-haired Queen Georgina dutifully and silently following him out of the Great Hall. The other guests remained, but now milled about from table to table, chatting with far more ease than they had while the king was present.

Dorian was on his feet, Roland still beside him as they spoke to three remarkably pretty young courtiers. Roland said something that set the girls giggling and blushing behind their lace fans, and Dorian's lips stretched toward a smile.

He *couldn't* like Roland. She had nothing more than gut feeling and Chaol's story to go by, but . . . there was something about Roland's emerald eyes that made her want to pull Dorian as far away from him as possible. Dorian was playing a dangerous game, too, she realized. As Crown Prince, he had to walk a careful line with certain people. Perhaps she'd speak to Chaol about it.

Celaena frowned. Telling Chaol could lead to tedious explanations. Maybe she'd just warn Dorian herself once this dinner was over. She had ended things with him romantically, but she still cared about him. Despite his history with women, he was everything that a prince should be: intelligent, kind, charming. Why hadn't Elena approached *him* for her tasks?

Dorian couldn't possibly know what his father was up to—no, he couldn't act the way he did if he knew that his father had such sinister intent. And maybe he shouldn't ever know.

No matter what she felt for him, Dorian would rule. And maybe his father would someday reveal his power and force Dorian to make a choice about what sort of ruler he wanted to become. But she was in no hurry to have Dorian make that choice; not yet. When he did, she could only pray that he would be a better king than his father.

⁘

Dorian knew Celaena was watching him. She'd been stealing glances at him throughout the whole insufferable dinner. But she'd also been looking at Chaol, and when she did, he could have sworn that her whole face changed—became softer, more contemplative.

She lounged against a pillar by the patio doors, cleaning her nails with a dagger. Thank the Wyrd his father had left, because he was fairly certain the king would have flayed her for it.

Roland said something else to the three ladies in front of them—girls whose names Dorian had heard and immediately forgotten—and they giggled again. Roland certainly rivaled him for charm. And it seemed that Roland's mother had come with him to find the young lord a bride—a girl with land and money that would add to Meah's importance. Dorian didn't have to ask Roland to know that until his wedding night, his cousin would enjoy all of the benefits of living in the castle as a young lord.

Listening to him flirt, watching him grin at these girls, Dorian didn't know whether he wanted to punch Roland or walk away. But years of living in this festering court kept Dorian from doing anything but looking gloriously bored.

He glanced at Celaena again, only to see her watching Chaol, whose eyes were in turn fixed on Roland. Sensing Dorian's attention, Celaena met his gaze.

Nothing. Not a hint of emotion. Dorian's temper flared, so fast that he found himself struggling for control. Especially as she looked away again—and her focus returned to the captain. And stayed there. *Enough.*

Not bothering to say good-bye to Roland or the girls, he strode out of the Great Hall. He had better, more important things to worry about than what Celaena felt for his friend. He was the Crown Prince of the largest empire in the world. His entire existence was bound to the crown and the glass throne that would someday be his. She'd ended things *because* of that crown and throne—because she wanted a freedom he could never give her.

"Dorian," someone called as he entered the hallway. He didn't have to turn around to know it was Celaena. She caught up to him, easily matching the brisk pace he hadn't realized he'd set. He didn't even know *where* he was going, only that he needed to get out of the Great Hall. She touched his elbow, and he hated himself for savoring the touch.

"What do you want?" he asked.

They passed beyond the busy halls and she tugged on his arm, slowing him down. "What's wrong?"

"Why would anything be wrong?"

How long have you been yearning for him? was what he really wanted to ask. Damn him for caring. Damn him for every moment he'd spent with her.

"You look like you could splatter someone against a wall."

He raised an eyebrow. He hadn't been making a face.

"When you get angry," she explained, "your eyes get this . . . cold look. Glazed."

"I'm fine."

They kept walking, and she kept following him to . . . to wherever he was going. The library, he decided, turning down a passageway. He'd go to the royal library.

"If you have something to say," he drawled, putting his temper on a tight leash, "then just say it."

"I don't trust your cousin."

He paused, the shining hallway around them empty. "You don't even know him."

"Call it instinct."

"Roland is harmless."

"Maybe. But maybe not. Maybe he has his own agenda in being here. And you're too smart to be a pawn in anyone's game, Dorian. He's from Meah."

"And?"

"*And* Meah is a small, insignificant port city. It means he's got little to lose and a *lot* to gain. That makes people dangerous. Ruthless. He'll use you, if he can."

"The same way an assassin from Endovier used me to become King's Champion?"

Her lips thinned. "Is that what you think I did?"

"I don't know what to think." He turned away.

She snarled—actually *snarled*—at him. "Well, let me tell you what *I* think, Dorian. I think you're used to getting what you want—who you want. And just because you couldn't get who you wanted this *one* time—"

He whirled toward her. "You know nothing about what I wanted. You didn't even give me the chance to tell you."

She rolled her eyes. "I'm not having this conversation right now. I came to warn you about your cousin, but you clearly don't care. So don't expect *me* to care when you find yourself nothing more than a puppet. If you aren't one already."

He opened his mouth, so close to exploding he could have punched the nearest wall, but Celaena was already striding off.

Celaena stood in front of the bars to Kaltain Rompier's cell.

The once-beautiful lady was curled against the wall, her dress soiled and her dark hair unbound and matted. She had buried her face in her arms, but Celaena could still see that her skin gleamed with sweat and had a slightly grayish hue. And the smell . . .

She hadn't seen her since the duel; since the day Kaltain had drugged Celaena's water with bloodbane so she would die at Cain's hands. Once she'd defeated Cain, Celaena had left without witnessing the screaming fit that Kaltain had thrown. So she'd missed the moment where Kaltain had accidentally confessed to poisoning her, claiming to have been manipulated by her former beau, Duke Perrington. The duke had denied her accusations, and Kaltain had been sent down here to await her punishment.

Two months later, it seemed that they still didn't know what to do with her—or didn't care.

"Hello, Kaltain," Celaena said quietly.

Kaltain lifted her head, her black eyes gleaming in recognition. "Hello, Celaena."

CHAPTER 9

Celaena took a step closer to the bars. A bucket for relieving herself, a bucket of water, the crumbs of her last meal, and moldy hay that formed a rough pallet; that was all Kaltain had been given.

All she deserves.

"Come to laugh?" Kaltain said. Her voice, which had once been rich and cultured, was little more than a hoarse whisper. It was freezing down here—it was a wonder Kaltain hadn't fallen ill already.

"I have some questions for you," Celaena said, keeping her words soft. Though the guards hadn't challenged her right to enter the dungeons, she didn't want them eavesdropping.

"I'm busy today." Kaltain smiled, leaning her head against the stone wall. "Come back tomorrow." She looked so much younger with her ebony hair unbound. She couldn't be much older than Celaena herself.

Celaena dropped into a crouch, one hand braced against the bars for balance. The metal was bitingly cold. "What do you know about Roland Havilliard?"

Kaltain looked toward the stone ceiling. "He's visiting?"

"He's been appointed to the king's council."

Kaltain's night-dark eyes met Celaena's. There was a hint of madness there—but also wariness and exhaustion. "Why ask me about him?"

"Because I want to know if he can be trusted."

Kaltain wheezed a laugh. "*None* of us can be trusted. Especially not Roland. The things I've heard about him are enough to turn even your stomach, I bet."

"Like what?"

Kaltain smirked. "Get me out of this cell and I might tell you."

Celaena returned the smirk. "How about I walk inside that cell and find another way to get you to talk?"

"*Don't*," she whispered, shifting enough so that Celaena could see the bruises circling her wrists. They looked unnervingly like handprints.

Kaltain tucked her arms into the folds of her skirts. "The night watch looks the other way when Perrington visits."

Celaena bit the inside of her lip. "I'm sorry," she said, and meant it. And she would mention it to Chaol when she saw him next; make sure he had a word with the night watch.

Kaltain rested her cheek on her knee. "He's ruined everything. And I don't even know why. Why not just send me home instead?" Her voice had taken on a faraway quality that Celaena recognized too well from her time in Endovier. Once the memories and the pain and the fear took over, there would be no chance of talking to her.

She asked quietly, "You were close to Perrington. Did you ever overhear anything about his plans?" A dangerous question, but if anyone might tell her, it would be Kaltain.

But the girl was staring at nothing and didn't reply.

Celaena stood. "Good luck."

Kaltain just shivered, tucking her hands under her arms.

She should let Kaltain freeze to death for what she'd tried to do to her. She should walk out of the dungeons smiling, because for *once* the right person was locked away.

"They encourage the crows to fly past here," Kaltain murmured, more to herself than to Celaena. "And my headaches are worse every day. Worse and worse, and full of all of those flapping wings."

Celaena kept her face blank. She couldn't hear anything—no caws, and certainly no flapping wings. Even if there were crows, the dungeon was so far underground that there was no way of hearing them here. "What do you mean?"

But Kaltain had already curled in on herself again, conserving as much warmth as she could. Celaena didn't want to think about how frigid the cell must be at night; she knew what it felt like to curl up like that, desperate for any kernel of warmth, wondering whether you'd wake up in the morning, or if the cold would claim you before then.

Not giving herself the time to reconsider, Celaena unfastened her black cloak. She threw it through the bars, aiming carefully to avoid the long-dried vomit that was caked onto the stones. She'd also heard about the girl's opium addiction— —being locked away without a fix had to have driven her close to insanity, if she wasn't mad to begin with.

Kaltain stared at the cloak that landed in her lap, and Celaena pivoted to return down the narrow, icy corridor and up to the warmer levels above.

"Sometimes," Kaltain said softly, and Celaena paused. "Sometimes I think they brought me here. Not to marry Perrington, but for another purpose. They want to use me."

"Use you for what?"

"They never say. When they come down here, they never tell me what they want. I don't even remember. It's all just . . . fragments. Shards of a broken mirror, each gleaming with its own individual image."

She was mad. Celaena clamped down the urge to make a cutting remark, the memory of Kaltain's bruises staying her tongue. "Thank you for your help."

Kaltain wrapped Celaena's cloak around herself. "Something is coming," she whispered. "And I am to greet it."

Celaena loosed the breath she hadn't realized she'd been holding. This conversation was pointless. "Good-bye, Kaltain."

The girl only laughed softly, and the sound followed Celaena long after she'd left the freezing dungeons behind.

"Those *bastards*," Nehemia spat, clenching her teacup so hard Celaena thought the princess would shatter it. They sat together in her bed, a large breakfast tray spread between them. Fleetfoot watched their every bite, ready to devour any stray crumbs. "How could the guards just turn their backs like that? How can they keep her in such conditions? Kaltain is a member of the court—and if they treat *her* like that, then I can't begin to imagine how they treat criminals from the other classes." Nehemia paused, glancing apologetically at Celaena.

Celaena shrugged and shook her head. After seeing Kaltain, she'd gone out to stalk Archer, but a snowstorm had struck, so fierce that visibility was nearly impossible. After an hour of trying to track him through the snow-swept city, she'd given up and come back to the castle.

The storm had continued all night, leaving a blanket of snow too deep for Celaena to take her usual morning run with Chaol. So she'd invited Nehemia to join her for breakfast in bed, and the princess—who was now thoroughly sick of snow—was more than happy to dash to Celaena's rooms and hop under the warm covers.

Nehemia set down her tea. "You have to tell Captain Westfall about how she's being treated."

Celaena finished her scone and leaned back in her fluffed-up pillows. "I already did. He dealt with it." No need to mention that after Chaol had returned to his bedroom, where Celaena had been reading, his tunic was rumpled, his knuckles were raw, and there was a deadly sort of gleam in his chestnut eyes that told Celaena the dungeon guard was going to have some serious changes—and new members.

"You know," Nehemia mused, using her foot to gently shove Fleetfoot away as the dog tried to snatch some food off their tray, "the courts weren't always like this. There was a time when people valued honor and loyalty—when serving a ruler wasn't about obedience and fear." She shook her head, her gold-tipped braids tinkling. In the early morning sun, her hazelnut skin was smooth and lovely. Honestly, it was a tad unfair that Nehemia naturally looked so beautiful—especially at the crack of dawn.

Nehemia went on. "I think such honor faded from Adarlan generations ago, but before Terrasen fell, its royal court was the one that set the example. My father used to tell me stories of Terrasen's court—of the warriors and lords who served King Orlon in his inner circle, of the unrivaled power and bravery and loyalty of his court. That was why the King of Adarlan targeted Terrasen first. Because it was the strongest, and because if Terrasen had been given the chance to raise an army against him, Adarlan would have been annihilated. My father still says that if Terrasen were to rise again, it might stand a chance; it would be a genuine threat to Adarlan."

Celaena looked toward the hearth. "I know," she managed to get out.

Nehemia turned to look at her. "Do you think another court like that could ever rise again? Not just in Terrasen, but anywhere? I've heard the court in Wendlyn still follows the old ways, but they're across the ocean, and do us no good. They looked in the other direction while the king enslaved our lands, and they still refuse all calls for aid."

Celaena forced herself to snort, to wave her hand in dismissal. "This is an awfully heavy discussion for breakfast." She filled her mouth with toast. When she dared a glance at the princess, Nehemia's expression remained contemplative. "Any news about the king?"

Nehemia clicked her tongue. "Only that he's added that little grub, Roland, to his council, and Roland seems to have been given the task of handling *me*. Apparently, I've been too pushy with Minister Mullison, the councilman responsible for dealing with Calaculla's labor camp. Roland is supposed to placate me."

"I can't tell who I feel worse for: you or Roland."

Nehemia jabbed her in the side, and Celaena chuckled, batting her hand away. Fleetfoot used their temporary distraction to swipe a piece of bacon right off the platter, and Celaena squawked. "You brazen thief!"

But Fleetfoot leapt off the bed, scuttled to the hearth, and stared right at Celaena as she gobbled down the rest of the bacon.

Nehemia laughed, and Celaena found herself joining in before she tossed Fleetfoot another piece of bacon. "Let's just stay in bed all day," Celaena said, throwing herself back onto the pillows and nestling into the blankets.

"I certainly wish I could," Nehemia said, sighing loudly. "Alas, I have things to do."

And so did she, Celaena realized. Like preparing for her dinner that evening with Archer.

CHAPTER 10

Dorian shivered as he entered the kennels that afternoon, brushing snow from his red cloak. Beside him, Chaol puffed air into his cupped hands, and the two young men hurried farther inside, the straw-coated floors crunching underfoot. Dorian hated winter—the intolerable cold and the way his boots never seemed completely dry.

They had chosen to enter the castle through the kennels because it was the easiest way to avoid Hollin, Dorian's ten-year-old brother, who had returned from school that morning and was already shrieking demands at anyone unfortunate enough to cross his path. Hollin would never look for them here. He hated animals.

They strode through the chorus of barking and whining, Dorian pausing every now and then to greet a favorite hound. He could have spent the rest of the day here—if only to avoid the court dinner in honor of Hollin. "I can't believe my mother pulled him out of school," he muttered.

"She missed her son," Chaol said, still rubbing his hands together, though the kennels were deliciously warm compared to outside. "And now that there's this movement growing against your father, he wants Hollin where we can keep an eye on him until it gets sorted out."

Until Celaena kills all the traitors, was what Chaol didn't need to say.

Dorian sighed. "I don't even want to imagine what sort of absurd gift my mother bought him. Do you remember the last one?"

Chaol grinned. It was hard *not* to remember the last gift Georgina had bought her younger son: four white ponies with a tiny golden carriage for Hollin to drive about himself. He'd trampled half of the queen's favorite garden.

Chaol led them toward the doors at the far end of the kennels. "You can't avoid him forever." Even as the captain spoke, Dorian could see him scanning, as he always did, for any sign of danger, any threat. After so many years, Dorian was used to it, but it still rankled his pride a little.

They passed through the glass doors and into the castle. To Dorian, the hall was warm and glowing; wreaths and garlands of evergreen still decorated archways and tabletops. To Chaol, he supposed, an enemy could be waiting anywhere.

"Maybe he's changed in the past few months—matured a little," Chaol said.

"You said that last summer, and I almost punched his teeth out."

Chaol shook his head. "Thank the Wyrd my brother was always too afraid of me to talk back."

Dorian tried not to look surprised. Since Chaol had abdicated his title as heir of Anielle, he hadn't seen his family in years, and rarely spoke about them.

Dorian could have gleefully killed Chaol's father for disowning him, refusing even to see Chaol when he brought his family to Rifthold for an important meeting with the king. Even though Chaol had never said it, Dorian knew the scars went deep.

Dorian sighed loudly. "Remind me again why I'm going to this dinner tonight?"

"Because your father will kill you *and* me if you don't show up and formally greet your brother."

"Maybe he'd hire Celaena to do it."

"*She* has dinner plans tonight. With Archer Finn."

"Isn't she supposed to kill him?"

"She wants information, apparently." A heavy pause. "I don't like him."

Dorian stiffened. They had managed, at least for the afternoon, to not talk about her—and for those few hours, it had been like nothing had ever changed between them. But things *had* changed. "I don't think you need to worry about Archer stealing her away—especially if he's going to be dead by the end of the month." It came out sharper and colder than he intended.

Chaol cut a glance at him. "You think *that's* what I'm worried about?"

Yes. And it's obvious to everyone except the two of you.

But he didn't want to have this conversation with Chaol, and Chaol sure as hell didn't want to have this conversation with him, so Dorian just shrugged. "She'll be fine, and you'll laugh at yourself for worrying. Even if he's as well-guarded as she claims, she's the Champion for a reason, right?"

Chaol nodded, though Dorian could still see the worry in his eyes.

⌒

Celaena knew the scarlet dress was a little scandalous. And she knew that it was definitely *not* appropriate for winter, given how low the front dipped, and how much lower the back went. Low enough to reveal through the black lace mesh that she wasn't wearing a corset beneath it.

But Archer Finn had always liked women who were daring with

their clothes, who were ahead of the trend. And this dress, with its close-fitting bodice, long, tight sleeves, and gently flowing skirt, was about as new and different as it came.

Which was why, when she ran into Chaol on her way out of her rooms, she wasn't very surprised when he stopped dead and blinked. Then blinked again.

Celaena smiled at him. "Hello to you, too."

Chaol stood in the hallway, his bronze eyes traveling down the front of her dress, then up again. "You're not wearing that."

She snorted and walked past him, deliberately giving him a view of the far more provocative back. "Oh, yes. I am."

Chaol fell into step beside her as she made her way down to the front gate and the waiting carriage. "You're going to catch your death."

She slung her ermine cloak around her. "Not with this, I won't."

"Do you even have any weapons with you?"

She stomped down the main staircase that led to the entrance hall. "*Yes*, Chaol, I have weapons. And I'm wearing this dress *because* I want Archer to ask the same thing. To think I don't have any on me."

There were indeed knives strapped to her legs, and the pins sweeping her hair into a curling cascade down one shoulder were long and razor-sharp—commissioned, to her delight, by Philippa, so she didn't need to "go traipsing around with cold metal jammed between your breasts."

"Oh," was all Chaol said. They reached the main entrance in silence, and Celaena slipped on her kid gloves as they neared the towering double doors that opened onto the courtyard. She was just about to walk down the front steps when Chaol touched her shoulder.

"Be careful," he said, examining the carriage, the driver, the footman. They seemed to pass inspection. "Don't put yourself at risk."

"I do this for a living, you know." She never should have told him about her capture, never should have let him see her as vulnerable, because now he'd just worry about her and doubt her and irritate her to no end. She didn't know why she did it, but she shook off his touch and hissed, "I'll see you tomorrow."

He stiffened as if he'd been struck, his teeth flashing. "What do you mean, *tomorrow?*"

Again, that stupid, bright anger took over, and she gave him a slow smile. "You're a smart boy," she said, stalking down the steps to the carriage. "Figure it out yourself."

Chaol kept staring as though he didn't know her, his body so very still. She wouldn't have him thinking her vulnerable, or foolish, or inexperienced—not when she'd worked so hard and sacrificed so much to get to this point. Maybe it had been a mistake to let him in; because the idea of him thinking that she was weak, that she needed to be protected, made her want to shatter someone's bones.

"Good night," she said, and before she could reconsider all that she'd just implied, she got into the carriage and drove away.

She'd worry about Chaol later. Tonight, her focus was on Archer—and on getting the truth out of him.

Archer was waiting inside an exclusive dining room, frequented by the elite of Rifthold. Most of the tables were already occupied, the patrons' fine clothes and jewels glimmering in the dim light.

As the servant at the front helped her out of her cloak, she made sure that she was angled away from Archer—so he could get an eyeful of the exquisite black lace that covered the open back (and mostly concealed her scars from Endovier). She felt the eyes of the servant on her, too, but pretended not to notice.

Archer let out a breath, and she turned to find him grinning, slowly shaking his head.

"I think 'stunning,' 'beautiful,' and 'dazzling' are the words you're looking for," she said. She took his arm as they were escorted to a table tucked into an alcove of the ornate room.

Archer ran a finger along the red velvet sleeve of her gown. "I'm glad to see your taste matured along with the rest of you. And with your arrogance, it seems."

She would have smiled anyway, she told herself.

Once they were seated, had the menu recited to them, and ordered the wine, Celaena found herself staring into that exquisite face. "So," she said, leaning back in her seat, "how many ladies want to kill me tonight for monopolizing your time?"

He gave a laugh like a tickle of breath. "If I told you, you'd be bolting back to the castle."

"You're still that popular?"

Archer waved a hand, taking a sip from his wine. "I still have my debts to Clarisse," he said, naming the most influential and prosperous madam in the capital. "But . . . yes." A twinkle gleamed in his eye. "And what of your surly friend? Should I watch my back tonight, too?"

This was all a dance, a prelude to what would come later. She winked at him. "He knows better than to try to keep me locked up."

"Wyrd help the man who does. I still remember what a hellion you were."

"And here I was thinking you found me charming."

"In the way a mountain cat's cub is charming, I suppose."

She laughed and drank a small sip of her wine. She had to keep her head as clear as possible. When she set her glass on the table, she found Archer giving her that contemplative, sad look he'd given her yesterday. "Can I ask how you came to work for him?" She knew he meant the king—and also knew he was aware they weren't the only people in the dining room. He would have made a good assassin.

Perhaps the king's suspicions weren't so far-fetched.

But she'd prepared for this question and countless others, so she gave him a wicked smile and said, "Turns out my skills are better suited to aiding the empire than they are to mining. Working for him and working for Arobynn are nearly the same." That wasn't a lie, actually.

Archer gave a slow, considering nod. "Our professions have always been similar, yours and mine. I can't tell which is worse: training us for the bedroom, or the battlefield."

If she recalled correctly, he'd been twelve when Clarisse had discovered him as an orphan running wild in the capital's streets and invited him to train with her.

And when he turned seventeen and had the Bidding Party for his virginity, there had been rumors of actual brawls breaking out among would-be patronesses.

"I can't tell, either. They're equally horrible, I suppose." She lifted her wineglass in a toast. "To our esteemed owners."

His eyes lingered on her for a moment before he lifted his glass and murmured, "To *us*." The sound of his voice was enough to make her skin heat, but the look in his eyes as he said it, the curve of that divine mouth . . . He was a weapon, too. A beautiful, deadly weapon.

He leaned over the edge of the table, pinning her to the spot with his stare. A challenge—and an intimate invitation.

Gods above and Wyrd save me.

She actually needed to take a long sip from her wine this time. "It's going to take more than a few sultry glances to make me your willing slave, Archer. You should know better than to try the tricks of your trade on me."

He let out a low, rumbling laugh that she felt in her core. "And I think you know well enough to realize when I'm not actually using them. If I *were*, then we would have left the restaurant already."

"That's a bold, bold claim. I don't think you'd want to go head-to-head with me when it comes to tricks of the trade."

"Oh, I want to do a lot of things with you."

She'd never been so grateful to see a servant in her life, and never realized that a bowl of soup could be so immensely interesting.

Since she'd dismissed her carriage just to spite Chaol and back up her insinuation, Celaena wound up in Archer's carriage after dinner. The meal itself had been pleasant enough—talk of old acquaintances, the theater, books, the miserable weather. All comfortable, safe topics, though he'd kept looking at her like she was his prey and this was one long hunt.

They sat beside each other on the bench of the carriage, close enough that she could smell whatever fine cologne he wore—an elegant, tantalizing blend that made her think of silk sheets and candlelight. So she turned her mind to what she was about to do.

The carriage rolled to a stop, and Celaena glanced out the small window to see a familiar, beautiful townhouse. Archer looked at her and gently twined her fingers with his before raising her hand to his lips. It was a soft, slow kiss that burned through her. He murmured onto her skin. "Do you want to come inside?"

She swallowed hard. "Don't you want a night off?" This was not what she'd expected. And . . . and this was *not* what she wanted, flirting aside.

He lifted his head but still held her hand, his thumb caressing small circles into her flame-hot skin. "It's immensely different when it's my choice, you know."

Someone else might have missed it, but she'd also grown up without choices, and recognized the glimmer of bitterness. She eased her hand out of his. "Do you hate your life?" Her words were barely more than a whisper.

He looked at her—*truly* looked at her, as though he somehow hadn't seen her until just now. "Sometimes," he said, and then his eyes shifted to the window behind her and the townhouse beyond it. "But some-day," he went on, "someday, I'll have enough money to pay off Clarisse forever—to really be *free*—and live on my own."

"You'd leave behind being a courtesan?"

He gave her a half smile that was more real than any expression she'd seen him give tonight. "By that point, I'll either be rich enough that I won't ever have to work, or old enough that no one will want to hire me."

She had a flicker of memory from a time when, just for a moment, she'd been free; when the world had been wide open and she'd been about to enter it with Sam at her side. It was a freedom that she was still working for, because even though she'd tasted it only for a heart-beat, it had been the most exquisite heartbeat she'd ever experienced.

She took a steadying breath and looked him in the eye. It was time. "The king sent me to kill you."

CHAPTER 11

His training with the assassins must have paid off, because Archer was across the carriage and brandishing a hidden dagger between them before she could blink. "Please," he breathed, his chest rising and falling in uneven patterns. "Please, Laena." She opened her mouth, ready to explain everything, but he was gasping down breaths, his eyes wide. "I can pay you."

A small, wretched part of her was fairly smug at the sight of him cowering. But she held up her hands, showing him she was unarmed—at least as far as he could see. "The king thinks you're part of a rebel movement that's interrupting his agenda."

A harsh, barked laugh—so raw that none of the smooth, lovely man was even recognizable in the sound. "I'm not part of any movement! Wyrd damn me, I might be a whore, but I'm not a *traitor*!" She kept her hands where he could see them, and opened her mouth to tell him to shut up, sit down, and listen. But he went on. "I don't know anything about a movement like that—I haven't even *heard* of anyone who'd dare try to get in the way of the king. But—but . . ." His panting evened out. "If you spare me, I can feed you information about a group that I *know* is starting to gather power in Rifthold."

"The king is targeting the wrong people?"

"I don't know," he said quickly, "but this group . . . this one, he'd probably want to know more about. It seems like they recently learned that the king might be planning some new horror for us all—and they want to try to stop him."

If she were a nice, decent person, she'd tell him to take the time to calm himself, to right his mind. But she wasn't a nice, decent person, and his panic was giving his tongue free rein, so she let him go on.

"I've only heard my clients whispering about it, every now and then. But there's a group that's formed, right here in Rifthold, and they want to put Aelin Galathynius back on Terrasen's throne."

Her heart stopped beating. Aelin Galathynius, the lost heir of Terrasen.

"Aelin Galathynius is dead," she breathed.

Archer shook his head. "They don't think so. They say she's alive, and that she's raising an army against the king. She's looking to reestablish her court, to find what's left of King Orlon's inner circle."

She just stared at him, willing her fingers to unclench, willing air into her lungs. If it were true . . . No, it wasn't true. If these people actually claimed to have met the heir to the throne, then she *had* to be an imposter.

Was it mere coincidence that Nehemia had mentioned Terrasen's court that morning? That Terrasen was the one force capable of standing against the king—if it could get to its feet again, with or without the true heir? But Nehemia had sworn to never lie to her; if she'd known anything, she would have said it.

Celaena closed her eyes, though she was aware of Archer's every movement. In the darkness, she pulled herself together, shoved down that desperate, foolish hope until nothing but an ageless fear blanketed it again.

She opened her eyes. Archer was gaping at her, his face white as death.

"I have no intention of killing you, Archer," she said. He sagged against the bench, releasing his grip on the dagger. "I'm going to give you a choice. You can fake your own death right now and flee the city before dawn. *Or* I can give you until the end of the month—four weeks. Four weeks to discreetly get your affairs in order; I assume you have money tied up in Rifthold. But the time comes at a cost: I'll keep you alive only if you can get me information about whatever this Terrasen rebel movement is—and whatever they know about the king's plans. At the end of the month, you *will* fake your death, and you *will* leave this city, go someplace far away, and never use the name Archer Finn again."

He stared carefully, warily, at her. "I'll need the rest of the month to untangle my money." He loosed a breath, then rubbed his face with his hands. After a long moment, he said, "Perhaps this is a blessing in disguise. I'll get to be free of Clarisse and start my life anew elsewhere." Though he gave her a wobbly smile, his eyes were still haunted. "Why did the king even suspect me?"

She hated herself for feeling such pity for him. "I don't know. He just handed me a piece of paper with your name on it, and said you were a part of some movement to upset his plans—whatever those may be."

Archer snorted. "I only wish I could be that sort of man."

She studied him: the strong jaw, the broad frame, all suggested strength. But what she'd seen just now—that was not strength. Chaol had known right away what sort of man Archer was. Chaol had seen through the illusion of strength—and she hadn't. Shame heated her cheeks, but she made herself speak again. "You truly think you can uncover information about this—this movement from Terrasen?" Even though the heir had to be an imposter, the movement itself was worth looking into. Elena had said to look for clues; she might find some here.

Archer nodded. "There's a ball tomorrow night at a client's house; I've heard him and his friends murmuring about the movement. If I sneak you into the party, it might give you a chance to look around his office. Maybe you'll even find *real* traitors at the party—not just suspects."

And some ideas about what the king might be up to. Oh, this information could be *very* useful.

"Send along the details to the castle tomorrow morning, care of Lillian Gordaina," she told him. "But if this party turns out to be a load of nonsense, I'll reconsider my offer. Don't make me look the fool, Archer."

"You're Arobynn's protégée," he said quietly, opening the carriage door and keeping his distance as best he could while he exited. "I wouldn't dare."

"Good," she said. "And Archer?" He paused, a hand on the carriage door. She leaned forward, letting a bit of that wicked darkness shine through her eyes. "If I find out that you aren't being discreet—if you draw too much attention to yourself or attempt to flee—I *will* end you. Is that clear?"

He gave her a low bow. "I am your eternal servant, milady." And then he gave her a smile that made her wonder whether she'd regret her decision to let him live. Leaning into the carriage bench, she thumped on the ceiling, and the driver headed to the castle. Though she was exhausted, she had one last thing to do before bed.

She knocked once, then opened the door to Chaol's bedroom just wide enough to peer in. He was standing frozen before the fireplace, as if he'd been in the middle of pacing.

"I thought you'd be asleep," she said, slipping inside. "It's past twelve."

He folded his arms across his chest, his captain's uniform rumpled and unbuttoned at the collar. "Then why bother stopping by? I thought you weren't coming home tonight, anyway."

She pulled her cloak tighter around her, her fingers digging into the soft fur. She lifted her chin. "Turns out Archer wasn't as dashing as I remembered. Funny how a year in Endovier can change the way you see people."

His lips tugged upward, but his face remained solemn. "Did you get the information you wanted?"

"Yes, and then some," she said. She explained what Archer had told her (pretending that he'd accidentally given her the information, of course). She explained the rumors surrounding the lost heir of Terrasen, but left out the bits about Aelin Galathynius seeking to reestablish her court and raise an army. And about Archer not really being in the movement. Oh, and about wanting to uncover the king's true plans.

When she finished telling Chaol about the upcoming ball, he walked up to the mantel and braced his hands against it, staring at the tapestry hanging on the wall above. Though it was faded and worn, she instantly recognized the ancient city nestled into the side of a mountain above a silver lake: Anielle, Chaol's home.

"When are you going to tell the king?" he asked, turning his head to look at her.

"Not until I know if this is actually real—or until I use Archer to get as much information as I can before I kill him."

He nodded, pushing off the mantel. "Just be careful."

"You keep saying that."

"Is there something wrong with saying it?"

"Yes, there is! I'm not some silly fool who can't protect herself or use her head!"

"Did I ever imply that?"

"No, but you keep saying 'be careful' and telling me how you worry, and insisting you help me with things, and—"

"Because I *do* worry!"

"Well, you shouldn't! I'm just as capable of looking after myself as you are!"

He took a step toward her, but she held her ground. "Believe me, Celaena," he snarled, his eyes flashing, "I know you can look after yourself. But I worry because I *care*. Gods help me, I know I shouldn't, but I do. So I will *always* tell you to be careful, because I will *always* care what happens."

She blinked. "Oh," was all she managed.

He pinched the bridge of his nose and squeezed his eyes shut, then took a long, deep breath.

Celaena gave him a sheepish smile.

CHAPTER 12

The masque was held in a riverfront estate along the Avery, and was so packed that Celaena had no trouble slipping in with Archer. Philippa had managed to find her a delicate white gown, made up of layers of chiffon and silk patterned like overlapping feathers. A matching mask obscured the upper half of her face, and ivory feathers and pearls had been woven into her hair.

It was fortunate it was a masquerade and not a normal party, since she certainly recognized a few faces in the crowd. They were mostly other courtesans she'd once known, along with Madame Clarisse. During the carriage ride here, Archer had promised that Arobynn Hamel wasn't attending, and neither was Lysandra—a courtesan with whom Celaena had a long, violent history, and someone she was fairly certain she'd kill if she ever saw again. As it was, just seeing Clarisse floating through the party, arranging liaisons between her courtesans and the guests, was enough to set Celaena on edge.

While she had come as a swan, Archer had dressed as a wolf—his tunic pewter, his slender pants dove gray, and his boots shining black. His wolf mask covered all but his sensual lips, which were currently parted in a rather wolfish smile as he squeezed the hand she had on his arm.

"Not the grandest party we've ever been to," he said, "but Davis has the best pastry chef in Rifthold."

Indeed, throughout the room, tables were overflowing with the most beautiful, decadent-looking pastries she'd ever seen. Pastries stuffed with cream, cookies dusted with sugar, and chocolate, chocolate, chocolate beckoning to her everywhere. Perhaps she'd swipe a few before she left. It was an effort to return her gaze to Archer. "How long has he been your client?"

That wolfish smile flickered. "A few years now. Which is how I noticed the change in his behavior." His voice dropped to a whisper, the words tickling her ear as he leaned in. "He's more paranoid, eats less, and holes up in his office any chance he gets."

At the other end of the domed ballroom, massive windows faced a patio overlooking a glittering stretch of the Avery. She could imagine those doors thrown wide in summer, and how lovely it would be to dance alongside the riverbank under the stars and city lights.

"I have about five minutes before I need to make my rounds," Archer said, his eyes following Clarisse as she patrolled the room. "She'll expect an auction for me on a night like this." Celaena's stomach turned over, and she found herself reaching for his hand. But he just gave her a bemused smile. "Just a few more weeks, right?" There was still enough bitterness that she squeezed his fingers reassuringly.

"Right," she swore.

Archer jerked his chin toward a stocky, middle-aged man holding court with a group of well-dressed people. "That's Davis," he said under his breath. "I haven't seen much during my visits, but I think he might be a key leader in this group."

"You're assuming that based on glimpsing some papers in the house?"

Archer slid his hands into his pockets. "One night about two months ago, I was here when three of his friends came over—all of them clients of mine, too. It was urgent, they said, and when Davis slipped out of the bedroom . . ."

She gave him a half smile. "You somehow accidentally overheard everything?"

Archer smiled back, but it faded as he again looked at Davis, who was pouring wine for the people assembled around him, including some young women who looked a year or two shy of sixteen. Celaena's own smile vanished as well. This was a side of Rifthold that she hadn't missed in the least.

"They spent more time ranting about the king than making plans. And regardless of what they might claim, I don't think they truly care about Aelin Galathynius. I think they just want to find a ruler who best serves *their* interests—and maybe they only want her to raise an army so their businesses can thrive during the war that would ensue. If they aid her, give her badly needed supplies . . ."

"Then she'd owe them. They want a puppet queen, not a true ruler." Of course—of course they would want something like that. "Are they even *from* Terrasen?"

"No. Davis's family was, years ago, but he's spent his whole life in Rifthold. If he claims loyalty to Terrasen, it's only a half truth."

She ground her teeth. "Self-serving bastards."

Archer shrugged. "That may be true. But they've also rescued a good number of would-be victims from the king's gallows, apparently. The night his friends burst into the house, it was because they'd managed to save one of their informants from being interrogated by the king. They smuggled him out of Rifthold before dawn broke the next day."

Did Chaol know about this? Given how he'd reacted to killing Cain, she didn't think torturing and hanging traitors were a part of his duties—or were even mentioned to him. Or Dorian, for that matter.

But if Chaol wasn't in charge of interrogating possible traitors, then who was? Was this person the source who had given the king his latest list of traitors to the crown? Oh, there were too many things to consider, too many secrets and tangled webs.

Celaena asked, "Do you think you can get me into Davis's office right now? I want to look around."

Archer smirked. "My darling, why do you think I brought you over here?" He smoothly led her to a nearby side door—a servants' entrance. No one noticed as they slipped through, and if they had, Archer's hands roaming over her bodice, her arms, her shoulders, her neck, would suggest that they were going through the door for some privacy.

A seductive smile on his face, Archer tugged her down the small hallway, then up the stairs, always taking care to keep his hands moving on her lest anyone see them. But all the servants were preoccupied, and the upstairs hall was clear and quiet, its wood-paneled walls and red carpeting immaculate. The paintings here—several from artists she recognized—were worth a small fortune. Archer moved with a stealth that probably came from years of slipping in and out of bedrooms. He led her to a set of locked double doors.

Before she could pull one of Philippa's pins from her hair to unlock it, a pick appeared in Archer's hand. He gave her a conspirator's grin. A heartbeat after that, the office door swung open, revealing a room lined with bookshelves over an ornate blue carpet, with potted ferns scattered throughout. A large desk sat in the center, two armchairs before it, and a chaise sprawled near a darkened fireplace. Celaena paused in the doorway, pressing on her bodice just to feel the slender dagger tucked inside. She brushed her legs together, checking the two daggers strapped to her thighs.

"I should go downstairs," Archer said, glancing at the hallway behind them. The sounds of a waltz floated up from the ballroom. "Try to be quick."

She raised an eyebrow, even though the mask covered her features. "Are you telling me how to do my job?"

He leaned in, brushing his lips against her neck. "I wouldn't dream of it," he said onto her skin. Then he turned and was gone.

Celaena quickly shut the door, then strode to the windows at the other side of the room and closed the curtains. The dim light shining beneath the door was enough to see by as she moved to the ironwood desk and lit a candle. The evening papers, a stack of response cards from tonight's masque, a personal expenses ledger . . .

Normal. Completely normal. She searched the rest of the desk, rifling through the drawers and knocking on every surface to check for trick compartments. When that yielded nothing, she walked to one of the bookcases, tapping the books to see whether any were hollowed out. She was about to turn away when a title caught her eye.

A book with a single Wyrdmark written on the spine in bloodred ink.

She pulled it out and rushed to the desk, setting down the candle as she opened the book.

It was full of Wyrdmarks—every page covered with them, and with words in a language she didn't recognize. Nehemia had said it was secret knowledge—that the Wyrdmarks were so old they'd been forgotten for centuries. Titles like this had been burned with the rest of the books on magic. She had found one in the palace library—*The Walking Dead*—but that had been a fluke. The art of using the Wyrdmarks was lost; only Nehemia's family knew how to properly use their power. But here, in her hands . . . She flipped through the book.

Someone had written a sentence on the inside of the back cover, and Celaena brought the candle closer as she peered at what had been scribbled.

It was a riddle—or some strange turn of phrase:

It is only with the eye that one can see rightly.

But what in hell did it mean? And what was Davis, some half-corrupt businessman, doing with a book on Wyrdmarks, of all things? If he was trying to interfere with the king's plans . . . For the sake of Erilea, she prayed the king had never even heard of Wyrdmarks.

She memorized the riddle. She would write it down when she returned to the castle—maybe ask Nehemia if she knew what it meant. Or if she'd heard of Davis. Archer might have given her vital information, but he obviously didn't know everything.

Fortunes had been broken upon the loss of magic; people who had made their living for years by harnessing its power were suddenly left with nothing. It seemed natural for them to seek out another source of power, even though the king had outlawed it. But what—

Footsteps sounded down the hall. Celaena swiftly put the book back on the shelf, then looked to the window. Her dress was too big, and the window too small and high, for her to easily make it out that way. And with no other exit . . .

The lock in the double doors clicked.

Celaena leaned against the desk, whipping out her handkerchief, bowing her shoulders, and starting a miserable sniffle-sob as Davis entered his study.

The short, solid man paused at the sight of her, the smile that had been on his face fading. Thankfully, he was alone. She popped up, doing her best to look embarrassed. "Oh!" she said, dabbing at her eyes with her kerchief through the holes in her mask. "Oh, I'm sorry, I—I needed a place to be alone for a moment and they s-s-said I could come in here."

Davis's eyes narrowed, then shifted to the key in the lock. "How did you get in?" A smooth, slippery voice, dripping with calculation—and a hint of fear.

She let out a shuddering sniffle. "The housekeeper." Hopefully, the poor woman wouldn't be flayed alive after this. Celaena hitched her voice, stumbling and rushing through the words. "My-my betrothed l-l-left m-me."

Honestly, she sometimes wondered if there was something a bit wrong with her for being able to cry so easily.

Davis took her in again, his lip curling—not out of sympathy, she realized, but from disgust at this silly, weepy woman sniffling about her fiancé. As if it would be a colossal waste of his precious time to comfort a person in pain.

The thought of Archer having to serve these people who looked at him like he was a toy to be used until he was broken . . . She focused on her breathing. She just had to get out of here without raising Davis's suspicions. One word to the guards down the hall, and she'd be in more trouble than she wanted—and might possibly drag Archer down with her.

She let out another shudder-sniffle.

"There is a ladies' powder room on the first floor," Davis said, stepping toward her—to escort her out. Perfect.

As he approached he pulled off the bird mask he wore, revealing a face that had probably been handsome in its youth. Age and too much drinking had pummeled it into saggy cheeks, thinning straw-blond hair, and a dull complexion. Capillaries had burst on the tip of his nose, staining it a purplish-red that offset his watery gray eyes.

He stopped close enough to touch her and held out a hand. She dabbed at her eyes one more time, then slipped her handkerchief back into her dress pocket. "Thank you," she whispered, looking at the floor as she took his hand. "I—I am sorry for intruding."

She heard his sudden intake of breath before she caught the flash of metal.

She had him disabled and on the floor in a heartbeat—but not fast enough to avoid the sting of Davis's dagger slicing into her forearm. The yards of fabric that made up her dress were cumbersome as she pinned him to the carpet, a thin line of blood welling up and trickling down her bare arm.

"No one has the keys to this study," Davis hissed, despite his prone position. Brave, or foolish? "Not even my housekeeper."

Celaena shifted her hand, going for the points in his neck that would render him unconscious. If she could hide her forearm, then she could still slip out of here unnoticed.

"What were you looking for?" Davis demanded, his breath reeking of wine as he wriggled against her hold. She didn't bother to answer, and he surged up, trying to dislodge her. She slammed her weight into him, lifting her hand to deliver the blow.

Then he chuckled softly. "Don't you want to know what was on that blade?"

She could have ripped his face off with her fingernails for the silken smile he gave her. In a smooth, swift movement, she snatched up his dagger and sniffed.

She'd never forget that musky smell, not in a thousand lifetimes: gloriella, a mild poison that caused hours of paralysis. It had been used the night she was captured to knock her down, to make her helpless to fight back as she was handed over to the king's men and thrown into the royal dungeons.

Davis's smile turned triumphant. "Just enough to knock you out until my guards arrive—and bring you to a more private location." Where she'd be tortured, he didn't need to add.

Bastard.

How much had she been exposed to? The cut was shallow and

short. But she knew the gloriella was already racing through her, just as it had on the days after she'd lain beside Sam's broken corpse, smelling the musky smoke still clinging to him. She had to go. *Now.*

She shifted her free hand to knock him out, but her fingers felt brittle, disconnected; and despite being short, he was *strong*. Someone must have trained him, because in a too-fast movement he grabbed her wrists, twisting her to the ground. She slammed into the carpet so hard the air was knocked from her lungs, her head spun, and she lost her grip on the dagger. The gloriella was acting fast—too fast. She had to get out.

A bolt of panic went through her, pure and undiluted. Her confounded dress got in the way, but she focused what little control remained on bringing up her legs and kicking—so hard he let go for a moment.

"Bitch!" He lunged for her again, but she'd already grabbed his poisoned dagger. A heartbeat later, he was clutching his neck as his blood sprayed on her, on her dress, on her hands.

He collapsed to the side, grasping at his throat as though he could hold it together, keep his life's blood from spewing. He was making a familiar gurgling noise, but Celaena didn't give him the mercy of ending it as she staggered to her feet. No, she didn't even give him a parting glance as she took the dagger and ripped the skirts of her gown up to her knees. A moment after that she was at his office window, studying the guards and parked carriages below, each thought fuzzier than the last as she climbed onto the ledge.

She didn't know how she made it, or how long it took, but suddenly she was on the ground and sprinting toward the open front gate.

The guards or footmen or servants started shouting. She was running—running as fast as she could, losing control of her body with each heartbeat that pumped the gloriella through her.

They were in the wealthy part of the city—near the Royal Theater—and she scanned the skyline, searching, searching for the glass castle. There! The glowing towers had never seemed more beautiful, more welcoming. She had to get back.

Her vision blurring, Celaena gritted her teeth and ran.

She had enough awareness to snatch a cloak off a drunk dozing on a corner and wipe the blood from her face, even though it took several tries to keep her hands steady as she ran. Once the cloak concealed her ruined dress, she made for the main gates of the castle grounds—where the guards recognized her, though the lights were too dim for them to look closely. The wound had been short and shallow; she could make it. She just had to get inside, get to safety . . .

But she stumbled on the winding road leading up to the castle, and her run turned into a staggering walk before she even got to the castle itself. She couldn't go in the front like this, not unless she wanted everyone to see—not unless she wanted everyone to know who was responsible for Davis's death.

She swayed with every step as she made for a side entrance, where studded iron doors were left partially open to the night—the barracks. Not the best place to enter, but good enough. Maybe the guards would be discreet.

One foot in front of the other. Just a little farther . . .

She didn't remember getting to the barracks doors, only the bite of the metal studs as she pushed them open. The light of the hall burned her eyes, but at least she was inside . . .

The door to the mess hall was open, and the sounds of laughter and clinking mugs floated toward her. Was she numb from the cold, or was it the gloriella taking over?

She had to tell someone what antidote to give her—just tell someone . . .

One hand braced against the wall, the other holding her cloak tightly around her, she slipped past the mess hall, every breath lasting a lifetime. No one stopped her; no one even looked her way.

There was one door down this hall that she had to reach—one room where she'd be safe. She kept her hand on the stone wall, counting the doors she passed. So close. Her cloak caught on the handle of a door as she passed by and ripped away.

But she made it to that door, to the room where she'd be safe. Her fingers didn't quite feel the grain of the wood as she pushed against the door and swayed on the threshold.

Bright light, a blur of wood and stone and paper . . . and through the haze, a face she knew, gaping at her from behind a desk.

A choked noise came out of her throat, and she looked down at herself long enough to see the blood covering her white dress, her arms, her hands. In the blood, she could see Davis, and the open gash across his throat. "Chaol," she moaned, seeking that familiar face again.

But he was already running, smashing through his office. He bellowed her name as her knees buckled and she fell. She saw only the golden brown of his eyes and held on long enough to whisper, "Gloriella," before everything tilted and went black.

CHAPTER 13

It was one of the longest nights of Chaol's life.

Every second had passed by with horrific clarity—every agonizing second as Celaena lay there on the floor of his office, her bodice covered in so much blood that he couldn't tell where she was bleeding. And with all the stupid layers of frills and pleats, he couldn't see the entry wounds.

So he'd lost it. Utterly lost it. There was no thought in his head beyond a roaring panic as he shut the door, took out his hunting knife, and ripped open her dress right there.

But there were no wounds, only a sheathed stiletto that clattered to the floor and a scratch on her forearm. With the dress ripped away, there was hardly any blood on her. And that's when the panic cleared enough for him to remember what she'd whispered: *gloriella*.

A poison used to temporarily paralyze victims.

Everything from then on became a series of steps: quietly

summoning Ress; telling the young, talented guard to keep his mouth shut and to find whatever healers were closest; wrapping her in his cloak so no one could see the blood on her skin; scooping her up and carrying her to her rooms; barking orders at the healers; and finally pinning her down on the bed as they forced the antidote down her throat until she choked on it. Then the long, long hours spent holding her as she vomited, twisting her hair back, snarling at anyone who entered the room.

When she was sleeping soundly at last, he sat by her, still watching over her as he sent Ress and his most trustworthy men into the city and warned them not to come back without answers. When they did return and told him about the businessman apparently murdered by his own poisoned dagger, Chaol pieced together enough of what had happened to be sure of one thing:

He was glad Davis was dead. Because if Davis had survived, Chaol would have gone back to finish the job himself.

Celaena awoke.

Her mouth was bone dry and her head pounded, but she could move. She could wiggle her toes and her fingers, and she recognized the smell of the sheets well enough to know that she was in her bed, in her room, and that she was safe.

Her eyelids were heavy as she opened them, blinking away the blurriness that still lingered. Her stomach ached, but the gloriella had worn off. She looked to her left, as if she'd somehow known, even in sleep, where he was.

Chaol dozed in the chair, his arms and legs sprawled out, his head tipped back, exposing the unbuttoned collar of his tunic and the strong column of his throat. From the angle of the sunlight, it was probably around dawn.

"Chaol," she rasped.

He was instantly awake and alert, leaning toward her as if he, too, always knew where she was. When he saw her, the hand that had lurched toward his sword relaxed. "You're awake," he said, his voice a dark rumble, laced with temper. "How are you feeling?"

She looked at herself; someone had washed away the blood and put her in a nightgown. Just moving her head made everything spin. "Horrible," she admitted.

He put his head in his hands, bracing his elbows on his knees. "Before you say anything else, just tell me this: did you kill Davis because you were snooping in his office, he caught you, and then cut you with a drugged blade?" A flash of teeth, a flicker of rage in those golden-brown eyes.

Her insides twisted up at the memory, but she nodded.

"Very well," he said, standing up.

"Are you going to tell the king?"

He crossed his arms, coming to the edge of the bed and staring down at her. "No." Again, that volatile temper burned in his eyes. "Because I don't feel like having to argue that you're still capable of spying without getting caught. My men will keep their mouths shut, too. But the next time you do *anything* like this, I am going to throw you in the dungeons."

"For killing him?"

"For scaring the hell out of me!" He ran his hands through his hair, pacing for a moment, then whirled, pointing at her. "Do you know what you looked like when you showed up?"

"I'll hazard a guess and say . . . bad?"

A flat stare. "If I hadn't burned your dress, I'd make you look at it right now."

"You burned my dress?"

He splayed his arms. "You want proof of what you did lying around?"

"You could get in trouble for covering for me like this."

"I'll deal with it if it comes to that."

"Oh? You'll deal with it?"

He leaned over the bed, bracing his hands on the mattress as he snarled in her face. "Yes. I'll *deal* with it."

She gulped, but her mouth was so dry she had nothing to swallow. Beyond his anger, there was enough lingering fear in his eyes that she winced. "It was that bad?"

He slumped onto the edge of the mattress. "You were sick. Really sick. We didn't know how much gloriella was in the wound, so the healers erred on the safe side and gave you a strong dose of the antidote—which caused you to spend a few hours with your head in a bucket."

"I don't remember any of that. I barely remember getting back to the castle."

He shook his head and stared at the wall. Dark smudges lay under his eyes, stubble coated his jaw, and utter exhaustion lined every inch of his body. He probably hadn't fallen asleep until a little while ago.

She'd hardly known where she was going while the gloriella tore through her; all she'd known was that she had to get someplace *safe*.

And somehow, she had wound up exactly where she knew she'd be safest.

CHAPTER
14

Celaena absolutely hated that it took a fair amount of courage to enter the royal library after coming upon that . . . *thing* a few nights ago. And more than that, she hated that the encounter had turned her favorite place in the castle into something unknown and possibly deadly.

She felt a little foolish as she shoved open the towering oak doors to the library, armed to the teeth—most of her weapons concealed from sight. No need to have someone start asking why the King's Champion was going into the library looking like she was walking onto a killing field.

Not feeling at all inclined to go into Rifthold after last night, she'd opted to spend the day digesting what she'd learned in Davis's office and searching for any connection between that book of Wyrdmarks and the king's plans. And since she'd only seen *one* hint of something being amiss in the castle . . . Well, she'd steeled her nerve to try to learn what that thing had been looking for in the library. Or if there was any hint of where it had gone.

The library looked as it had always had: dim, cavernous, achingly beautiful in its ancient stone architecture and endless corridors lined with books. And totally silent.

She knew there were a few scholars and librarians about, but they mostly kept to their private studies. The size of the place was overwhelming; it was a castle in itself.

What had that thing been doing here?

She craned her head back to take in the two upper levels, both bordered with ornate railings. Iron chandeliers cast light and shadow throughout the main chamber in which she stood. She loved this room—loved the scattering of heavy tables and red velvet chairs, and the worn couches sprawled before massive hearths.

Celaena paused beside the table she had always used when researching the Wyrdmarks—a table at which she'd spent hours with Chaol.

Three levels that she could see. Plenty of places to hide on all of them—rooms and alcoves and half-crumbling staircases.

What about *beneath* this level? The library was probably too far away to connect to the tunnels attached to her rooms, but there could be *more* forgotten places beneath the castle. The polished marble floor gleamed under her feet.

Chaol had said something once about a legend regarding a *second* library underground—in catacombs and tunnels. If *she* were doing something that she didn't want others to find out about, if she were some foul creature who needed a place to hide . . .

Maybe she was a fool for looking into it, but she had to know. Maybe this thing would be able to give her some clues as to what was going on in this castle.

She headed for the nearest wall and was soon swallowed up in the gloom of the stacks. It took her a few minutes to reach the perimeter wall, which was interspersed with bookcases and chipped writing desks. She pulled a piece of chalk from her pocket and drew an *X* on one of the desks. Most of the library would probably look the same after a while; it would be helpful to know when she'd made a full sweep of the perimeter. Even if it took her hours to cover it all.

She passed stack after stack of books, some of the cases plain, some of them ornately carved. Sconces were few and far enough apart that she often had to take several steps in near darkness. The floor had turned from gleaming marble to ancient gray blocks, and the scrape of her boots against stone was the only sound. It felt as if it'd been the only sound for a thousand years.

But someone must have come down this passageway to light the sconces. So if she became lost, she might not stay that way forever.

Not that getting lost was a possibility, she reassured herself as the silence of the library became a living thing. She'd been trained to mark and remember pathways and exits and turns. She'd be fine.

Odds were that she had to go as far back into the library as possible—to a place where even the scholars didn't bother going.

There had been a day, she recalled—a day when she'd been poring over *The Walking Dead*, and she'd *felt* something under her boots. Chaol had later revealed that he'd been dragging his dagger along the floor to spook her, but the initial vibration had been . . . *different*.

Like someone drawing a claw along stone.

Stop it, she told herself. *Stop it now. Your imagination is absurd. It was just Chaol teasing you.*

She didn't know how long she'd been walking when she finally hit another wall: a corner. The bookcases here were all carved from ancient wood, their ends shaped into sentries—guards forever protecting the books held between them. It was here that the sconces ran out—and a glance down the back wall of the library revealed utter darkness.

Thankfully, one of the scholars had left a torch beside the last sconce. It was small enough that it wouldn't burn the whole damn library down, but also too small to last long.

She could end it now, and go back to her rooms to contemplate ways to pry information from Archer's clients. One wall had been explored—one wall that revealed nothing. She could do the back wall tomorrow.

But she was here already.

Celaena picked up the torch.

Dorian jerked awake at the sound of a clock chiming, and found himself sweating despite the fierce cold in his bedroom.

It was odd enough that he'd fallen asleep, but the frigid temperature was what struck him as most unusual. His windows were all sealed, his door shut.

And yet his shallow breaths clouded in front of him.

He sat up, his head aching.

A nightmare—of teeth and shadows and glinting daggers. Just a nightmare.

Dorian shook his head, the temperature in the room already increasing. Perhaps it had only been a rogue draft. The nap was just the product of staying up too late last night; the nightmare probably triggered by hearing from Chaol about Celaena's encounter.

He gritted his teeth. Her job wasn't without risk—and though he was furious about what had happened, he had a feeling she'd only push him away further if he yelled at her about it.

Dorian shook off the last bit of the cold and walked to his dressing room to change his wrinkled tunic. As he turned, he could have sworn he caught a glimpse of a faint ring of frost around where his body had lain on the couch.

But when he looked back to see it more fully, there was nothing there.

⁓

Celaena heard a distant clock chime somewhere—and didn't quite believe it when she heard the time. She'd been here for three hours. *Three hours*. The back wall wasn't like the side wall; it dipped and curved and had closets and alcoves and little study rooms full of mice and dust. And just when she'd been about to draw an *X* on the wall and call it a day, she noticed the tapestry.

She saw it only because it was the sole bit of decoration she'd encountered along the wall. Considering how the last six months of her life had gone, part of her just *knew* that it had to mean something.

There was no depiction of Elena, or a stag, or anything lovely and green.

No; this tapestry, woven from red thread so dark it looked black, depicted . . . nothing.

She touched the ancient strands, marveling at the hue, so deep that it seemed to swallow her fingers in its darkness. The hair on the back of her neck rose, and Celaena put a hand on her dagger as she pulled the tapestry aside. She swore. And swore again.

Another secret door greeted her.

Glancing around the stacks, listening for any footsteps or rustle of clothing, Celaena pushed it open.

A breeze, musty and thick, floated past her from the depths of the spiral stairwell revealed by the open door. The light of her torch reached only a few feet inside, illuminating ornately carved walls depicting a battle.

There was a thin groove in the marble wall, a channel barely three inches deep. It curved along the entire length of the wall, extending beyond the limits of her sight. She swiped her finger in the groove; it was smooth as glass and held a faint residue of something slimy.

A small silver lamp hung from the wall, and she put her torch in its place as she took down the lamp, liquid splashing inside. "Clever," she murmured.

Smiling to herself, making sure her torch was far enough away, Celaena placed the slender nozzle of the lamp into the groove and tipped. Oil poured out and traveled down the chute. Celaena grabbed her torch and touched it to the wall. Instantly, the groove glowed with fire, providing a thin line of light all the way down the dark and cob-webbed stairwell. A hand on her hip, she stared down, admiring the engraved surface of the walls.

She doubted anyone would come looking for her, but she still put the tapestry back into its original position and took out one of her long daggers. As she descended, the images of battle shifted and moved in the firelight, and she could have sworn that the stone faces turned to watch her go. She stopped looking at the walls.

A breath of cold air brushed her face, and she at last spied the bottom of the stair. It was a dark corridor that smelled of aged and rotting things. A torch lay discarded at the bottom of the step, covered with enough cobwebs to reveal that no one had been down here in a long, long time.

Unless that thing can see in the dark.

She shoved away that thought, too, and picked up the torch, igniting it on the illuminated wall of the stairwell.

Cobwebs hung from the arched ceiling, grazing over the cobblestone floor. Rickety bookcases lined the hallway, the shelves crammed full of books so worn that Celaena couldn't read the titles. Scrolls and pieces of parchment were stuffed into every nook and cranny or lay unrolled on the sagging wood, as if someone had just walked away from reading them. Somehow, it was more of a tomb than Elena's resting place.

She walked down the corridor, stopping occasionally to examine the scrolls. They were maps and receipts from kings long since turned to dust.

Castle records. All this walking and fretting, and all you've discovered is useless castle records. That's probably what that creature was after: an ancient king's grocery bill.

Beginning a chant of truly despicable curses, Celaena waved her torch before her and walked on until a hallway appeared on the left.

It had to lead even lower than Elena's tomb—but how deep? There was a lantern and a groove in the wall, so Celaena once again lit the spiraling passage. This time, the gray stone depicted a forest. A forest, and—

Fae. It was impossible to miss those delicately pointed ears and elongated canines. The Fae lounged and danced and played music, content to bask in their immortality and ethereal beauty.

No, the king and his cronies *couldn't* know about this place, because they certainly would have defaced these carvings by now. Celaena didn't need a historian to know that this stairwell was old—far older than the one through which she had just descended, perhaps even older than the castle itself.

Why *had* Gavin picked this site to build his castle? Had there been something here before?

Or something beneath it worth hiding?

A cold sweat slithered down her spine as she peered into the stairwell. Against all odds, another breeze wafted up from below. Iron. It smelled like iron.

The images on the walls flickered as she descended the spiral staircase. When she at last reached the bottom, she took a shallow breath and ignited a torch from a nearby bracket. She was in a long hallway paved in gray stones. There was only one door in the center of the left-hand wall, and no exit save for the stairs behind her.

She scanned the hall. Nothing. Not even a mouse. After observing for another moment, she stepped down it, igniting the few torches on the wall as she went.

The iron door was unremarkable, though undeniably impenetrable. Its studded surface was like a slab of starless sky.

Celaena stretched out a hand, but stopped before her fingers could graze the metal.

Why *was* it made entirely of iron?

Iron was the one element immune to magic; she remembered that much. There had been so many kinds of magic-wielders ten years ago— people whose power was believed by some to have long ago originated from the gods themselves, despite the King of Adarlan's claim that magic was an affront to the divine. Wherever it came from, magic had countless variations: abilities to heal, to shape-shift, to summon flame or water or storm, to encourage the growth of crops and plants, to glimpse the future, and on and on. Most of those gifts had been watered down over the millennia, but for some rare strong ones, when they held on to their power too long, the iron in their blood caused fainting spells. Or worse.

She had seen hundreds of doors in the castle—doors of wood, of bronze, of glass—but never one of solid iron. This one was ancient, from a time when an iron door *meant* something. So was this supposed to keep someone out—or to keep something in?

Celaena touched the Eye of Elena, scanning the door again. It yielded no answers about what might be behind it, so she clamped a hand around the handle and pulled.

It was locked. There was no keyhole in sight. She ran a hand along the grooves. Perhaps it had rusted shut?

She frowned. No sign of rust, either.

Celaena stepped back, studying the door. Why put a handle on it if there was no way of opening it? And why use a lock unless there was something worthwhile hidden behind it?

She turned away, but the amulet warmed against her skin, and a flicker of light shone through her tunic. Celaena paused.

It could have been the flicker of the torch, but . . . Celaena studied the slender gap between the door and the stone. A shadow—darker than the blackness beyond—lingered on the other side.

Slowly, drawing out her thinnest and flattest dagger with her free hand, she set the torch down and lay on her stomach, as close to the door as she dared. Just shadows—it was just shadows. Or rats.

Either way, she had to know.

With absolute silence, she slid the shining dagger under the door. The reflection along the blade revealed nothing but darkness—darkness and torchlight.

She shifted the dagger, pushing it just a bit farther beneath.

Two gleaming, green-gold orbs flashed in the shadows beyond.

She lunged back, swiping the dagger with her, biting down on her lip to keep from cursing aloud. *Eyes.* Eyes gleaming in the dark—eyes like an . . . an . . .

She sighed through her nose, relaxing slightly. Eyes like an animal. Like a rat. Or a mouse. Or some feral cat.

Still, she crept forward again, holding her breath as she angled the blade under the door to scan the darkness.

Nothing. Absolutely nothing.

She watched the dagger's blade for a full minute, waiting for those eyes to reappear.

But whatever it was had scuttled off.

A rat. It was probably a rat.

Still, Celaena couldn't shake the chill that had wrapped around her, or ignore the warmth of the amulet at her neck. Even if there wasn't a creature behind that door, answers lay behind it. And she'd find them— just not today. Not until she was ready.

Because there might be ways to get through that door. And

considering how old this place was, she had a feeling that the power that had sealed it was connected to the Wyrdmarks.

But if there *was* something behind the door . . . She shifted the fingers of her right hand as she picked up her torch, studying the arc of scars left by the ridderak's bite.

It was just a rat. And she had no interest—*none*—in being proven wrong right now.

CHAPTER 15

The Great Hall was packed at dinner that night. Though Celaena usually preferred to eat in her rooms, when she heard that Rena Goldsmith would be performing during the meal to honor Prince Hollin's return, she crammed herself into one of the long tables in the back. It was the only place where the lesser nobility, some of Chaol's higher-born men, and any others who wanted to brave the viper's nest of the court were allowed to sit.

The royal family dined at their table atop the dais in the front of the hall with Perrington, Roland, and a woman who looked like she might be Roland's mother. From the other side of the room, Celaena could hardly see little Prince Hollin, but he seemed to be pale, rotund, and blessed with a head full of ebony curls. It seemed rather unfair to put Hollin next to Dorian—where comparisons could easily be made—and though she'd heard every nasty rumor about Hollin, she couldn't help but feel a shred of pity for the boy.

Chaol, to her surprise, opted to sit beside her, five of his men joining them at the table. Though there were several guards posted around the room, she had no doubt that the ones at her table were just as alert and watchful as those stationed by the doors and dais. Her tablemates were all polite to her—wary, but polite. They didn't mention what had happened last night, but they did quietly ask how she was feeling. Ress, who had guarded her during the competition, seemed genuinely relieved that she was better, and was the chattiest of them all, gossiping as much as any old court hen.

"And *then*," Ress was saying, his boyish face set with fiendish delight, "just as he got into her bed, stark naked as the day he was born, her *father* walked in"—winces and groans came from the guards, even Chaol himself—"and he *dragged* him out of bed by his feet, took him down the hall, and dumped him down the stairs. He was shrieking like a pig the whole time."

Chaol leaned back in his seat, crossing his arms. "You would be, too, if someone were dragging your naked carcass across the ice-cold floor." He smirked as Ress tried to deny it. Chaol seemed so comfortable with the men, his body relaxed, eyes alight. And they respected him, too—always glancing at him for approval, for confirmation, for support. As Celaena's chuckle faded, Chaol looked at her, his brows high. "You're one to laugh. You moan about the cold floors more than anyone I know."

She straightened as the guards gave hesitant smiles. "If I recall correctly, *you* complain about them every time I wipe the floor with you when we spar."

"Oho!" Ress cried, and Chaol's brows rose higher. Celaena gave him a grin.

"Dangerous words," Chaol said. "Do we need to go to the training hall to see if you can back them up?"

"Well, as long as your men don't object to seeing you knocked on your ass."

"We certainly do *not* object to that," Ress crowed. Chaol shot him a look, more amused than warning. Ress quickly added, "Captain."

Chaol opened his mouth to reply, but then a tall, slim woman walked onto the small stage erected along one side of the room.

Celaena craned her neck as Rena Goldsmith floated across the wooden platform to where a massive harp and a man with a violin waited. She'd seen Rena perform only once before—years ago, at the Royal Theater, on a cold winter night like this. For two hours, the theater was so still that it seemed as if everyone had stopped breathing. Rena's voice had floated through Celaena's head for days afterward.

From their table, Celaena could hardly see Rena—just enough to tell that she wore a long green dress (no petticoats, no corset, no ornamentation save for the woven leather belt circling her narrow hips), and that her red-gold hair was unbound. Silence rippled through the hall, and Rena curtsied to the dais. When she took her seat before the green-and-gold harp, the spectators were waiting. But how long would the court's interest hold?

Rena nodded to the reedy violinist, and her long, white fingers began plucking out a melody on the harp. After a few notes the rhythm established itself, followed by the slow, sad sweep of the violin. They wove together, blending, lifting up, up, up, until Rena opened her mouth.

And when she sang, the whole world faded.

Her voice was soft, ethereal, the sound of a lullaby half-remembered. The songs she sang, one by one, held Celaena in place. Songs of distant lands, of forgotten legends, of lovers forever waiting to be reunited.

Not a single soul stirred in the hall. Even the servants remained along the walls and in doorways and alcoves. Rena paused between songs only long enough to allow a heartbeat of applause before the harp and the violin began anew, and she hypnotized them all once more.

And then Rena looked toward the dais. "This song," she said softly, "is in honor of the esteemed royal family who invited me here tonight."

This song was an ancient legend—an old poem, actually. One Celaena hadn't heard since childhood, and never set to music.

She heard it now as if for the first time: the story of a Fae woman blessed with a horrible, profound power that was sought by kings and lords in every kingdom. While they used her to win wars and conquer nations, they all feared her—and kept their distance.

It was a bold song to sing; dedicating it to the king's family was even bolder. But the royals made no outcry. Even the king just stared blankly at Rena as though she weren't singing about the very power he'd outlawed ten years ago. Perhaps her voice could conquer even a tyrant's heart. Perhaps there was an unstoppable magic inherent in music and art.

Rena went on, spinning the ageless story of the years that the Fae woman served those kings and lords, and the loneliness that consumed her bit by bit. And then, one day, a knight came, seeking her power on behalf of his king. As they traveled to his kingdom, his fear turned to love—and he saw her not for the power she wielded, but for the woman beneath. Of all the kings and emperors who had come courting her with promises of wealth beyond imagining, it was the knight's gift, of seeing her for who she was—not *what* she was—that won her heart.

Celaena didn't know when she began crying. Somehow she skipped a breath, and it set her lips wobbling. She shouldn't cry, not here, not with these people around her. But then a warm, calloused hand grasped hers beneath the table, and she turned her head to find Chaol looking at her. He smiled slightly—and she knew he understood.

So Celaena looked at her Captain of the Guard and smiled back.

Hollin was squirming beside him, hissing and grousing about how bored he was and what a stupid performance this was, but Dorian's attention was on the long table in the back of the hall.

Rena Goldsmith's unearthly music wove through the cavernous

space, wrapping them in a spell that he would have called magic had he not known better. But Celaena and Chaol just sat there, staring at each other.

And not just staring, but something more than that. Dorian stopped hearing the music.

She had never looked at him like that. Not once. Not even for a heartbeat.

Rena was finishing her song, and Dorian tore his eyes away from them. He didn't think anything had happened between them, not yet. Chaol was stubborn and loyal enough to never make his move—or to even realize that he looked at Celaena the same way she looked at him.

Hollin's complaining grew louder, and Dorian took a long, long breath.

He would move on. Because he would not be like the ancient kings in the song and keep her for himself. She deserved a loyal, brave knight who saw her for what she was and did not fear her. And *he* deserved someone who would look at him like that, even if the love wouldn't be the same, even if the girl wouldn't be her.

So Dorian closed his eyes, and took another long breath. And when he opened his eyes, he let her go.

⁓

Hours later, the King of Adarlan stood at the back of the dungeon chamber as his secret guards dragged Rena Goldsmith forward. The butcher's block at the center of the room was already soaked with blood. Her companion's headless corpse lay a few feet away, his blood trickling toward the drain in the floor.

Perrington and Roland stood silent beside the king, watching, waiting.

The guards shoved the singer to her knees before the stained stone. One of them grabbed a fistful of her red-gold hair and yanked, forcing her to look at the king as he stepped forward.

"It is punishable by death to speak of or to encourage magic. It is an affront to the gods, and an affront to me that you sang such a song in my hall."

Rena Goldsmith just stared at him, her eyes bright. She hadn't struggled when his men grabbed her after the performance or even screamed when they'd beheaded her companion. As if she'd been expecting this.

"Any last words?"

A queer, calm rage settled over her lined face, and she lifted her chin. "I have worked for ten years to become famous enough to gain an invitation to this castle. Ten years, so I could come here to sing the songs of magic that you tried to wipe out. So I could sing those songs, and *you* would know that we are still here—that you may outlaw magic, that you may slaughter thousands, but we who keep the old ways still remember."

Behind him, Roland snorted.

"Enough," the king said, and snapped his fingers.

The guards shoved her head down on the block.

"My daughter was sixteen," she went on. Tears ran over the bridge of her nose and onto the block, but her voice remained strong and loud. "Sixteen, when you burned her. Her name was Kaleen, and she had eyes like thunderclouds. I still hear her voice in my dreams."

The king jerked his chin to the executioner, who stepped forward.

"My sister was thirty-six. Her name was Liessa, and she had two boys who were her joy."

The executioner raised his ax.

"My neighbor and his wife were seventy. Their names were Jon and Estrel. They were killed because they dared try to protect my daughter when your men came for her."

Rena Goldsmith was still reciting her list of the dead when the ax fell.

CHAPTER 16

Celaena dipped her spoon into her porridge, tasted it, then dumped in a mountain of sugar. "I much prefer eating breakfast together than going out in the freezing cold." Fleetfoot, her head on Celaena's lap, huffed loudly. "I think she does, too," she added with a grin.

Nehemia laughed softly before taking a bite of her bread. "It seems like this is the only time of day either of us gets to see you," she said in Eyllwe.

"I've been busy."

"Busy hunting down the conspirators on the king's list?" A pointed glance in her direction; another bite of toast.

"What do you want me to say?" Celaena stirred the sugar into her porridge, focusing on that instead of the look on her friend's face.

"I want you to look me in the eye and tell me that you think your freedom is worth this price."

"Is *this* why you've been so on edge lately?"

Nehemia set down her toast. "How can I tell my parents about you? What excuses can I make that will convince them that my friendship with the *King's Champion*"—she used the common-tongue language for the two words, spitting them out like poison—"is in any way an honorable thing? How can I convince them that your soul isn't rotted?"

"I didn't realize that I needed parental approval."

"You are in a position of power—and knowledge—and yet you just obey. You obey and you do not question, and you work only toward one goal: *your* freedom."

Celaena shook her head and looked away.

"You turn from me because you know it's true."

"And what is so wrong with wanting my freedom? Haven't I suffered enough to deserve it? So what if the means are unpleasant?"

"I won't deny that you have suffered, Elentiya, but there are thousands more who have also suffered—and suffered more. And they do not sell themselves to the king to get what they, too, deserve. With each person you kill, I am finding fewer and fewer excuses for remaining your friend."

Celaena flung her spoon down on the table and stalked to the fireplace. She wanted to rip down the tapestries and the paintings and smash all the silly little baubles and ornaments she'd bought to decorate her room. Mostly she just wanted to make Nehemia stop looking at her like that—like she was just as bad as the monster who sat on that glass throne. She took a breath, then another, listening for signs of anyone else in her chambers, then turned.

"I haven't killed anyone," she said softly.

Nehemia went still. "What?"

"I haven't killed anyone." She remained where she was standing, needing the distance between them to get the words out right. "I faked all of their deaths and helped them flee."

Nehemia ran her hands over her face, smearing the powdered gold she'd dusted on her eyelids. After a moment, she lowered her fingers. Her dark, lovely eyes were wide. "You haven't killed a single person he's ordered you to kill?"

"Not a single one."

"What about Archer Finn?"

"I offered Archer a bargain: I give him until the end of the month to get his affairs in order before he fakes his death and flees, and he gives me information about the *actual* enemies of the king." She could tell Nehemia the rest of it later—the king's plans, the library catacombs—but mentioning those things now would only bring up too many questions.

Nehemia took a sip of her tea, the liquid inside the cup sloshing as her hands shook. "He'll kill you if he finds out."

Celaena looked to the balcony doors, where a beautiful day was dawning in the wide-open world beyond. "I know."

"And this information that Archer is giving you—what will you do with it? What sort of information is it?"

Celaena briefly explained what he'd told her about the people involved in putting Terrasen's lost heir back on the throne, even telling her what had happened with Davis. Nehemia's face paled. When Celaena finished, Nehemia took another trembling sip of tea. "And you trust Archer?"

"I think he values his life more than he values anything else."

"He's a courtesan; how can you be sure you can trust him?"

Celaena slipped back into her chair, Fleetfoot curling between her feet. "Well, *you* trust *me*, and I'm an assassin."

"It's not the same."

Celaena looked to the tapestry along the wall to her left, and the chest of drawers in front of it. "While I'm telling you all the things that could get me executed, there's something else that I should bring up."

Nehemia followed her line of sight to the tapestry. After a moment, she let out a gasp. "Is that—that's *Elena* in the tapestry, isn't it?"

Celaena smiled crookedly and crossed her arms. "That's not even the worst of it."

⁓

As they walked down to the tomb, Celaena told Nehemia about everything that had occurred between her and Elena since Samhuinn—and all the adventures that had befallen her. She showed her the room where Cain had summoned the ridderak, and as they approached the tomb, Celaena winced as she remembered one miserable new detail.

"Brought a friend?"

Nehemia yelped. Celaena greeted the bronze, skull-shaped door knocker. "Hello, Mort."

Nehemia squinted at the skull. "How is this—" She looked over her shoulder at Celaena. "How is this possible?"

"Ancient spells and nonsense," Celaena said, cutting off Mort as he began to recite the story of how King Brannon created him. "Someone used a spell with the Wyrdmarks."

"Someone!" Mort sputtered. "That *someone* is—"

"Shut it," Celaena said, and flung open the tomb door, letting Nehemia inside. "Save it for someone who cares."

Mort huffed what sounded like a violent stream of curses, and Nehemia's eyes twinkled as they entered the tomb. "It's incredible," the princess whispered, gazing at the walls where the Wyrdmarks had been written.

"What does it say?"

" 'Death, Eternity, Rulers,' " Nehemia recited. "Standard tomb posturing." She continued moving through the room. As Nehemia strode about, Celaena leaned against a wall and slumped to the ground. Sighing, she rubbed her heel against one of the raised stars on the floor, examining the curve that they made across the room.

Do they make a constellation?

Celaena rose to her feet and stared down. Nine of the stars made up a familiar pattern—the Dragonfly. Her brows rose. She'd never realized it before. A few feet away another constellation lay on the floor—the Wyvern. It sat at the head of Gavin's sarcophagus.

A symbol of Adarlan's house, as well as the second constellation in the sky.

Celaena followed the line that the shapes made, weaving through the tomb. The night sky passed beneath her feet, and by the time she reached the final constellation, she would have collided with the wall had Nehemia not grabbed her by the arm.

"What is it?"

Celaena was staring down at the last constellation—the Stag, Lord of the North. The symbol of Terrasen, Elena's home country. The constellation faced the wall, and its head seemed to be pointed upward, as though it were looking at something . . .

Celaena followed the stag's stare, up through the dozens of Wyrdmarks that covered the wall, until—

"By the Wyrd. Look at this," she said, pointing.

An eye, no larger than her palm, was etched into the wall. A hole was bored in its center, a perfectly crafted puncture that had been carefully concealed within the eye. The Wyrdmark itself made a face, and while the other eye was filled in and smooth, this one held a hollowed-out iris.

It is only with the eye that one can see rightly. There was no way she was that lucky—it was surely no more than coincidence. Calming her growing excitement, she lifted onto her toes to see into the eye.

How had she not noticed this before? She took a step back, and the Wyrdmark faded into the wall. She stepped back onto the constellation, and it appeared again.

"You can only see the face when you stand on the stag," Nehemia whispered.

Celaena ran her hands over the face, feeling for any cracks or slight breezes that might suggest a door into another room. Nothing. With a deep breath, she rose onto her toes and faced the eye, her dagger held aloft in case anything leapt out at her. Nehemia chuckled softly. And Celaena conceded a smile as she put her eye against the stone and peered into the gloom.

There was nothing. Just a distant wall, illuminated by a small shaft of moonlight.

"It's just—just a blank wall. Does that make any sort of sense?" She'd been jumping to conclusions—trying to see things and make connections that weren't there. Celaena stepped away so Nehemia could see for herself. "Mort!" she hollered while the princess looked. "What the hell is that wall? Does it make any sense to you why it would be here?"

"No," Mort said dully.

"Don't lie to me."

"Lie to you? To *you*? Oh, I couldn't lie to *you*. You asked me whether it makes sense, and I said no. You must learn to ask the right questions before you can receive the right answers."

Celaena growled. "What sort of question might I ask to receive the right answer?"

Mort clicked his tongue. "I'll have none of that. Come back when you have some proper questions."

"You promise you'll tell me then?"

"I'm a door knocker; it's not in my nature to make promises."

Nehemia stepped away from the wall and rolled her eyes. "Don't listen to his teasing. I can't see anything, either. Perhaps it is just a prank. Old castles are full of nonsense intended only to confuse and bother later generations. But—all these Wyrdmarks . . ."

Celaena took a too-short breath, and then made the request that she'd been contemplating for some time now. "Could you—could you teach me how to read them?"

"Oho!" cackled Mort from the hall. "Are you sure you're not too dim to understand?"

Celaena ignored him. She hadn't told Nehemia about Elena's latest demand to uncover the king's source of power, because she knew what Nehemia's response would be: listen to the dead queen. But the Wyrdmarks seemed so *connected* to everything, somehow—even to that eye riddle and this stupid trick wall. And perhaps if she learned how to use them, then she could unlock the iron door in the library and find some answers beyond it. "Maybe . . . maybe just the basics?"

Nehemia smiled. "The basics are the hardest part."

Usefulness aside, it was a forgotten secret language, a system for accessing a strange power. Who *wouldn't* want to learn about it? "Morning lessons instead of our walk, then?"

Nehemia beamed, and Celaena felt a twinge of guilt for not telling her about the catacombs as the princess said, "Of course."

When they left, Nehemia spent a few minutes studying Mort— mostly asking him questions about his creation spell, which he claimed to have forgotten, then claimed was too private, then claimed she had no business hearing.

After Nehemia's near-infinite patience wore thin, they cursed Mort soundly and stormed back upstairs, where Fleetfoot was anxiously waiting in the bedroom. The dog refused to set foot in the secret passage—probably because of some foul stench left over from Cain and his creature. Even Nehemia hadn't been able to coax her downstairs with them.

Once the door was closed and hidden, Celaena leaned against her desk. The eye in the tomb hadn't been the solution to the riddle. Now she wondered if Nehemia might have a better sense of what it was about.

"I found a book on Wyrdmarks in Davis's office," she told Nehemia. "I can't tell if it's a riddle or a proverb, but someone wrote this on the inside back cover: *It is only with the eye that one can see rightly.*"

Nehemia frowned. "Sounds like an idle lord's nonsense to me."

"But do you think it's just coincidence that he was a part of this movement against the king and had a book on Wyrdmarks? What if this is some sort of riddle about them?"

Nehemia snorted. "What if Davis wasn't even *in* this group? Perhaps Archer had his information wrong. I bet that book had been there for years—and I bet Davis didn't even know it existed. Or maybe he saw it in a bookshop and bought it to look daring."

But maybe he didn't—and maybe Archer was on to something. She would question him when she saw him next. Celaena fiddled with the chain of her amulet—then went rod-straight. The Eye. "Do you think it could be *this* Eye?"

"No," Nehemia said. "It wouldn't be that easy."

"But—" Celaena pushed off the desk.

"Trust me," Nehemia said. "It's a coincidence—just like that eye in the wall. 'The eye' could refer to anything—anything at all. Having eyes plastered all over things used to be quite popular centuries ago as a ward against evil. You'll drive yourself mad, Elentiya. I can do some research on the subject, but it might take a while before I find anything."

Celaena's face warmed. Fine; maybe she was wrong. She didn't want to believe Nehemia, didn't want to think that the riddle could be *that* impossible to solve, but . . . the princess knew far more about ancient lore than she did. So Celaena sat down at her breakfast table again. Her porridge had gone cold, but she ate it anyway. "Thank you," she said in between mouthfuls as Nehemia sat down again, too. "For not exploding on me."

Nehemia laughed. "Elentiya, I'm honestly surprised you told me."

An opening and closing door, then footsteps, then Philippa knocked and bustled in, carrying a letter for Celaena. "Good morning, beautiful ladies," she clucked, making Nehemia grin. "A letter for our most esteemed Champion."

Celaena beamed at Philippa and took it, and her smile grew as she read the contents once the servant left. "It's from Archer," she told Nehemia. "He's given me some names of people who might be involved in this movement—people associated with Davis." She was a little shocked he'd risk putting it all in a letter. Perhaps she needed to teach him a thing or two about code-writing.

Nehemia had stopped smiling, though. "What sort of man just hands out this information like it's nothing more than morning gossip?"

"A man who wants his freedom and has had enough of serving pigs." Celaena folded the letter and stood. If the men on this list were anything like Davis, then perhaps handing them over to the king and using them as leverage wouldn't be so horrible after all. "I should get dressed; I need to go into the city." She was halfway to her dressing room when she turned. "We'll have our first lesson over breakfast tomorrow?"

Nehemia nodded, digging into her food again.

~

It took her all day to hunt down the men—to learn where they lived, whom they spoke to, how well-guarded they were. None of it yielded anything useful.

She was tired and cranky and hungry when she trudged back to the castle at sundown, and her mood only took a turn for the worse when she arrived at her rooms and found a note from Chaol. The king had commanded her to be on guard duty yet again for the royal ball that night.

CHAPTER 17

Chaol knew Celaena was in a foul mood without even having to speak to her. Actually, he hadn't dared speak to her since before the ball had started, other than to position her outside on the patio, hidden in the shadows of a pillar. A few hours in the winter night would cool her down.

From his spot inside, tucked into an alcove near a servants' entrance, he could keep an eye on the glittering ball in front of him, as well as the assassin standing watch just outside the towering balcony doors. Not that he didn't trust her—but having Celaena in one of these moods always set *him* on edge, too.

She was currently leaning against the pillar, arms crossed—*not* hiding in the shadows as he'd told her to. He could see the tendrils of her breath curling in the night air, and the moonlight glinting off the hilt of one of the daggers she wore at her side.

The ballroom had been decorated in hues of white and glacier blue, with swaths of silk floating from the ceiling and ornate glass baubles hanging between. It was something out of a winter dream, and it was in honor of Hollin, of all people. A few hours of entertainment and a small fortune spent for a boy who was currently sulking on his little glass throne, shoveling sweets down his throat as his mother smiled at him.

He'd never tell Dorian, but Chaol dreaded the day when Hollin would grow into a man. A spoiled child was easy enough to deal with, but a spoiled, cruel leader would be another matter entirely. He hoped that between him and Dorian, they could check whatever corruption was already rotting away in Hollin's heart—once Dorian ascended to the throne.

The heir was on the dance floor, fulfilling his obligation to court and crown by dancing with whatever ladies demanded his attention. Which, not surprisingly, was almost all of them. Dorian played his role well and smiled throughout the waltzes, a graceful and competent partner, never once complaining or turning any lady away. The dance finished, Dorian bowed to his partner, and before he could take one step, another courtier was curtsying in front of him. If Chaol had been in Dorian's shoes, he would have winced, but the prince just grinned, took the lady's hand, and swept her around the floor.

Chaol glanced outside again and straightened. Celaena wasn't by the pillar.

He stifled a snarl. Tomorrow, they were going to have a nice, long chat about the rules and the consequences of abandoning posts while on guard duty.

A rule that he was also breaking, he realized as he slipped from the alcove and out the door that had been left ajar to allow fresh air into the toasty ballroom.

Where in hell had she gone? Perhaps she'd actually seen some sign of trouble—not that there'd ever been an attack on the palace, and not that anyone would ever be foolish enough to try during a royal ball.

But he still put a hand on the hilt of his sword as he approached the columns at the top of the stairs leading down into the frosted garden. She'd been standing right here, and—

Chaol spotted her.

Well, she'd certainly abandoned her post. But not to face some potential threat.

Chaol crossed his arms. Celaena had left her post to *dance*.

The music was loud enough that it reached them out here, and at the foot of the steps, Celaena waltzed with herself. She even held the edge of her dark cloak in one hand as if it were the skirts of a ball gown, her other hand poised on the arm of an invisible partner. He didn't know if he should laugh, yell, or just go back inside and pretend he'd never seen it.

She turned, an elegant sweeping motion that brought her to face him, and halted.

Well, the last option was no longer a possibility. Laughter or yelling, then. Though neither felt appropriate now.

Even in the moonlight, he could see her scowl. "I'm bored to tears and nearly dead with cold," she said, dropping her cloak.

He remained atop the stairs, watching her.

"And it's your fault," she went on, stuffing her hands into her pockets. "You made me come out here, and someone left the balcony door open so I could hear all that lovely music." The waltz was still playing, filling the frozen air around them with sound. "So you should really reconsider who's to blame. It was like putting a starving man in front of a feast and telling him not to eat. Which, by the way, you actually *did* when you made me go to that state dinner."

She was babbling, and her face was dark enough for him to know she was beyond mortified that he'd caught her. He bit his lip to keep from smiling and walked down the four steps to the gravel path of the garden. "You're the greatest assassin in Erilea, and yet you can't stand watch for a few hours?"

"What's there to watch?" she hissed. "Couples sneaking out to fondle each other between the hedges? Or His Royal Highness, dancing with every eligible maiden?"

"You're jealous?"

She barked a laugh. "No! Gods, no. But I can't say it's particularly fun to watch him. Or watch any of them enjoying themselves. I think I'm more jealous of that giant buffet no one is even touching."

He chuckled and glanced up the stairs, to the patio and the ballroom doors beyond. He should be back inside already. But here he was, toeing that line he couldn't stay away from.

He'd managed to stay on this side of it last night, even though seeing her cry during Rena Goldsmith's song had stirred him so bone deep it was like he'd found a part of him he hadn't even realized was missing. He'd made them run an extra mile this morning, not to punish her for it, but because he couldn't stop thinking about the way she'd looked at him.

She sighed loudly and studied the moon. It was so bright it drowned out the stars. "I heard the music and I just wanted to dance for a few minutes. To just . . . forget everything for one waltz and pretend to be a normal girl. So"—she glared at him now—"go ahead and snarl and snap at me about it. What will my punishment be? Three extra miles tomorrow? An hour of drills? The rack?"

There was a sort of bleak bitterness in her words that didn't sit well with him. And yes, they *would* have a conversation about abandoning posts, but right now—right now . . .

Chaol stepped up to the line.

"Dance with me," he said, and held out his hand to her.

Celaena stared at Chaol's outstretched hand. "What?"

The moonlight caught in his golden eyes, setting them shining. "What didn't you understand?"

Nothing. Everything. Because when he'd said it, it hadn't been the way Dorian had asked her to dance at the Yulemas ball. That had merely been an invitation. But this . . . His hand remained reaching toward her.

"As far as I recall," she said, lifting her chin, "at Yulemas, *I* asked *you* to dance, and you flat-out refused me. You said it was too *dangerous* for us to be seen dancing together."

"Things are different now." Again, another layered statement she couldn't begin to sort through now.

Her throat tightened, and she looked at his extended hand, flecked with callouses and scars.

"Dance with me, Celaena," he said again, his voice rough.

When her eyes found his, she forgot about the cold, and the moon, and the glass palace looming above them. The secret library and the king's plans and Mort and Elena faded into nothing. She took his hand, and there was only the music and Chaol.

His fingers were warm, even through his gloves. He slid his other hand around her waist as she braced one of hers on his arm. She looked up at him when he began to move—a slow step, then another, and another, easing into the steady rhythm of the waltz.

He stared back at her, neither of them smiling—somehow beyond smiling at that moment. The waltz built, louder, faster, and Chaol steered her into it, never stumbling.

Her breathing turned uneven, but she couldn't look away from him, couldn't stop dancing. The moonlight and the garden and the golden glow from the ballroom blurred together, now miles away. "We'll never be a normal boy and girl, will we?" she managed to say.

"No," he breathed, eyes blazing. "We won't."

And then the music exploded around them, and Chaol took her with it, spinning her so that her cloak fanned out around her. Each step was flawless, lethal, like that first time they'd sparred together so many months ago. She knew his every move and he knew hers, as though they'd been dancing this waltz together all their lives. Faster, never faltering, never breaking her stare.

The rest of the world quieted into nothing. In that moment, after ten long years, Celaena looked at Chaol and realized she was home.

Dorian Havilliard stood at the ballroom window, watching Celaena and Chaol dance in the garden beyond, their dark cloaks flowing around them like they were no more than two wraiths spinning through the wind. After hours of dancing, he'd finally managed to get free of the ladies demanding his attention, and had come to the window to get some much-needed fresh air.

He'd intended to go outside, but then he'd seen them. That had been enough to still his steps—but not enough to make him walk away. He knew he should. He should walk away and pretend he hadn't seen it, because even though it was just a dance . . .

Someone stepped beside him, and he glanced over in time to see Nehemia stop at the window. After months of being scarce around the court due to the rebel massacre in Eyllwe, she'd made an appearance tonight. She was resplendent in a cobalt gown with gold-thread accents, her hair coiled and braided in a coronet atop her head. Her delicate golden earrings glittered in the light of the chandelier, drawing his eye to her elegant neck. Nehemia was easily the most stunning woman in the ballroom, and he hadn't failed to notice how many men—and women—had been watching her all night.

"Don't cause trouble for them," she said quietly, her accent still thick, but much improved since she'd arrived in Rifthold. Dorian raised an eyebrow. Nehemia traced an invisible pattern on the glass pane. "You and I . . . We will always stand apart. We will always have . . ." She searched for the word. "Responsibilities. We will always have burdens that no one else can ever understand. That they"—she inclined her head toward Chaol and Celaena—"will never understand. And if they did, then they would not want them."

They would not want us, is what you mean.

Chaol spun Celaena, and she flowed smoothly through the air before snapping back into his arms.

"I've already decided to move on," Dorian said with equal quiet. It was the truth. He'd awoken this morning feeling lighter than he had in weeks.

Nehemia nodded, the gold and jewels in her hair twinkling. "Then I thank you for that." She traced another symbol on the window. "Your cousin, Roland, told me that your father has approved Councilman Mullison's plans to swell Calaculla's ranks—to expand the labor camp to accommodate more . . . people."

He kept his face blank. There were far too many eyes on them. "Roland told you that?"

Nehemia lowered her hand from the window. "He wants me to tell my father that I support his agenda—to get my father to make the expansion as easy as possible. I refused. He says there's a council meeting tomorrow where they will vote on Mullison's plans. I'm not allowed to attend."

Dorian focused on his breathing. "Roland had no right to do that. Any of it."

"Would you stop it, then?" Her dark eyes were fixed on his face. "Speak to your father at the council meeting; convince the others to say no."

No one except for Celaena dared speak to him like that. But her boldness had nothing to do with his response as Dorian said, "I can't."

His face warmed as the words came out, but it was true. He couldn't tackle Calaculla, not without causing a lot of trouble for both himself and Nehemia. He'd already convinced his father to leave Nehemia alone. Demanding he shut down Calaculla could force him to choose sides—and make a choice that could destroy everything he had.

"You can't, or you will not?" Dorian sighed, but she cut him off. "If Celaena were shipped to Calaculla, would you free her? Would you put a stop to the camp? When you took her from Endovier, did you think twice about the thousands you left behind?" He had, but . . . but not for as long as he should have. "Innocents work and die in Calaculla and Endovier. By the thousands. Ask Celaena about the graves they dig there, Prince. Look at the scars on her back, and realize that what she went through is a *blessing* compared to what most endure." Perhaps he'd just gotten used to her accent, but he could have sworn she was speaking more clearly. Nehemia pointed at the garden, at Celaena and Chaol, who had stopped dancing and were talking now. "If she was sent back, would you free her?"

"Of course I would," he said carefully. "But it's complicated."

"There is nothing complicated. It is the difference between right and wrong. The slaves in those camps have people who love them just as much as you loved my friend."

He glanced around them. Ladies were eagerly watching from behind their fans, and even his mother had noticed their lengthy conversation. Outside, Celaena had resumed her post by the pillar. At the other end of the room, Chaol slipped through one of the patio doors and took up his spot in an alcove, his face blank, as if the dance had never happened. "This isn't the place for this conversation."

Nehemia stared at him for a long moment before nodding. "You have power in you, Prince. More power than you realize." She touched his chest, tracing a symbol there, too, and some of the court ladies gasped. But Nehemia's eyes were locked on his. "It sleeps," she whispered, tapping his heart. "In here. When the time comes, when it awakens, do not be afraid." She removed her hand and gave him a sad smile. "When it is time, I will help you."

With that, she walked away, the courtiers parting, then swallowing up her wake. He stared after the princess, wondering what her last words had meant.

And why, when she had said them, something ancient and slumbering deep inside of him had opened an eye.

CHAPTER 18

Celaena sat in the parlor of Archer's townhouse, frowning at the crackling fireplace. She hadn't touched the tea the butler had laid out for her on the low-lying marble table, though she'd certainly indulged in two creampuffs and one chocolate torte while waiting for Archer to return. She could have come back later, but it was freezing outside, and after standing on guard duty last night, she was exhausted. And in need of anything to distract her from reliving that dance with Chaol.

After the waltz had finished, he'd merely told her that if she abandoned her post again, he'd break a hole through the ice in the trout pond and toss her in. And then, as though he hadn't just danced with her in a way that made her knees tremble, he stalked back inside and left her to suffer in the cold. He hadn't even mentioned the dance this morning during their run. Maybe she'd just imagined the whole thing. Maybe the frigid night air had made her stupid.

She'd been distracted during her first Wyrdmarks lesson with

Nehemia that morning and had earned a fair amount of scolding as a result. She blamed the complex, near-nonsensical language. She'd learned a few languages before—enough to get by in places where Adarlan's language laws hadn't taken root—but Wyrdmarks were completely different. Trying to learn them while also trying to unravel the labyrinth that was Chaol Westfall was impossible.

Celaena heard the front door open. Muffled words, hurried footsteps, and then—Archer's beautiful face popped in. "Just give me a moment to freshen up."

She stood. "That won't be necessary. This won't take long."

Archer's green eyes glimmered, but he slipped into the parlor, shutting the mahogany door behind him.

"Sit," she told him, not particularly caring that this was his house. Archer obeyed, taking a seat in the armchair across from the couch. His face was flushed from the cold, making his lovely eyes seem even greener.

She crossed her legs. "If your butler doesn't stop listening at the keyhole, I'm going to cut off his ears and shove them down his throat."

There was a muffled cough, followed by retreating footsteps. Once she was sure no one else was listening, she leaned back into the couch cushions. "I need more than a list of names. I need to know what, exactly, they're planning—and how much they know about the king."

Archer's face paled. "I need more time, Celaena."

"You have little more than three weeks left."

"Give me five."

"The king only gave me a month to kill you. I already have a hard time convincing everyone you're a difficult target. I can't give you more time."

"But I need it to wrap up things here in Rifthold and to get you more information. With Davis dead, they're all being extra careful. No one is talking. No one dares whisper anything."

"Do they know Davis was a mistake?"

"Mistakes happen often enough in Rifthold for us to know that most of them are anything *but* mistakes." He ran his hands through his hair. "Please. Just a little more time."

"I don't have any to give you. I need more than names, Archer."

"What about the Crown Prince? And the Captain of the Guard? Perhaps they have the information you need. You're close with both of them, aren't you?"

She bared her teeth at him. "What do you know about them?"

Archer gave her a steady, calculating look. "You think I didn't recognize the Captain of the Guard the day you just happened to run into me outside of the Willows?" His attention flicked to her side, where her hand currently rested on a dagger. "Have you told them about your plan to keep me alive?"

"No," she said, her grip on the dagger relaxing. "No, I haven't. I don't want to involve them."

"Or is it because you don't actually trust either of them?"

She shot to her feet. "Don't presume to know anything about me, Archer."

She stalked to the door and flung it open. The butler was nowhere to be seen. She looked over her shoulder at Archer, whose eyes were wide as he watched her. "You have until the end of the week—*six* days—to get me more information. If you don't give me anything by then, my next visit won't be nearly as pleasant."

Not giving him the time to reply, she stormed out of the room, grabbed her cloak from the front closet, and strode back out onto the icy city streets.

⁓

The maps and figures in front of Dorian had to be wrong. Someone had to be playing a joke, because there was no way Calaculla had *this* many slaves. Seated at the long table in his father's council chamber,

Dorian glanced at the men around him. None looked surprised, none looked upset. Councilman Mullison, who had taken a special interest in Calaculla, was practically beaming.

He should have fought to get Nehemia into this council meeting. But there was probably nothing she could say right now that would have any impact on a decision that had clearly already been made.

His father was smiling faintly at Roland, his head propped on a fist. The black ring on the king's hand glinted in the dim light from the beastly fireplace, that mouth-shaped hearth that seemed poised to devour the room.

From his spot beside Perrington, Roland gestured to the map. Another black ring glinted on Roland's hand—the same as the one Perrington wore, too. "As you can see, Calaculla can't support the current number of slaves. There are too many to even fit in the mines as it is—and though we have them digging for new deposits, the work has been stagnant." Roland smiled. "*But*, slightly to the north, right along the southern edge of Oakwald, our men have discovered an iron deposit that seems to cover a large area. It's close enough to Calaculla that we could erect a few new buildings to house additional guards and overseers, bring in even more slaves if we want, and start work on it right away."

Impressed murmurs, and a nod from his father to Roland made Dorian's jaw clench. Three matching rings; three black rings to signify— what? That they were bound in some way to each other? How had Roland gotten past his father's and Perrington's defenses so quickly? Because of his support of a place like Calaculla?

Nehemia's words from the night before kept ringing in his head. He'd seen the scars on Celaena's back up close—a brutal mess of flesh that made him sick with rage to look at. How many like her were rotting away in these labor camps?

"And where will the slaves sleep?" Dorian suddenly asked. "Will you build shelter for them, too?"

Everyone, including his father, turned to look at him. But Roland just shrugged. "They're slaves. Why shelter them, when they can sleep in the mines? Then we wouldn't waste time bringing them in and out every day."

More murmurs and nods. Dorian stared at Roland. "If we have a surplus of slaves, then why not let some of them go? Surely they're not all rebels and criminals."

A growl from down the table—his father. "Watch your tongue, Prince."

Not a father to his son, but a king to his heir. Still, that icy rage was growing, and he kept seeing Celaena's scars, her too-thin body the day they'd pulled her out of Endovier, her gaunt face and the hope and desperation mingling in her eyes. He heard Nehemia's words: *What she went through is a* blessing *compared to what most endure.*

Dorian peered down the table at his father, whose face was dark with irritation. "Is this the plan? Now that we've conquered the continent, you'll throw everyone into Calaculla or Endovier, until there's no one left in the kingdoms but people from Adarlan?"

Silence.

The rage dragged him down to the place where he'd felt that flicker of ancient power when Nehemia had touched his heart. "You keep tightening the leash, and it's going to snap," Dorian said to his father, then looked across the table to Roland and Mullison. "How about *you* spend a year in Calaculla, and when you're done, you two can sit here and tell me about your plans for expansion."

His father slammed his hands on the table, rattling the glasses and pitchers. "You will mind your mouth, Prince, or you will be thrown out of this room before the vote."

Dorian shot out of his seat. Nehemia had been right. He hadn't looked at the others in Endovier. He hadn't let himself. "I've heard enough," he snarled at his father, at Roland and Mullison, at Perrington, and at all the lords and men in the room. "You want my vote? Then here it is: *No*. Not in a thousand years."

His father growled, but Dorian was already walking across the red marble floor, past that horrible fireplace, out the doors, and into the bright halls of the glass castle.

He didn't know where he was going, only that he felt freezing cold—a cold that fueled the calm, glittering rage. He took flight after flight of stairs down into the stone castle, then long hallways and narrow staircases until he found a forgotten hall where there were no eyes to see him as he drew back his fist and punched the wall.

The stone cracked under his hand.

Not a small crack, but a spiderweb that kept growing and growing toward the window on the right, until—

The window exploded, glass showering everywhere as Dorian dropped into a crouch and covered his head. Air rushed in, so cold his eyes blurred, but he just knelt there, fingers in his hair, breathing, breathing, breathing as the anger ebbed out of him.

It wasn't possible. Maybe he'd just hit the wall in the wrong spot, and the damn thing was so ancient that it had only been waiting for something like this to happen. He'd never heard of stone cracking that way—spreading out like a living thing—and then the window . . .

Heart racing, Dorian lowered his hands from his head and looked at them. There wasn't a bruise or a cut, or even a trace of pain. But he'd hit that wall as hard as he could. He could have—*should* have— broken his hand. Yet his knuckles were unharmed—only white from gripping his fingers in a tight fist.

On trembling legs, Dorian rose and surveyed the damage.

The wall had splintered, but remained intact. The ancient window, however, had shattered completely. And around him, around where he had crouched . . .

A perfect circle, clean of debris, as if the glass and wood had showered everything but him.

It wasn't possible. Because magic—

Magic . . .

Dorian dropped to his knees and was violently sick.

Curled on the couch beside Chaol, Celaena took a sip of her tea and frowned. "Can't you hire a servant like Philippa, so we can have someone bring us treats?"

Chaol raised an eyebrow. "Don't you ever stay in your own rooms anymore?"

No. Not if she could help it. Not with Elena and Mort and all that nonsense just a secret door away. Ordinarily, she might have sought sanctuary in the library, but not now. Not when the library held so many secrets it made her head spin to think about them. For a moment, she wondered if Nehemia had discovered anything about the riddle in Davis's office. She'd have to ask her tomorrow.

She kicked Chaol in the ribs with a sock-covered foot. "All I'm saying is that I'd like some chocolate cake every now and then."

He closed his eyes. "And an apple tart, and a loaf of bread, and a pot of stew, and a mountain of cookies, and a—" He chuckled as she put her foot against his face and pushed. He grabbed her foot and wouldn't let go when she tried yanking her leg back. "It's true, and you know it, *Laena*."

"So what if it is? Haven't I earned the right to eat as much as I want, whenever I want?" She wrenched her foot out of his grasp as the smile faded from his face.

"Yes," he said quietly, his voice barely audible over the crackling fire. "You have." After a few moments of silence, he stood up and walked to the door.

She sat up on her elbows. "Where are you going?"

He opened the door. "To get you chocolate cake."

When he returned, and after they'd both eaten half of the cake he'd swiped from the kitchens, Celaena lay back on the couch, a hand on her full belly. Chaol was already sprawled across the cushions, sleeping soundly. Staying up until the middle of the night at the ball, then awakening for their sunrise run this morning had been exhausting. Why hadn't he just canceled the run?

You know, the courts weren't always like this, Nehemia had said. *There was a time when people valued honor and loyalty—when serving a ruler wasn't about obedience and fear. . . . Do you think another court like that could ever rise again?*

Celaena hadn't given Nehemia an answer. She hadn't wanted to talk about it. But looking at Chaol now, at the man he was, and the man he was still becoming . . .

Yes, she thought. *Yes, Nehemia. It could rise again, if we could find more men like him.*

But not in a world with this king, she realized. He'd crush a court like that before Nehemia could muster one. If the king were gone, then the court that Nehemia dreamed of could change the world. That court could undo the damage of a decade of brutality and terror; it could restore the lands ravaged by conquest and renew the hearts of the kingdoms that shattered when Adarlan marched in.

And in that world . . . Celaena swallowed hard. She and Chaol would never be a normal boy and girl, but perhaps in that world they could make a life of their own. She *wanted* that life. Because even though he'd pretended nothing had happened after the dance they'd shared last night, something had. And maybe it had taken her this long to realize it, but this man—she wanted that life *with* him.

The world Nehemia dreamed about, and the world Celaena sometimes dared let herself consider, was nothing more than a shred of hope and a memory of what the kingdoms had once been. But perhaps the rebel movement truly knew about the king's plans and how to ruin them—how to destroy him, with or without Aelin Galathynius and whatever army they claimed she was raising.

Celaena sighed and eased off the couch, gently shifting Chaol's legs so she didn't disturb him. She turned back, though—just once, leaning down to brush her fingers through his short hair, then graze them along his cheek. Then she quietly slipped from his room, taking the remnants of the chocolate cake with her.

⟡

She was wondering whether eating the rest of the chocolate cake would make her severely sick when she turned down her hallway and spotted Dorian sitting on the floor outside her rooms. He looked over when he saw her, his eyes going to the cake in her hands. Celaena blushed and lifted her chin. They hadn't spoken since their argument over Roland. Perhaps he'd come to apologize. Served him right.

But as she neared and Dorian got to his feet, she took one look at the expression in his sapphire eyes and knew he wasn't here for an apology.

"It's a bit late for a visit," she said by way of greeting.

Dorian put his hands in his pockets and leaned against the wall. His face was pale, his eyes haunted, but he gave her half a smile. "It's a bit late for chocolate cake, too. Been raiding the kitchens?"

She remained outside her rooms, running an eye over him. He looked fine—no bruises, no signs of injury—yet something was off. "What are you doing here?"

He avoided her gaze. "I was looking for Nehemia, but her servants said she was out. I thought they meant here; then I thought you two might be out for a stroll."

"I haven't seen her since this morning. Is there something you want from her?"

Dorian took a ragged breath, and Celaena suddenly realized just how *cold* it was in the hallway. How long had he been sitting here on the freezing floor? "No," he said, shaking his head as if convincing himself of something. "No, there isn't."

He began walking away. She started speaking before she knew she'd opened her mouth. "Dorian. What's wrong?"

He turned. For a heartbeat, there was something in his eyes that reminded her of a world long since burned—a glimmer of color and power that still stalked the edges of her nightmares. But he blinked, and it was gone. "Nothing. There's nothing wrong at all." He strode away, hands still in his pockets. "Enjoy your cake," he said over his shoulder, and then was gone.

CHAPTER 19

Chaol stood before the king's throne, almost boring *himself* to tears as he gave yesterday's report. He tried not to think about last night—how the brief touch of Celaena's fingers through his hair and on his face had sent a pang of desire through him so strong he'd wanted to grab her and pin her on the couch. It had taken all his self-control to keep his breathing steady, to keep pretending that he was asleep. After she'd left, his heart had been pounding so hard it took him an hour to calm enough to actually sleep.

Looking at the king now, Chaol was glad he'd controlled himself. The line between him and Celaena was there for a reason. Crossing it could call into question his loyalty to the king before him—not to mention the way it would impact his friendship with Dorian. The prince had made himself scarce this past week; Chaol would have to make a point today to go see him.

Dorian and the king were where his loyalty lay. Without his

loyalty, he was no one. Without it, he'd given up his family, his title, for nothing.

Chaol finished explaining his security plans for the carnival that would arrive today, and the king nodded. "Very well, Captain. Make sure your men watch the castle grounds, too. I know what sort of filth likes to travel with these carnivals, and I don't want them wandering around."

Chaol bowed his head. "Consider it done."

Normally, the king would dismiss him with a grunt and a wave, but today, the man merely studied him, an elbow propped on the arm of his glass throne. After a moment of silence—during which Chaol wondered if a castle spy had somehow been looking through the keyhole when Celaena touched him—the king spoke.

"Princess Nehemia needs to be watched."

Of all the things the king could have said, this was not what Chaol had expected. But he kept his face blank and did not question the words that implied so much.

"Her . . . influence is starting to be felt in these halls. And I am beginning to wonder if perhaps the time has come to remove her back to Eyllwe. I know that we already have some men watching her, but I also received word that there was an anonymous threat on her life."

Questions roared through him, along with a rising sense of dread. Who had threatened her? What had Nehemia said or done to warrant the threat?

Chaol stiffened. "I haven't heard anything about that."

The king smiled. "No one has. Not even the princess herself. It seems she's made some enemies outside the palace as well."

"I'll have extra guards watch her rooms and patrol her wing of the castle. I'll alert her immediately of—"

"There is no need to alert her. Or anyone." The king gave him a pointed look. "She might try to use the fact that someone wants her dead as a bargaining chip—might try to make herself into a martyr of sorts. So tell your men to stay quiet."

He didn't think Nehemia would do that, but Chaol kept his mouth shut. He'd tell his men to be discreet.

And he wouldn't tell the princess—or Celaena. Just because he was friendly with Nehemia, just because she was Celaena's friend, it didn't change anything. While he knew that Celaena would be furious that he didn't tell her, he was the Captain of the Guard. He had fought and sacrificed nearly as much as Celaena had to get to this position. He'd let her get too close by asking her to dance—he'd let himself get too close.

"Captain?"

Chaol blinked, then bowed low. "You have my word, Your Majesty."

Dorian panted, swinging the sword through the air in a precise parry that sent the guard scrambling. His third match, and his third opponent about to go down. He hadn't slept last night, nor had he been able to sit still this morning. So he'd come to the barracks, hoping to have someone wear him down enough for exhaustion to take over.

He parried and deflected the guard's assault. It had to be a mistake. Maybe he'd dreamed it all up. Maybe it had just been a combination of the right elements at the wrong time. Magic was *gone*, and there was no reason that he should have that power, when not even his father had been gifted with magic. Magic had been dormant in the Havilliard bloodline for generations.

Dorian got past the guard's defense in an easy maneuver, though when the young man raised his hands in defeat, the prince had to wonder if he'd let him win. The thought sent a growl rippling through him.

He was about to demand another match when someone sauntered over to them. "Mind if I join?"

Dorian stared at Roland, whose rapier looked like it had hardly ever been used. The guard took one look at Dorian's face, bowed, and found someplace else to be. Dorian watched his cousin, the black ring on Roland's finger. "I don't think you want to dance with me today, cousin."

"Ah," Roland said, frowning. "About yesterday . . . I'm sorry for that. Had I known the labor camps were such a sensitive matter for you, I never would have broached the subject or worked with Councilor Mullison. I called off the vote after you left. Mullison was furious."

Dorian raised his brows. "Oh?"

Roland shrugged. "You were right. I don't know anything about what it's like in those camps. I only took up the cause because Perrington suggested that I work with Mullison, who stood to gain a lot from the expansion because of his ties to the iron industry."

"And I'm supposed to believe you?"

Roland gave him a winning smile. "We *are* family, after all."

Family. Dorian had never really considered himself to be in an actual family. And certainly not now. If anyone found out about what had happened in that hallway yesterday, about the magic he might have, his father would kill him. He had a second son, after all. Families weren't exactly supposed to think like that, were they?

Dorian had gone looking for Nehemia last night out of desperation, but in the light of morning, he was grateful he hadn't seen her. If the princess had that sort of information about him, she could use it to her advantage—blackmail him all she wanted.

And Roland . . . Dorian began walking **away**. "Why don't you save your maneuvering for someone who cares?"

Roland kept pace beside him. "Ah, but who else is more worthy than my own cousin? What greater challenge than winning you over to my schemes?" Dorian shot him a warning glare and found the young man grinning. "If only you'd seen the chaos that erupted after you left," Roland went on. "As long as I live, I'll never forget the look on your father's face when you growled at them all." Roland laughed, and, despite himself, Dorian found a smile tugging on his lips. "I thought the old bastard would combust right there."

Dorian shook his head. "He's hanged men for calling him such names, you know."

"Yes, but when you're as handsome as I am, dear cousin, you'd be surprised by how much more you can get away with."

Dorian rolled his eyes, but considered his cousin for a few moments. Roland might be close with Perrington and his father, but . . . perhaps he'd just been pulled into Perrington's schemes and needed someone to steer him right. And if his father and the other councilmen thought that they could use Roland to win support for their dark dealings, well, then it was time for Dorian to play the game, too. He could turn his father's pawn against him. Between the two of them, surely they could sway enough of the council to oppose more unsavory proposals.

"You really called off the vote?"

Roland waved a hand. "I think you're right that we're pushing our luck with the other kingdoms. If we want to keep control, we need to find a balance. Shoving them into slavery won't help; it might just turn more people toward rebellion."

Dorian nodded slowly, and paused. "I have somewhere to be," he lied, sheathing his sword, "but perhaps I'll see you in the hall for dinner."

Roland gave him an easy smile. "I'll try to muster up a few lovely ladies to keep us company."

Dorian waited until Roland was around the corner before heading outside, where the chaos of the courtyard sucked him up. The carnival his mother had commissioned for Hollin—her belated Yulemas present to him—had finally arrived.

It was not a massive carnival; only a few black tents, a dozen cage wagons, and five covered wagons had been set up in the open courtyard. The whole thing felt rather somber, despite the fiddler sawing away and the merry shouts of the workers scrambling to finish setting up the tents in time to surprise Hollin that evening.

People hardly looked Dorian's way as he meandered through the throng. Then again, he was dressed in sweaty, old clothes and had his cloak wrapped tightly around him. Only the guards—highly trained and aware of everything—noticed him, but they understood his need for anonymity without being told.

A stunningly beautiful woman walked out of one of the tents—blond, slender, tall, and dressed in fine riding clothes. A mountain-sized man also emerged, carrying long poles of iron that Dorian doubted most men could even lift.

Dorian passed by one of the large covered wagons, pausing at the words written in white paint on its side:

THE CARNIVAL OF MIRRORS!

SEE ILLUSIONS AND REALITY COLLIDE!

He frowned. Had his mother even put a moment's consideration into the gift, into how it might appear, the message it would send? Carnivals, with their illusions and tricks, always pushed the limit of outright treason. Dorian snorted. Perhaps *he* belonged in one of these cages.

A hand landed on his shoulder, and Dorian whirled to find Chaol smiling at him. "I thought I'd find you here." He wasn't surprised in the least that Chaol had recognized him.

Dorian was about to smile back when he noticed who was with the captain. Celaena was standing at one of the covered cages, listening through the black velvet curtains to whatever was inside. "What are you two doing here so early? The unveiling's not until nightfall." Nearby, the gargantuan man began hammering foot-long spikes into the frozen earth.

"She wanted a walk, and—" Chaol suddenly gave a violent curse. Dorian didn't particularly want to, but he followed after Chaol as he stalked to Celaena and yanked her arm away from the black curtain. "You'll lose your hand like that," the captain warned her, and she glared at him.

Then she gave Dorian a close-lipped smile that felt more like a wince. He hadn't lied to her last night about wanting to see Nehemia. But he'd also found himself wanting to see her—until she appeared with that ridiculous half-eaten cake, which she clearly had plans to devour in private.

He couldn't begin to imagine how she'd look at him if she found out he might—*might*, he kept telling himself—have some trace of magic within him.

Nearby, the beautiful blond woman perched on a stool and began playing the lute. He knew that the men—and guards—starting to flock to her weren't just there for the lovely music.

Chaol shifted on his feet, and Dorian realized that they'd been standing there silently, not saying anything. Celaena crossed her arms. "Did you find Nehemia last night?"

He had a feeling she already knew the answer, but he said, "No. I went back to my room after I saw you."

Chaol looked at Celaena, who merely shrugged. What did *that* mean?

"So," Celaena said, surveying the carnival, "do we really have to wait for your brother before we can see what's inside all these cages? Looks like the performers are already starting."

And they were. All sorts of jugglers and sword-swallowers and fire-breathers milled about, while tumblers balanced on impossible things: chair backs, poles, a bed of nails.

"I think this is just practice," Dorian said, and he hoped he was right, because if Hollin learned that anyone had started without his approval . . . Dorian would make sure he was far away from the castle when that tantrum occurred.

"Hmm," Celaena said, and walked deeper into the teeming carnival.

Chaol was watching the prince warily. There were questions in Chaol's eyes—questions that Dorian had no intention of answering—so he strode after Celaena, because leaving the carnival would feel too much like drawing a line. They made their way to the last and largest wagon in the rough semicircle of tents and cages.

"Welcome! Welcome!" shouted an old woman, bent and gnarled with age, from a podium at the foot of its stairs. A crown of stars adorned her silver hair, and though her tanned face was saggy and speckled, there was a spark in her brown eyes.

"Look into my mirrors and see the future! Let me examine your palm so I might tell you myself!" The old woman pointed with a knotted cane at Celaena. "Care to have your fortune told, girl?" Dorian blinked—then blinked again at the sight of the woman's teeth. They were razor-sharp, like a fish's, and made of metal. Of—of iron.

Celaena pulled her green cloak tightly around her, but remained staring at the crone.

Dorian had heard the legends of the fallen Witch Kingdom, where bloodthirsty witches had overthrown the peaceful Crochan Dynasty and then ripped apart the kingdom stone by stone. Five hundred years later, songs were still sung of the deadly wars that had left the Ironteeth Clans the only ones standing on a killing field, dead Crochan queens all around them. But the last Crochan queen had cast a spell to ensure that as long as Ironteeth banners flew, no bit of soil would yield life to them.

"Come into my wagon, dear heart," the old woman crooned at Celaena, "and let old Baba Yellowlegs take a look into your future." Sure enough, peeking out from beneath her brown robe were saffron-colored ankles.

Celaena's face had drained of color, and Chaol went to her side and took her elbow. Despite the way the protective gesture made Dorian's gut twist, he was glad Chaol had done it. But this was all just a sham—that woman had probably put on a fake set of iron teeth and sheer yellow stockings, and called herself Baba Yellowlegs to make carnival patrons hand over good coin.

"You're a witch," Celaena said, her voice strangled. She didn't think it was a sham, apparently. No, her face was still white as death. Gods—was she actually scared?

Baba Yellowlegs laughed, a crow's cackle, and bowed. "The last-born witch in the Witch Kingdom." To Dorian's shock, Celaena took a step back, closer to Chaol now, a hand going to the necklace she always wore. "Care to have your fortune read *now*?"

"No," Celaena said, almost leaning into Chaol.

"Then get out of my way and let me go about my business! I've never seen such a cheap crowd!" Baba Yellowlegs snarled, and lifted her head to look over them. "Fortunes! Fortunes!"

Chaol took a step toward her, a hand on his sword. "Don't be so rude to your customers."

The crone smiled, her teeth glinting in the afternoon light as she sniffed at him. "And what would a man who smells of the Silver Lake do to an innocent old witch like me?"

A chill went down Dorian's spine, and it was Celaena's turn to grab on to Chaol's arm as she tried to pull him away. But Chaol refused to move. "I don't know what sort of sham you're running, old woman, but you'd best mind your tongue before you lose it."

Baba Yellowlegs licked her razor-sharp teeth. "Come and get it," she purred.

Challenge flashed in Chaol's eyes, but Celaena was still so pale that Dorian took her by the arm, leading her away. "Let's go," he said, and the old woman shifted her eyes to him. If she could indeed tell things about them, then the *last* place he wanted to be was here. "Chaol, let's go."

The witch was grinning at him as she used a long, metallic nail to pick out something from her teeth. "Hide from fate all you like," Baba Yellowlegs said as they turned away. "But it shall soon find you!"

~

"You're shaking."

"No, I'm not," Celaena hissed, batting Chaol's hand from her arm. It was bad enough that Dorian was there, but for Chaol to witness her coming face-to-face with Baba Yellowlegs . . .

She knew the stories—legends that had given her brutal nightmares as a child, a firsthand account that a former friend had once told her. Given how that friend had foully betrayed and nearly killed her, Celaena had hoped that the horrific stories about the Ironteeth witches were just more lies. But seeing that woman . . .

Celaena swallowed hard. Seeing that woman, feeling the sense of *otherness* that radiated from her, Celaena had no trouble believing that these witches were capable of consuming a human child until nothing but clean-picked bones remained.

Frozen down to her core now, she followed Dorian as he strode away from the carnival. While she'd been standing in front of that wagon, all she'd wanted, for some reason, was to get inside it. Like there was something waiting for her within. And that crown of stars the witch had been wearing . . . And then her amulet had started feeling heavy and warm, the way it had the night she'd seen that person in the hall.

If she ever came back to the carnival, she would bring Nehemia with her, just to see if Yellowlegs was indeed what she claimed to be. She didn't give a damn about what was in the cages. Not anymore, not with Yellowlegs to hold her interest. She followed Dorian and Chaol without hearing a single word they said until they had somehow arrived at the royal stables, and Dorian was leading them inside.

"I was going to give it to you on your birthday," he said to Chaol, "but why wait another two days?"

Dorian stopped before a stall. Chaol exclaimed, "Are you out of your mind?"

Dorian grinned—an expression she hadn't seen in so long that it made her remember late nights spent tangled up with him, the warmth of his breath on her skin. "What? You deserve it."

A night-black Asterion stallion stood within the pen, staring at them with ancient, dark eyes.

Chaol was backing away, hands raised. "This is a gift for a prince, not—"

Dorian clicked his tongue. "Nonsense. I'll be offended if you don't accept."

"I can't." Chaol shifted pleading eyes to Celaena, but she shrugged.

"I had an Asterion mare once," she admitted, and both of them blinked. Celaena went up to the stall and held out her fingers, letting the stallion sniff her. "Her name was Kasida." She smiled at the memory, stroking the stallion's velvet-soft nose. "It meant 'Drinker of the Wind' in the dialect of the Red Desert. She looked like a storm-tossed sea."

"How did *you* get an Asterion mare? They're worth even more than the stallions," Dorian said. It was the first normal-sounding question he'd asked her in weeks.

She looked over her shoulder at them and flashed a fiendish grin. "I stole her from the Lord of Xandria." Chaol's eyes grew wide, and Dorian cocked his head. It was so comical that she started laughing. "I swear on the Wyrd it's the truth. I'll tell you the story some other time." She backed away, nudging Chaol toward the pen. The horse huffed at his fingers, and beast and man looked at each other.

Dorian was still watching her with narrowed brows, but when she caught him staring, he turned to Chaol. "Is it too early to ask what you'll be doing for your birthday?"

Celaena crossed her arms. "We have plans," she said before Chaol could reply. She didn't mean to sound so sharp, but—well, she'd been planning the night for a few weeks now.

Chaol looked at her over a shoulder. "We do?"

Celaena gave him a venomously sweet smile. "Oh, yes. It might not be an Asterion stallion, but . . ."

Dorian's eyes flashed. "Well, I hope you have fun," he interrupted.

Chaol quickly looked back at the horse as Celaena and Dorian faced each other. Whatever familiar expressions he'd once worn were now gone. And part of her—the part that had spent so many nights looking forward to seeing that handsome face—truly mourned it. Looking at him became difficult.

She left them in the stables with a brief good night, congratulating Chaol on his new gift. She didn't dare turn in the direction of the carnival, where the sound of the crowd suggested that Hollin had made his appearance and unveiled the cages. Instead, she sprinted up the stairs to the warmth of her rooms, trying to shut out the image of the witch's iron teeth, and the way she'd called after them with those words about fate, so similar to what Mort had said on the night of the eclipse . . .

Perhaps it was intuition, or perhaps it was because she was a miserable person who couldn't even trust the advice of a friend, but she wanted to go back to the tomb. Alone. Maybe Nehemia was wrong about the amulet being irrelevant. And she was tired of waiting for her friend to find the time to research the eye riddle.

She'd go back just once, and never tell Nehemia. Because the hole in the wall was shaped like an eye, its iris removed to form a space that would perfectly fit the amulet she wore around her neck.

CHAPTER 20

"Mort," Celaena said, and the skull knocker opened an eye.

"It's terribly rude to wake someone when they're sleeping," he said drowsily.

"Would you have preferred it if I had knocked on your face?" He glared at her. "I need to know something." She held out the amulet. "This necklace—does it truly have power?"

"Of course it does."

"But it's thousands of years old."

"So?" Mort yawned. "It's magic. Magical things rarely age as normal objects do."

"But what does it *do*?"

"It protects you, as Elena said. It guards you from harm, though you certainly seem to do your best to get *into* trouble."

Celaena opened the door. "I think I know what it does." Perhaps it was mere coincidence, but the riddle had been worded so specifically. Perhaps Davis had been looking for the same thing Elena wanted her to find: the source of the king's power. This could be the first step toward uncovering that.

"You're probably wrong," Mort said as she walked by. "I'm just warning you."

She didn't listen. She went right up to the hollow eye in the wall and stood on tiptoe to look through. The wall on the other side was still blank. Unfastening her necklace, Celaena carefully lifted the amulet to the eye, and—

It fit. Sort of. Her breath caught in her throat, and Celaena leaned up against the hole, peering through the delicate gold bands.

Nothing. No change on the wall, or on the giant Wyrdmark. She turned the necklace upside down, but it was the same. She tried it on either side, backward, angled—but nothing. Just the same blank stone wall, illuminated by a shaft of moonlight from some vent above. She pushed against the stone, feeling for any door, any moveable panel.

"But it's the Eye of Elena! 'It is only with the eye that one can see rightly'! What other eye is there?"

"You could rip out your own and see if it fits," Mort sang from the doorway.

"Why won't it work? Do I need to say a spell?" She glanced at the sarcophagus of the queen. Perhaps the spell would be triggered by ancient words—words hiding right under her nose. Wasn't that always how these things happened? She refitted the amulet into the stone. "Ah!" she called into the night air, reciting the words engraved at Elena's feet. "Time's Rift!"

Nothing happened.

Mort cackled. She snatched the amulet out of the wall. "Oh, I hate this! I hate this stupid tomb, and I hate these stupid riddles and mysteries!" Fine—fine. Nehemia was right that the amulet was a dead end. And she was a wretched, horrible friend for being so distrustful and impatient.

"I told you it wouldn't work."

"Then what *will* work? That riddle *does* reference something in this tomb—behind that wall. Doesn't it?"

"Yes, it does. But you still haven't asked the proper question."

"I've asked you *dozens* of questions! And you won't give me any answers!"

"Come back another—" he started, but Celaena had already stalked up the stairs.

Celaena stood on the barren edge of a ravine, a chill northern wind ruffling her hair. She'd had this dream before; always this setting, always this night of the year.

Behind her sloped a rocky, wasted plain, and before her stretched a chasm so long it disappeared into the starlit horizon. Across the ravine was a lush, dark wood, rustling with life.

And on the grassy lip of the other side stood the white stag, watching her with ancient eyes. His massive antlers glowed in the moonlight, wreathing him in ivory glory, just as she remembered. It had been on a chill night like this that she'd spotted him through the bars of her prison wagon on the way to Endovier, a glimmer of a world before it was burned to ash.

They watched each other in silence.

She took a half step closer to the edge, but paused as loose pebbles trickled free, tumbling into the ravine. There was no end to the darkness in that ravine. No end, and no beginning, either. It seemed to breathe, pulsing with whispers of faded memories, forgotten faces. Sometimes, it felt as though the darkness stared back at her—and the face it wore was her own.

Beneath the dark, she could have sworn she heard the rushing of a half-frozen river, swollen with melting snow off the Staghorns. A flash of white, the thud of hooves on soft earth, and Celaena looked up from the ravine. The stag had come closer, his head now angled, as if inviting her to join him.

But the ravine only seemed to grow wider, like the maw of a giant beast opening to devour the world.

So Celaena did not cross, and the stag turned away, his steps near silent as he disappeared between the tangled trees of the ageless wood.

~

Celaena awoke to darkness. The fire was nothing but cinders, and the moon had set.

She studied the ceiling, the faint shadows cast by the city lights in the distance. It was always the same dream, always this one night.

As if she could ever forget the day when everything she had loved had been wrenched from her, and she'd awoken covered in blood that was not her own.

She got out of bed, Fleetfoot leaping down beside her. She walked a few steps, then paused in the center of the room, staring into the dark, into the endless ravine still beckoning to her. Fleetfoot nuzzled her bare legs, and Celaena reached down to stroke the hound's head.

They remained there for a moment, gazing into that blackness without end.

Celaena left the castle long before dawn broke.

~

When Celaena didn't meet Chaol at the barracks door that dawn, he gave her ten minutes before stalking up to her rooms. Just because she didn't feel like going out in the cold wasn't an excuse to be lax with her training. Not to mention he was particularly interested in hearing the story about how she'd stolen an Asterion mare from the Lord of Xandria. He smiled at the thought, shaking his head. Only Celaena would have the nerve to do something like that.

His smile faded when he reached her chambers and found Nehemia sitting at the small table in the foyer, a cup of steaming tea before her. There were some books piled in front of the princess, and she looked up from one of them as he entered. Chaol bowed. The princess just said, "She is not here."

Celaena's bedroom door was open wide enough to reveal that the bed was empty and already made. "Where is she?"

Nehemia's eyes softened, and she picked up a note that was lying among the books. "She has taken today off," she said, reading from the note before setting it down. "If I were to guess, I'd say that she is as far away from the city as she can get in half a day's ride."

"Why?"

Nehemia smiled sadly. "Because today is the tenth anniversary of her parents' death."

CHAPTER 21

Chaol's breath caught. He remembered her screaming at the duel with Cain, when Cain had taunted her about the brutal murder of her parents—when she'd awoken covered in their blood. She'd never told him anything else, and he hadn't dared ask. He knew she'd been young, but he hadn't realized she'd been only eight. *Eight*.

Ten years ago, Terrasen had been in upheaval, and anyone who had defied Adarlan's invading forces had been slaughtered. Entire families had been dragged out of their homes and murdered. His stomach clenched. What horrors had she witnessed that day?

Chaol ran a hand over his face. "She told you about her parents in her note?" Maybe it held a shred more information—anything for him to better understand what sort of woman he'd be facing when she returned, what sort of memories he'd have to contend with.

"No," Nehemia said. "She didn't tell me. But I know." She watched him with a calculated stillness, a switch to the defensive that he recognized. What sort of secrets was she protecting for her friend? And what sort of secrets did Nehemia herself keep that had caused the king to have her watched? The fact that he didn't know anything about it, about how much the king knew, enraged him to no end. And then there was the other question: who had threatened the princess's life? He'd ordered more guards to look after her, but so far, there had been no sign of anyone wanting to harm her.

"How do you know about her parents?" he asked.

"Some things you hear with your ears. Others, you hear with your heart." He looked away from the intensity in her eyes.

"When is she coming back?"

Nehemia returned to the book in front of her. It looked like it was filled with strange symbols; vaguely familiar markings that tickled at his memory. "She said she won't be back until after nightfall. If I were to guess, I'd say she didn't want to spend one moment of daylight in this city—especially in this castle."

In the home of the man whose soldiers had probably butchered her family.

Chaol took the morning training run alone. He ran through the mist-shrouded game park until his very bones were exhausted.

In the misty foothills above Rifthold, Celaena strode between the trees of the small forest, barely more than a sliver of darkness winding through the woods. She had been walking since before dawn, letting Fleetfoot follow as she would. Today, even the forest seemed silent.

Good. Today was not a day for the sounds of life. Today was for the hollow wind rustling branches, for the rushing of a half-frozen river, for the crunch of snow under her boots.

On this day last year, she'd known what she had to do—had seen every step with such brutal clarity that it had been easy when the time came. She'd once told Dorian and Chaol that she'd snapped that day in the Salt Mines of Endovier, but it was a lie. *Snapped* implied too human a feeling; nothing like the cold, hopeless rage that had taken hold and shut everything down when she'd awoken from the dream of the stag and the ravine.

She found a large boulder nestled between the bumps and hollows and sank down on its smooth, ice-cold top, Fleetfoot soon sitting beside her. Wrapping her arms around the dog, Celaena looked out into the still forest and remembered the day she'd unleashed herself upon Endovier.

Celaena panted through her bared teeth as she yanked the pickax out of the overseer's stomach. The man gurgled blood, clutching at his gut as he looked to the slaves in supplication. But one glance from Celaena, one flash of eyes that showed she had gone beyond the edge, kept the slaves at bay.

She merely smiled down at the overseer as she swung the ax into his face. His blood sprayed her legs.

The slaves still stayed far away when she brought down the ax upon the shackles that bound her ankles to the rest of them. She didn't offer to free them, and they didn't ask; they knew how useless it would be.

The woman at the end of the chain gang was unconscious. Her back poured blood, split open by the iron-tipped whip of the dead overseer. She would die by tomorrow if her wounds were not treated. Even if they were, she'd probably die from infection. Endovier amused itself like that.

Celaena turned from the woman. She had work to do, and four overseers had to pay a debt before she was done.

She stalked from the mine shaft, pickax dangling from her hand. The two guards at the end of the tunnel were dead before they realized what was happening. Blood soaked her clothes and her bare arms, and Celaena wiped it from her face as she stormed down to the chamber where she knew the four overseers worked.

She had marked their faces the day they'd dragged that young Eyllwe woman behind the building, marked every detail about them as they used her, then slit her throat from ear to ear.

Celaena could have taken the swords from the fallen guards, but for these four men, it had to be the ax. She wanted them to know what Endovier felt like.

She reached the entrance to their section of the mines. The first two overseers died when she heaved the ax into their necks, slashing back and forth between them. Their slaves screamed, backing against the walls as she raged past them.

When she reached the other two overseers, she let them see her, let them try to draw their blades. She knew it wasn't the weapon in her hands that made them stupid with panic, but rather her eyes—eyes that told them they had been tricked these past few months, that cutting her hair and whipping her hadn't been enough, that she had been baiting them into forgetting that Adarlan's Assassin was in their midst.

But she had not forgotten a second of pain, nor what she had seen them do to the others—to that young woman from Eyllwe, who had begged to gods who did not save her.

The men died too quickly, but Celaena had one more task to complete before she would meet her end. She prowled back up the main tunnel that led out of the mines. Guards foolishly came rushing out of tunnel mouths to meet her.

She surged upward, hacking and swinging. Two more guards went down, and she took up their swords, leaving the ax behind. The slaves didn't cheer as their oppressors fell; they just watched in silence, understanding. This was not a fight for escape.

The light of the surface made her blink, but she was ready. Her eyes having to adjust to the sun would be her greatest weakness. That was why she had waited until the softer light of afternoon. Twilight would have been better, but that time of day was too heavily guarded, and there were too many slaves about then that could be caught in the crossfire. This last hour of full daylight, when the warm sun lulled many to sleep, was when the sentries went lax on watch before the evening inspection.

The three sentries at the entrance to the mines didn't know what was happening below. Everyone was always screaming in Endovier. Everyone sounded the same when they died. And the three sentries screamed just like the others.

And then she was running, sprinting for the death that beckoned to her, making for the towering stone wall at the other end of the compound.

Arrows whizzed past, and she zigzagged. They wouldn't kill her, by order of the king. An arrow through the shoulder or leg, maybe. But she'd make them reconsider their orders once the carnage was too massive to ignore.

Other sentries came rushing from everywhere, and her blades were a song of steel fury as she cut through them. Silence settled over Endovier.

She took a gash in her leg—deep, but not deep enough to cut the tendon. They still wanted her able to work. But she wouldn't work—not again, not for them. When the body count was high enough, they'd have no choice but to put that arrow through her throat.

But then she neared the gate, and the arrows stopped.

She started laughing when she found herself surrounded by forty guards, and laughed even more when they called for irons.

She was laughing when she lashed out one last time—one final attempt to touch the wall. Four more went down in her wake.

She was still laughing when the world went black and her fingers hit the rocky ground—barely an inch away from the wall.

⁓

Chaol stood from his seat at her foyer table as the door quietly opened. The outside hall was dark, the lights burned out; most of the castle asleep and tucked into their beds. He'd heard the clock chime midnight some time ago, but he knew it wasn't exhaustion weighing down

Celaena's shoulders when she slipped into her rooms. Her eyes were purple beneath, her face wan, lips colorless.

Fleetfoot rushed to him, tail wagging, and licked him a few times on the hand before she trotted into the bedroom, leaving them alone.

Celaena glanced once at him, her turquoise-and-gold eyes weary and haunted, and began unfastening her cloak as she walked past him into the bedroom.

Wordlessly, he followed her, if only because she hadn't had a hint of warning or reproach in her expression—rather a bleakness that suggested she wouldn't have cared if she'd found the King of Adarlan himself in her rooms.

She removed her coat and then her boots, leaving them wherever she happened to discard them. He looked away as she unbuttoned her tunic and walked into the dressing room. A moment later, she walked back out, wearing a nightgown that was far more modest than her usual lacy attire. Fleetfoot had already hopped into bed, sprawling against the pillows.

Chaol swallowed hard. He should have given her privacy instead of waiting here. If she'd wanted him to be here, she would have written him a note.

Celaena stopped before the dim fireplace and used the poker to stir the coals before tossing another two logs on. She stared down at the flames. Her back was still to him when she spoke.

"If you're trying to figure out what to say to me, don't bother. There's nothing that can be said, or done."

"Then let me keep you company." If she realized how much he knew, she didn't care to ask how.

"I don't want company."

"Want and need are different things." Nehemia, probably, should have been here—another child of a conquered kingdom. But he didn't want Nehemia to be the one she turned to. And despite his loyalty to the king, he couldn't turn away from her—not today.

"So you're just going to stay here all night?" She flicked her eyes to the couch between them.

"I've slept in worse places."

"I think my experience with 'worse places' is a lot more horrible than yours." Again, that twisting in his gut. But then she looked through the open bedroom door to the foyer table, and her brows rose. "Is that . . . chocolate cake?"

"I thought you might need some."

"*Need*, not *want*?"

A ghost of a smile was on her lips, and he almost sagged in relief as he said, "For you, I'd say that chocolate cake is most definitely a *need*."

She crossed from the fireplace to where he stood, stopping a hand's breadth away and staring up at him. Some of the color had returned to her face.

He should step back, put more distance between them. But instead, he found himself reaching for her, a hand slipping around her waist and the other twining itself through her hair as he held her tightly to him. His heart thundered through him so hard he knew she could feel it. After a second, her arms came up around him, her fingers digging into his back in a way that made him realize how close they stood.

He shoved that feeling down, even as the silken texture of her hair against his fingers made him want to bury his face in it, and the smell of her, laced with mist and night, had him grazing his nose against her neck. There were other kinds of comfort that he could give her than mere words, and if she needed that kind of distraction . . . He shoved down that thought, too, swallowing it until he nearly choked on it.

Her fingers were moving down his back, still digging into his muscles with a fierce kind of possession. If she kept touching him like that, his control was going to slip completely.

And then she pulled back, just far enough to look up at him again, still so close their breath mingled. He found himself gauging the distance between their lips, his eyes flicking between her mouth and her eyes, the hand he had entwined in her hair stilling.

Desire roared through him, burning down every defense he'd put up, erasing every line he'd convinced himself he had to maintain.

And then she said, so quietly it was hardly more than a murmur, "I can't tell if I should be ashamed of wanting to hold you on this day, or grateful that, despite what happened before now, it somehow brought me to you."

He was so startled by the words that he let go, let go and stepped back. He had his obstacles to overcome, but so did she—perhaps more obstacles than he'd even realized.

He had no response to what she'd said. But she didn't give him time to think of the right words before she walked to the chocolate cake in the foyer, plunked down in the chair, and dug in.

CHAPTER 22

The silence of the library wrapped around Dorian like a heavy blanket, interrupted only by the turning of pages as he read through his family's extensive genealogical charts, records, and histories. He couldn't be the only one; if he truly did have magic, then what about Hollin? It had taken until now to manifest, so perhaps it wouldn't reveal itself in Hollin for another nine years. Hopefully by then, he'd figure out how to suppress it and teach Hollin to do the same. He might not be fond of his brother, but he didn't wish the boy dead—especially not the kind of death their father would give them if he learned what dwelled in their blood. Beheading, dismemberment, then burning. Complete annihilation.

No wonder the Fae had fled the continent. They had been powerful and wise, but Adarlan had military might and a frantic public looking for any solution to the famine and poverty that had plagued the kingdom for decades. It hadn't just been the armies that had made the Fae run—no, it was also the people who had lived in an uneasy truce with them, as well as the mortals gifted with magic, for generations. How would those people react if they knew that the heir to the throne was plagued by the same powers?

Dorian ran a finger down his mother's family tree. It was dotted with Havilliards along the way; a close mingling of their two families for the past few centuries that had given rise to numerous kings.

But he'd been here for three hours now, and none of the rotting old books held any mention of magic-wielders. In fact, there had been a drought in the line for centuries. Several gifted people had married into the bloodline, but their children hadn't been born with the power, no matter what manner of gifts their parents possessed. Was it coincidence, or divine will?

Dorian closed the book and stalked back into the stacks. He reached the section along the back wall that held all the genealogical records and pulled out the oldest book he could find—one that held records dating back to the founding of Adarlan itself.

There, on the top of the family tree, was Gavin Havilliard, the mortal prince who had taken his war band into the depths of the Ruhnn Mountains to challenge the Dark Lord Erawan. The war had been long and brutal, and in the end, only a third of the men who had ridden in with Gavin came out of those mountains. But Gavin also emerged from that war with his bride—the princess Elena, the half-Fae daughter of Brannon, Terrasen's first king. It was Brannon himself who gave Gavin the territory of Adarlan as a wedding gift—and a reward for the prince and princess's sacrifices during the war. And since then, no Fae blood had bred into their line. Dorian followed the tree down and down. Just long-forgotten families whose lands were now called by different names.

Dorian sighed, set down the book, and browsed through the stack. If Elena *had* gifted the line with her power, then perhaps answers could be found elsewhere . . .

He was surprised to see the book sitting there, given how his father had destroyed that noble house ten years ago. But there it was: a history of the Galathynius line, starting with the Fae King Brannon himself. Dorian flipped through the pages, his brows raised high. He'd known the line was blessed with magic, but *this* . . .

It was a powerhouse. A bloodline so mighty that other kingdoms had lived in terror of the day the Lords of Terrasen would come to claim their lands.

But they never had.

While they'd been gifted, they'd never once pushed their borders—even when wars came to their doorstep. When foreign kings had threatened them, the retribution had been swift and brutal. But always, no matter what, they kept to their borders. Kept the peace.

As my father should have done.

Despite all their power, though, the Galathynius family had fallen, and their noble lords with them. In the book he held, no one had bothered to mark the houses his father had exterminated, or the survivors sent into exile. Without the heart or the knowledge to do it himself, Dorian closed the book, grimacing as all those names burned in his vision. What sort of throne would he inherit someday?

If the heir of Terrasen, Aelin Galathynius, had lived, would she have become a friend, an ally? His bride, perhaps?

He'd met her once, in the days before her kingdom became a charnel house. The memory was hazy, but she'd been a precocious, wild girl—and had set her nasty, brutish older cousin on him in order to teach Dorian a lesson for spilling tea on her dress. Dorian rubbed his neck. Of course, as fate would have it, her cousin wound up becoming Aedion Ashryver, his father's prodigy general and the fiercest warrior in the north. He'd met Aedion a few times over the years, and at each encounter with the haughty young general, he'd gotten the distinct impression that Aedion wanted to kill him.

And with good reason.

Shuddering, Dorian replaced the book and stared at the bookcase, as if it would yield any answers. But he already knew there was nothing here that could help him.

When the time comes, I will help you.

Did Nehemia know what dwelt inside him? She had acted so strangely that day at the duel, drawing symbols in the air and then fainting. And then there had been the moment when that mark had burned on Celaena's brow . . .

A clock chimed somewhere in the library, and he glanced down the aisle. He should go. It was Chaol's birthday, and he should at least say hello to his friend before Celaena whisked him off. Of course he hadn't been invited. And Chaol hadn't tried to suggest that Dorian was welcome, either. What did she plan to do, exactly?

The temperature in the library dropped, a frozen draft blowing in from a distant corridor.

Not that he cared. He'd meant it when he swore to Nehemia that he was done with Celaena. And maybe he should have told Chaol that he could have her. Not that she'd ever belonged to him—or that she'd even tried to suggest that he belonged to her.

He could let go. He *had* let go. He'd let go. Let go. Let—

Books flew from their shelves, dozens upon dozens bursting into flight, and this time, they slammed into him as he staggered back toward the end of the row. He shielded his face, and when the sound of leather and paper stopped, Dorian braced a hand on the stone wall behind him and gaped.

Half of the books in the row had been tossed off their shelves and scattered about, as if thrown by some invisible force.

He rushed to them, shoving volumes back onto their shelves in no order whatsoever, working as fast as he could before one of the crotchety royal librarians came hobbling over to see what the noise was about. It took him a few minutes to put them all back, his heart pounding so hard he thought he'd be sick again.

His hands trembled—and not just with fear. No, there was some force still running through him, begging him to unleash it again, to open himself up . . .

Dorian crammed the last book back onto the shelf and took off at a run.

He could tell no one. Trust no one.

When he reached the main hall of the library, he slowed to a walk, feigning a lazy carelessness. He even managed to smile at the old, withered librarian who bowed to him as he passed. Dorian gave him a friendly wave before striding out the towering oak doors.

He could trust no one.

That witch at the carnival—she hadn't recognized him as the prince. Still, her gift had rung true, at least when talking to Chaol. It was a risk, but perhaps Baba Yellowlegs had the answers he needed.

Celaena wasn't nervous. She had nothing—absolutely nothing—to be worried about. It was just a dinner. A dinner she'd spent weeks arranging whenever she had a spare moment while spying on those men in Rifthold. A dinner at which she'd be alone. With Chaol. And after last night . . .

Celaena took a surprisingly shaky breath and checked herself in the mirror one last time. The dress was pale blue, almost white, and encrusted with crystal beading that made the fabric look like the shimmering surface of the sea. Perhaps it was a bit much, but she'd told Chaol to dress well, so hopefully he'd be wearing something nice enough to make her feel less self-conscious.

Celaena huffed. Gods above, she *was* feeling self-conscious, wasn't she? It was ridiculous, really. It was just a dinner. Fleetfoot was with

Nehemia for the night, and—and if she didn't leave now, she'd be late.

Refusing to let herself sweat another second longer, Celaena grabbed her ermine cloak from where Philippa had left it on the ottoman in the center of her dressing room.

When she reached the entrance hall, Chaol was already waiting for her by the doors. Even from across the massive space, she could tell his eyes were on her as she descended the stairs. Not surprisingly, he wore black—but at least it wasn't his uniform. No, his tunic and pants looked to be of fine make, and it seemed like he'd even run a comb through his short hair.

He watched her every step across the hall, his face unreadable. At last she stopped in front of him, the cold air from the open doors biting into her face. She hadn't gone for their run this morning, and he hadn't come to drag her outside. "Happy birthday," she said before he could object to her clothes.

His eyes rose to her face, and he gave her a half smile, that unreadable, closed-off expression vanishing. "Do I even want to know where you're taking me?"

She grinned at him, her nerves melting away. "Somewhere utterly inappropriate for the Captain of the Guard to be seen." She inclined her head toward the carriage that waited outside the castle doors. Good. She'd threatened to flay the driver and footmen alive if they were late. "Shall we?"

As they rode through the city, sitting on opposite sides of the carriage, they talked about anything *but* last night—the carnival, Fleetfoot, Hollin's daily tantrums. They even debated whether spring would start showing itself at last. When they reached the building—an old apothecary—Chaol raised his brows. "Just wait," she said, and led him into the warmly lit shop.

The owners smiled at her, beckoning them up the narrow stone staircase. Chaol said nothing as they went up and up the stairs, past the second level, and the third, until they reached a door at the uppermost landing. The landing was small enough that he brushed against the skirts of her gown, and when she turned to him, one hand on the doorknob, she gave him a small smile. "It might not be an Asterion stallion, but . . ."

She opened the door, stepping aside so he could enter.

Wordlessly, he walked in.

She'd spent hours arranging everything, and in the daylight it had looked lovely, but at night . . . It was exactly as she'd imagined it would be.

The roof of the apothecary was an enclosed glass greenhouse, filled with flowers and potted plants and fruit trees that had been hung with little glittering lights. The whole place had been transformed into a garden out of an ancient legend. The air was warm and sweet, and by the windows overlooking the expanse of the Avery River stood a small table set for two.

Chaol surveyed the room, turning in place. "It's the Fae woman's garden—from Rena Goldsmith's song," he said softly. His golden eyes were bright.

She swallowed hard. "I know it's not much —"

"No one has ever done anything like this for me." He shook his head in awe, looking back at the greenhouse. "No one."

"It's just a dinner," she said, rubbing her neck and walking to the table, if only because the urge to go to him was so strong that she needed a table between them.

He followed her, and an instant later, two servants appeared to pull out their chairs for them. She smiled a little as Chaol's hand shot to his sword, but upon seeing that they were *not* being ambushed, he gave her a sheepish glance and sat down.

The servants poured two glasses of sparkling wine, then bustled off for the food that they'd spent all day preparing in the apothecary's kitchen. She'd managed to hire the cook from the Willows for the night—for a fee that had made her consider punching the woman's throat. It was worth it, though. She lifted her flute of wine.

"Many happy returns," she said. She'd had a little speech prepared, but now that they were here, now that his eyes were so bright, and he was looking at her the way he had last night . . . all the words went right out of her head.

Chaol lifted his glass and drank. "Before I forget to say it: Thank you. This is . . ." He examined the glittering greenhouse again, then looked out to the river beyond the glass walls. "This is . . ." He shook his head once more, setting down his glass, and she caught a glimmer of silver in his eyes that made her heart clench. He blinked it away and looked back at her with a small smile. "No one has thrown me a birth-day party since I was a child."

She scoffed, fighting past the tightness in her chest. "I'd hardly call this a *party*—"

"Stop trying to downplay it. It's the greatest gift I've been given in a long while."

She crossed her arms, leaning back in her chair as the servants arrived, bringing their first course—roast boar stew. "Dorian got you an Aste-rion stallion."

Chaol was staring down at his soup, brows high. "But Dorian doesn't know what my favorite stew is, does he?" He glanced up at her, and she bit her lip. "How long have you been paying attention?"

She became very interested in her stew. "Don't flatter yourself. I just bullied the castle's head cook to tell me what dishes you favored."

He snorted. "You might be Adarlan's Assassin, but even *you* couldn't bully Meghra. If you'd tried, I think you'd be sitting there with two black eyes and a broken nose."

She smiled, taking a bite of stew. "Well, *you* might think you're mysterious and brooding and stealthy, Captain, but once you know where to look, you're a fairly easy book to read. Every time we have roast boar stew, I can barely get a spoonful before you've eaten the whole tureen."

He tipped his head back and laughed, and the sound sent heat coursing through every part of her. "And here I was, thinking I'd managed to hide my weaknesses so well."

She gave him a wicked grin. "Just wait until you see the other courses."

When they'd eaten the last crumb of chocolate-hazelnut cake and drunk the last of the sparkling wine, and when the servants had cleared everything away and bid their farewells, Celaena found herself standing on the small balcony at the far edge of the roof, the summer plants buried under a blanket of snow. She held her cloak close to her as she stared toward the distant spot where the Avery met the ocean, Chaol beside her, leaning against the iron railing.

"There's a hint of spring in the air," he said as a mild wind whipped past them.

"Thank the gods. Any more snow and I'll go mad."

In the glow of the lights from the greenhouse, his profile was illuminated. She'd meant the dinner to be a nice surprise—a way to tell him how much she appreciated him—but his reaction . . . How long had it been since he felt cherished? Apart from that girl who had treated him so foully, there was also the matter of the family that had shunned him just because he wanted to be a guard, and they were too proud to have a son serve the crown in that manner.

Did his parents have any idea that in the entire castle, in the entire kingdom, there was no one more noble and loyal than him? That the boy they'd thrown out of their lives had become the sort of man that kings and queens could only dream of having serve in their courts? The sort of man that she hadn't believed existed, not after Sam, not after everything that had happened.

The king had threatened to kill Chaol if she didn't obey his orders. And, considering how much danger she was putting him in right now, and how much she wanted to gain—not just for herself, but for *them* . . .

"I have to tell you something," she said softly. Her blood roared through her ears, especially as he turned to her with a smile. "And before I tell you, you have to promise not to go berserk."

The smile faded. "Why do I have a bad feeling about this?"

"Just promise." She clenched the railing, the cold metal biting into her bare hands.

He studied her carefully, then said, "I'll try."

Fair enough. Like a damned coward, she turned away from him, focusing on the distant ocean instead.

"I haven't killed any of the people the king commanded me to assassinate."

Silence. She didn't dare look at him.

"I've been faking their deaths and smuggling them out of their homes. Their personal effects are given to me after I approach them with my offer, and the body parts come from sick-houses. The only person that I've actually killed so far is Davis, and he wasn't even an official target. At the end of the month, once Archer has gotten his affairs in order, I'll fake his death, and Archer will get on the next ship out of Rifthold and sail away."

Her chest was so tight it hurt, and she slid her eyes to him.

Chaol's face was bone white. He backed away, shaking his head. "You've gone mad."

CHAPTER 23

He must have heard her incorrectly. Because there was no possible way that she could be *that* brash, that foolish and insane and idealistic and brave.

"Have you lost your senses completely?" His words rose into a shout, a riot of rage and fear that rushed through him so fast he could hardly think. "He'll kill you! He will *kill* you if he finds out."

She took a step toward him, that spectacular dress glinting like a thousand stars. "He *won't* find out."

"It's only a matter of time," he gritted out. "He has spies who are watching *everything*."

"And you'd rather I kill innocent men?"

"Those men are traitors to the crown!"

"Traitors!" She barked a laugh. "Traitors. For refusing to grovel before a conqueror? For sheltering escaped slaves trying to get home? For daring to believe in a world that's better than this gods-forsaken place?" She shook her head, some of her hair escaping. "I will not be his butcher."

And he hadn't wanted her to. From the second she'd been crowned Champion, he'd been sick at the thought of her doing what the king had commanded she do. But *this* . . . "You swore an *oath* to him."

"And how many oaths did *he* swear to foreign rulers before he marched in with his armies and destroyed everything? How many oaths did he swear when he ascended the throne, only to spit on those promises?"

"He will *kill you*, Celaena." He grabbed her by the shoulders and shook her. "He'll kill you, and make *me* do it as punishment for being your friend." That was the terror that he grappled with—the fear that plagued him, the thing that had kept him on this side of the line for so long.

"Archer has been giving me real information—"

"I don't give a damn about Archer. What information could that conceited ass have that could possibly help you?"

"This secret movement from Terrasen actually exists," she said with maddening calm. "I could use the information I've gathered about it to bargain with the king to let me go—or just give me a shorter contract. Short enough that if he ever finds out the truth, I'll be long gone."

He growled. "He could have you whipped just for being that impertinent." But then the last part of her words registered, hitting him like a punch to the face. *I'll be long gone.* Gone. "Where will you go?"

"Anywhere," she said. "As far away as I can get."

He could hardly breathe, but he managed to say, "And what would you do?"

She shrugged, and both of them realized that he'd been gripping her shoulders. He eased his grip, but his fingers ached to grab her again, as though it would somehow keep her from leaving. "Live my life, I suppose. Live it the way I want to, for once. Learn how to be a normal girl."

"How far away?"

Her blue-and-gold eyes flickered. "I'd travel until I found a place where they'd never heard of Adarlan. If such a place exists."

And she would never come back.

And because she was young, and so damn clever and amusing and wonderful, wherever she made her home, there would be some man who would fall in love with her and who would make her his wife, and *that* was the worst truth of all. It had snuck up on him, this pain and terror and rage at the thought of anyone else with her. Every look, every word from her . . . He didn't even know when it had started.

"We'll find that place, then," he said quietly.

"What?" Her brows narrowed.

"I'll go with you." And though he hadn't asked, they both knew those words held a question. He tried not to think of what she'd said last night—of the shame she'd felt holding him when he was a son of Adarlan and she was a daughter of Terrasen.

"What about being Captain of the Guard?"

"Perhaps my duties aren't what I expected them to be." The king kept things from him; there were so many secrets, and perhaps he was little more than a puppet, part of the illusion that he was starting to see through . . .

"You love your country," she said. "I can't let you give all that up." He caught the glimmer of pain and hope in her eyes, and before he knew what he was doing, he'd closed the distance between them, one hand on her waist and the other on her shoulder.

"I would be the greatest fool in the world to let you go alone."

And then there were tears rolling down her face, and her mouth became a thin, wobbling line.

He pulled back, but didn't let her go. "Why are you crying?"

"Because," she whispered, her voice shaking, "you remind me of how the world ought to be. What the world *can* be."

There had never been any line between them, only his own stupid fear and pride. Because from the moment he'd pulled her out of that mine in Endovier and she had set those eyes upon him, still fierce despite a year in hell, he'd been walking toward this, walking to *her*.

So Chaol brushed away her tears, lifted her chin, and kissed her.

⁓

The kiss obliterated her.

It was like coming home or being born or suddenly finding an entire half of herself that had been missing.

His lips were hot and soft against hers—still tentative, and after a moment, he pulled back far enough to look into her eyes. She trembled with the need to touch him everywhere at once, to feel him touching *her* everywhere at once. He would give up everything to go with her.

She twined her arms around his neck, her mouth meeting his in a second kiss that knocked the world out from under her.

⁓

She didn't know how long they stood on that roof, tangled up in each other, mouths and hands roving until she moaned and dragged him through the greenhouse, down the stairs, and into the carriage waiting outside. And then there was the ride home, where he did things to her neck and ear that made her forget her own name. They managed to straighten themselves out as they reached the castle gates, and kept a respectable distance as they walked back to her room, though every inch of her felt so alive and burning that it was a miracle she made it back to her door without pulling him into a closet.

But then they were inside her rooms, and then at her bedroom door, and he paused as she took his hand to lead him in. "Are you sure?"

She lifted a hand to his face, exploring every curve and freckle that had become so impossibly precious to her. She had waited once before—waited with Sam, and then it had been too late. But now, there was no doubt, no shred of fear or uncertainty, as if every moment between her and Chaol had been a step in a dance that had led to this threshold.

"I've never been so sure of anything in my life," she told him. His eyes blazed with hunger that matched her own, and she kissed him again, tugging him into her bedroom. He let her pull him, not breaking the kiss as he kicked the door shut behind them.

And then there was only them, and skin against skin, and when they reached that moment when there was nothing more between them at all, Celaena kissed Chaol deeply and gave him everything she had.

Celaena awoke as dawn poured into her room. Chaol still held her to him, just as he had all night, as if she would somehow slip away during sleep. She smiled to herself, pressing her nose against his neck and breathing him in. He shifted, just enough for her to know that he'd awoken.

His hands began moving, twining themselves in her hair. "There's no way in hell I'm getting out of this bed and going for a run," he murmured onto her head. She chuckled quietly. His hands grazed lower, down her back, not even stumbling over the scar tissue. He'd kissed every scar on her back, on her entire body, last night. She smiled against his neck. "How are you feeling?"

Like she was everywhere and nowhere all at once. Like she'd somehow been half-blind all her life and could now see everything clearly. Like she could stay here forever and be content. "Tired," she admitted. He tensed. "But happy."

She almost whined when he let go of her long enough to prop himself up on an elbow and stare down at her face. "You're all right, though?"

She rolled her eyes. "I'm pretty certain 'tired, but happy' is a normal reaction after one's first time." And she was pretty certain she'd have to talk to Philippa about a contraceptive tonic as soon as she dragged herself out of bed. Because Gods above, a baby . . . She snorted.

"What?"

She just shook her head, smiling. "Nothing." She ran her fingers through his hair. A thought hit her, and her smile faded. "How much trouble will you get in for this?"

She watched his muscled chest expand as he took a deep breath, dipping his head to rest his brow on her shoulder. "I don't know. Maybe the king won't care. Maybe he'll dismiss me. Maybe worse. It's hard to tell; he's unpredictable like that."

She chewed her lip and ran her hands down his powerful back. She'd longed to touch him like this for so long—longer than she'd realized. "Then we'll keep it secret. We spend enough time together that no one should notice the change."

He lifted himself again, peering into her eyes. "I don't want you to think I'm agreeing to keep it secret because I'm ashamed in any way."

"Who said anything about shame?" She gestured down to her naked body, even though it was covered by the blanket. "Honestly, I'm surprised you're not strutting about, boasting to everyone. *I* certainly would be if I'd tumbled *me*."

"Does your love for yourself know no bounds?"

"Absolutely none." He leaned down to nip at her ear, and her toes curled. "We can't tell Dorian," she said quietly. "He'll figure it out, I bet, but . . . I don't think we should tell him outright."

He paused his nibbling. "I know." But then he pulled back, and she winced inwardly as he studied her again. "Do you still—"

"No. Not for a long while." The relief in his eyes made her kiss him. "But he'd be another complication if he knew." And there was no telling how he'd react, given how tense things had been between them. He was important enough in Chaol's life that she didn't want to ruin that relationship.

"So," he said, flicking her nose, "how long have *you* wanted—"

"I don't see how that's any of your business, Captain Westfall. And I won't tell you until you tell me."

He flicked her nose again, and she batted away his fingers. He caught her hand in his, holding it up so he could look at her amethyst ring—the ring she never took off, not even to bathe. "The Yulemas ball. Maybe earlier. Maybe even Samhuinn, when I brought you this ring. But Yulemas was the first time I realized I didn't like the idea of you with—with someone else." He kissed the tips of her fingers. "Your turn."

"I'm not telling you," she said. Because she had no idea; she was still figuring out when it had happened, exactly. It somehow felt as if it had *always* been Chaol, even from the very beginning, even before they'd ever met. He began to protest, but she pulled him back down on top of her. "And that's enough talking. I might be tired, but there are still plenty of things to do instead of going for a run."

The grin Chaol gave her was hungry and wicked enough that she shrieked when he yanked her under the blankets.

CHAPTER 24

Dorian walked past the black tents of the carnival, wondering for the umpteenth time if this was the greatest mistake of his life. He'd lost the nerve to come yesterday, but after yet another sleepless night, he'd decided to see the old witch and deal with the consequences later. If he wound up on the executioner's block because of it, he'd surely kick himself for being so brash, but he had exhausted every other way of finding out why he was plagued by magic. This was his only option.

He found Baba Yellowlegs sitting on the back steps of her giant wagon, a chipped plate heaped with roast chicken parts resting on her knees, a pile of clean-licked bones littering the ground below.

She lifted her yellowed eyes to him, iron teeth glinting in the noontime sun as she bit into a chicken leg. "Carnival's closed for lunch."

He swallowed his irritation. Getting answers relied on two things: being on her good side, and her not knowing who he was.

"I was hoping you'd have a few moments to answer some questions."

The chicken leg cracked in two. He tried not to cringe at the slurping sounds as she sucked out the marrow. "Customers who have questions during lunch pay double."

He reached into his pocket and fished out the four gold coins he'd brought. "I hope this will buy me all the questions I want—and your discretion."

She chucked the clean half of the leg onto the pile and set to work on the other, sucking and gnawing. "I bet you wipe your ass with gold."

"I don't think that would be very comfortable."

Baba Yellowlegs hissed a laugh. "Very well, lordling. Let's hear your questions."

He leaned in close enough to set his gold on the top step beside her, keeping well away from her withered form. She smelled atrocious, like mildew and rotted blood. But he kept his face blank and bored as he pulled back. The gold vanished with a swipe of a gnarled hand.

Dorian glanced around. Workers were scattered throughout the carnival, all of them settled down for the midday meal wherever they could find seats. None of them, he noticed, sat anywhere near the black-painted wagon. They didn't even look this way.

"You're truly a witch?"

She picked up a chicken wing. *Crack. Crunch.* "The last-born witch of the Witch Kingdom."

"That would make you over five hundred years old."

She gave him a smile. "It's a marvel I've stayed so young, isn't it?"

"So it's true: witches really are blessed with the long lifespans of the Fae."

She tossed another bone at the foot of the wooden steps. "Fae or Valg. We never learned which one."

Valg. He knew that name. "The demons who stole Fae to breed with them; which made the witches, right?" And, if he recalled correctly, the beautiful Crochan witches had taken after their Fae ancestors—while the three clans of Ironteeth witches took after the race of demons that had invaded Erilea at the dawn of time.

"Why would a lordling as pretty as you bother yourself with such wicked stories?" She peeled the skin off the breast of the chicken and guzzled it down, smacking her withered lips together.

"When we're not wiping our asses with gold, we need to find *some* way to amuse ourselves. Why not learn a little history?"

"Indeed," the witch said. "So, are you going to dance around it all day while I bake in this miserable sun, or are you going to ask what you really came here to learn?"

"Is magic truly gone?"

She didn't even look up from her plate. "*Your* kind of magic is gone, yes. But there are other, forgotten powers that work."

"What sort of powers?"

"Powers that lordlings have no business knowing. Now ask your next question."

He gave her a playful, wounded face that had the old woman rolling her eyes. She made him want to run in the other direction, but he had to get through this, had to keep up the charade for as long as he could.

"Could one person somehow have magic?"

"Boy, I've traveled from one shore of this continent to the other, across every mountain, and into the dark, shadowy places where men still fear to tread. There is no magic left anymore; even the surviving Fae can't access their powers. Some of them remain trapped in their animal forms. Miserable wretches. Taste like animals, too." She laughed, a crow's caw that made the hair on the back of his neck rise. "So, no— one person could *not* be the exception to the rule."

He kept up his careful mask of idle boredom. "And if someone discovered that they suddenly had magic . . . ?"

"Then they'd be a damn fool, and asking for a hanging."

He already knew that. That wasn't what he was asking. "But if it were true—hypothetically. How would that even be possible?"

She paused her eating, cocking her head. Her silver hair gleamed like fresh snow, offsetting her tanned face. "We don't know how or why magic vanished. I hear rumors every now and then that the power still exists on other continents, but not here. So that's the real question: why did magic vanish only here, and not across the whole of Erilea? What crimes did we commit to make the gods curse us like that, to take away what they had once given us?" She tossed the rib cage of the chicken onto the ground. "*Hypothetically*, if someone had magic and I wanted to learn why, I'd start by figuring out why magic left in the first place. Maybe that would explain how there could be an exception to the rule." She licked the grease off her deadly fingers. "Strange questions from a lordling dwelling in the glass castle. Strange, strange questions."

He gave her a half grin. "Stranger still that the last-born witch of the Witch Kingdom would stoop low enough to spend her life doing carnival tricks."

"The gods that cursed these lands ten years ago damned the witches centuries before that."

It might have been the clouds that passed over the sun, but he could have sworn that he saw a darkness gleaming in her eyes—a darkness that made him wonder if she was even older than she let on. Perhaps her "last-born witch" title was a lie. A fabrication to conceal a history so violent that he couldn't imagine the horrors she'd committed during those long-ago witch wars.

Against his will, he found himself reaching for the ancient force slumbering inside him, wondering if it would somehow shield him from Yellowlegs the way it had from the shattering window. The thought made him queasy.

"Any other questions?" she said, licking her iron nails.

"No. Thank you for your time."

"Bah," she spat, and waved him off.

He walked away, and got no farther than the nearest tent when he saw the sun glinting off a golden head, and Roland walked toward him, away from the table where he'd been talking to that stunning blond musician who'd played the lute the other night. Had he followed him here? Dorian frowned, but gave his cousin a nod in greeting as Roland fell into step beside him.

"Getting your fortune read?"

Dorian shrugged. "I was bored."

Roland looked over his shoulder to where Baba Yellowlegs's caravan wagon was parked. "That woman makes my blood run cold."

Dorian snorted. "I think that's one of her talents."

Roland glanced at him sidelong. "Did she tell you anything interesting?"

"Just the normal nonsense: I'll soon meet my true love, a glorious destiny awaits me, and I'll be rich beyond imagining. I don't think she knew who she was talking to." He surveyed the Lord of Meah. "And what are you doing here?"

"I saw you heading out and thought you might want company. But then I saw where you were going and decided to keep well away."

Either Roland was spying on him, or he was telling the truth; Dorian honestly couldn't tell. But he'd made a point to be pleasant to his cousin during the past few days—and at every council meeting, Roland had backed whatever decision Dorian made without hesitation. The irritation on Perrington and his father's faces was an unexpected delight, too.

So Dorian didn't question Roland about why he'd followed him, but when he glanced back at Baba Yellowlegs, he could have sworn the old woman was grinning at him.

It had been a few days since Celaena had tracked her targets. Cloaked in darkness, she stood in the shadows of the docks, not quite believing what she was seeing. All the men on her list, all the ones she'd been following, the ones who might know what the king was up to—were *leaving*. She'd seen one of them sneak into an unmarked carriage and had followed him here, where he'd boarded a ship set to depart at the midnight tide. And then, to her dismay, the other three had shown up, too, their families in tow, before they were quickly ushered belowdecks.

All those men, all that information she'd been gathering, just—

"I'm sorry," a familiar voice said behind her, and she whirled to find Archer approaching. How was he so stealthy? She hadn't even heard him getting close. "I had to warn them," he said, his eyes on the ship getting ready to depart. "I couldn't live with their blood on my hands. They have children; what would become of them if you handed over their parents to the king?"

She hissed, "Did you organize this?"

"No," he said softly, the words barely audible above the shouts of the sailors untying the ropes and readying the oars. "A member of the organization did. I mentioned that their lives might be in jeopardy, and he had his men get them on the next ship out of Rifthold."

She put a hand on her dagger. "Part of this bargain relies on you giving me useful information."

"I know. I'm sorry."

"Would you rather I just faked your death now and put you on that ship as well?" Perhaps she'd find another way to convince the king to release her earlier.

"No. This won't happen again."

She highly doubted that, but she leaned back against the wall of the building and crossed her arms, watching Archer observe the ship. After a moment, he turned to her. "Say something."

"I don't have anything to say. I'm too busy debating whether I should just kill you and drag your carcass before the king." She wasn't bluffing. After last night with Chaol, she was starting to wonder whether simplicity would be best. Anything to keep Chaol from getting ensnared in a potential mess.

"I'm sorry," Archer said again, but she waved him off and watched the readying ship.

It was impressive that they'd organized an escape so quickly. Perhaps they weren't all fools like Davis. "The person you mentioned this to," she said after a while. "He's a leader of the group?"

"I think so," Archer said quietly. "Or high up enough that when I dropped the hint about these men, he was able to organize an escape immediately."

She chewed on the inside of her cheek. Perhaps Davis had been a fluke. And maybe Archer was right. Maybe these men just wanted a ruler who would better suit their tastes. But whatever their financial and political motives might be, when innocent people had been threatened, they'd mobilized and gotten them to safety. Few people in the empire dared to do that—and fewer still were getting away with it.

"I want new names and more information by tomorrow night," she told Archer as she turned away from the docks, heading back toward the castle. "Or else I'll toss your head at the king's feet and let him decide whether he wants me to dump it in the sewer or spike it on the front gates." She didn't wait for Archer's reply before she faded into the shadows and fog.

She took her time going back to the castle, thinking about what she'd seen. There was never absolute good or absolute evil (though the king was definitely the exception). And even if these men were corrupt in some ways, they were also saving lives.

While it was absurd that they claimed to have contact with Aelin Galathynius, she couldn't help but wonder if there really were forces gathering in the heir's name. If somewhere, in the past decade, members of the powerful royal court of Terrasen had managed to hide. Thanks to the King of Adarlan, Terrasen no longer had a standing army—just whatever forces were camped throughout the kingdom. But those men *did* have some resources. And Nehemia had said that if Terrasen ever got to its feet again, it would pose a real threat to Adarlan.

So maybe she wouldn't even have to do anything. Maybe she wouldn't have to risk her life, or Chaol's. Maybe, just maybe, whatever their motives, these people could find a way to stop the king—and free all of Erilea as well.

A slow, reluctant smile spread across her face, and it only grew wider as she walked to the glowing glass castle, and to the Captain of the Guard who awaited her there.

It had been four days since Chaol's birthday, and he'd spent every night since then with Celaena. And afternoons, and mornings. And every moment they could spare from their individual obligations. Unfortunately, this meeting with his chief guards wasn't optional, but as he listened to the men's reports, his thoughts kept drifting back to her.

He'd barely breathed during that first time, and he'd done his best to be gentle, to make it as painless for her as possible. She'd still winced, and her eyes had gleamed with tears, but when he'd asked if she needed to stop, she'd just kissed him. Again and again. All through that first night he'd held her and allowed himself to imagine that this was how every night for the rest of his life would be.

And every night since then, he'd traced the scars down her back, silently swearing oath after oath that someday, he'd go back to Endovier and rip that place down stone by stone.

"Captain?"

Chaol blinked, realizing someone had asked him a question, and shifted in his chair. "Say that again," he ordered, refusing to let himself blush.

"Do we need extra guards at the carnival?"

Hell, he didn't even know why they were asking that. Had there been some incident? If he asked, then they'd definitely know he hadn't been listening.

He was spared from looking like a fool when someone knocked on the door to the small meeting room in the barracks, and then a golden head popped in.

Just seeing her made him forget the world around them. Everyone in the room shifted to look at the door, and as she smiled, he fought the urge to smash in the faces of the guards who looked at her so appreciatively. These were his men, he told himself. And she *was* beautiful—and she scared them half to death. Of course they would look, and appreciate.

"Captain," she said, remaining on the threshold. There was color high on her cheeks that set her eyes sparkling, making him think of how she looked when they were tangled up with each other. She inclined her head toward the hall. "The king wants to see you."

He would have felt a jolt of nerves, would have started to think the worst, had he not caught that glimmer of mischief in her eyes.

He stood from his seat, bowing his head to his men. "Decide among yourselves about the carnival, and report back to me later," he said, and quickly left the room.

He kept a respectable distance until they rounded a corner into an empty hallway and he stepped closer, needing to touch her.

"Philippa and the servants are gone until dinner," she said huskily.

He ground his teeth at the effect her voice had on him, like someone dragging an invisible finger down his spine. "I've got meetings for the rest of the day," he managed to say. It was true. "I've got another one in twenty minutes." Which he'd surely be late for if he followed her, considering how long it would take to walk to her rooms.

She paused, frowning at him. But his eyes drifted to the small wooden door just a few feet away. A broom closet. She followed his attention, and a slow smile spread across her face. She turned toward it, but he grabbed her hand, bringing his face close to hers. "You're going to have to be *very* quiet."

She reached the knob and opened the door, tugging him inside. "I have a feeling that *I'm* going to be telling *you* that in a few moments," she purred, eyes gleaming with the challenge.

Chaol's blood roared through him, and he followed her into the closet and wedged a broom beneath the handle.

"A broom closet?" Nehemia said, grinning like a fiend. *"Really?"*

Celaena lay sprawled on Nehemia's bed and tossed a chocolate-covered raisin into her mouth. "I swear it on my life."

Nehemia leapt onto the mattress. Fleetfoot jumped up beside her and practically sat on Celaena's face as she wagged her tail at the princess.

Celaena gently shoved the dog aside, and smiled so broadly that her face hurt. "Who knew I'd been missing out on such fun?" And gods above, Chaol was . . . well, she blushed to think about just how much she enjoyed him after her body had adjusted. Just the touch of his fingers on her skin could turn her into a feral beast.

"I could have told you that," Nehemia said, reaching over Celaena to grab a chocolate from the dish on the nightstand. "Though I think the real question is, who would have guessed that the solemn Captain of the Guard could be so passionate?" She lay down beside Celaena, also smiling. "I'm happy for you, my friend."

Celaena smiled back. "I think . . . I think I'm happy for me, too."

And she was. For the first time in years, she was truly *happy*. The feeling curled around every thought, a tendril of hope that grew with each breath. She was afraid to look at it for too long, as though acknowledging it would somehow cause it to disappear. Perhaps the world would never be perfect, perhaps some things would never be right, but maybe she stood a chance of finding her own sort of peace and freedom.

She felt the shift in Nehemia before the princess even said a word, like a current in the air somehow chilled. Celaena looked over to find Nehemia staring up at the ceiling. "What's wrong?"

Nehemia ran a hand over her face, letting out a deep breath. "The king has asked me to speak to the rebel forces. To convince them to back down. Or else he'll butcher them all."

"He threatened to do that?"

"Not directly, but it was implied. At the end of the month, he's sending Perrington to the duke's keep in Morath. I don't doubt for one minute that he wants Perrington at the southern border so he can monitor things. Perrington is his right hand. So if the duke decides the rebels need to be dealt with, he has permission to use whatever force is necessary to put them down."

Celaena sat up, folding her legs beneath her. "So you're going back to Eyllwe?"

Nehemia shook her head. "I don't know. I need to be here. There are . . . there are things that I need to do here. In this castle and in this city. But I cannot abandon my people to another massacre."

"Can your parents or your brothers deal with the rebels?"

"My brothers are too young and untried, and my parents have enough on their hands in Banjali." The princess sat up, and Fleetfoot rested her head on Nehemia's lap, stretching out between them—and giving Celaena a few kicks with her hind legs in the process. "I have grown up knowing the weight of my crown. When the king invaded Eyllwe all those years ago, I knew that I would someday have to make choices that would haunt me." She cupped her forehead in a palm. "I didn't think it would be this hard. I cannot be in two places at once."

Celaena's chest tightened, and she put a hand on Nehemia's back.

No wonder Nehemia had been so slow about looking into the eye riddle. Shame colored her cheeks.

"What will I do, Elentiya, if he kills another five hundred people? What will I do if he decides to set an example by butchering everyone in Calaculla? How can I turn my back on them?"

Celaena had no answer. She'd spent the week lost in thoughts of Chaol. Nehemia had spent her week trying to balance the fate of her kingdom. And Celaena had clues littering the ground at her feet—clues that might help Nehemia in her cause against the king, and a command from Elena that she'd practically ignored.

Nehemia took her hand. "Promise me," she said, her dark eyes shining. "Promise me that you'll help me free Eyllwe from him."

Ice shot through Celaena's veins. "*Free* Eyllwe?"

"Promise me that you'll see my father's crown restored to him. That you'll see my people returned from Endovier and Calaculla."

"I'm just an assassin." Celaena pulled her hand out of Nehemia's. "And the kind of thing you're talking about, Nehemia . . ." She got off the bed, trying to control her rapid heartbeat. "That would be madness."

"There is no other way. Eyllwe *must* be freed. And with you helping me, we could start to gather a host to—"

"*No.*" Nehemia blinked, but Celaena shook her head. "No," she repeated. "Not for all the world would I help you muster an army against him. Eyllwe has been hit hard by the king, but you barely got a taste of the kind of brutality he unleashed elsewhere. You raise a force against him, and he'll butcher you. I won't be a part of that."

"So what will you be a part of, *Celaena*?" Nehemia stood, jostling Fleetfoot from her lap. "What will you stand for? Or will you only stand for yourself?"

Her throat ached, but Celaena forced the words out. "You have no idea what sort of things he can do to you, Nehemia. To your people."

"He massacred five hundred rebels and their families!"

"And he destroyed my *entire* kingdom! You daydream about the power and honor of Terrasen's royal court, yet you don't realize what it means that the king was able to destroy them. They were the strongest court on the continent—they were the strongest court on *any* continent, and he killed them all."

"He had the element of surprise," Nehemia countered.

"And now he has an army that numbers in the *millions*. There is nothing that can be done."

"When will you say *enough*, Celaena? What will make you stop running and face what is before you? If Endovier and the plight of my people cannot move you, what will?"

"I am *one person*."

"One person chosen by Queen Elena—one person whose brow burned with a sacred mark on the day of that duel! One person who, despite the odds, is still breathing. Our paths crossed for a reason. If you are not gods-blessed, then who is?"

"This is ridiculous. This is folly."

"Folly? Folly to fight for what is right, for people who cannot stand up for themselves? You think soldiers are the worst he can send?" Nehemia's tone softened. "There are far darker things gathering on the horizon. My dreams have been filled with shadows and wings—the booming of wings soaring between mountain passes. And every scout and spy we send into the White Fang Mountains, into the Ferian Gap, *does not come back*. Do you know what the people say in the valleys below? They say they can hear wings, too, riding the winds through the Gap."

"I don't understand a word you're saying." But Celaena had seen that thing outside the library.

Nehemia stalked to her, grabbing her by the wrists. "You do understand. When you look at him, you sense that there is a greater, twisted power around him. How did such a man conquer so much of the continent so quickly? With military might alone? How is it that Terrasen's court fell so quickly, when its retainers had been trained for generations to be warriors? How did the most powerful court in the world get wiped out within a matter of days?"

"You're tired and upset," Celaena said as calmly as she could, trying not to think of how similar Nehemia's and Elena's words were. She shook off the princess's grip. "Maybe we should talk about this later—"

"I don't want to talk about this later!"

Fleetfoot whined, wedging herself between them.

"If we do not strike now," Nehemia went on, "then whatever he is brewing will only grow more powerful. And then we will be beyond any chance of hope."

"There is no hope," Celaena said. "There is no hope in standing against him. Not now, not ever." That was a truth she'd slowly been realizing. If Nehemia and Elena were right about this mysterious power source, then how could they ever overthrow him? "And I will not be a part of whatever plan you have. I will not help you get yourself killed, and bring down even more innocent people in the process."

"You will not help because all you care about is *yourself*."

"And so what if I do?" Celaena splayed her arms. "So what if I want to spend the rest of my life in peace?"

"There can never be any peace—not while he reigns. When you said you weren't killing the men on his list, I thought you were finally taking a step toward making a stand. I thought that when the time came, I could count on you to help me start planning. I didn't realize that you were doing it just to keep your own conscience clean!"

Celaena began storming toward the door.

Nehemia clicked her tongue. "I didn't realize that you're just a coward."

Celaena looked over her shoulder. "Say that again."

Nehemia didn't flinch. "You're a coward. You are nothing more than a coward."

Celaena's fingers clenched into fists. "When your people are lying dead around you," she hissed, "don't come crying to me."

She didn't give the princess the chance to reply before she stalked out of the room, Fleetfoot close on her heels.

CHAPTER 25

"One of them has to break," the queen said to the princess. "Only then can it begin."

"I know," the princess said softly. "But the prince isn't ready. It has to be her."

"Then do you understand what I am asking of you?"

The princess looked up, toward the shaft of moonlight spilling into the tomb. When she looked back at the ancient queen, her eyes were bright. "Yes."

"Then do what needs to be done."

The princess nodded and walked out of the tomb. She paused on the threshold, the darkness beyond beckoning to her, and turned back to the queen. "She won't understand. And when she goes over the edge, there will be nothing to pull her back."

"She will find her way back. She always does."

Tears formed, but the princess blinked them away. "For all our sakes, I hope you're right."

CHAPTER 26

Chaol hated hunting parties. Many of the lords could barely handle a bow, let alone be stealthy. It was painful to watch them—and the poor hounds bursting through the brush, trying to scatter game that the lords would miss anyway. Usually, just to get things over with, he would discreetly kill a few animals and then pretend Lord So-and-So had done it. But the king, Perrington, Roland, and Dorian were all out in the game park today, which meant he had to keep close to them.

Whenever he rode close enough to the lords to overhear their laughing and gossiping and harmless scheming, he sometimes let himself wonder if that was how he would have wound up had he not chosen this path. He hadn't seen his younger brother in years; had his father allowed Terrin to turn into one of these idiots? Or had his father sent him to train as a warrior, as all lords of Anielle had done in the centuries after the wild mountain men had preyed upon the city on the Silver Lake?

As Chaol trailed behind the king, his new Asterion stallion

earning many admiring and envious glances from the hunting party, Chaol allowed himself to consider—for one heartbeat—what his father would make of Celaena. His mother was a gentle, quiet woman, whose face had become a blurred memory in the years since he'd last seen her. But he still remembered her lilting voice and soft laugh, and the way she'd sung him to sleep when he was ill. Even though their marriage had been arranged, his father had wanted someone like his mother— someone submissive. Which meant that someone like Celaena . . . He cringed to even consider his father and Celaena in a room together. Cringed, and then smiled, because *that* was a battle of wills that could go down in legend.

"You're distracted today, Captain," the king said as he emerged from between the trees. He was massive; the king's size always surprised Chaol, for some reason.

He was flanked by two of Chaol's guards—one of which was Ress, who looked more nervous than triumphant at being selected to protect the king today, though he was trying his hardest not to show it. It was why Chaol had also chosen Dannan, the other guard—older and weathered and possessing near-legendary patience. Chaol bowed to his sovereign, and then gave Ress a slight nod of approval. The young guard sat up straighter, but remained alert—his focus now upon their surroundings, the lords riding nearby, the sounds of dogs and arrows.

The king pulled his black horse alongside Chaol's, falling into a meandering walk. Ress and Dannan fell back a respectable pace, still close enough to intercept any lurking threat. "Whatever will my lords do without you to kill their quarry for them?"

Chaol tried to hide his smile. Perhaps he hadn't been as discreet as he thought. "Apologies, milord."

Atop his warhorse, the king looked every inch the conqueror he was. There was something in his eyes that sent a chill down Chaol's spine—and made him realize why so many foreign rulers had offered him their crowns instead of facing him in battle.

"I am having the Princess of Eyllwe questioned in my council room tomorrow night," the king said quietly enough that only Chaol could hear, turning his stallion to follow after the pack of hounds that rushed through the thawing woods. "I want six men outside the room. Make sure there are no complications or interruptions." The look the king gave him suggested exactly the sort of complication he had in mind—Celaena.

Chaol knew it was risky to ask questions, but he said, "Is there anything specific that I should prepare my men for?"

"No," the king said, nocking an arrow to his bow and firing at a pheasant that surged up from the brush. A clean shot—right through the eye. "That will be all."

The king whistled to his hounds and followed after the prey he'd killed, Ress and Dannan close behind.

Chaol stilled his stallion, watching the mountain of a man ride through the thicket. "What was that about?" Dorian said, suddenly beside him.

Chaol shook his head. "Nothing."

Dorian reached over his shoulder to the quiver strapped there and drew an arrow. "I haven't seen you for a few days."

"I've been busy." Busy with his duties, and busy with Celaena. "I haven't seen you around, either." He made himself meet Dorian's gaze.

Dorian's lips were pursed, his face stony as he quietly said, "I've been busy, too." The Crown Prince turned his horse away, heading in another direction, but paused. "Chaol," he said, looking over his shoulder. Dorian's eyes were frozen, his jaw clenched. "Treat her well."

"Dorian," he started, but the prince rode off to join Roland. Suddenly alone in the teeming forest, Chaol watched his friend disappear.

⁓

Chaol didn't tell Celaena what the king had said, though part of him twisted until it hurt. The king wouldn't hurt Nehemia—not when she was such a public and well-liked figure. Not when he'd warned Chaol about that anonymous threat to Nehemia's life. But he had a feeling that whatever was going to be said in the council room wasn't going to be pleasant.

Celaena knowing or not knowing made no difference, he told himself as he lay curled around her in his bed. Even if Celaena knew, even if she told Nehemia, it wouldn't stop the conversation from taking place, and it wouldn't make the nameless threat go away. No, it would just make things worse if they knew—worse for all of them.

Chaol sighed, untangling his legs from Celaena's as he sat up and grabbed his pants from where he'd thrown them on the floor. She stirred, but didn't move. That was a miracle in itself, he realized—that she felt safe enough to sleep soundly with him.

He paused to gently kiss her head, then picked up the rest of his clothes from around the room and dressed, even though the clock had chimed only three not long ago.

Perhaps it was a test, he thought as he slipped out the door of his chambers. Perhaps the king was testing Chaol to see where his loyalties lay—if he could still trust him. And if he learned that Celaena and Nehemia were aware of the interrogation tomorrow, then there would be only one way for them to have learned . . .

He just needed some fresh air, to feel the briny breeze off the Avery on his face. He'd meant it when he told Celaena about someday leaving Rifthold with her. And he'd go to his death defending her secret about the men she wasn't killing.

Chaol reached the dark, silent gardens and strode between the hedges. He'd kill any man who hurt Celaena; and if the king ever gave *him* the order to dispatch her, then he'd plunge his sword into his own heart before he would obey. His soul was bound to hers by some unbreakable chain. He snorted, imagining what his father would think when he learned that Chaol had taken Adarlan's Assassin for his wife.

The thought stopped Chaol dead in his tracks. She was only eighteen. He forgot that sometimes, forgot that he was older than her, too. And if he asked her to marry him right now . . . "Gods above," he muttered, shaking his head. That day was a long way off.

But he couldn't help imagining it—the glimmer of the future and how it would be to forge a life together, to call her his wife, to hear her call him husband, to raise a brood of children who would probably be far too clever and talented for their own good (and for Chaol's sanity).

He was still envisioning that impossibly beautiful future when someone grabbed him from behind and pressed something cold and reeking against his nose and mouth, and the world went black.

CHAPTER 27

Chaol wasn't in his bed when she awoke, and Celaena thanked the gods for their small mercies, because she was certainly too worn out to bother running. His side of the bed was cold enough that she knew he'd left hours before—probably to fulfill his duties as Captain of the Guard.

She lay there for a while, content to daydream, to imagine a time when they could have whole, uninterrupted days with each other. When her stomach started growling, she decided it was a sign that she should drag herself out of bed. She'd taken to leaving some clothes in his room, so she bathed and dressed before returning to her own chambers.

Over breakfast, a list of names arrived from Archer—written in code, as she'd asked—with more men to hunt down. She just hoped he wouldn't squeal on her again. Nehemia didn't show up for their daily lesson on the Wyrdmarks, though Celaena wasn't surprised by that, either.

She didn't particularly feel like talking to her friend—and if the princess was foolish enough to think of starting a rebellion . . . She'd stay well enough away from Nehemia until she came to her senses. It did halt her hope of finding a way to use the Wyrdmarks to get through that secret door in the library, but that could wait—at least until both of their tempers had cooled.

After spending the day in Rifthold stalking the men on Archer's list, Celaena returned to the castle, eager to tell Chaol what else she'd learned. But he didn't show up for dinner. It wasn't that unusual for him to be busy, so she dined alone, and curled up on the couch in her bedroom with a book.

She probably needed some *rest*, too, since the Wyrd knew she hadn't been getting any sleep this past week. Not that she minded.

When the clock struck ten and he still hadn't come to her, she found herself walking to his rooms. Perhaps he was waiting for her there. Perhaps he'd just fallen asleep without meaning to.

But she hurried down the halls and stairs, her palms turning slicker with each step. Chaol was the Captain of the Guard. He held his own against her every day. He'd *bested* her in their first sparring match. Yet Sam had been her equal in many ways, too. And he'd still been caught and tortured by Rourke Farran—still died the most brutal death she'd ever seen. And if Chaol . . .

She was running now.

Like Sam, Chaol was admired by almost everyone. And when they'd taken Sam from her, it hadn't been because of anything Sam had done.

No, they'd done it to get at *her*.

She reached his rooms, part of her still praying that she was just being paranoid, that he'd be sleeping in the bed, that she could curl up with him and make love to him and hold him through the night.

But then she opened the door to his bedroom and saw a sealed note addressed to her on the table beside the door—placed atop his sword, which hadn't been there this morning. It was placed casually enough that the servants might have just assumed it was a note from Chaol himself—and that nothing was wrong. She ripped open the red seal and unfolded the paper.

WE HAVE THE CAPTAIN. WHEN YOU'RE TIRED OF STALKING US, COME FIND US HERE.

It listed the address for a warehouse in the slums of the city.

BRING NO ONE, OR THE CAPTAIN WILL DIE BEFORE YOU SET FOOT IN THE BUILDING. IF YOU FAIL TO ARRIVE BY TOMORROW MORNING, WE'LL LEAVE WHAT'S LEFT OF HIM ON THE BANKS OF THE AVERY.

She stared at the letter.

Every one of the restraints she'd locked into place after she'd rampaged through Endovier snapped free.

An icy, endless rage swept through her, wiping away everything except the plan that she could see with brutal clarity. *The killing calm*, Arobynn Hamel had once called it. Even he had never realized just how calm she could get when she went over the edge.

If they wanted Adarlan's Assassin, they'd get her.

And Wyrd help them when she arrived.

⁓

Chaol didn't know why they'd chained him up, only that he was thirsty and had a pounding headache, and that the irons holding him against the stone wall weren't going to budge. They threatened to beat him every time he tried pulling against them. They'd already knocked him about enough to convince him they weren't bluffing.

They. He didn't even know who they were. They all wore long robes and hoods that concealed their masked faces. Some of them were armed to the teeth. They spoke in murmurs, all of them growing increasingly on-edge as the day passed.

From what he could tell, he had a split lip and would have some bruises on his face and ribs. They hadn't asked questions before unleashing two of their men on him, though he hadn't been entirely cooperative once he'd awoken and found himself here. Celaena would be impressed by just how creative his curses had been before, during, and after that initial beating.

In the passing hours, he'd moved only once to relieve himself in the corner, since when he asked to use the washroom, they just stared at him. And they'd watched him the entire time, hands on their swords. He'd tried not to snort.

They were waiting for something, he realized with a strange clarity as the day stretched into evening. The fact that they hadn't killed him yet suggested that they wanted some sort of ransom.

Maybe it was a rebel group, seeking to blackmail the king. He'd heard of nobility being captured for that reason. And heard the king himself order the rebels to kill the petty lord or lady, because he would not yield to traitorous filth.

Chaol didn't allow himself to consider that possibility, even as he began saving up his strength for whatever stand he'd make before he met his end.

Some of his captors whispered in rapid arguments, but they were usually silenced by others who told them to wait. He was just pretending to doze off when another of these arguments occurred, a hissing back and forth about whether they should just free him, and then—

"She has until dawn. She'll show up."

She.

That word was the worst thing he'd ever heard.

Because there was only one *she* who would bother to show up for him. One *she* that he could be used against.

"You hurt her," he said, his voice hoarse from a day without water, "and I'll rip you apart with my bare hands."

There were thirty of them, half fully armed, and they all turned to him.

He bared his teeth, even though his face ached. "You so much as *touch* her, and I'll gut you."

One of them—tall, with two swords crossed over his back—approached. Even though his face was obscured, Chaol recognized him by his weapons as one of the men who had beaten him earlier. He stopped just beyond where Chaol's feet could kick.

"Good luck with that," the man said. By his voice, he could have been anywhere from twenty to forty. "You'd better pray to whatever gods you favor that your little assassin cooperates."

He growled, pulling against the chains. "What do you want from her?"

The warrior—he was a warrior, Chaol could tell by the way he moved—cocked his head. "None of your business, *Captain*. And keep your mouth shut when she arrives, or else I'll cut out your filthy royal tongue."

Another clue. The man hated royals. Which meant that these people . . .

Had Archer known how dangerous this rebel group was? When he got free, he'd kill him for letting Celaena get tangled up with them. And then he'd make sure that the king and his secret guards got their hands on all of these bastards.

Chaol yanked on the chains, and the man shook his head. "Do that, and I'll knock you out again. For the Captain of the Royal Guard, you were far too easy to capture."

Chaol's eyes flashed. "Only a coward captures men the way you did."

"A coward? Or a pragmatist?"

Not an uneducated warrior, then. Someone with schooling, if he could use vocabulary like that.

"How about a damned fool?" Chaol said. "I don't think you realize who you're dealing with."

The man clicked his tongue. "If you were that good, you would be more than the Captain of the Guard."

Chaol let out a low, breathy laugh. "I wasn't talking about me."

"She's just one girl."

Though his guts were twisting at the thought of her in this place, with these people, though he was considering every possible way to get himself and Celaena out of here alive, he gave the man a grin. "Then you're *really* in for a surprise."

CHAPTER 28

Her rage took her to a place where she only knew three things: that Chaol had been taken from her, that she was a weapon forged to end lives, and that if Chaol was hurt, no one was going to walk out of that warehouse.

She made it across the city quickly and efficiently, a predator's stealth keeping her steps quiet on the cobblestone streets. They'd told her to arrive alone, and she'd obeyed.

But they hadn't said anything about arriving unarmed.

So she'd taken every weapon she could fit onto her, including Chaol's sword, which was strapped across her back with a second sword of her own, the two hilts within easy reach over her shoulders. From there down, she was a living armory.

When she neared the slums, her features concealed with a dark cloak and heavy hood, she scaled the side of a ramshackle building until she reached the roof.

They hadn't said anything about using the front door of the warehouse, either.

She stalked across the roofs, her supple boots finding easy purchase on the crumbling emerald shingles, listening, watching, *feeling* the night around her. The usual sounds of the slums greeted her as she approached the enormous two-story warehouse: half-feral orphans screeching to each other, the splatter of drunks pissing against buildings, harlots calling out to prospective hires . . .

But there was a silence around the wooden warehouse, a bubble of quiet that told her the place had enough men out front that the usual slum denizens stayed away.

The nearby rooftops were empty and flat, the gaps between buildings easily jumpable.

She didn't care what this group wanted with her. She didn't care what sort of information they expected to twist from her. When they had taken Chaol, they'd made the biggest mistake of their lives. The last mistake, too.

She reached the roof of the building beside the warehouse and dropped into a crawl before she reached the ledge and peered over.

In the narrow alley directly below, three cloaked men patrolled. On the street beyond lay the front doors to the warehouse, light spilling from the cracks to reveal at least four men outside. No one was even looking at the roof. Fools.

The wooden warehouse was a giant open space three stories high, and through the open second-level window in front of her, she could see all the way to the floor below.

The mezzanine wrapped around much of the second level, and stairs led onto the third level and roof beyond—a possible escape route, if the front door wasn't an option. Ten of the men were heavily armed, and six archers were positioned around the wooden mezzanine, arrows all pointed at the first floor below.

There was Chaol, chained to one of the wooden walls.

Chaol, his face bruised and bleeding, his clothes ripped and dirty, his head hanging between his shoulders.

The ice in her gut spread through her veins.

She could scale the building to the roof, then come down from the third floor. But that would take time, and no one was looking at the open window before her.

She tipped her head back and gave the moon a wicked smile. She'd been called Adarlan's Assassin for a reason. Dramatic entrances were practically her art form.

Celaena eased back from the ledge and strode away a few paces, judging how far and fast she'd need to run. The open window was wide enough that she wouldn't need to worry about shattering glass or her swords catching on the frame, and the mezzanine had a guardrail to stop her if she overshot her landing.

She had made a jump like this once before, on the night when her world had been shattered completely. But on that night, Sam had already been dead for days, and she'd leapt through the window of Rourke Farran's house for pure revenge.

This time, she wouldn't fail.

The men weren't even looking at the window when she hurtled through. And by the time she landed on the mezzanine and rolled into a crouch, two of her daggers were already flying.

⁓

Chaol caught the glint of moonlight on steel in the heartbeat before she leapt through the second-level window, landing atop the mezzanine and hurling two daggers at the archers nearest to her. They went down, and she went up—two more daggers thrown at two more archers. He didn't know if he should watch them or watch her as she gripped the mezzanine railing and flipped over it, landing on the ground below just as several arrows struck where her hands had held the rail.

The men in the room were shouting, some fleeing for the safety of pillars and the exit while others rushed at her, weapons drawn. And he could only watch in horror and awe as she drew two swords—one of them his—and unleashed herself upon them.

They didn't stand a chance.

In the fray of bodies, the remaining two archers didn't dare loose arrows that might hit one of their own—another intentional move on her part, he knew. Chaol yanked on his chains again and again, his wrists aching; if he could just get to her, the two of them could—

She was a whirlwind of steel and blood. As he watched her cut through the men as though they were stalks of wheat in a field, he understood how she had gotten so close to touching Endovier's wall that day. And at last—after all these months—he saw the lethal predator he'd expected to find in the mines. There was nothing human in her eyes, nothing remotely merciful. It froze his heart.

The guard who had been taunting him all day remained nearby, twin swords drawn, waiting for her.

One of the hooded men had gotten far enough away from her to start shouting: "Enough! *Enough!*"

But Celaena didn't listen, and as Chaol hurled himself forward, still trying to dislodge the chains from the wall, she cleared a path through the men, leaving moaning bodies in her wake. To his credit, his tormentor stood his ground as she stalked toward him.

"*Don't shoot!*" the hooded man was ordering the archers. "*Don't shoot!*"

Celaena paused in front of the guard, pointing a blood-drenched sword at him. "Get out of my way, or I'll cut you into pieces."

His guard, the fool, snorted, lifting his swords a little higher. "Come and get him."

Celaena smiled. But then the hooded man with the ancient voice was rushing to them, arms spread to show he wasn't armed. "Enough! Put down your weapons," he told the guard. The guard faltered, but Celaena's swords remained at the ready. The old man took one step toward Celaena. "Enough! We have enough enemies as it is! There are worse things out there to face!"

Celaena slowly turned to him, her face splattered with blood and eyes blazing bright. "No, there aren't," she said. "Because I'm here now."

⁓

Blood that was not her own drenched her clothes, her hands, her neck, but all she could see were the archers ready on the mezzanine above her, and the foe still standing between her and Chaol. *Her* Chaol.

"Please," the hooded man said, pulling off his hood and mask to reveal a face that matched his ancient voice. Short-cropped white hair, laugh lines around his mouth, and crystal-clear gray eyes that were wide with pleading. "Perhaps our methods were wrong, but—"

She pointed a sword at him, and the masked guard between her and Chaol straightened. "I don't care who you are and what you want. I'm taking him now."

"Please listen," the old man said softly.

She could feel the ire and aggression rolling off the hooded guard in front of her, see how tightly, eagerly, he clutched the hilts of his twin swords. She wasn't ready for the bloodletting to end, either. She wasn't ready to give in at all.

So she knew exactly what would happen when she turned to the guard and gave him a lazy grin.

He charged. As she met his swords, the men who were outside burst in, steel flashing. And then there was nothing but metal ringing and the shouts of the injured going down around her, and she was soaring through them, delighting in the feral song that sang through her blood and bones.

Someone was shouting her name, though—a familiar voice that wasn't Chaol's, and as she turned, she saw the flash of a steel-tipped arrow shooting for her, then a glint of golden-brown hair, and then—

Archer hit the ground, the arrow that was meant for her in his shoulder. It took all of two movements to drop one sword and draw the dagger from her boot, hurling it at the guard who had fired. By the time she looked at Archer, he was getting to his feet, putting himself between her and the wall of men, one arm splayed in front of her— facing *her*. Protecting the men.

"This is a misunderstanding," he said to her, panting. Blood from the wound in his shoulder leaked down his black robes. *Robes.* The same robes that these men wore.

Archer was a part of this group; Archer had set her up.

And then that rage, the rage that blurred the events of the night she'd been captured with the events of this night, that made Chaol's and Sam's faces bleed together, seized her so fiercely that she reached for another dagger strapped to her waist.

"*Please*," Archer said, taking a step toward her, wincing as the movement made the arrow shift. "Let me explain." As she saw the blood trickle down his robes, saw the agony and fear and desperation in his eyes, her rage flickered.

"Unchain him," she said, her voice filled with deadly calm. "Now."

Archer refused to break her stare. "Hear me out first."

"*Unchain him now.*"

Archer jerked his chin to the guard who had foolishly launched the last attack against her. Limping, but surprisingly still in one piece, and, still possessing his twin blades, the guard slowly unshackled the Captain of the Guard.

Chaol was on his feet in an instant, but she noted the way he swayed, the wince he tried to hide. Still, he managed to stare down the hooded guard who stood before him, eyes gleaming with the promise of violence. The guard just stepped back, reaching for his swords again.

"You have one sentence to convince me not to kill you all," she said to Archer as Chaol came to her side. "One sentence."

Archer began shaking his head, looking between her and Chaol, his eyes filled not with fear or anger or pleading, but sorrow.

"I have been working with Nehemia to lead these people for the past six months."

Chaol stiffened, but Celaena blinked. It was enough for Archer to know he'd passed the test. He jerked his head to the men around him. "Leave us," he said, his voice thundering with an authority she hadn't heard him use before. The men listened, those still on their feet dragging their injured companions away. She didn't let herself consider how many were dead.

The old man who had exposed his face to her was staring with a mixture of awe and disbelief, and she wondered what sort of monster she looked at that moment. But when he noticed her attention, he bowed his head to her and left with the others, taking that impulsive, brash guard with him.

Alone, she pointed her sword at Archer again, taking a step closer, keeping Chaol behind her. Of course, the Captain of the Guard stepped right up to her side.

Archer said, "Nehemia and I have been leading this movement together. She came here to organize us—to assemble a group that could go into Terrasen and start gathering forces against the king. And to uncover what the king truly plans to do to Erilea."

Chaol tensed, and Celaena clamped down on her surprise. "That's impossible."

Archer snorted. "Is it? Why is it that the princess is so busy all the time? Do *you* know where she goes at night?"

The frozen rage flickered again, slowing, slowing, slowing the world down.

And then she remembered: remembered how Nehemia convinced her not to look into the riddle she'd found in Davis's office and had been so slow and forgetful about her promise to research the riddle; remembered the night Dorian had come to her rooms because Nehemia had been out, and he hadn't been able to find her anywhere in the castle; remembered Nehemia's words to her before their fight, about how she had important matters in Rifthold to look after, things as important as Eyllwe . . .

"She comes here," Archer said. "She comes here to feed us all of the information that you confide in her."

"If she's part of your group," Celaena ground out, "then where is she?"

Archer drew his word and pointed it at Chaol. "Ask him."

A sharp pain twisted in her gut. "What is he talking about?" she asked Chaol.

But Chaol was staring at Archer. "I don't know."

"Lying bastard," Archer snapped, and bared his teeth with a savagery that made him, for once, look anything but attractive. "My sources told me that the king informed you over a week ago of the threat to Nehemia's life. When were you planning on telling anyone about that?" He turned to Celaena. "We brought him here because he was ordered to question Nehemia about her behavior. We wanted to know what kind of questions he'd been commanded to ask. And because we wanted *you* to see what sort of man he really is."

"That's not true," Chaol spat. "That's a damned lie. You haven't asked me one thing, you gutter-born piece of filth." He turned pleading eyes to Celaena. The words were still sinking in, each more awful than the next. "I knew about the anonymous threat to Nehemia's life, yes. But I was told that she would be questioned by the *king*. Not me."

"And we realized that," Archer said. "Moments before you arrived, Celaena, we realized the captain wasn't the one. But it's not questioning that they're going to be doing tonight, is it, Captain?" Chaol didn't answer—and she didn't care why.

She was pulling away from her body. Inch by inch. Like a tide ebbing from the shore.

"I just sent men to the castle a moment ago," Archer went on. "Perhaps they can stop it."

"Where is Nehemia?" she heard herself asking, from lips that felt far away.

"That's what my spy discovered tonight. Nehemia insisted on staying in the castle, to see what kind of questions they wanted to ask her, to see how much they suspected and knew—"

"*Where is Nehemia?*"

But Archer just shook his head, his eyes bright with tears. "They aren't going to question her, Celaena. And by the time my men get there, I think it will be too late."

Too late.

Celaena turned to Chaol. His face was stricken and pale.

Archer shook his head again. "I'm sorry."

CHAPTER 29

Celaena hurtled through the city streets, discarding her cloak and heavier weapons as she went, anything to give her additional speed, anything to get her back to the castle before Nehemia... Before Nehemia—

A clock began sounding somewhere in the capital, and a lifetime passed between each booming peal.

It was late enough that the streets were mostly deserted, but the people who saw her kept well out of her way as she sprinted past, her lungs nearly shattering. She pushed that pain away, willing strength into her legs, praying to whatever gods still cared to give her swiftness and strength. Who would the king use? If not Chaol, then who?

She didn't care if it was the king himself. She'd destroy them. And that anonymous threat to Nehemia—she'd sort that out, too.

The glass castle loomed closer, its crystalline towers glowing with a pale greenish light.

Not again. Not again, she told herself with each step, each pound of her heart. *Please.*

She couldn't take the front gate. The guards there would surely stop her or cause a ruckus that might prompt the unknown assassin to act faster. There was a high stone wall bordering one of the gardens; it was closer, and far less monitored.

She could have sworn she heard hooves thundering after her, but there was nothing in the world except her and the distance to Nehemia. She neared the stone wall surrounding the garden, her blood roaring in her ears as she made a running jump for it.

She hit the side as silently as she could, her fingers and feet immediately finding purchase, digging in so hard her fingernails cracked. She scrambled up and over the wall before the guards even looked her way.

She landed on the gravel path of the garden, falling onto her hands. Somewhere in the back of her mind she registered pain in her palms, but she was already running again, careening toward the glass doors that led to the castle. Patches of snow glowed blue in the moonlight. She'd go to Nehemia's room first—go there and lock Nehemia up safely, and then take down the bastard who was coming for her.

Archer's men could go to hell. She'd dispatched them in a matter of heartbeats. Whoever had been sent to hurt Nehemia—that person was *hers*. Hers to take apart bit by bit, until she ended them. She would throw their remnants at the feet of the king.

She flung open one of the glass doors. There were guards loitering about, but she'd picked this entrance because they knew her—and knew her face. She didn't expect to glimpse Dorian, though, chatting with them. His sapphire eyes were nothing more than a glimmer of color as she sprinted by.

She could hear shouts from behind her, but she wouldn't stop, couldn't stop. *Not again. Never again.*

She hit the stairs, taking them by twos and threes, her legs trembling. Just a bit farther—Nehemia's rooms were only one level up, and two hallways over. She was Adarlan's Assassin—she was Celaena Sardothien. She would not fail. The gods owed her. The Wyrd owed her. She would not fail Nehemia. Not when there were so many awful words left between them.

Celaena hit the top of the stairs. The shouts behind her grew; people were calling her name. She would stop for no one.

She turned down the familiar hallway, nearly sobbing with relief at the sight of the wooden door. It was shut; there were no signs of forced entry.

She drew her two remaining daggers, summoning the words she'd need to quickly explain to Nehemia how and where to hide. When her assailant arrived, Nehemia's only task would be to keep quiet and concealed. Celaena would deal with the rest. And she'd enjoy the hell out of it.

She reached the door and slammed into it, exploding through the locks.

The world slowed to the beat of an ancient, ageless drum.

Celaena beheld the room.

The blood was everywhere.

Before the bed, Nehemia's bodyguards lay with their throats cut from ear to ear, their internal organs spilling out onto the floor.

And on the bed . . .

On the bed . . .

She could hear the shouts growing closer, reaching the room, but their words were somehow muffled, as though she were underwater, the sounds coming from the surface above.

Celaena stood in the center of the freezing bedroom, gazing at the bed, and the princess's broken body atop it.

Nehemia was dead.

PART TWO

The Queen's Arrow

CHAPTER 30

Celaena stared at the body.

An empty body, artfully mutilated, so cut up that the bed was almost black with blood.

People had rushed into the room behind her, and she smelled the faint tang as someone was sick nearby.

But she just stayed there, letting the others fan out around her as they rushed to assess the three cooling bodies in the room. That ancient, ageless drum—her heartbeat—pulsed through her ears, drowning out any sound.

Nehemia was gone. That vibrant, fierce, loving soul; the princess who had been called the Light of Eyllwe; the woman who had been a beacon of hope—just like that, as if she were no more than a wisp of candlelight, she was gone.

When it had mattered most, Celaena hadn't been there.

Nehemia was gone.

Someone murmured her name, but didn't touch her.

There was a gleam of sapphire eyes in front of her, blocking out her vision of the bed and the dismembered body atop it. Dorian. Prince Dorian. There were tears running down his face. She reached out a hand to touch them. They were oddly warm against her freezing, distant fingers. Her nails were dirty, bloody, cracked—so gruesome against the smooth white cheek of the prince.

And then that voice from behind her said her name again.

"Celaena."

They had done this.

Her bloody fingers slid down Dorian's face, to his neck. He just stared at her, suddenly still.

"Celaena," that familiar voice said. A warning.

They had done this. They had betrayed her. Betrayed Nehemia. They had taken her away. Her nails brushed Dorian's exposed throat.

"*Celaena,*" the voice said.

Celaena slowly turned.

Chaol stared at her, a hand on his sword. The sword she'd brought to the warehouse—the sword she'd left there. Archer had told her that Chaol had known they were going to do this.

He had known.

She shattered completely, and launched herself at him.

⁓

Chaol had only enough time to release his sword as she lunged, swiping for his face with a hand.

She slammed him into the wall, and stinging pain burst from the four lines she gouged across his cheek with her nails.

She reached for the dagger at her waist, but he grasped her wrist. Blood slid down his cheek, down his neck.

His guards shouted, rushing closer, but he hooked a foot behind hers, twisting as he shoved, and threw her to the ground.

"*Stay back*," he ordered them, but it cost him. Pinned beneath him, she slammed a fist up beneath his jaw, so hard his teeth sang.

And then she was snarling, snarling like some kind of wild animal as she snapped for his neck. He reared back, throwing her against the marble floor again. "*Stop.*"

But the Celaena he knew was gone. The girl he'd imagined as his wife, the girl he'd shared a bed with for the past week, was utterly gone. Her clothes and hands were caked with the blood of the men in the warehouse. She wedged a knee up, pounding it between his legs so hard he lost his grip on her, and then she was on top of him, dagger drawn, plunging down toward his chest—

He grabbed her wrist again, crushing it in his hand as the blade hovered over his heart. Her whole body trembled with effort, trying to shove it the remaining few inches. She reached for her other dagger, but he caught that wrist, too.

"*Stop.*" He gasped, winded from the blow she'd landed with her knee, trying to think past that blinding pain. "Celaena, *stop.*"

"Captain," one of his men ventured.

"*Stay back*," he snarled again.

Celaena threw her weight into the dagger she held aloft, and gained an inch. His arms strained. She was going to kill him. She was truly going to kill him.

He made himself look into her eyes, look at the face so twisted with rage that he couldn't find her.

"Celaena," he said, squeezing her wrists so hard that he hoped the pain registered somewhere—wherever she had gone. But she still wouldn't loosen her grip on the blade. "Celaena, I'm your friend."

She stared at him, panting through gritted teeth, her breath coming quicker and quicker before she roared, the sound filling the room, his blood, his world: "*You will* never *be my friend. You will always be my* enemy."

She bellowed the last word with such soul-deep hatred that he felt it like a punch to the gut. She surged again, and he lost his grip on the wrist that held the dagger. The blade plunged down.

And stopped. There was a sudden chill in the room, and Celaena's hand just *stopped*, as though it had been frozen in midair. Her eyes left his face, but Chaol couldn't see who it was she hissed at. For a heart-beat, it seemed as if she was thrashing against some invisible force, but then Ress was behind her, and she was too busy struggling to notice as the guard slammed the pommel of his sword into her head.

As Celaena fell atop him, a part of Chaol fell along with her.

CHAPTER 31

Dorian knew that Chaol had no choice, no other way out of the situation, as his friend carried Celaena out of that bloody chamber, into the servants' stairwell, and down, down, down, until they reached the castle dungeons. He tried not to look at Kaltain's curious, half-mad face as Chaol laid Celaena in the cell beside hers. As he locked the cell door.

"Let me give her my cloak," Dorian said, reaching to unfasten it.

"Don't," Chaol said quietly. His face was still bleeding. She'd gouged four lines across his cheek with her nails. Her *nails*. Gods above.

"I don't trust her with anything in there except hay." Chaol had already taken the time to remove her remaining weapons—including six lethal-looking hairpins from her braid—and checked her boots and tunic for any hidden ones.

Kaltain was smiling faintly at Celaena. "Don't touch her, don't talk to her, and don't look at her," Chaol said, as if there wasn't a wall of bars separating the two women. Kaltain just huffed and curled up on her side. Chaol barked orders to the guards about food and water rations, and how often the watch was to be changed, and then stalked from the dungeon.

Dorian silently followed. He didn't know where to begin. There was grief sweeping down on him in waves as he realized again and again that Nehemia was dead; there was the sickness and terror of what he'd seen in that bedroom; and there was the horror and relief that he'd somehow used his power to stop Celaena's hand before she stabbed Chaol, and that no one except Celaena had noticed.

And when she'd hissed at him . . . he'd seen something so savage in her eyes that he shuddered.

They were halfway up the winding stone stairs out of the dungeons when Chaol suddenly slumped onto a step, putting his head in his hands. "What have I done?" Chaol whispered.

And despite whatever was changing between them, he couldn't walk away from Chaol. Not tonight. Not when he, too, needed someone to sit next to. "Tell me what happened," Dorian said quietly, taking a seat on the stair beside him and staring into the gloom of the stairwell.

So Chaol did.

Dorian listened to his tale of kidnapping, of some rebel group trying to use him to get Celaena to trust them, of Celaena breaking into the warehouse and cutting down men like they were nothing. How the king had told Chaol of an anonymous threat to Nehemia a week ago and ordered him to keep an eye on Nehemia. How the king wanted the princess questioned and told Chaol to keep Celaena away tonight. And then Archer—the man she'd been dispatched to kill weeks ago—explaining that it had been code for Nehemia being assassinated. And then how Celaena ran from the slums all the way back here, to find that she'd been too late to save her friend.

There were things Chaol still wasn't telling him, but Dorian understood it well enough.

His friend was trembling—which was a horror in itself, another foundation slipping out from beneath their feet. "I've never seen anyone move like she did," Chaol breathed. "I've never seen anyone run that fast. Dorian, it was like . . ." Chaol shook his head. "I found a horse within *seconds* of her taking off, and she *still* outran me. Who can do that?"

Dorian might have dismissed it as a warped sense of time due to fear and grief, but he'd had *magic* coursing through his veins only moments ago.

"I didn't know this would happen," Chaol said, resting his forehead against his knees. "If your father . . ."

"It wasn't my father," Dorian said. "I dined with my parents tonight." He'd just come from that dinner when Celaena went flying past, hell burning in her eyes. That look had been enough for him to run after her, guards in tow, until Chaol nearly collided with them in the halls. "My father said he was going to talk to Nehemia later on, after dinner. From what I saw, this happened hours before that."

"But if your father didn't want her dead, who did? I had extra patrols on alert for any threat; I picked those men myself. Whoever did this got through them like they were nothing. Whoever did this . . ."

Dorian tried not to think of the murder scene. One of Chaol's guards had taken a look at the three bodies and vomited all over the floor. And Celaena had just stood there, staring at Nehemia, as if she'd been sucked out of herself.

"Whoever did this got some kind of sick delight out of it," Chaol finished. The bodies flashed through Dorian's mind again: carefully, artfully arranged.

"What does it mean, though?" It was easier to keep talking than to really consider what had happened. The way Celaena had looked at him without really seeing him, the way she'd wiped away his tears with a finger, then grazed her nails across his neck, as though she could sense the pulsing life's blood beneath. And when she'd launched herself at Chaol . . .

"How long will you keep her here?" Dorian said, looking down the stairs.

She had attacked the Captain of the Guard in front of his men. Worse than attacked.

"As long as it takes," Chaol said quietly.

"For what?"

"For her to decide not to kill us all."

～～

Celaena knew where she was before she awoke. And she didn't care. She was living the same story again and again.

The night she'd been captured, she'd also snapped, and come *so close* to killing the person she most wanted to destroy before someone knocked her out and she awoke in a rotting dungeon. She smiled bitterly as she opened her eyes. It was always the same story, the same loss.

A plate of bread and soft cheese, along with an iron cup of water, lay on the floor on the other side of the cell. Celaena sat up, her head throbbing, and felt the bump on the side of her skull.

"I always knew you'd wind up here," Kaltain said from the cell beside hers. "Did Their Royal Highnesses tire of you, too?"

Celaena pulled the tray closer, then leaned against the stone wall behind the pallet of hay. "I tired of them," she said.

"Did you kill anyone particularly deserving?"

Celaena snorted, closing her eyes against the pounding in her mind. "Almost."

She could feel the stickiness of the blood on her hands and beneath her nails. Chaol's blood. She hoped the four scratches scarred. She hoped she would never see him again. If she did, she'd kill him. He'd known the king wanted to question Nehemia. He'd known that the king—the most brutal and murderous monster in the world—had wanted to *question* her friend. And he hadn't told her. Hadn't warned her.

It wasn't the king, though. No—she had gathered enough in the few minutes she'd been in that bedroom to know this wasn't his handiwork. But Chaol had still been warned about the anonymous threat, had been aware that someone wanted to hurt Nehemia. And he hadn't told her.

He was so stupidly honorable and loyal to the king that he didn't even think that she could have done something to prevent this.

She had nothing left to give. After she'd lost Sam and been sent to Endovier, she'd pieced herself back together in the bleakness of the mines. And when she'd come here, she'd been foolish enough to think that Chaol had put the final piece into place. Foolish enough to think, just for a moment, that she could get away with being happy.

But death was her curse and her gift, and death had been her good friend these long, long years.

"They killed Nehemia," she whispered into the dark, needing someone, anyone, to hear that the once-bright soul had been extinguished. To know that Nehemia had been here, on this earth, and she had been all that was good and brave and wonderful.

Kaltain was silent for a long moment. Then she said quietly, as if she were trading one piece of misery for another, "Duke Perrington is going to Morath in five days, and I am to go with him. The king told me I can either marry him, or rot down here for the rest of my life."

Celaena turned her head, opening her eyes to find Kaltain sitting against the wall, grasping her knees. She was even dirtier and more haggard than she'd been a few weeks ago. She still clutched Celaena's cloak around her. Celaena said, "You betrayed the duke. Why would he want you for his wife?"

Kaltain laughed quietly. "Who knows what games these people play, and what ends they have in mind?" She rubbed her dirty hands on her face. "My headaches are worse," she mumbled. "And those wings—they never stop."

My dreams have been filled with shadows and wings, Nehemia had said; Kaltain, too.

"What has one to do with the other?" Celaena demanded, the words sharp and hollow.

Kaltain blinked, raising her brows as though she had no idea what she'd said. "How long will they keep you here?" she asked.

For trying to kill the Captain of the Guard? Forever, perhaps. She wouldn't care. Let them execute her.

Let them put an end to her, too.

Nehemia had been the hope of a kingdom, of many kingdoms. The court Nehemia had dreamed of would never be. Eyllwe would never be free. Celaena would never get the chance to tell her that she was sorry for the things she'd said. All that would remain were the last words Nehemia had spoken to her. The last thing her friend had thought of her.

You are nothing more than a coward.

"If they let you out," Kaltain said, both of them staring into the blackness of their prisons, "make sure that they're punished someday. Every last one of them."

Celaena listened to her own breathing, felt Chaol's blood under her nails, and the blood of all those men she'd hacked down, and the coldness of Nehemia's room, where all that gore had soaked the bed.

"They will be," Celaena swore to the darkness.

She had nothing left to give, except that.

It would have been better if she'd stayed in Endovier. Better to have died there.

Her body didn't feel quite like hers when she pulled the tray of food toward her, the metal scraping against the old, damp stones. She wasn't even hungry.

"They drugged the water with a sedative," Kaltain said as Celaena reached for the iron cup. "That's what they do for me, too."

"Good," Celaena said, and drank the entire thing.

Three days passed. And every meal they brought her was drugged with that sedative.

Celaena stared into the abyss that now filled her dreams, both sleeping and awake. The forest on the other side was gone, and there was no stag; only barren terrain all around, crumbling rocks and a vicious wind that whispered the words again and again.

You are nothing more than a coward.

So Celaena drank the drugged water every time they offered it, and let it sweep her away.

"She drank the water about an hour ago," Ress said to Chaol on the morning of the fourth day.

Chaol nodded. She was unconscious on the floor, her face gaunt. "Has she been eating?"

"A bite or two. She hasn't tried to escape. And she hasn't said one word to us, either."

Chaol unlocked the cell door, and Ress and the other guards tensed.

But he couldn't bear another moment without seeing her. Kaltain was asleep next door and didn't stir as he strode across Celaena's cell.

He knelt by Celaena. She reeked of old blood, and her clothes were stiff with it. His throat tightened.

In the castle above, it had been sheer pandemonium for the past several days. He had men combing the castle and city for Nehemia's assassin. He had gone before the king multiple times already to try to explain what happened: how he'd gotten himself kidnapped, and how, even with extra men watching Nehemia, someone had slipped past them all. He was stunned the king hadn't dismissed him—or worse.

The worst part was that the king seemed *smug*. He hadn't had to dirty his hands to get rid of a problem. His main annoyance was dealing with the uproar that was sure to happen in Eyllwe. He hadn't spared one moment to mourn Nehemia, or shown one flicker of remorse. It had taken a surprising amount of self-control for Chaol not to throttle his own sovereign.

But more than just his fate relied on his submission and good behavior. When Chaol had explained Celaena's situation to the king, he had barely looked surprised. He'd just said to get her in line, and left it at that.

Get her in line.

Chaol gently picked up Celaena, trying not to grunt at the weight, and carried her out of the cell. He'd never forgive himself for throwing her in this rotting dungeon, even though he hadn't had a choice. He hadn't even let himself sleep in his own bed—the bed that still smelled like her. He'd laid down on it that first night and realized what *she* was lying on, and opted for his couch instead. The least he could do right now was get her back to her own rooms.

But he didn't know how to get her in line. He didn't know how to fix what had been broken. Both inside of her, and between them.

His men flanked him as he brought her up to her rooms.

Nehemia's death hung around him, followed his every step. It had been days since he'd dared look in the mirror. Even if it hadn't been the king who had ordered Nehemia dead, if Chaol had warned Celaena about the unknown threat, at least she would have been looking out. If he'd warned Nehemia, her men would have been on alert, too. Sometimes the reality of his decision hit him so hard he couldn't breathe.

And then there was *this* reality, the reality he held in his arms as Ress opened the door to her rooms. Philippa was already waiting, beckoning him to the bathing chamber. He hadn't even thought of that—that Celaena might need to be cleaned up before getting into bed.

He couldn't meet the servant's gaze as he walked into the bathing chamber, because he knew the truth he'd find there.

He'd realized it the moment Celaena had turned to him in Nehemia's bedroom.

He had lost her.

And she would never, in a thousand lifetimes, let him in again.

CHAPTER 32

Celaena awoke in her own bed, and knew there would be no more sedatives in her water.

There would be no more breakfast conversations with Nehemia, nor would there be any more lessons on the Wyrdmarks. There would be no more friends like her.

She knew without looking that someone had scrubbed her clean. Blinking against the brightness of the sunlight in her room—her head instantly pounding after days in the darkness of the dungeon—she found Fleetfoot sleeping pressed against her. The dog lifted her head to lick Celaena's arm a few times before going back to sleep, her nose nestled between Celaena's elbow and torso. She wondered if Fleetfoot could sense the loss, too. She'd often wondered if Fleetfoot loved the princess more than her.

You are nothing more than a coward.

She couldn't blame Fleetfoot. Outside of this rotten, festering court and kingdom, the rest of the world had loved Nehemia. It was hard not to. Celaena had adored Nehemia from the moment she'd laid eyes on her, like they were twin souls who had at last found each other. A soul-friend. And now she was gone.

Celaena put a hand against her chest. How absurd—how utterly absurd and useless—that her heart still beat and Nehemia's didn't.

The Eye of Elena was warm, as if trying to offer some comfort. Celaena let her hand drop back to her mattress.

She didn't even try to get out of bed that day, after Philippa coaxed her into eating and let slip that she'd missed Nehemia's funeral. She'd been too busy guzzling down sedatives and hiding from her grief in the dungeons to be present when they put her friend in the cold earth, so far from the sun-warmed soil of Eyllwe.

You are nothing more than a coward.

So Celaena didn't get out of bed that day. And she didn't get out of it the next.

Or the next.

Or the next.

CHAPTER
33

The mines in Calaculla were stifling, and the slave girl could only imagine how much worse they would become when the summer sun was overhead.

She had been in the mines for six months—longer than anyone else had ever survived, she'd been told. Her mother, her grandmother, and her little brother hadn't lasted a month. Her father hadn't even made it to the mines before Adarlan's butchers had cut him down, along with the other known rebels in their village. Everyone else had been rounded up and sent here.

She'd been alone for five and a half months now; alone, yet surrounded by thousands. She couldn't remember the last time she'd seen the sky, or the grasslands of Eyllwe undulating in a cool breeze.

She would see them both again, though—the sky and the grasslands. She knew she would, because she'd stayed awake on nights she was supposed to have been sleeping, listening through the cracks in the floorboards as her father and his fellow rebels talked of ways to bring down Adarlan, and of Princess Nehemia, who was in the capital at that very moment, working for their freedom.

If she could just hold on, if she could just keep drawing breath, she might make it until Nehemia accomplished her goal. She would make it, and then bury her dead; and when the mourning months were over, she would find the nearest rebel group and join them. With every Adarlanian life she took, she would say the names of her dead again, so that they would hear her in the afterlife and know they were not forgotten.

She swung her pickax into the unforgiving wall of stone, her breath ragged in her parched throat. The overseer lounged against a nearby wall, sloshing water in his canteen, waiting for the moment when one of them would collapse, just so he could unfurl that whip of his.

She kept her head down, kept working, kept breathing.

She would make it.

She didn't know how much time passed, but she felt the ripple go through the mines like a shudder in the earth. A ripple of stillness, followed by wails.

She felt it coming, swelling up toward her, closer and closer with each turned head and murmured words.

And then she heard it—the words that changed everything.

Princess Nehemia is dead. Assassinated by Adarlan.

The words were past her before she had time to swallow them.

There was a scrape of leather against rock. The overseer would tolerate the pause for only a few seconds longer before he started swinging.

Nehemia is dead.

She stared down at the pickax in her hands.

She turned, slowly, to look into the face of her overseer, the face of Adarlan. He cocked his wrist, pronged whip ready.

She felt her tears before she realized they were falling, sliding through six months' worth of filth.

Enough. The word screamed through her, so loudly she began to shake.

Silently, she began to recite the names of her dead. And as the overseer raised his whip, she added her name to the end of that list and swung her ax into his gut.

CHAPTER 34

"Any changes in her behavior?"

"She got out of bed."

"And?"

Standing in the sunlit hall of the upper levels of the glass castle, Ress's usually jovial face was grim. "And now she's sitting in a chair in front of the fire. It's the same as yesterday: she got out of bed, sat in the chair all day, then got back into bed at sundown."

"Is she still not speaking?"

Ress shook his head, keeping his voice low as a courtier passed by. "Philippa says she just sits there and stares at the fire. Won't speak. Still barely touches her food." Ress's eyes grew warier as they took in the healing cuts that ran down Chaol's cheek. Two had already scabbed and would fade, but there was a long, surprisingly deep one that was still tender. Chaol wondered whether it would scar. He'd deserve it if it did.

"I'm probably overstepping my bounds—"

"Then don't say it," Chaol growled. He knew exactly what Ress would say: the same thing Philippa said, and anyone who saw him and gave him that pitying glance. *You should try talking to her.*

He didn't know how word had gotten out so quickly that she'd tried to kill him, but it seemed they all knew how deep the break between him and Celaena went. He'd thought the two of them had been discreet, and he knew Philippa wasn't a gossip. But perhaps what he felt for her had been written all over him. And what she now felt for *him* . . . He resisted the urge to touch the cuts on his face.

"I still want the watch posted outside her door and windows," he ordered Ress. He was on his way to another meeting; another shouting match about how they should deal with the fallout in Eyllwe over the princess's death. "Don't stop her if she leaves, but try to slow her down a bit."

Long enough for word to get to him that she'd finally left her rooms. If anyone was going to intercept Celaena, if anyone would confront her about what happened to Nehemia, it would be him. Until then, he'd give her the space she needed, even if it killed him not to speak to her. She'd become entwined in his life—from the morning runs to the lunches to the kisses she stole from him when no one was looking—and now, without her, he felt hollow. But he still didn't know how he'd ever look her in the eye.

You will always be my *enemy.*

She'd meant it.

Ress nodded. "Consider it done."

The young guard saluted as Chaol headed for the meeting room. There would be other meetings today—lots of meetings, since the debate was still raging over how Adarlan should react to Nehemia's death. And though he hated to admit it, he had other things to worry about than Celaena's unending grief.

The king had summoned his southern lords and retainers to Rifthold.

Including Chaol's father.

⁓

Dorian usually didn't mind Chaol's men. But he *did* mind being followed around, day and night, by guards who were on the lookout for any threat. Nehemia's death had proved that the castle was not impregnable. His mother and Hollin were sequestered in her chambers, and many of the nobility had either left the city or were lying low, too.

Except Roland. Though Roland's mother had fled back to Meah the morning after the princess was assassinated, Roland stayed, insisting that Dorian would need his support now more than ever. And he was right. At the council meetings, which grew more and more crowded as the southern lords arrived, Roland backed every point and objection that Dorian made. Together they argued against sending more troops into Eyllwe in case of revolt, and Roland seconded Dorian's proposal that they should publicly apologize to Nehemia's parents for her death.

His father had exploded when Dorian suggested that, but Dorian had still written her parents a message, expressing his deepest condolences. His father could go to hell for all he cared.

And that was starting to be a problem, he realized as he sat in his tower room and flipped through all the documents he had to read before tomorrow's meeting with the southern lords. He had spent so long being careful to avoid defying his father, but what sort of man could he call himself if he blindly obeyed?

A smart man, a part of him whispered, flickering with that cold, ancient power.

At least his four guards stayed outside his rooms. His private tower was high enough that no one could reach the balcony, and only one stair led up and down. Easily defensible. But it also made for an easy cage.

Dorian stared at the glass pen on his desk. The night Nehemia had died, he hadn't intended to stop Celaena's wrist in midair. He'd just known that the woman he'd loved was about to kill his oldest friend over a misunderstanding. He'd been too far away to grab her as she plunged the blade down, but then . . . it was like a phantom arm reached out from within him and wrapped around her wrist. He could *feel* her blood-crusted skin, as if he himself were touching her.

But he hadn't known what he was doing. He'd just acted on gut feeling and desperation and need.

He had to learn to control this power, whatever it was. If he could control it, then he could keep it from appearing at inopportune times. Like when he was in those damned council meetings and his temper rose, and he felt the magic stirring in response.

Dorian took a deep breath, focusing on the pen, willing it to move. He'd stopped Celaena midstrike, he'd thrown a wall of books into the air—he could move a pen.

It didn't move.

After staring at it until his eyes nearly crossed, Dorian groaned and leaned back in his chair, covering his eyes with his hands.

Maybe he'd gone insane. Maybe he'd just imagined the whole thing.

Nehemia had once promised to be there when he needed help—when some power in him awoke. She had known.

Had her assassin, in killing Nehemia, also killed any hope he had of finding answers?

~

Celaena had only started sitting in the chair because Philippa had come in yesterday and complained about the dirty sheets. She might have told Philippa to go to hell, but then she considered who had last shared this bed with her, and was suddenly glad to have them replaced. Any trace of him, she wanted gone.

As the sun finished setting, she sat before the fire, staring into the glowing embers that grew brighter as the world darkened.

Time was shifting and ebbing around her. Some days had passed in an hour, others a lifetime. She had bathed once, long enough to wash her hair, and Philippa had watched the whole time to make sure she didn't drown herself instead.

Celaena ran a thumb over the armrest of the chair. She had no intention of ending her life. Not before she did what needed to be done.

The shadows in the room grew, and the embers seemed to breathe as she watched them. Breathing with her, pulsing with each heartbeat.

In these days of silence and sleep, she'd realized one thing: the assassin had come from outside the palace.

Perhaps they had been hired by whoever had initially threatened Nehemia's life—perhaps not. But they weren't associated with the king.

Celaena gripped the arms of the chair, her nails digging into the polished wood. It hadn't been one of Arobynn's assassins, either. She knew his style, and it wasn't this monstrous. She again went over the details of the bedroom, now branded into her mind.

She did know one killer this monstrous.

Grave.

She'd learned as much about him as she could when she'd faced him in the competition to become King's Champion. She'd heard what he did to the bodies of his victims.

Her lips pulled back from her teeth.

Grave knew the palace; he'd trained here just as she had. And he'd known, too, just whom he was murdering and dismembering—and what it would mean to her.

A familiar, dark fire rippled in her gut, spreading through her, dragging her down into an abyss without end.

Celaena Sardothien stood from her chair.

CHAPTER 35

There would be no candles for these midnight deeds, no ivory horn to signal the start of this hunt. She dressed in her darkest tunic and slid a smooth black mask into her cloak pocket. All of her weapons, even the hairpins, had been removed from her rooms. She knew without checking that the doors and windows were being watched. Good. This was not the sort of hunt that began at the front door.

Celaena locked her bedroom and spared a glance at Fleetfoot, who cowered under the bed as she hauled open the secret door. The dog was still quietly whining as Celaena strode into the passage.

She didn't need a light to make her way down to the tomb. She knew the path by memory now, each step, each turn.

Her cloak whispered against the steps. Down and down she went.

It was war upon them all. Let them tremble in fear at what they had awoken.

Moonlight spilled onto the landing, illuminating the open door of the tomb and Mort's little bronze face.

"I'm sorry about your friend," he said with surprising sorrow as she stalked toward him.

She didn't reply. And she didn't care how he knew. She just kept walking, through the door and between the sarcophagi, to the heap of treasure piled in the back.

Daggers, hunting knives—she took whatever she could strap onto her belt or tuck into her boots. She took a handful of gold and jewels and shoved that into a pocket, too.

"What are you doing?" Mort demanded from the hallway.

Celaena approached the stand that displayed Damaris, sword of Gavin, first King of Adarlan. The hollowed-out golden pommel glinted in the moonlight as she pulled the scabbard from the stand and strapped it across her back.

"That is a *sacred* sword," Mort hissed, as though he could see inside.

Celaena smiled grimly as she stalked back to the door, flinging her hood over her head.

"Wherever you are going," Mort went on, "whatever you plan to do, you debase that sword by taking it from here. Aren't you afraid of angering the gods?"

Celaena just laughed quietly before she took the stairs, savoring each step, each movement that brought her closer to her prey.

~

She relished the burn in her arms as she hauled the sewer grate up, rotating the ancient wheel until it was fully raised, dripping with filth, and the water beneath the castle flowed freely into the small river outside. She tossed a piece of broken stone into the river beyond the archway, listening for guards.

Not a sound, not a scrape of armor or a whisper of warning.

An assassin had killed Nehemia, an assassin with a taste for the grotesque and a desire for notoriety. Finding Grave would take only a few questions.

She tied the chain around the lever, testing its strength, and checked to ensure that Damaris was tightly strapped to her back. Then, gripping the castle stones, she swung around the wall, slithering sideways. She didn't bother to glance up at the castle as she eased around the bank of the river and dropped onto the frozen ground.

Then she vanished into the night.

Cloaked in darkness, Celaena stalked through the streets of Rifthold. She made no sound as she passed through dim alleys.

Only one place could provide the answers she wanted.

Sewage and puddles of excrement lay beneath every window of the slums, and the cobblestone streets were cracked and misshapen after many hard winters. The buildings leaned against each other, some so ramshackle that even the poorest citizens had abandoned them. On most streets, the taverns overflowed with drunks and whores and everyone else who sought temporary relief from their miserable lives.

It made no difference how many saw her. None would bother her tonight.

The cape billowed behind her, her face remaining expressionless beneath her obsidian mask as she moved through the streets. The Vaults was just a few blocks away.

Celaena's gloved hands clenched. Once she found out where Grave was hiding, she'd turn his skin inside out. Worse than that, actually.

She stopped before a nondescript iron door in a quiet alley. Hired thugs stood watch outside; she flashed them the silver entrance fee, and they opened the door for her. In the subterranean warren below, one could find the cutthroats, the monsters, and the damned of Adarlan. The filth came here to exchange stories and make deals, and it was here that any whisper of Nehemia's assassin would be found.

Grave had undoubtedly received a large fee for his services, and could be counted on to now be recklessly spending his blood money—a spree that would not go unnoticed. He wouldn't have left Rifthold—oh, no. He *wanted* people to know he killed the princess; he wanted to hear himself named the new Adarlan's Assassin. He wanted Celaena to know, too.

As she headed down the steps into the Vaults, the reek of ale and unwashed bodies hit her like a stone to the face. She hadn't been in this sort of festering den for a long while.

The main chamber was strategically lit: a chandelier hung in the center of the room, but there was little light to be found along the walls for those who sought not to be seen. All laughter halted as she strode between the tables. Red-rimmed eyes followed her every step.

She didn't know the identity of the new crime lord who ruled over this place, and didn't care. Her business wasn't with him, not tonight. She didn't allow herself to look at the many fighting pits that occupied the distant end of the chamber—pits where crowds were still gathered, cheering for whoever fought with fists and feet within.

She'd been to the Vaults before, many times in those final days before her capture. Now that Ioan Jayne and Rourke Farran were dead, the place seemed to have passed into new ownership without losing any of its depravity.

Celaena walked right up to the barkeep. He didn't recognize her, but she didn't expect him to—not when she'd been so careful to hide her identity all those years.

The barkeep was already pale, and his sparse hair had become even sparser over the past year and a half. He tried to peer beneath her cowl as she halted at the bar, but the mask and hood kept her features hidden.

"Drink?" he asked, wiping sweat from his brow. Everyone in the bar was still watching her, either discreetly or outright.

SARAH J. MAAS

"No," she said, her voice contorted and deep beneath the mask.

The barkeep gripped the edge of the counter. "You—you're back," he said quietly, as more heads turned. "You escaped."

So he did recognize her, then. She wondered if the new owners held a grudge against her for killing Ioan Jayne—and how many bodies she'd have to leave in her wake if they decided to start a fight right here, right now. What she planned to do tonight already broke enough rules, crossed too many lines.

She leaned on the bar, crossing one ankle over the other. The barkeep mopped his brow again and poured her a brandy. "On the house," he said, sliding it to her. She caught it in her hand, but didn't drink it. He wet his lips, then asked, "How—how did you escape?"

People leaned back in their chairs, straining to hear. Let them spread rumors. Let them hesitate before crossing her path. She hoped Arobynn heard, too. She hoped he heard and stayed the hell away from her.

"You'll soon discover that," she said. "But I have need of you."

His brows lifted. "Me?"

"I have come to inquire after a man." Her voice was scratchy and hollow. "A man who recently earned a large sum of gold. For the assassination of the Eyllwe princess. He goes by the name of Grave. I need to know where he is."

"I don't know anything." The barkeep's face turned even paler.

She reached into a pocket and pulled out a glittering fistful of ancient jewels and gold. All eyes watched them now.

"Allow me to repeat my question, barkeep."

The assassin who called himself Grave ran.

He didn't know how long she'd been hunting him. It had been well over a week since he'd killed the princess; a week, and no one had even looked his way. He thought he'd gotten away with it—and had even started wondering whether he should have been more cre-ative with the body, if he should have left some sort of calling card behind. But all that had changed tonight.

He'd been drinking at the counter of his favorite tavern when the packed room had suddenly gone quiet. He'd turned to see her in the doorway as she called out his name, looking more wraith than human. His name hadn't even finished echoing in the room before he burst into a sprint, escaping through the back exit and into the alley. He couldn't hear footsteps, but he knew she was behind him, melting in and out of shadows and mist.

He took alleys and side streets, leaping over walls, zigzagging across the slums. Anything to shake her, to wear her down. He'd make his final stand in a quiet street. There, he would take out the blades strapped to his skin and make her pay for the way she'd humiliated him in the competition. The way she had sneered at him, the way she'd broken his nose and tossed her handkerchief onto his chest.

Haughty, stupid bitch.

He staggered as he rounded a corner, his breath ragged and raw. He had only three daggers hidden on him. He'd make them count, though. When she'd appeared at the tavern, he had immediately taken note of the broadsword hovering over one of her shoulders and the assortment of gleaming, wicked-looking blades strapped to her hips. But he could make her pay, even if he only had a few blades.

Grave was halfway down the cobblestone alley when he realized it was a dead end, the far wall too high to climb. Here, then. He'd soon have her begging for mercy before he cut her into little, little pieces. Drawing one of his daggers, he smiled and turned to the open street behind him.

Blue mist drifted by, and a rat scurried across the narrow passage. There was no noise, only the sounds of distant revelry. Perhaps he had lost her. Those royal fools had made the biggest mistake of their lives when they crowned her Champion. His client had said as much when he'd hired Grave.

He waited a moment, still watching the open street entrance, and then allowed himself to breathe, surprised to find that he was a little disappointed.

King's Champion indeed. It hadn't been hard to lose her at all. And now he would go home, and he'd receive another job offer in a matter of days. And then another. And another. His client had promised him that the offers would come. Arobynn Hamel would curse the day he had rejected Grave from the Assassins Guild for being too cruel with his prey.

Grave chuckled, flipping his dagger in his hands. Then she appeared.

She came through the fog, no more than a sliver of darkness. She didn't run—she just walked with that insufferable swagger. Grave surveyed the buildings surrounding them. The stone was too slippery, and there were no windows.

One step at a time, she approached. He would really, *really* enjoy making her suffer as much as the princess had.

Smiling, Grave retreated to the end of the alley, only stopping when his back hit the stone wall. In a narrower space, he could overpower her. And in this forgotten street, he could take his own sweet time doing what he wanted.

Still she approached, and the sword at her back whined as she drew it. The moonlight glinted off the long blade. Probably a gift from her princeling lover.

Grave pulled his second dagger from his boot. This wasn't a frilly, ridiculous competition run by nobility. Here, any rules applied.

She didn't say anything when she neared.

And Grave didn't say anything to her as he rushed at her, swiping for her head with both blades.

She stepped aside, dodging him with maddening ease. Grave

lunged again. But faster than he could follow she ducked and slashed her sword across his shins.

He hit the wet ground before he felt the pain. The world flashed black and gray and red, and agony tore at him. A dagger still left in his hand, he scuttled backward toward the wall. But his legs wouldn't respond, and his arms strained to pull him through the damp filth.

"Bitch," he hissed. *"Bitch."* He hit the wall, blood pouring from his legs. Bone had been sliced. He would not be able to walk. He could still find a way to make her pay, though.

She stopped a few feet away and sheathed her sword. She drew a long, jeweled dagger.

He swore at her, the filthiest word he could think of.

She chuckled, and faster than a striking asp, she had one of his arms against the wall, the dagger glinting.

Pain ripped through his right wrist, then his left as it, too, was slammed into the stone. Grave screamed—truly screamed—as he found his arms pinned to the wall by two daggers.

His blood was nearly black in the moonlight. He thrashed, cursing her again and again. He would bleed to death unless he pulled his arms from the wall.

With otherworldly silence, she crouched before him and lifted his chin with another dagger. Grave panted as she brought her face close to his. There was nothing beneath the cowl—nothing of this world. She had no face.

"Who hired you?" she asked, her voice like gravel.

"To do what?" he asked, almost sobbing. Maybe he could feign innocence. He could talk his way out, convince this arrogant whore he had nothing to do with it . . .

She turned the dagger, pressing it into his neck. "To kill Princess Nehemia."

"N-n-no one. I don't know what you're talking about."

And then, without even an intake of breath, she buried another dagger he hadn't realized she'd been holding into his thigh. So deep he felt the reverberation as it hit the cobblestones beneath. His scream shattered out of him, and Grave writhed, his wrists rising farther on the blades.

"Who hired you?" she asked again. Calm, so calm.

"Gold," Grave moaned. "I have gold."

She drew yet another dagger and shoved it into his other thigh, piercing again to the stone. Grave shrieked—shrieked to gods who did not save him. "Who hired you?"

"I don't know what you're talking about!"

After a heartbeat, she withdrew the daggers from his thighs. He almost soiled himself at the pain, at the relief.

"Thank you." He wept, even as he thought of how he would punish her. She sat back on her heels and stared at him. "Thank you."

But then she brought up another dagger, its edge serrated and glinting, and hovered it close to his hand.

"Pick a finger," she said. He trembled and shook his head. *"Pick a finger."*

"P-please." A wet warmth filled the seat of his pants.

"Thumb it is."

"N-no. I . . . I'll tell you everything!" Still, she brought the blade closer, until it rested against the base of his thumb. *"Don't!* I'll tell you everything!"

CHAPTER 36

Dorian was just starting to feel his temper fray after hours of debate when the doors to his father's council room were thrown open and Celaena prowled in, her dark cape billowing behind her. All twenty men at the table fell silent, including his father, whose eyes went straight to the thing dangling from Celaena's hand. Chaol was already striding across the room from his post by the door. But he, too, stopped when he beheld the object she carried.

A head.

The man's face was still set in a scream, and there was something vaguely familiar about the grotesque features and mousy brown hair that she gripped. It was hard to be certain as it swung from her gloved fingers.

Chaol put a hand on his sword, his face pale as death. The other guards in the room drew their blades, but didn't move—wouldn't move, until Chaol or the king commanded them.

"What is this?" the king demanded. The councilmen and assembled lords were gaping.

But Celaena was smiling as her eyes locked onto one of the ministers at the table, and she walked right toward him.

And no one, not even Dorian's father, said anything as she set the severed head atop the minister's stack of papers.

"I believe this belongs to you," she said, releasing her grip on the hair. The head lolled to the side with a thud. Then she patted—*patted*—the minister's shoulder before rounding the table and plopping into an empty chair at one end, sprawling across it.

"Explain yourself," the king growled at her.

She crossed her arms, smiling at the minister, whose face had turned green as he stared at the head before him.

"I had a little chat with Grave about Princess Nehemia last night," she said. Grave, the assassin from the competition—and Minister Mullison's Champion. "He sends his regards, minister. He also sends this." She tossed something onto the long table: a small golden bracelet, engraved with lotus blossoms. Something Nehemia would have worn. "Here's a lesson for you, Minister, from one professional to another: cover your tracks. And hire assassins without personal connections to you. And perhaps try *not* to do it so soon after you've publicly argued with your target."

Mullison was looking at the king with pleading eyes. "I didn't do this." He recoiled from the severed head. "I have no idea what she's talking about. I'd never do something like this."

"That's not what Grave said," Celaena crooned. Dorian could only stare at her. This was different from the feral creature she'd become the night Nehemia had died. What she was right now, the edge on which she was balancing . . . Wyrd help them all.

But then Chaol was at her chair, grasping her elbow. "What the hell do you think you're doing?"

Celaena looked up at him and smiled sweetly. "Your job, apparently." She shook off his grip with a thrash, then got out of her seat, stalking around the table. She pulled a piece of paper out of her tunic and tossed it in front of the king. The impertinence in that throw should have earned her a trip to the gallows, but the king said nothing.

Following her around the table, a hand still on his sword, Chaol watched her with a face like stone. Dorian began praying they wouldn't come to blows—not here, not again. If it riled his magic and his father saw . . . Dorian wouldn't even *think* of that power when he was in a room with so many potential enemies. He was sitting beside the person who would give the order to have him put down.

His father took the paper. From where he sat, Dorian could see that it was a list of names, at least fifteen long.

"Before the unfortunate death of the princess," she said, "I took it upon myself to eliminate some traitors to the crown. My target," she said, and he knew his father was aware she meant Archer, "led me right to them."

Dorian couldn't look at her for a moment longer. This couldn't be the whole truth. But she hadn't gone after them to hunt them down, she'd gone to save Chaol. So why lie now? Why pretend she'd been hunting them? What sort of game was she playing?

Dorian looked across the table. Minister Mullison was still trembling at the severed head in front of him. He wouldn't have been surprised if the minister vomited right there. *He* was the one who had made the anonymous threat against Nehemia's life?

After a moment, his father looked up from the list and surveyed her. "Well done, Champion. Well done indeed."

Then Celaena and the King of Adarlan smiled at each other, and it was the most terrifying thing Dorian had ever seen.

"Tell my exchequer to give you double last month's payment," the king said. Dorian felt his gorge rise—not just for the severed head and her blood-stiffened clothing, but also for the fact that he could not, for the life of him, find the girl he had loved anywhere in her face. And from Chaol's expression, he knew his friend felt the same.

Celaena bowed dramatically to the king, flourishing a hand before her. Then, with a smile devoid of any warmth, she stared down Chaol before stalking from the room, her dark cape sweeping behind her.

Silence.

And then Dorian's attention returned to Minister Mullison, who merely whispered, "Please," before the king ordered Chaol to have him dragged to the dungeons.

Celaena wasn't done—not nearly. Perhaps the bloodletting was over, but she still had another person to visit before she could return to her bedroom and wash off the stink of Grave's blood.

Archer was resting when she arrived at his townhouse, and his butler didn't dare stop her as she strode up the carpeted front steps, stormed down the elegant wood-paneled hallway, and flung open the double doors to what could only have been his room.

Archer jolted in bed, wincing as he put a hand to his bandaged shoulder. Then he took in her appearance, the daggers still strapped to her waist. He went very, very still.

"I'm sorry," he said.

She stood at the foot of his bed, staring down at him, at his wan face and injured shoulder. "You're sorry, Chaol's sorry, the whole damn world is sorry. Tell me what you and your movement want. Tell me what you know about the king's plans."

"I didn't want to lie to you," Archer said gently. "But I needed to know that I could trust you before I told you the truth. Nehemia"—she tried not to wince at the name—"said you could be trusted, but I needed to know for sure. And I needed you to trust me, too."

"So you thought kidnapping Chaol would make me *trust* you?"

"We kidnapped him because we thought he and the king were planning to hurt her. I needed you to come to that warehouse and hear from Westfall's lips that he was aware there had been threats to her safety and he didn't tell you; to realize that *he* is the enemy. If I'd known you would go so berserk, I never would have done it."

She shook her head. "That list you sent me yesterday, of the men from the warehouse—they're truly dead?"

"You killed them, yes."

Guilt punched through her. "For my part, I am sorry." And she was. She'd memorized their names, tried to recall their faces. She would carry the weight of their deaths forever. Even Grave's death, what she'd done to him in that alley; she'd never forget that, either. "I gave their names to the king. It should keep him from looking in your direction for a little while longer—five days at most."

Archer nodded, sinking back into the pillows.

"Nehemia really worked with you?"

"It was why she came to Rifthold—to see what could be done about organizing a force in the north. To give us information directly from the castle." As Celaena had always suspected. "Her loss . . ." He closed his eyes. "We can't replace her."

Celaena swallowed.

"But you could," Archer said, looking at her again. "I know you came from Terrasen. So part of you has to realize that Terrasen *must* be free."

You are nothing more than a coward.

She kept her face blank.

"Be our eyes and ears in the castle," Archer whispered. "Help us. Help us, and we can find a way to save everyone—to save *you*. We don't know what the king plans to do, only that he somehow found a source of power *outside* magic, and that he's probably using that power to create monstrosities of his own. But to what end, we don't know. That's what Nehemia was trying to discover—and it's knowledge that could save us all."

She would digest all that later—much later. For now, she stared at Archer, then looked down at her blood-stiffened clothing. "I found the man who killed Nehemia."

Archer's eyes widened. "And?"

She turned to walk out of the room. "And the debt has been paid. Minister Mullison hired him to get rid of a thorn in his side—because she put him down one too many times in council meetings. The minister is now in the dungeons, awaiting his trial."

And she would be there for every minute of that trial, and the execution afterward.

Archer loosed a sigh as she put her hand on the doorknob.

She looked over her shoulder at him, at the fear and sadness on his face. "You took an arrow for me," she said quietly, gazing at the bandages.

"It was the least I could do after I caused that whole mess."

She chewed on her lip and opened the door. "We have five days until the king expects you to be dead. Prepare yourself and your allies."

"But—"

"But nothing," she interrupted. "Consider yourself fortunate that I'm not going to rip out your throat for the stunt you pulled. Arrow or no arrow, and regardless of my relationship with Chaol, you lied to me. And kidnapped my friend. If it hadn't been for that—for *you*—I would have been at the castle that night." She fixed him with a stare. "I'm done with you. I don't want your information, I'm not going to *give* you information, and I don't particularly care what happens to you once you leave this city, as long as I never see you again."

She took a step into the hallway.

"Celaena?"

She looked over her shoulder.

"I am sorry. I know how much you meant to her—and she to you."

The weight she'd been avoiding since she'd gone to hunt Grave suddenly fell on her, and her shoulders drooped. She was so tired. Now that Grave was dead, now that Minister Mullison was in the dungeon, now that she had no one left to maim and punish—she was so, *so* tired.

"Five days; I'll be back in five days. If you aren't prepared to leave Rifthold, then I won't bother faking your death. I'll kill you before you know I'm in the room."

Chaol kept his face blank and his shoulders thrown back as his father surveyed him. The small breakfast room in his father's suite was sunny and silent; pleasant, even, but Chaol remained in the doorway as he looked at his father for the first time in ten years.

The Lord of Anielle looked mostly the same, his hair a bit grayer, but his face still ruggedly handsome, far too similar to Chaol's for his own liking.

"The breakfast is growing cold," his father said, waving a broad hand to the table and the empty chair across from him. His first words.

Chaol clenched his jaw so hard it hurt as he walked across the bright room and slid into the chair. His father poured himself a glass of juice and said without looking at him, "At least you fill out your uniform. Thanks to your mother's blood, your brother is all gangly limbs and awkward angles."

Chaol bristled at the way his father spat "your mother's blood," but made himself pour a cup of tea, then butter a slice of bread.

"Are you just going to keep quiet, or are you going to say something?"

"What could I possibly have to say to you?"

SARAH J. MAAS

His father gave him a thin smile. "A polite son would inquire after the state of his family."

"I haven't been your son for ten years. I don't see why I should start acting like one now."

His father's eyes flicked to the sword at Chaol's side, examining, judging, weighing. Chaol reined in the urge to walk out. It had been a mistake to accept his father's invitation. He should have burned the note he received last night. But after he'd ensured that Minister Mullison was locked up, the king's lecture about Celaena making a fool out of him and his guards had somehow worn through his better judgment.

And Celaena . . . He had no idea how she'd gotten out of her rooms. None. The guards had been alert and had reported no noise. The windows hadn't been opened, and neither had her front door. And when he asked Philippa, she only said that the bedroom door had been locked all night.

Celaena was keeping secrets again. She'd lied to the king about the men she'd killed in the warehouse to rescue him. And there were other mysteries lurking around her, mysteries that he'd better start figuring out if he was to stand a chance of surviving her wrath. What his men had reported about the body that had been found in that alley . . .

"Tell me what you've been up to."

"What do you wish to know?" Chaol said flatly, not touching his food or drink.

His father leaned back in his seat—a movement that had once made Chaol start sweating. It usually meant that his father was about to focus all of his attention on him, that he would judge and consider and dole out punishment for any weakness, any missteps. But Chaol was a grown man now, and he answered only to his king.

"Are you enjoying the position you sacrificed your lineage to attain?"

"Yes."

2

72

"I suppose I have you to thank for being dragged to Rifthold. And if Eyllwe rises up, then I suppose we can all thank you as well."

It took every ounce of will he had, but Chaol just took a bite from his bread and stared at his father.

Something like approval flickered in the man's eyes, and he took a bite of his own bread before he said, "Do you have a woman, at least?"

The effort it took to keep his face blank was considerable. "No."

His father smiled slowly. "You were always a horrible liar."

Chaol looked toward the window, toward the cloudless day that was revealing the first hint of spring.

"For your sake, I hope she's at least of noble blood."

"For my sake?"

"You might have spat on your lineage, but you are still a Westfall—and we do not marry scullery maids."

Chaol snorted, shaking his head. "I'll marry whomever I please, whether she's a scullery maid or a princess or a slave. And it'll be none of your damn business."

His father folded his hands in front of him. After a long silence, he said quietly, "Your mother misses you. She wants you home."

The breath was knocked out of him. But he kept his face blank, his tone steady, as he said, "And do you, Father?"

His father stared right at him—through him. "If Eyllwe rises up in retaliation, if we find ourselves facing a war, then Anielle will need a strong heir."

"If you've groomed Terrin to be your heir, then I'm sure he'll do just fine."

"Terrin is a scholar, not a warrior. He was born that way. If Eyllwe rebels, there is a good chance that the wild men in the Fangs will rise up, too. Anielle will be the first place they sack. They've been dreaming of revenge for too long."

Chaol wondered just how much this was grating on his father's pride, and part of him truly wanted to make him suffer for it.

But he'd had enough of suffering, and enough of hatred. And he hardly had any fight left in him now that Celaena had made it clear she'd sooner eat hot coals than look at him with affection in her eyes. Now that Celeana was—gone. So he just said, "My position is here. My life is here."

"Your people need you. They *will* need you. Would you be so selfish as to turn your back on them?"

"The way my father turned his back on me?"

His father smiled again, a cruel, cold thing. "You disgraced your family when you gave up your title. You disgraced me. But you have made yourself useful these years—made the Crown Prince rely upon you. And when Dorian is king, he'll reward you for it, won't he? He could make Anielle a duchy and bless you with lands large enough to rival Perrington's territory around Morath."

"What is it that you really want, Father? To protect your people, or to use my friendship with Dorian to your gain?"

"Would you throw me in the dungeons if I said both? I hear you like to do that to the people who dare provoke you these days." And then there was that gleam in his eyes that told Chaol just how much his father already knew. "Perhaps if you do, your woman and I can exchange notes about the conditions."

"If you want me back in Anielle, you're not doing a very good job of convincing me."

"Do I *need* to convince you? You failed to protect the princess, and that has created the possibility of war. The assassin who was warming your bed now wants nothing more than to spill your innards on the ground. What's left for you here, except more shame?"

Chaol slammed his hands on the table, rattling the dishes. *"Enough."*

He didn't want his father knowing anything about Celaena, or about the remaining fragments of his heart. He wouldn't let his servants change the sheets on his bed because they still smelled like her, because he went to sleep dreaming that she was still lying beside him.

"I have worked for ten years to be in this position, and it'll take far more than a few taunts from you to get me back to Anielle. And if you think Terrin is weak, then send him to me for training. Maybe here he'll learn how real men act."

Chaol shoved his chair away from the table, rattling the dishes again, and stormed to the door. Five minutes. He'd lasted less than five minutes.

He paused in the doorway and looked back at his father. The man was smiling faintly at him, still taking him in, still assessing how useful he would be. "You talk to her—you so much as look in her direction," Chaol warned, "and, father or not, I'll make you wish you'd never set foot in this castle."

And though he didn't wait to hear what his father had to say, Chaol left with the sinking feeling that he'd somehow just stepped right into his father's snare.

CHAPTER 37

There was no one else to carry out this task, not with Eyllwe soldiers and ambassadors still on their way to retrieve Nehemia's body from where it lay interred in the royal plot. As Celaena opened the door to the room that had smelled of blood and pain, she saw that someone had cleaned away all traces of gore. The mattress was gone, and Celaena paused in the doorway as she surveyed the skeleton of the bed frame. Perhaps it would be best to leave Nehemia's belongings to the people who came to bring her back to Eyllwe.

But would they be friends of hers? The thought of strangers touching Nehemia's belongings, packing them away like any other objects, made her wild with grief and rage.

Almost as wild as she'd been earlier today, when she'd walked into her own dressing room and ripped every gown off its hanger, pulled out every pair of shoes, every tunic, every ribbon and cloak and thrown them into the hallway.

She'd burned the dresses that reminded her most of Nehemia, the dresses she'd worn at their lessons, at their meals, and on their walks around the castle. It was only when Philippa came in to scold her about the smoke that Celaena had relented, allowing her to take whatever clothing survived and donate it. But it had been too late to stop Celaena from burning the dress she'd worn the night of Chaol's birthday. That gown had burned first.

And when her dressing room was empty, she shoved a bag of gold into Philippa's hands and told her to go buy some new clothes. Philippa had only given her a sad look—another thing that made Celaena sick—and left.

It took Celaena an hour to gently, carefully pack up Nehemia's clothes and jewelry, and she tried not to dwell too long on the memories that accompanied each item. Or the lotus-blossom smell that clung to everything.

When she had sealed all the trunks, she went to Nehemia's desk, which was still littered with papers and books as if the princess had only stepped outside for a moment. As she reached for the first paper, her eyes fell upon the arc of scars around her right hand—the teeth marks of the ridderak.

The papers were covered with scribblings in Eyllwe and—and Wyrdmarks.

Countless Wyrdmarks, some in long lines, some forming symbols like the ones Nehemia had traced underneath Celaena's bed all those months ago. How had the king's spies not taken these? Or had he not even bothered to have her rooms searched? She started stacking them into a pile. Perhaps she could still learn some things about the marks, even if Nehemia were—

Dead, she made herself think. *Nehemia is dead.*

Celaena looked at the scars on her hand again and was about to turn from the desk when she spotted a familiar-looking book half tucked beneath some papers.

It was the book from Davis's office.

This copy was older, more damaged, but it was the same book. And written on the inside cover was a sentence in Wyrdmarks—such basic marks that even Celaena could understand them.

Do not trust—

The final symbol, though, was a mystery. It looked like a wyvern—the Royal Seal. Of course she shouldn't trust the King of Adarlan.

She flipped through the book, scanning it for any information. Nothing.

And then she turned to the back cover. And there, Nehemia had written—

It is only with the eye that one can see rightly.

It was scribbled in the common tongue, then in Eyllwe, then in some other languages that Celaena didn't recognize. Different translations—as if Nehemia had wondered whether the riddle held any meaning in another tongue. The same book, the same riddle, the same writing in the back.

An idle lord's nonsense, Nehemia had said.

But Nehemia . . . Nehemia and Archer led the group to which Davis had belonged. Nehemia had *known* Davis; known him and *lied* about it, lied about the riddle, and—

Nehemia had promised. Promised that there would be no more secrets between them.

Promised and lied. Promised and deceived her.

She fought down a scream as she tore through every other piece of paper on the desk, in the room. Nothing.

What else had Nehemia lied about?

It is only with the eye . . .

Celaena touched her necklace. Nehemia had known about the tomb. If she had been feeding information to this group, and had encouraged Celaena to look into the eye carved into the wall . . . then Nehemia had been looking, too. But after the duel, she'd returned the Eye of Elena to Celaena; if Nehemia had needed it, she would have kept it. And Archer hadn't mentioned knowing anything about this.

Unless this wasn't the eye the riddle referenced.

Because . . .

"By the Wyrd," Celaena breathed, and rushed out of the room.

Mort hissed when she appeared at the door to the tomb. "Plan on desecrating any other sacred objects tonight?"

Carrying a satchel full of papers and books that she'd grabbed from her rooms, Celaena merely patted his head as she walked by. His bronze teeth clanked against each other as he sought to bite her.

The tomb was filled with moonlight bright enough to see by. And there, directly across the tomb from the eye in the wall, was another eye, golden and gleaming.

Damaris. It was Damaris, the Sword of Truth. Gavin could see nothing but what was right—

It is only with the eye that one can see rightly.

"Am I so blind?" Celaena dumped her leather satchel on the floor, the books and papers spilling across the stones.

"It appears so!" Mort sang. The eye-shaped pommel was the exact size . . .

Celaena lifted the sword from its stand and unsheathed it. The Wyrdmarks on the blade seemed to ripple. She rushed back to the wall.

"In case you didn't realize," called Mort, "you're supposed to hold the eye against the hole in the wall and look through it."

"I know *that*," snapped Celaena.

And so, not daring to breathe the entire time, Celaena lifted the pommel to the hole until both eyes were evenly aligned. She stood on her toes and peered in—and groaned.

It was a poem.

A lengthy poem.

Celaena fished out the parchment and charcoal she'd stashed in her pocket and copied down the words, darting to and from the wall as she read, memorized, double-checked, and then recorded. It was only when she had finished the last stanza that she read it aloud.

> *By the Valg, three were made,*
> *Of the Gate-Stone of the Wyrd:*
> *Obsidian the gods forbade*
> *And stone they greatly feared.*
>
> *In grief, he hid one in the crown*
> *Of her he loved so well,*
> *To keep with her where she lay down*
> *Inside the starry cell.*
>
> *The second one was hidden*
> *In a mountain made of fire,*
> *Where all men were forbidden*
> *Despite their great desires.*
>
> *Where the third lies*
> *Will never be told*
> *By voice or tongue*
> *Or sum of gold.*

Celaena shook her head. More nonsense. And the rhyme with "Wyrd" and "feared" was off. Not to mention the break in the rhyme scheme in the final lines.

"Since you *clearly* knew that the sword could be used to read the riddle," she said to Mort, "then why don't you save me some trouble and tell me what the hell this one's about?"

Mort sniffed. "It sounds to *me* like it's a riddle giving the location of three very powerful items."

She read through the poem again. "But three *what*? Sounds like the second thing is hidden in—in a volcano? And the first and third ones . . ." She gritted her teeth. "'Gate-Stone of the Wyrd' . . . What is this a riddle for? And why is it here?"

"Isn't *that* the question of the millennia!" Mort crowed as Celaena walked back to the papers and books she'd scattered at the other end of the tomb. "You'd better clean up the mess you brought down here, or I'll ask the gods to send some wicked beastie after you."

"Already happened; Cain beat you to it months ago." She replaced Damaris in its stand. "Too bad the ridderak didn't take *you* off the door when he burst through." A thought hit her, and she stared at the wall in front of her—where she'd once fallen to avoid being ripped apart. "Who was it that moved the carcass of the ridderak?"

"Princess Nehemia, of course."

Celaena twisted to look toward the doorway. "Nehemia?"

Mort made a choking sound and cursed his loose tongue.

"Nehemia was—Nehemia was *here*? But I only brought her to the tomb . . ." Mort's bronze face gleamed in the light of the candle she'd set before the door. "You're telling me that Nehemia came here after the ridderak attacked? That she knew about this place all along? And you're only telling me *now*?"

Mort closed his eyes. "Not my business."

Another deceit. Another mystery.

"I suppose if Cain could get down here, then there are other entrances," she said.

"Don't ask me where they are," Mort said, reading her mind. "I've never left this door." She had a feeling it was another lie; he always seemed to know about the layout of the tomb and when she was touching things she shouldn't be.

"Then what use are you? Brannon just made you to piss everyone off?"

"He *did* have a sense of humor like that."

The thought of Mort actually having known the ancient Fae king made her quake inside. "I thought you had *powers*. You can't just speak some nonsense words and have the meaning of the riddle be revealed to me?"

"Of course not. And isn't the journey more important than the end?"

"No," she spat. Spewing a concoction of curses that could have curdled milk, Celaena tucked the paper into her pocket. She would need to study this riddle at length.

If these items were things that Nehemia was looking for, things that she'd lied about to keep secret . . . Celaena might be able to accept that Archer and his friends were capable of good, but she certainly didn't trust them to hold an object with the power that the riddle mentioned. If they were already looking, then perhaps it was in her best interest to find the items before anyone else. Nehemia hadn't figured out that the eye riddle referred to Damaris, but had she known what the three objects were? Maybe she'd pursued the eye riddle because she was trying to find the objects before the king did.

The king's plans—had they been to find these things?

She picked up her candle and strode from the room.

"Has the questing spirit seized you at last?"

"Not yet," she said as she walked by. Once she found out what the three items were, then maybe she'd consider finding a way to go after them. Even if the only volcanoes she knew about were in the Desert Peninsula, and there was no way in hell the king would let her go off on her own for such a long trip.

"It's a pity that I'm attached to this door," sighed Mort. "Imagine all the trouble you'll get into while trying to solve the riddle!"

He was right; and as Celaena walked up the winding stair, she found herself wishing that he actually could move about. Then she'd at least have one person to discuss this with. If she did have to go hunt these things down, whatever they were, then she'd have no one to go with her. There was no one who knew the truth.

The truth.

She snorted. What truth was there now? That she had no one left to talk to? That Nehemia had lied through her teeth about so many things? That the king might be searching for an earth-shattering source of power? That he might already *have* something like this? Archer had mentioned a source of power *outside* of magic; was that what these things were? Nehemia had to have known . . .

Celaena slowed, the candle guttering in a damp breeze through the stairwell, and slumped onto a step, bracing her arms on her knees.

"What else were you hiding, Nehemia?" she whispered into the darkness.

Celaena didn't need to turn to know who sat behind her when something silver and glimmering shone in the corner of her eye.

"I thought you were too exhausted to come here," she said to the first Queen of Adarlan.

"I can only stay for a few moments," Elena said, her dress rustling as she took a seat a few steps up from Celaena. It seemed a distinctly un-queenlike thing to do.

Together, they stared into the gloom of the stairwell, Celaena's breathing the only sound. She supposed Elena didn't need to breathe—didn't make any sounds unless she wanted to.

Celaena gripped her knees. "What was it like?" she asked quietly.

"Painless," Elena said with equal quiet. "Painless, and easy."

"Were you frightened?"

"I was a very old woman, surrounded by my children, and their children, and their children's children. I had nothing to be afraid of when the time came."

"Where did you go?"

A soft laugh. "You know I can't tell you that."

Celaena's lips wobbled. "She didn't die an old woman in her bed."

"No, she didn't. But when her spirit left her body, there was no more pain—no more fear. She is safe now."

Celaena nodded. Elena's dress rustled again, and then she was on the step beside her, an arm around her shoulders. She hadn't realized how cold she was until she found herself leaning into Elena's warmth.

The queen didn't say anything as Celaena buried her face in her hands and wept at last.

There was one last thing she had to do. Perhaps the hardest and the worst of all the things she had done since Nehemia had died.

The moon was overhead, casting the world in silver. Even though they didn't recognize her in her current attire, the night watch at the royal mausoleum hadn't stopped her as she passed through the iron gates at the back of one of the castle gardens. Nehemia wouldn't be entombed inside the white marble building, though; inside was for the royal family.

Celaena walked around the domed building, feeling as if the wyverns carved into the side stared at her as she passed.

The few people still active at this hour had quickly looked away as she made her way here. She didn't blame them. A black dress and a sheer, flowing black veil spoke enough about her grief, and kept everyone at a long, long distance. As though her sorrow were a plague.

But she didn't give a damn what the others thought; the mourning clothes weren't for them. She rounded the back of the mausoleum and beheld the rows of graves in the gravel garden behind it, the pale and worn stones illuminated by the moon. Statues depicting everything from mourning gods to dancing maidens marked the resting places of distinguished nobility, some so lifelike they seemed to be people frozen in stone.

It had not snowed since before Nehemia's murder, so it was easy enough to spot the grave by the upturned earth before it.

There were no flowers, not even a headstone. Just fresh soil and a sword thrust into the earth—one of the curved swords of Nehemia's fallen guards. Apparently, no one had bothered to give her anything more, not when she would be retrieved and brought back to Eyllwe.

Celaena stared at the dark, tilled earth, a chill wind rustling her veil.

Her chest ached, but this was the one last thing she had to do, the one last honor she could give her friend.

Celaena tilted her head to the sky, closed her eyes, and began to sing.

⌇

Chaol had told himself that he was only following Celaena to make sure she didn't hurt herself or anyone else, but as she'd neared the royal mausoleum, he followed for other reasons.

The night provided good cover, but the moon was bright enough to keep him back, far enough away so she wouldn't see or hear his approach. But then he saw where she had stopped, and realized he had no right to be here for this. He'd been about to turn away when she lifted her face to the moon and sang.

It was not in any language that he knew. Not in the common tongue, or in Eyllwe, or in the languages of Fenharrow or Melisande or anywhere else on the continent.

This language was ancient, each word full of power and rage and agony.

She did not have a beautiful voice. And many of the words sounded like half sobs, the vowels stretched by the pangs of sorrow, the consonants hardened by anger. She beat her breast in time, so full of savage grace, so at odds with the black gown and veil she wore. The hair on the back of his neck stood as the lament poured from her mouth, unearthly and foreign, a song of grief so old that it predated the stone castle itself.

And then the song finished, its end as brutal and sudden as Nehemia's death had been.

She stood there for a few moments, silent and unmoving.

He was about to walk away when she half turned to him.

Her thin silver circlet shimmered in the moonlight, weighing down a veil so concealing that only he had recognized her.

A breeze whipped past them, making the branches of the trees moan and creak, setting her veil and skirts billowing to one side.

"Celaena," he pleaded. She didn't move, her stillness the only sign that she'd heard him. And that she had no interest in talking.

What could he ever say to repair the rift between them, anyway? He'd kept information from her. Even if he hadn't been directly responsible for Nehemia's death, if either girl had been more alert, they might have had their own defenses prepared. The loss she felt, the stillness with which she watched him—it was all his fault.

If the punishment for that was losing her, then he'd endure it.

So Chaol walked away, her lament still echoing through the night around him, carried on the wind like the pealing of distant bells.

CHAPTER
38

The dawn was chill and gray as Celaena stood in the familiar field of the game park, a large stick dangling between her gloved fingers. Fleetfoot sat before her, her tail slashing through the long, dried grass that poked up through the remaining layer of snow. But the hound didn't whine or bark for the stick to be thrown.

No, Fleetfoot just kept sitting there, watching the palace far behind them. Waiting for someone who was never going to arrive.

Celaena stared across the barren field, listening to the sighing grasses. No one had tried to stop her from leaving her rooms last night—or this morning. Yet even though the guards were gone, whenever she left her room, Ress had an uncanny habit of *accidentally* running into her.

She didn't care if he reported her movements to Chaol. She didn't even care that Chaol had been spying on her at Nehemia's grave last night. Let him think what he would about the song.

With a sharp intake of breath, she hurled the stick as hard as she could, so far it blended in with the cloudy morning sky. She didn't hear it land.

Fleetfoot turned to look up at Celaena, her golden eyes full of question. Celaena reached down to stroke the warm head, the long ears, the slender muzzle. But the question remained.

Celaena said, "She's never coming back."

The dog kept waiting.

Dorian had spent half the night in the library, searching in forgotten crevices, scouring every dark corner, every hidden nook, for any books on magic. There were none. It wasn't surprising, but given how many books were in the library, and how many twisting passageways there were, he was a little disappointed that *nothing* of worth could be found.

He didn't even know what he would *do* with a book like that once he found it. He couldn't bring it back to his rooms, since his servants were likely to find it there. He would probably have to put it back in its hiding place and return to it whenever he could.

He was scanning a bookshelf built into a stone alcove when he heard footsteps. Immediately, just as he'd rehearsed, he took out the book he'd tucked into his jacket and leaned against the wall, opening to a random page.

"It's a little dark for reading," a female voice said. She sounded so normal, so like herself that Dorian nearly dropped the book.

Celaena was standing a few feet away, arms crossed. Pitter-pattering feet echoed against the floors, and a moment later Dorian braced himself against the wall as Fleetfoot flung herself at him, all wagging tail and bountiful kisses. "Gods, you're huge," he told the dog. She licked his cheek one last time and sprinted off down the hall. Dorian watched her go, brows raised. "I'm fairly certain that whatever she's about to do, it won't make the librarians happy."

"She knows to stick to the poetry and mathematics books."

Celaena's face was grave and pale, but her eyes shone with faint amusement. She wore a dark blue tunic he'd never seen before, with golden embroidery that glinted in the dim light. In fact, her whole outfit looked new.

The silence that settled between them made him shift on his feet. What could he possibly say to her? The last time they'd been this close, she'd grazed her nails across his neck. He'd had nightmares about that moment.

"Can I help you find anything?" he asked her. Keep it normal, keep it simple.

"Crown Prince *and* royal librarian?"

"*Unofficial* royal librarian," he said. "A title hard-won after many years of hiding here to avoid stuffy meetings, my mother, and . . . well, everything else."

"And here I was, thinking you just hid in your little tower."

Dorian laughed softly, but the sound somehow killed the amusement in her eyes. As if the sound of merriment was too raw against the wound of Nehemia's death. *Keep it simple*, he reminded himself. "So? Is there a book I can help you find? If that's a list of titles in your hand, then I could look them up in the catalog."

"No," she said, folding the papers in half. "No, there's no book. I just wanted a walk."

And he'd just come to a dark corner of the library to read.

But he didn't push it, if only because she could easily start asking *him* questions, too. If she remembered what had happened when she attacked Chaol, that is. He hoped she didn't.

There was a muffled shriek from somewhere in the library, followed by a string of howled curses and the familiar pitter-patter of paws on stone. Then Fleetfoot came sprinting down the row, a scroll of paper in her jaws.

"Wicked beast!" a man was shouting. "Come back here at once!"

Fleetfoot just zoomed on by, a blur of gold.

A moment later, when the little librarian came waddling into view and asked if they'd seen a dog, Celaena only shook her head and said that she *had* heard something—from the opposite direction. And *then* she told him to keep his voice down, because this was a *library*.

His eyes shooting daggers at her, the man huffed and scuttled away, his shouting a bit softer.

When he was gone, Dorian turned to her, brows high on his head. "That scroll could have been invaluable."

She shrugged. "He looked like he could use the exercise."

And then she was smiling. Hesitantly at first, then she shook her head, and the smile bloomed wide enough to show her teeth.

It was only when she looked at him again that he realized he'd been staring, trying to sort out the difference between this smile and the smile she'd given his father the day she'd put Grave's head on the council table.

As if she could read his thoughts, she said, "I apologize for my behavior lately. I haven't . . . been myself."

Or she'd just been a part of herself that she usually kept on a tight, tight leash, he thought. But he said, "I understand."

And from the way her eyes softened, he knew that was all he'd ever needed to say.

Chaol wasn't hiding from his father. He wasn't hiding from Celaena. And he wasn't hiding from his men, who now felt some ridiculous urge to look after *him*.

But the library *did* offer a good amount of refuge and privacy.

Maybe answers, too.

The head librarian wasn't in the little office tucked into one of the walls of the library. So Chaol had asked an apprentice. The gawking youth pointed, gave some vague directions, and told him good luck.

Chaol followed the boy's directions up a sweeping flight of black marble stairs and along the mezzanine rail. He was about to turn down an aisle of books when he heard them speaking.

Actually, he heard Fleetfoot's prancing first, and looked over the marble rail in time to see Celaena and Dorian walking toward the towering main doors. They were a comfortable, casual distance apart, but . . . but she was talking. Her shoulders were relaxed, her gait smooth. So different from the woman of shadow and darkness that he'd seen yesterday.

What were the two of them doing here—together?

It wasn't his business. Frankly, he was grateful that she was talking to *anyone*, and not burning her clothes or butchering rogue assassins. Still, something twanged in his heart that Dorian was the one beside her.

But she was talking.

So Chaol quickly turned from the balcony rail and walked deeper into the library, trying to shove the image from his mind. He found Harlan Sensel, the head librarian, huffing and puffing down one of the main paths through the library, shaking a fistful of paper shreds at the air around him.

Sensel was so busy cursing that he hardly noticed when Chaol stepped in his path. The librarian had to tilt his head back to see Chaol, and then frowned at him.

"Good, you're here," Sensel said, and resumed walking. "Higgins must have sent word."

Chaol had no idea what Sensel was talking about. "Is there some issue that you need assistance with?"

"Issue!" Sensel waved the shredded papers. "There are feral *beasts* running amok in my library! Who let that—that *creature* in here? I demand that they pay!"

Chaol had had a feeling that Celaena had something to do with this. He just hoped she and Fleetfoot were out of the library before Sensel reached the office.

"What sort of scroll was damaged? I'll see to it that they replace it."

"Replace it!" Sensel sputtered. "Replace *this*?"

"What, exactly, is it?"

"A letter! A letter from a *very* close friend of mine!"

He bit back his annoyance. "If it's just a letter, then I don't think the creature's owner can offer a payment. Though perhaps they'd be happy to donate a few books in—"

"Throw them in the dungeons! My library has become little more than a circus! Did you know that there's a cloaked person skulking about the stacks at all hours of the night? *They* probably unleashed that horrible beast in the library! So track them down and—"

"The dungeons are full," Chaol lied. "But I'll look into it." While Sensel finished his rant about the truly exhausting hunt he'd gone on to retrieve the letter, Chaol debated whether he should just leave.

But he had questions, and once they reached the mezzanine and he was certain that Celaena, Fleetfoot, and Dorian were long gone, he said, "I have a question for you, sir."

Sensel preened at the honorific, and Chaol tried his best to look uninterested.

"If I wanted to look up funeral dirges—laments—from other kingdoms, where would be the best place to start?"

Sensel gave him a confused look, then said, "What a dreadful subject."

Chaol shrugged and took a shot in the dark. "One of my men is from Terrasen, and his mother recently died, so I'd like to honor him by learning one of their songs."

"Is that what the king pays you to do—learn sad songs with which to serenade your men?"

He almost snorted at the idea of serenading his men, but shrugged again. "Are there any books where those songs might be?"

Even a day later, he couldn't get the song out of his head, couldn't stop the chill that went up his neck when its words echoed through his mind. And then there were those other words, the words that had changed everything: *You will always be my* enemy.

She was hiding something—a secret she kept locked up so tight that only the horror and shattering loss of that night could have made her slip in such a way. So the more he could discover about her, the better chance he stood of being prepared when the secret came to light.

"Hmm," the little librarian said, walking down the main steps. "Well, most of the songs were never written down. And why would they be?"

"Surely the scholars in Terrasen recorded some of them. Orynth had the greatest library in Erilea at one time," Chaol countered.

"That they did," Sensel said, a twinge of sorrow in his words. "But I don't think anyone ever bothered to write down their dirges. At least, not in a way that would have made it here."

"What about in other languages? My guard from Terrasen mentioned something about a dirge he once heard sung in another tongue— though he never learned what it was."

The librarian stroked his silver beard. "Another language? Everyone in Terrasen speaks the common tongue. No one's spoken a different language there for a thousand years."

They were close to the office, and he knew that once they arrived, the little bastard would probably shut him out until he'd brought Fleetfoot to justice. Chaol pressed a bit harder. "So there are no dirges in Terrasen that are sung in a different language?"

"No," he said, drawing out the word as he pondered. "But I once heard that in the high court of Terrasen, when the nobility died, they sang their laments in the language of the Fae."

Chaol's blood froze and he almost tripped, but he managed to keep walking and say, "Would these songs have been known by everyone—not just the nobility?"

"Oh, no," Sensel said, only half-listening as he recited whatever history was in his head. "Those songs were sacred to the court. Only those of noble blood ever learned or sang them. They were taught and sung in secret, their dead buried by the light of the moon, when no other ears could hear them. At least, that's what rumor claimed. I'll admit to my own morbid curiosity in that I'd hoped to hear them ten years ago, but by the time the slaughter had ended, there was no one left in those noble houses to sing them."

No one, except . . .

You will always be my enemy.

"Thank you," Chaol got out, then quickly turned away, walking toward the exit. Sensel called after him, demanding his oath that he'd find the dog and punish it, but Chaol didn't bother to reply.

Which house did she belong to? Her parents hadn't just been murdered—they were part of the nobility who had been executed by the king.

Slaughtered.

She'd been found in their bed—after they'd been killed. And then she must have run until she found the place where a Terrasen nobleman's daughter could hide: the Assassins' Keep. She'd learned the only skills that could keep her safe. To escape death, she'd become death.

Regardless of what territory her parents had lorded over, if Celaena ever took up the mantle she'd lost, and if Terrasen ever got to its feet . . .

Then Celaena could become a powerhouse—potentially capable of standing against Adarlan. And that made Celaena more than just his enemy.

It made her the greatest threat he'd ever encountered.

CHAPTER 39

Crouched in the shadow of a chimney atop a pretty little townhouse, Celaena watched the home next door. For the last thirty minutes, people had been slipping inside, all cloaked and hooded—looking like nothing more than cold patrons eager to get out of the freezing night.

She'd meant it when she told Archer she wanted nothing to do with him or his movement. And honestly, there was a part of her that wondered whether she should just kill them all and toss their heads at the king's feet. But Nehemia had been a part of this group. And even if Nehemia had pretended she didn't know anything about these people . . . they were still her people. She hadn't lied to Archer when she told him that she'd bought him a few extra days; after turning over Councilor Mullison, the king didn't hesitate to grant her a bit more time to kill the courtesan.

A snow flurry gusted up, veiling her view of the front of Archer's townhouse. To anyone else, the gathering would seem like a dinner party for his clients. She knew only a few of the faces—and bodies—that hurried up the steps, people who hadn't fled the kingdom or been killed by her the night everything went to hell.

There were many more, however, whose names she didn't know. She recognized the guard who had stood between her and Chaol at the warehouse—the man who had been so eager for a fight. Not by his face, which had been masked that night, but by the way he moved, and by the twin swords strapped to his back. He still wore a hood, but she could see shoulder-length dark hair gleaming beneath it, and what looked like the tan skin of a young man.

He paused at the bottom step, turning to quietly utter commands to the two hooded men flanking him. With a nod, they vanished into the night.

She contemplated trailing one of them. But she'd come here only to check on Archer, to see what he was up to. She planned to keep checking on him until the moment he got on that boat and sailed away. And once he was gone, once she'd given the king his fake corpse . . . She didn't know what she'd do then.

Celaena slipped farther behind the brick chimney as one of the guards scanned the rooftops for any signs of trouble before continuing on his way—to watch one end of the street, if she guessed correctly.

She stayed in the shadows for a few hours, moving to the rooftop across the street to better watch the front of the house, until the guests started leaving, one by one, looking for all the world like drunken revelers. She counted them, and marked what directions they went in and who walked with them, but the young man with the twin swords didn't emerge.

She might have convinced herself that he was another client of Archer's, even his lover, had the stranger's two guards not returned and slipped inside.

As the front door opened, she caught a glimpse of a tall, broad-shouldered young man arguing with Archer in the foyer. His back was to the door, but his hood was off—confirming that he did indeed have night-black shoulder-length hair and was armed to the teeth. She could see nothing else. His guards immediately flanked him, keeping her from getting a closer look before the door shut again.

Not very careful—not very inconspicuous.

A moment later, the young man stormed out, hooded once more, his two men at his side. Archer stood in the open doorway, his face visibly pale, arms crossed. The young man paused at the bottom of the steps, turning to give Archer a particularly vulgar gesture.

Even from this distance, Celaena could see the smile that Archer gave the man in return. There was nothing kind in it.

She wished she'd been close enough to hear what they'd said, to understand what this was all about.

Before, she would have trailed the young stranger to seek out the answers.

But that was before. Now . . . now, she didn't particularly care.

It was hard to care, she realized as she started the trek back to the castle. Incredibly hard to care, when you didn't have anyone left to care about.

Celaena didn't know what she was doing at this door. Even though the guards at the foot of the tower had let her pass after checking her thoroughly for weapons, she didn't doubt for one moment that word would go right to Chaol.

She wondered if he'd dare stop her. If he'd ever dare to utter another word to her. Last night, even from the distance at the moonlit graveyard, she'd seen the still-healing cuts on his cheek. She didn't know whether they filled her with satisfaction or guilt.

Every little bit of interaction was draining, somehow. How exhausted would she be after tonight?

Celaena sighed and knocked on the wooden door. She was five

minutes late—minutes she'd spent debating whether she truly wanted to accept Dorian's offer to dine with him in his rooms. She'd almost eaten dinner in Rifthold instead.

There was no answer to her knock at first, so she turned away, trying to avoid looking at the guards posted on the landing. It was stupid to come here, anyway.

She had just taken a step down the spiral staircase when the door opened.

"You know, I think this is the first time you've been to my little tower," Dorian said.

Foot still in the air, Celaena collected herself before looking over her shoulder at the Crown Prince.

"I was expecting more doom and gloom," she said, walking back to the door. "It's quite cozy."

He held the door open and nodded to his guards. "No need to worry," he told them as Celaena walked into the prince's chambers.

She'd expected grandeur and elegance, but Dorian's tower was—well, "cozy" was a good way to describe it. A bit shabby, too. There was a faded tapestry, a soot-stained fireplace, a moderate-size four-poster bed, a desk heaped with papers by the window, and books. Stacks and mountains and towers and columns of books. They covered every surface, every bit of space along the walls.

"I think you need your own personal librarian," she muttered, and Dorian laughed.

She hadn't realized how much she missed that sound. Not just his laugh, but her own, too; *any* laugh, really. Even if it felt wrong to laugh these days, she missed it.

"If my servants had their way, these would all go to the library. They make dusting rather hard." He stooped to pick up some clothes he'd left on the floor.

"From the mess, I'm surprised to hear you even *have* servants."

Another laugh as he carried the pile of clothes toward a door. It opened just wide enough to reveal a dressing room nearly as big as her own, but she saw no more than that before he chucked the clothes inside and shut the door. Across the room, another door had to lead to a bathing chamber. "I have a habit of telling them to go away," he said.

"Why?" She walked to the worn red couch before the fireplace and pushed off the books that were piled there.

"Because *I* know where everything in this room is. All the books, the papers—and the moment they start cleaning, those things get hopelessly organized and tucked away, and I can never find them again." He was straightening the red cloth of his bedspread, which looked rumpled enough to suggest he'd been sprawled across it until she'd knocked.

"Don't you have people who dress you? I would have thought that Roland would be your devoted servant, at least."

Dorian snorted, plumping his pillows. "Roland's tried. Thankfully, he's been suffering from awful headaches lately and has backed off." That was good to hear—sort of. The last she'd bothered to check, the Lord of Meah had indeed become close to Dorian—a friend, even. "And," Dorian went on, "aside from my refusal to find a bride, my mother's greatest annoyance is my refusal to be dressed by lords eager to win my favor."

That was unexpected. Dorian was always so well dressed that she assumed he had people doing it for him.

He went to the door to tell the guards to have their dinner brought up. "Wine?" he asked from the window, where a bottle and a few glasses were kept.

She shook her head, wondering where they would even eat their food. The desk wasn't an option, and the table before the fireplace was a miniature library on its own. As if in answer, Dorian began clearing the table. "Sorry," he said sheepishly. "I meant to clear a space to eat before you got here, but I got wrapped up in reading."

She nodded, and silence fell between them, interrupted only by the thud and hiss of him moving books.

"So," Dorian said quietly, "can I ask why you decided to join me for dinner? You've made it pretty clear that you didn't want to spend any time with me—and I thought you had work to do tonight."

Actually, she'd been downright awful to him. But he kept his back to her, as though the question didn't matter.

And she didn't quite know why the words came out, but she spoke the truth anyway. "Because I have nowhere else to go."

Sitting in her rooms in silence made the pain worse, going to the tomb only frustrated her, and the thought of Chaol still hurt so badly she couldn't breathe. Every morning, she walked Fleetfoot by herself, then ran alone in the game park. Even the girls who had once lined the garden pathways, waiting for Chaol, had stopped showing up.

Dorian nodded, looking at her with kindness she couldn't stand. "Then you will always have a place here."

⤸

While their dinner was quiet, it wasn't lachrymose. But Dorian could still see the change in her—the hesitation and consideration behind her words, the moments when she thought he wasn't looking and an endless sorrow filled her eyes. She kept talking to him, though, and answered all his questions.

Because I have nowhere else to go.

It wasn't an insult, not the way she'd said it. And now that she was dozing on his couch, the clock having recently chimed two, he wondered what was keeping her from going back to her own rooms. Clearly, she didn't want to be alone—and maybe she needed to be in a place that didn't remind her of Nehemia.

Her body was a patchwork of scars; he'd seen it with his own eyes. But these new scars might go deeper: the pain of losing Nehemia, and the different, but perhaps just as agonizing, loss of Chaol.

An awful part of him was glad she'd cut out Chaol. He hated himself for it.

⌇

"There has to be something more here," Celaena said to Mort as she combed through the tomb the following afternoon.

Yesterday, she'd read the riddle until her eyes ached. Still it offered no hint about what the objects might be, where precisely they were concealed, or why the riddle had been hidden so elaborately in the tomb. "Some sort of clue. Something that connects the riddle to the rebel movement and Nehemia and Elena and all the rest." She paused between the two sarcophagi. Sunlight spilled in, setting the dust motes shimmering. "It's staring me in the face, I know it."

"I'm afraid I can't be of service," Mort sniffed. "If you want an instant answer, you should find yourself a seer or an oracle."

Celaena slowed her pacing. "You think if I read this to someone with the gift of clairvoyance, they might be able to . . . see some different meaning that I'm missing?"

"Perhaps. Though as far as I know, when magic vanished, those with the gift of Sight lost it, too."

"Yes, but *you're* still here."

"So?"

Celaena looked at the stone ceiling as if she could see through it, all the way to the ground above. "So perhaps other ancient beings might retain some of their gifts, too."

"Whatever it is you're thinking, I guarantee it's a bad idea."

Celaena gave him a grim smile. "I'm pretty sure you're right."

CHAPTER 40

Celaena stood before the caravans, watching as the tents were taken apart. Fortunate timing.

She ran a hand through her unbound hair and straightened her brown tunic. Finery would have attracted too much attention. And even if it was just for an hour, she couldn't help but savor the feeling of anonymity, of blending in with the carnival workers, these people who had the dust of a hundred kingdoms on their clothes. To have that sort of freedom, to see the world bit by bit, to travel each and every road . . . Her chest tightened.

People streamed by, hardly glancing at her as she made her way to the black wagon. This could easily be folly, but what harm was there in asking? If Yellowlegs truly was a witch, then perhaps she had the gift of Sight. Perhaps she could make sense of the riddle in the tomb.

When Celaena reached the wagon, it was mercifully devoid of patrons. Baba Yellowlegs sat on the top stair, smoking a long bone pipe whose bowl was shaped like a screaming mouth. Pleasant.

"Come to look into the mirrors?" she said, smoke spilling from her withered lips. "Done running from fate at last?"

"I have some questions for you."

The witch sniffed her, and Celaena fought the urge to step back. "You do indeed stink of questions—and the Staghorn Mountains. From Terrasen, are you? What's your name?"

Celaena stuck her hands deep in her pockets. "Lillian Gordaina."

The witch spat on the ground. "What's your *real* name, Lillian?" Celaena stiffened. Yellowlegs crowed with laughter. "Come," she cawed, "want to have your fortune told? I can tell you who you'll marry, how many children you'll have, when you'll die . . ."

"If you're indeed as good as you claim, you know I'm not interested in those things. I'd like to talk to you instead," Celaena said, flashing the three gold coins in her palm.

"Cheap goat," Yellowlegs said, taking another long drag from the pipe. "That's all my gifts are worth to you?"

Perhaps this *would* be a waste of time. And money. And pride.

Celaena turned away with a scowl, shoving her hands into the pockets of her dark cloak.

"Wait," Yellowlegs said.

Celaena kept walking.

"The prince gave me four coins."

She paused and looked over her shoulder at the crone. A cold, clawed hand gripped her heart.

Yellowlegs smiled at her. "He had such interesting questions, too. He thought I didn't recognize him, but I can smell Havilliard blood a mile off. Seven gold pieces, and I'll answer your questions—and tell you his."

She'd sell Dorian's questions to her—to anyone? That familiar calm went through her. "How do I know you're not lying?"

Yellowlegs's iron teeth glinted in the light of the torches. "It would be bad for business if I were branded a liar. Would it make you more comfortable if I swore on one of your soft-hearted gods? Or perhaps on one of mine?"

Celaena studied the black wagon, swiftly braiding her hair back. One door, no back exit, no sign of trick panels. No way out, and plenty of warning in case someone came in. She checked her weapons—two long daggers, a knife in her boot, and three of Philippa's deadly hairpins. More than enough.

"Make it six coins," Celaena said softly, "and I won't report you to the guard for trying to sell the prince's secrets."

"Who says the guard won't be interested in them, too? You'd be surprised how many people want to know what truly interests the prince of the realm."

Celaena slammed six gold coins onto the step beside the tiny crone. "Three pieces for my questions," she said, bringing her face as close to Yellowlegs's as she dared. The reek from the woman's mouth was like carrion and stale smoke. "And three for your silence about the prince."

Yellowlegs's eyes gleamed, her iron nails clinking together as she stretched out a hand to grab the coins. "Get in the caravan." The door behind her swung open soundlessly. A dark interior lay beyond, speckled with patches of glimmering light. Yellowlegs snuffed out her bone pipe.

She'd been hoping for this—to get inside the caravan, and thus avoid having anyone see her with Yellowlegs.

The old woman groaned as she stood, a hand braced on her knee. "Care to tell me your name *now*?"

A chill wind blew from within the caravan, sliding along Celaena's neck. Carnival trick. "I'll ask the questions," Celaena said, and stalked up the steps into the caravan.

Inside, there were a few measly candles, whose light flickered along row after row, stack after stack, of mirrors. They were every shape, every size, some leaning against the walls, some propped against each other like old friends, some little more than shards clinging to their frames.

And everywhere else, wherever there was a bit of space, were papers and scrolls, jars full of herbs or liquids, brooms . . . junk.

In the gloom, the caravan stretched on much wider and longer than should have been possible. A winding path had been made between the mirrors, leading into the dark—a path that Yellowlegs was now treading, as if there were anywhere to go inside this strange place.

This can't be real—it must be an illusion of the mirrors.

Celaena glanced back toward the wagon door in time to see it snick shut. Her dagger was out before the sound had finished echoing through the wagon. Ahead, Yellowlegs chuckled, lifting the candle in her hand. Its holder seemed to be shaped like a skull mounted on some sort of longer bone.

Tacky, cheap carnival tricks, Celaena told herself again and again, her breath clouding in the chill air inside the wagon. None of it was real. But Yellowlegs—and the knowledge she offered—truly was.

"Come along, girl. Come sit with me where we might talk."

Celaena carefully stepped over a fallen mirror, keeping an eye on the bobbing skull-lantern—and on the door, any possible exits (none as far as she could see, but perhaps there was a trapdoor in the floor), and how the woman moved.

Surprisingly fast, she realized, and hurried to catch up to Yellow-legs. As she strode through the forest of mirrors, her reflection shifted everywhere. In one she appeared short and fat, in another tall and impossibly thin. In another she stood upside down, and in yet another she walked sideways. It was enough to give her a headache.

"Done gawking?" Yellowlegs said. Celaena ignored her, but sheathed her dagger as she followed the woman into a small sitting area before a dim, grated oven. No reason to have her weapon out—not when she still needed Yellowlegs to cooperate.

The sitting area lay in a rough circle cleared of junk and stacks of mirrors, with little more than a rug and a few chairs to make it hospitable. Yellowlegs hobbled over to the raised hearthstone, yanking a few logs from a tiny stack perched on the rim. Celaena remained on the edge of the worn red rug, watching as Yellowlegs threw open the iron grate of the oven, tossed in the wood, and slammed the grate shut again. Within seconds, light flared, made brighter still by the surrounding mirrors.

"The stones of this oven," Yellowlegs said, patting the curved wall of dark bricks like an old pet, "came from the ruins of the Crochan capital city. The wood of this wagon was hewn from the walls of their sacred schools. That's why my wagon is . . . unusual inside."

Celaena said nothing. It would have been easy to dismiss it as a bit of carnival dramatics, except she was seeing it for herself.

"So," Yellowlegs said, remaining standing as well, despite the aged wooden furniture scattered around them. "Questions."

Even though the air in the wagon was chill, the burning oven somehow made it instantly warm—warm enough for Celaena's layers of clothing to be uncomfortable. She'd been told a story once, on a hot summer night in the Red Desert; a story about what one of the long-lost Ironteeth witches had done to a young girl. What had been left of her.

Gleaming white bones. Nothing more.

Celaena glanced at the oven again and angled herself closer to the door. Across the small sitting area, more mirrors waited in the gloom— as if even the light of the fire couldn't reach them.

Yellowlegs leaned closer to the grate, rubbing her gnarled fingers in front of it. The firelight danced along her iron nails. "Ask away, girl."

What had Dorian wanted to know so badly? Had he come inside this strange, smothering place? At least he'd survived. If only because Yellowlegs wanted to use whatever information she'd gleaned from him. Foolish, foolish man.

Was she any different, though?

This might be her only chance to learn what she needed to know, despite the risk, despite how messy and complicated the aftermath might be.

"I found a riddle, and my friends have been debating its answer for weeks. We even have a bet going about it," she said as vaguely as she could. "Answer it, if you're so clever and all-knowing. I'll toss in an extra gold coin if you get it right."

"Impudent children. Wasting my time with this nonsense." Yellow-legs watched the mirrors now, as if she could see something Celaena couldn't.

Or as if she's already bored.

Some of the tightness in her chest loosening, Celaena pulled the riddle from her pocket and read it aloud.

When she was done, Yellowlegs slowly turned her head to Celaena, her voice low and rough. "Where did you find that?"

Celaena shrugged. "Give me the answer and I might tell you. What sort of objects does this riddle describe?"

"Wyrdkeys," Yellowlegs breathed, eyes glowing. "It describes the three Wyrdkeys to open the Wyrdgate."

Cold slithered down Celaena's spine, but she said, with more bravado than she felt, "Tell me what they are—the Wyrdkeys, the Wyrdgate. For all I know, you might be lying about the answer. I'd rather not be made a fool of."

"This information is not for the idle games of mortals," Yellowlegs snapped.

Gold gleamed in Celaena's palm. "Name your price."

The woman studied her from head to toe, sniffing once. "Nameless is my price," Yellowlegs said. "But gold will do for now."

Celaena set five extra gold coins down on the hearthstone, the heat from the flame singeing her face. Such a small fire, but she was already slick with sweat.

"Once you know this, there is no unknowing it," the witch warned. And from the gleam in Yellowlegs's eyes, Celaena knew that the old woman hadn't bought her lie about the bet for one heartbeat.

Celaena took a step closer. "Tell me."

Yellowlegs looked toward another mirror. "The Wyrd governs and forms the foundation of this world. Not just Erilea, but *all* life. There are worlds that exist beyond your knowledge, worlds that lie on top of each other and don't know it. Right now, you could be standing on the bottom of someone else's ocean. The Wyrd keeps these realms apart."

Yellowlegs began to hobble around the sitting area, lost in her own words.

"There are gates—black areas in the Wyrd that allow for life to pass between the worlds. There are Wyrdgates that lead to Erilea. All sorts of beings have come through them over the eons. Benign things, but also the dead and foul things that creep in when the gods are looking elsewhere."

Yellowlegs disappeared behind a mirror, her uneven steps echoing along. "But long ago, before humans overran this miserable world, a different sort of evil broke through the gates: the Valg. Demons from another realm, bent on the conquest of Erilea, and with the force of an endless army behind them. In Wendlyn, they fought against the Fae. Try as the immortal children might, they could not defeat them.

"Then the Fae learned that the Valg had done something unforgivable. They had taken a piece of a Wyrdgate with their dark magic, and split it into three slivers—three *keys*. One key for each of their kings. Using all three at once, the Valg Kings were able to open that Wyrdgate at will, to manipulate its power to strengthen their forces, to allow an endless line of soldiers to pour into the world. The Fae knew that they must stop it."

Celaena stared at the fire, at the mirrors, at the darkness of the wagon around her. The heat was smothering now.

"And so a small band of Fae set out to steal them from the Valg Kings," Yellowlegs said, her voice coming nearer again. "It was an impossible task; most of those fools didn't return.

"But the Wyrdkeys were indeed retrieved, and the Fae Queen Maeve banished the Valg to their realm. Yet for all her wisdom, Maeve couldn't discover how to put the keys back in the gate—and no forge, no steel, no weight could destroy them. So Maeve, believing that no one should have their power, sent them across the sea with Brannon Galathynius, first King of Terrasen, to hide on this continent. And thus the Wyrdgate remained protected, its power unused."

Silence fell. Even Yellowlegs's hobbling steps had slowed.

"So the riddle is a . . . a map to where the keys are hidden?" Celaena asked, trembling now as she realized just what kind of power Nehemia and the others had been after. Worse, what the *king* might be after.

"Yes."

Celaena licked her lips. "What might one do with the Wyrdkeys?"

"The person who holds all three Wyrdkeys would have control over the broken Wyrdgate—and all Erilea. They would be able to open and close the gate at will. They could conquer new worlds or let in all sorts of life to bend to their cause. But even one key could make someone immensely dangerous. Not enough power to open the gate, but enough to be a threat. You see, the keys themselves are pure power—power to be shaped as the wielder wills it. Tempting, isn't it?"

The words echoed through her, blending with Elena's command to find and destroy the source of evil. *Evil.* Evil that had arisen ten years ago, when a whole continent had suddenly found itself at the mercy of one man—a man who had somehow become unstoppable.

A source of power that existed outside of magic. "It can't be."

Yellowlegs only let out a confirming chuckle.

Celaena kept shaking her head, her heart beating so violently she could hardly breathe. "The king has some of the Wyrdkeys? That's how he was able to conquer the continent so easily?" But if he'd already done that—then what further plans did he have?

"Perhaps," Yellowlegs said. "If I were to wager my hard-earned gold, I'd say he has at least one."

Celaena scanned the dark, the mirrors, but saw only versions of herself looking back. She heard nothing but the crackling of the fire in the oven and her own uneven breathing.

Yellowlegs had stopped moving.

"Is there anything else?" Celaena demanded.

No response from the old woman.

"So you're going to take my money and run?" Celaena eased toward the winding path through the mirrors, and the door that now seemed impossibly far away. "What if I still have questions?" Her own movements in the mirrors sent her nerves jumping, but she kept alert and focused—reminded herself what she had to do. She drew both her daggers.

"You think steel can hurt me?" came a voice that slithered across each mirror until its origin was everywhere and nowhere.

"Here I was, thinking we were having a grand time," Celaena said, taking another step.

"Bah. Who can have a grand time when your guest is planning to kill you?"

Celaena smiled.

"Isn't that why you're moving toward the door?" Yellowlegs went on. "Not to escape, but to make sure *I* don't get past your clever, wicked daggers?"

"Tell me who else you've sold the prince's questions to and I'll let you go." Earlier, she'd been about to walk away—about to leave—when Yellowlegs's mention of Dorian had stopped her cold. Now she had no choice about what she had to do. What she *would* do to protect Dorian. It was what she'd realized last night: she did have someone left—one friend. And there was nothing she wouldn't do to keep him safe.

"And if I say that I've told no one?"

"I wouldn't believe you." Celaena spied the door at last. No sign of the witch. She paused, roughly in the center of the wagon. It would be easier to catch the woman here—easier to make it quick and clean.

"Pity," Yellowlegs said, and Celaena angled herself toward the disembodied voice. There *had* to be some hidden exit—but where? If Yellowlegs got out, if she told anyone what Dorian had asked (whatever it might be), if she told anyone what *Celaena* had asked . . .

All around Celaena, her reflection shifted and glimmered. Quick, clean, then she'd be gone.

"What happens," Yellowlegs hissed, "when the hunter becomes the hunted?"

From the corner of her eye, Celaena glimpsed the hunched form, chains sagging between the gnarled hands. She whirled toward the crone, dagger already flying—to disable, to get her down so she could—

The mirror shattered where Yellowlegs had been standing.

Behind her, there was a heavy clink, and a satisfied caw of laughter.

For all her training, Celaena wasn't fast enough to duck before the heavy chain whipped across the side of her head, and she slammed face-first into the floor.

CHAPTER 41

Chaol and Dorian stood on a balcony and watched the carnival be dismantled bit by bit. It would leave tomorrow morning, and then Chaol could finally have his men back to doing useful things. Like making sure no other assassins got into the castle.

But Chaol's most pressing problem was Celaena. Late last night, after the royal librarian had gone to bed, Chaol had returned to the library and found the genealogy records. Someone had gotten them all out of order, so it had taken him a while to locate the right one, but he at last found himself staring at the list of Terrasen's noble houses.

None of them bore the name of Sardothien, though that was little surprise. Part of him had always known that wasn't Celaena's true name. So he'd made a list—a list that now sat in his pocket, burning a hole through it—of all the noble houses she might have come from, houses with children at the time of Terrasen's conquest. There were at least six families that had survived . . . but what if she hailed from one that had been entirely slaughtered? When he had finished writing down the names, he was no closer to figuring out who she really was than he'd been at the start.

"So, are you going to ask me whatever it is you dragged me out here to ask, or am I just going to enjoy freezing my ass off for the rest of the night?" Dorian said.

Chaol raised a brow, and Dorian gave him a slight smile.

"How is she?" Chaol asked. He'd heard that they'd had dinner—and that she hadn't left his rooms until the middle of the night. Had it been a deliberate move on her part? Something to throw in his face, make him ache just a bit more?

"Coping," Dorian said. "Coping as best she can. And since I know you're too proud to ask it, I'll just tell you that no, she hasn't mentioned you. Nor do I think she will."

Chaol took a long breath. How could he convince Dorian to stay away from her? Not because he was jealous, but because Celaena might be more of a threat than Dorian could ever imagine. Only the truth would work, but . . .

"Your father is curious about you," Dorian said. "After the council meetings, he always asks me about you. I think he wants you back in Anielle."

"I know."

"Are you going to go with him?"

"Do you want me to?"

"It's not for me to decide."

Chaol clamped his teeth. He certainly wasn't going anywhere, not while Celaena was here. And not just because of who she actually was. "I have no interest in being Lord of Anielle."

"Men would kill for the kind of power that Anielle wields."

"I've never wanted it."

"No." Dorian braced his hands on the balcony rail. "No, you've never wanted anything for yourself, save for the position you have now, and Celaena."

Chaol opened his mouth, excuses already forming on his tongue.

"You think I'm blind?" Dorian asked, his gaze a frozen, ice blue. "Do you know why I approached her at the Yulemas ball? Not because I wanted to ask her to dance, but because I saw the way you two were looking at each other. Even then, I knew how you felt."

"You knew, and yet you asked her to dance." His hands clenched into fists.

"She's capable of making up her own mind. And she did." Dorian gave him a bitter smile. "About both of us."

Chaol took a steadying breath, calming his rising anger. "If you feel the way you do, then why let her stay shackled to your father? Why not find a way to get her out of her contract? Or are you just afraid that if you set her free, she'll never come back to you?"

"I'd be careful what you say," Dorian said softly.

But it was true. Even though he couldn't imagine a world without Celaena, Chaol knew he had to get her out of this castle. Yet he couldn't tell if it was for Adarlan's sake or her own.

"My father is temperamental enough to punish me—and her—if I try to broach that subject. I agree with you, I truly do: it's not right to keep her here. But you should still mind what you say." The Crown Prince of Adarlan stared him down. "And consider where your true loyalties lie."

Once, Chaol might have argued. Once, he might have protested that his loyalty to the crown was his greatest asset. But that blind loyalty and obedience had started this descent.

And it had destroyed everything.

⌒

Celaena knew she'd only been out for a few seconds, but it was long enough for Yellowlegs to yank her arms behind her back and get the chain around her wrists. Her head was pounding, and blood slid down the side of her neck, trickling into her tunic. Nothing too bad—she'd had worse wounds. Her weapons were gone, though, discarded somewhere in the wagon. Even the ones in her hair and clothes. And boots. Clever woman.

So she didn't give the witch a chance, not even a heartbeat, to realize she was conscious. With no warning, she surged her shoulders up, throwing back her head as hard as she could.

Bone cracked, and Yellowlegs howled, but Celaena had already twisted, getting her legs beneath her. Yellowlegs scrambled for the other end of the chain, fast as a viper. Celaena stomped on the length of chain between them, her other foot lashing out to meet Yellowlegs's face.

The woman went flying, as though she were made of nothing but dust and wind, tumbling into the shadows between mirrors.

Swearing under her breath, Celaena's wrists ached against the cold iron. But she'd been taught to free herself from worse. Arobynn had bound her up from head to toe and made her learn how to get loose, even if it meant spending two days prostrate on the ground in her own filth, or dislocating her shoulder to get out. So, not all that surprisingly, she had the chains off in a matter of seconds.

She yanked a handkerchief from her pocket and used it to snatch up a long mirror shard. Angling the glass, Celaena peered into the shadows where Yellowlegs had gone flying. Nothing. Just a smear of dark blood.

"Do you know how many young women I've trapped in this wagon in the past five hundred years?" Yellowlegs's voice was everywhere and nowhere. "How many Crochan witches I destroyed? They were warriors, too—such talented, beautiful warriors. They tasted like summer grass and cool water."

Confirming that Yellowlegs was a blue-blooded Ironteeth witch changed nothing, Celaena told herself. Nothing, except that she'd have to find a bigger weapon.

Celaena scanned the wagon—for the witch, for her lost daggers, for anything to use against the crone. Her gaze lifted to the shelves on the nearby wall. Books, crystal balls, paper, dead things in jars . . .

Celaena would have missed it if she'd blinked. It was coated in dirt, but still gleamed faintly in the light of the distant oven. Mounted on the wall above a woodpile was a long, single-bladed ax.

She smiled faintly as she yanked it off the wall. All around, Yellowlegs's image danced in the mirrors, a thousand possibilities for where she could be standing, watching, waiting.

Celaena swung the ax at the nearest one. Then the next. And the next.

The only way to kill a witch is to cut off her head. A friend had told her that once.

Celaena wove between the mirrors, smashing them as she went, the reflections of the crone vanishing until the real witch stood along the narrow pathway between Celaena and the hearth, the chain back in her hands.

Celaena hefted the ax over a shoulder. "One more chance," she breathed. "You agree to never say one word about me and Dorian, and I'll walk out of here."

"I can taste your lies," Yellowlegs said. Faster than should be possible, she came for Celaena, scuttling like a spider, the chain swinging from her fingers.

Celaena dodged the first whip of the chain. She heard the second before she saw it, and though it missed her, it struck a mirror and glass exploded everywhere. Celaena had no choice but to shield her eyes, to look away for one heartbeat.

It was enough.

The chain wrapped around her ankle, stinging and bruising, and then *yanked*.

The world tilted as Yellowlegs pulled her feet out from under her, and Celaena went crashing to the floor. Yellowlegs rushed for her, but

Celaena rolled across the shards, chain tangling around her, clinging to the ax with one hand, until her face brushed against the coarse fibers of the ancient rug before the oven.

There was a firm yank on the chain, and then another whipping sound. Metal slammed into Celaena's forearm, so hard that she lost her grip on the ax. She flipped onto her back, still tangled in the infernal chain, only to find the iron teeth of Baba Yellowlegs looming above her. In a flash, the witch slammed Celaena back down into the carpet.

The iron nails dug into her skin, drawing blood as the witch pinned her by the shoulder. "Hold still, you foolish girl," Yellowlegs hissed, grabbing for the length of the chain lying nearby.

The rug scratched against Celaena's fingers as she stretched for the fallen ax, just inches out of reach. Her arm throbbed mercilessly, her ankle, too. If she could just get the ax . . . Yellowlegs lunged for Celaena's neck, her teeth snapping.

Celaena threw herself to the side, narrowly dodging those iron teeth, and grabbed the ax at last. She hauled it up so hard that its blunt end slammed into the side of the old woman's face.

Yellowlegs was knocked away, collapsing in a heap of billowing brown robes. Celaena scrambled back and raised the weapon between them.

Pushing to her hands and knees, Yellowlegs spat dark blood— *blue* blood—onto the aged rug, her eyes blazing. "I am going to make you wish you'd never been born. Both you and your prince." And then Yellowlegs shot forward so fast Celaena could have sworn she was flying.

But she only got as far as Celaena's feet.

Celaena brought the ax down, throwing every bit of strength into her arms. Blue blood sprayed everywhere.

There was a smile on Baba Yellowlegs's decapitated head as it thudded to a stop.

Quiet fell. Even the fire, still burning so hot that she was sweating again, seemed to have gone silent. Celaena swallowed. Once. Twice.

Dorian couldn't know. Even though she wanted to scold him to high hell for asking questions that Yellowlegs had deemed valuable enough to sell to others, he couldn't know what had happened here. No one could.

When she at last found the strength to disentangle herself, her pants and boots were stained blue-black. Another outfit to be burned. She studied the body and the stained, soaking carpet. It hadn't been quick, but it could still be clean. A missing person was better than a decapitated corpse.

Celaena raised her eyes to the large oven grate.

CHAPTER 42

Mort chuckled when she staggered through the tomb door. "Witch Slayer, are you? Another lovely title to add to your repertoire."

"How do you know about that?" she asked, setting down her candle. She'd already burned her bloodied clothes. They had reeked as they burned—reeked like rotting flesh, just as Yellowlegs had. Fleetfoot had growled at the fireplace and tried to herd Celaena away by pressing her body against her legs.

"Oh, I can smell her on you," Mort said. "Smell her fury and wickedness."

Celaena peeled back the collar of her tunic to show the little cuts where Yellowlegs's nails had pierced the skin right above her collarbone. She'd cleaned them out, but had a feeling they would leave marks, a necklace of scars. "What do you make of those?"

Mort winced. "Those make me grateful I'm made of bronze."

"Will they harm me?"

"You killed a witch—and you're now marked by a witch. It will not be the usual sort of wound." Mort's eyes narrowed. "You understand that you may have just landed yourself in a heap of trouble."

Celaena groaned.

"Baba Yellowlegs was a leader—a queen to her clan," Mort went on. "When they destroyed the Crochan family, they joined with the Blackbeaks and the Bluebloods in the Ironteeth Alliance. They still honor those oaths."

"But I thought all the witches were gone—scattered to the winds."

"Gone? The Crochans and those who followed them have been in hiding for generations. But the clans in the Ironteeth Alliance still travel about, as Baba did. Though many more of them live in the ruined and dark places of the world, content in their wickedness. But I suspect that when the Yellowlegs learn of their matron's death, they will muster the Blackbeaks and the Bluebloods and demand answers from the king. And you will be fortunate if they do not come on their brooms and drag you into it."

She grimaced. "I hope you're wrong."

Mort's brows lowered slightly. "So do I."

Celaena spent an hour in the tomb, reading through the riddle on the wall, puzzling over Yellowlegs's words. Wyrdkeys, Wyrdgates . . . it was all so strange, so incomprehensible and terrifying. And if the king had them—if he even had *one* . . .

Celaena shuddered.

When staring at the riddle gave her no further answers, Celaena trudged back to her rooms for a much-needed nap.

At least she'd finally discovered a possible source of the king's power. But she still needed to learn more. And then the real question: what was the king planning to do with the keys that he had not done already?

She had a feeling she didn't want to know.

But the library catacombs might contain the answer to that most horrible of questions. There was a book she could use to gain access to that answer—a book that might have the unlocking spell she was looking for. And she knew that *The Walking Dead* would find her the moment she began looking for it.

Halfway up to her rooms, all plans for a nap vanished as Celaena turned back around and went to retrieve Damaris, and every other ancient blade she could carry.

⟳

He shouldn't be here. He was only asking for trouble—another fight that might wind up tearing the castle in two. And if Celaena attacked him again, Chaol knew with absolute certainty that he'd let her kill him, if she really wanted.

He didn't even know what he'd say to her. But he had to say something, if only to end the silence and the tension that kept him awake night after night and prevented him from focusing on his duties.

She wasn't in her rooms, but he went in anyway, wandering over to her desk. It was as messy as Dorian's, and covered in papers and books. He might have turned away had he not seen the strange symbols written on everything, symbols that reminded him of the mark he'd seen burn on her forehead at the duel. He'd somehow forgotten about it in the months that had gone by. Was it . . . was it something connected to her past?

Glancing over his shoulder, listening for any sign of Philippa or Celaena, he rifled through the documents. Just scribblings—drawings of the symbols and random underlined words. Perhaps they were no more than doodles, he tried to tell himself.

He was about to turn away when he caught sight of a document peeking out from a stack of books. It was written in careful calligraphy and signed by multiple people.

Easing it out from under the books, Chaol picked up the thick paper and read.

The world dropped out from beneath his feet.

It was Celaena's will. Signed two days before Nehemia's death.

And she'd given everything—every last copper—to him.

His throat tightened as he stared at the sum and the list of assets, including an apartment in a warehouse in the slums and all the wealth inside.

And she had signed it all to him, with only one request: that he consider giving some of it to Philippa.

"I'm not going to change it."

He whirled, finding her leaning against the doorframe, her arms crossed. Though the position was so familiar, her face was cold, blank. He let the document slip from his fingers.

The list of noble houses in his pocket became leaden. What if he'd been jumping to conclusions? Perhaps the song wasn't actually a dirge of Terrasen. Maybe it had been another language he'd never heard of.

She watched him like a cat. "It would be too much trouble to bother changing it," she went on. She wore a beautiful, ancient-looking blade at her side, along with a few daggers he'd never seen before. Where had she gotten them?

There were so many words trying to work their way out of him that he couldn't speak at all. All of that money—she'd left everything to him. Left it to him because of what she'd felt for him . . . even Dorian had seen it from the start.

"At least now," she said, pushing off the doorframe and turning away, "when the king sacks you for being so damn lousy at your job, you'll have something to fall back on."

He couldn't breathe. She hadn't just done it out of generosity. But rather because she knew that if he ever lost his position, he'd have to consider going back to Anielle, to his father's money. And that it'd kill part of him to do that.

But she'd have to be dead for him to see that money. Verifiably dead, and not a traitor to the crown, either—if she died a traitor, then all her assets had to go to the king.

And the only way she'd die a traitor would be for her to do what he feared: ally with this secret organization, find Aelin Galathynius, and return to Terrasen. This was a hint that she had no intention of doing that. She had no plans to reclaim her lost title, and posed no threat to Adarlan or Dorian. He'd been wrong. Yet again, he'd been wrong.

"Get out of my chambers," she said from the foyer, before striding into the gaming room and slamming the door behind her.

He hadn't wept when Nehemia died, or when he'd thrown Celaena in the dungeons, or even when she'd returned with Grave's head, utterly different from the woman he had grown to love so fiercely.

But when Chaol walked out, leaving that damning will behind him, he didn't even make it to his own room. He barely made it into an empty broom closet before the sobs hit.

CHAPTER 43

Celaena stood in the gaming room, staring at the pianoforte as she heard Chaol quickly leave. She hadn't played in weeks.

Originally, it had been just because she didn't have time. Because Archer and the tomb and Chaol had occupied every moment of her day. Then Nehemia had died—and she hadn't gone into this room once, hadn't wanted to look at the instrument, hadn't wanted to hear or make music ever again.

Shoving the encounter with Chaol out of her mind, Celaena slowly folded back the lid of the pianoforte and stroked the ivory keys.

But she couldn't push down, couldn't bring herself to make a sound. Nehemia should have been here—to help with Yellowlegs and the riddle, to tell her what to do with Chaol, to smile as Celaena played something particularly clever for her.

Nehemia was gone. And the world . . . it was moving on without her.

When Sam had died, she had tucked him into her heart, tucked him in alongside her other beloved dead, whose names she kept so secret she sometimes forgot them. But Nehemia—Nehemia wouldn't fit. It was as if her heart was too full of the dead, too full of those lives that had ended well before their time.

She couldn't seal Nehemia away like that, not when that blood-stained bed and those ugly words still haunted her every step, every breath.

So Celaena just hovered at the pianoforte, tracing her fingers over the keys again and again, and let the silence devour her.

An hour later, Celaena stood before the strange, second staircase at the end of the forgotten hall of ancient records, a clock chiming somewhere far in the library above. The images of Fae and flora danced along the fire-lit stairwell, spiraling out of sight, down and down into unknown depths. She'd found *The Walking Dead* almost immediately—discarded on a lonely table between some stacks. As though it had been waiting for her. And it had been the work of a few minutes to find a spell inside that claimed to unlock any door. She'd quickly memorized it, practicing a few times on a locked closet.

It had taken all of her self-control not to scream when she'd heard the lock snap free the first time. Or the second.

It was no wonder Nehemia and her family kept such power a secret. And no wonder the King of Adarlan had sought it out for himself.

Staring down into the stairwell, Celaena touched Damaris, then looked at the two jeweled daggers hanging from her belt. She was fine. No reason to be nervous. What sort of evil did she expect to find in a library, of all places?

Surely the king had better places to hide his dark dealings. At best, she'd find more hints as to whether he had any Wyrdkeys and where he kept them. At worst . . . she would run into the cloaked person she'd seen outside the library that night. But the glowing eyes she'd glimpsed on the other side of that door belonged to a rodent of some sort—nothing more. And if she was wrong . . . Well, whatever it was, after taking down the ridderak, *this* shouldn't be too hard, right?

Right. Celaena stepped forward, pausing on the landing.

Nothing. No feelings of terror, no otherworldly warnings. Not a thing.

She took another step, then another, holding her breath as she wound around the staircase until she could no longer see the top. She could have sworn that the etchings on the wall moved all around her, that the beautiful, feral faces of the Fae turned to look as she passed.

The only noises were her footsteps and the whispering of the torch flame. A chill ran down her spine, and Celaena stopped as the dark void of the hallway came into view.

She was at the sealed iron door a moment later. She didn't give herself the luxury of reconsidering her plan as she took out her piece of chalk and traced two Wyrdmarks onto the door, whispering the accompanying words at the same time. They burned on her tongue, but as she finished speaking, she heard a faint, dull *thud* as something in the door slid open.

She swore under her breath. The spell truly worked. She didn't want to think about all that implied, about how it was able to work on iron, the one element supposedly immune to magic. And not when there were so many awful spells contained in *The Walking Dead*—spells to summon demons, to raise the dead, to torture others until they begged for death . . .

With a firm tug, she yanked the door open, wincing as it whined across the gray stone floor. A stale, cold breeze ruffled her hair. She drew Damaris.

After checking and double-checking that she could not be locked inside, she crossed the threshold.

Her torch revealed a small staircase of about ten steps, which led down to another long, narrow passageway. Cobwebs and dust filled every inch of it, but it wasn't the neglected look of the place that made her pause.

Rather it was the doors, the dozens of iron doors that lined both sides of the hallway. All as nondescript as the door behind her, all revealing nothing of what might be behind them. At the opposite end of the hall, another iron door gleamed dully in the torchlight.

What was this place?

She descended the stairs. It was so silent. As if the very air held its breath.

She held her torch high, Damaris in her other hand, and approached the first iron door. It had no handle, the surface marked only by a single line. The door across from it had two marks. Numbers one and two. Odd numbers on the left, even on the right. She kept moving, igniting torch after torch, brushing away the curtains of cobwebs. As she walked farther down the hall, the numbers on the doors rose.

Is this some sort of dungeon?

But the floor held no traces of blood, no remnants of bones or weapons. It didn't even smell that bad—just dusty. Dry. She tried opening one of the doors, but it was firmly locked. All of the doors were locked. And some instinct told her to keep them that way.

Her head throbbed slightly with the beginnings of a headache.

The hallway went on and on, until she reached the door at the far end, the cells on either side numbered ninety-eight and ninety-nine.

Beyond them was a final, unmarked door. She set her torch in a bracket beside the last door and grabbed the ring on the door to pull it open. This one was significantly lighter than the first, but also locked.

And unlike the doors lining the hall, this one seemed to *ask* her to unlock it—as though it needed to be opened. So Celaena sketched the unlocking spell again, the chalk bone-white against the ancient metal. The door yielded without a sound.

Perhaps these were Gavin's dungeons. From the time of Brannon. That would explain the Fae depictions on the staircase above. Perhaps he'd used these iron-gated cells to imprison the demon-soldiers of Erawan's army. Or the wicked things Gavin and his war band hunted down . . .

Her mouth went dry as she passed through the second door and ignited the torches along the way. Again, the light revealed a small set of stairs leading down into a hallway. Yet this one veered to the right, and was significantly shorter. There was nothing in the shadows— just more and more locked iron doors on either side. It was so, so quiet . . .

She walked until she reached the door on the other end of the hall. Sixty-six cells this time, all sealed shut. She unlocked the end door with the Wyrdmarks.

She entered the third passageway, which also made a sharp right turn, and found it to be even shorter. Thirty-three cells.

The fourth hallway veered right again, and she counted twenty-two cells. The slight throbbing in her head turned into a full-on pounding, but it was so far to her rooms, and she *was* here already . . .

Celaena paused before the fourth end door.

It's a spiral. A labyrinth. Bringing you deeper and deeper inside, farther belowground . . .

She bit her lip but unlocked the door. Eleven cells. She increased her pace, and swiftly reached the fifth door. Nine cells.

She approached the sixth door and halted.

A different sort of chill went through her as she stared at the sixth portal.

The center of the spiral?

As the chalk met the iron door to form the Wyrdmarks, a voice in the back of her mind told her to run. And though she wanted to listen, she opened the door anyway.

Her torch revealed a hallway in ruin. Parts of the walls had caved in, and the wooden beams were left in splinters. Cobwebs stretched between the broken shafts of wood, and tattered scraps of cloth, impaled upon rock and beam, swayed in the slight breeze.

Death had been here. And not too long ago. If this place were as ancient as Gavin and Brannon, most of the cloth would be dust.

She looked at the three cells that lined the short hallway. There was one more door at the end, which hung crookedly on its one remaining hinge. Darkness filled the void beyond.

But it was the third cell that held her interest.

The iron door to the third cell had been smashed, its surface dented and folded in upon itself. But not from the outside.

Celaena raised Damaris before her as she faced the open cell.

Whoever had been within had broken loose.

A quick sweep of her torch across the threshold revealed nothing save for bones—piles of bones, most of them splintered beyond recognition.

She snapped her attention back to the hallway. Nothing moved.

Gingerly, she stepped into the cell.

Iron chains dangled from the walls, broken off where manacles would have been. The dark stone was covered in white marks; dozens and dozens of long, deep gouges in groups of four.

Fingernails.

She turned around to face the broken cell door. There were countless marks on it.

How could someone make such lines in iron? In stone?

She shuddered and quickly stepped out of the cell.

She glanced back the way she had come, which glowed with the torches she'd lit, and then at the dark, open space that led onward.

You're near the center of the spiral. Just see what it is—see if it yields any answers. Elena said to look for clues . . .

She swung Damaris in her hand a few times—only to loosen her wrist, of course. Rolling her neck, she entered the gloom.

There were no torch brackets here. The seventh portal revealed only a short passageway and one open door. An eighth gate.

The walls on either side of the eighth door were damaged and claw-marked. Her head gave a violent throb, then quieted as she stepped nearer.

Beyond the portal lay a spiral staircase that led upward, so high that she couldn't see the top. A straight ascent into darkness.

But to where?

The stairwell stank, and she held Damaris before her as she ascended the steps, taking care to avoid the fallen stones that littered the ground.

Up and up and up she climbed, grateful for all her training. Her headache only grew worse, but when she reached the top, she forgot about fatigue, forgot about pain.

She raised the torch. Shimmering obsidian walls surrounded her, reaching high, high, high—so high that she couldn't see the ceiling. She was inside some sort of chamber at the bottom of a tower.

Twining through the strange stone walls, greenish veins glittered in the torchlight. She had seen this material before. Seen it—

The king's ring. The ring on Perrington's finger. And Cain's . . .

She touched the stone, and a shock went through her, her head pounding so badly she gagged. The Eye of Elena gave a pulse of blue light but quickly died, as if the light itself had been sucked toward the stone and devoured.

She staggered back toward the stairs.

Gods above. What is this?

As if in response, a boom shuddered through the tower, so loud that she jumped back. It echoed and echoed, turning metallic.

She raised her gaze to the darkness above.

"I know where I am," she whispered as the sound subsided.

The clock tower.

CHAPTER 44

Dorian stared at the odd spiral staircase. Celaena had found the legendary catacombs beneath the library. Of course she had. If there were anyone in Erilea who could find something like that, it would be Celaena.

He'd been just about to go to lunch when he'd seen Celaena strut into the library, a sword strapped across her back. Perhaps he would have let her go about her own business were it not for her braided hair. Celaena *never* tied back her hair unless she was fighting. And when she was about to get messy.

It wasn't spying. And it wasn't sneaking. Dorian was merely curious. He followed her through long-forgotten hallways and rooms, always staying far behind, keeping his steps silent as Chaol and Brullo had taught him years ago. He'd followed until Celaena had disappeared down that staircase with a suspicious glance over her shoulder.

Yes, Celaena was up to something. And so Dorian had waited. One minute. Five minutes. Ten minutes before following after her. To make it seem like an accident if their paths crossed.

And now what did he see? Nothing but junk. Old parchment and books tossed around. Beyond was a second spiral staircase, lit in the same manner as the previous one.

A chill went through him. He didn't like any of this. What was Celaena doing here?

As if in answer, his magic screamed at him to run in the opposite direction—to find help. But the main library was a long way off, and by the time he could get there and back, something might happen. Something might already have happened . . .

Dorian quickly descended the staircase and found a dimly lit hallway with a single door left ajar, two marks written on it in chalk. When he saw the cell-lined hallway beyond, he froze. The iron reeked, somehow—and made his stomach turn.

"Celaena?" he called down the hallway. No response. "Celaena?" Nothing.

He had to tell her to get out. Whatever this place was, neither of them should be here. Even if the power in his blood wasn't screaming it, he would have known. He had to get her out.

Dorian descended the staircase.

⁓

Celaena half ran, half jumped down the stairs, getting away from the interior of the clock tower as fast as she could. Though it had been months since she had encountered the dead during the duel with Cain, the memory of being slammed into the dark wall of the tower was still too near. She could see the dead grinning at her, and recalled Elena's words on Samhuinn about the eight guardians in the clock tower and how she should stay far from them.

Her head ached so badly that she could barely focus on the steps beneath her feet.

What had been in there? This had nothing to do with Gavin, or Brannon. Maybe the dungeon had been built then, but this—all of this—had to be connected to the king. Because he had built the clock tower; built it out of—

Obsidian the gods forbade
And stone they greatly feared.

But—but the keys were supposed to be small. Not mammoth, like the clock tower. Not—

Celaena hit the bottom of the clock stairs and froze as she beheld the passage that contained the destroyed cell.

The torches had been extinguished. She looked behind her, toward the clock tower. The darkness seemed to expand, reaching for her. She wasn't alone.

Clutching her own torch, keeping her breathing steady, she crept along the ruined passage. Nothing—no sounds, no hint of another person in the passage. But . . .

Halfway down, she stopped again and set down the torch. She'd marked all the turns, counted her steps as she came here. She knew the way in the dark, could find her way back blindfolded. And if she wasn't alone down here, then her torch was a beacon. And she was in no mood to be a target. She put out the torch with a grind of her heel.

Complete darkness.

She lifted Damaris higher, adjusting to the dark. Only it wasn't wholly black. A faint glow issued from her amulet—a glow that allowed her to see only dim shapes, as if the darkness were too strong for the Eye. The hair on the back of her neck rose. The only other time she'd seen the amulet glow like that . . . Feeling along the wall with her other hand, not daring to turn around, she eased back toward the library.

There was a scrape of nail against stone, and then the sound of breathing.

It was not her own.

It peered out from the shadows of the cell, clutching at its cloak with taloned hands. Food. For the first time in months. She was so warm, so teeming with life. It skittered out of the cell past her as she continued her blind retreat.

Since they had locked it down here to rot, since they had gotten tired of playing with it, it had forgotten so many things. It had forgotten its own name, forgotten what it used to be. But it now knew more useful things—better things. How to hunt, how to feed, how to use those marks to open and close doors. It had paid attention during the long years; it had watched them make the marks.

And once they had left, it had waited until it knew they weren't coming back. Until *he* was looking elsewhere and had taken all his other things with him. And then it had begun opening the doors, one after another. Some shred of it remained mortal enough to always seal those doors shut, to come back here and form the marks that again locked the doors, to keep it contained.

But she had come here. She had learned the marks. Which meant she had to know—to know what had been done to it. She had to have been a part of it, the breaking and shattering and then the brutal rebuilding. And since she had come here . . .

It ducked into another shadow and waited for her to walk into its claws.

Celaena stopped her retreat as the breathing halted. Silence.

The blue light around her grew brighter.

Celaena put a hand to her chest.

The amulet flared.

⁓

It had been stalking the little men who lived above for weeks now, contemplating how they would taste. But there was always that cursed light near them, light that burned its sensitive eyes. There was always something that sent it skittering back here to the comfort of the stone.

Rats and crawling things had been its only food for too long, their blood and bones thin and tasteless. But this female . . . it had seen her twice before. First with that same faint, blue light at her throat—then a second time, when it hadn't seen her as much as *smelled* her from the other side of that iron door.

Upstairs, the blue light had been enough to keep it away—the blue light that had tasted of power. But down here, down in the shadow of the black, breathing stone, that light was diminished. Down here, now that it had put out the torches she'd ignited, there was nothing to stop it, and no one to hear her.

It had not forgotten, even in the twisted pathways of its memory, what had been done to it on that stone table.

With a dripping maw, it smiled.

⁓

The Eye of Elena burned bright as a flame, and there was a hiss in her ear.

Celaena whirled, striking before she could get a good look at the cloaked figure behind her. She glimpsed only a flash of withered skin and jagged, stumpy teeth before she sliced Damaris across its chest.

It screamed—screamed like nothing she had ever heard as the ragged cloth ripped, revealing a bony, misshapen chest peppered with scars. It slammed a clawed hand into her face as it fell, its eyes gleaming from the light of the amulet. An animal's eyes, capable of seeing in the dark.

The person—creature—from the hallway. From the other side of the door. She didn't even see where she had wounded it as she hit the ground. Blood rushed from her nose and filled her mouth. She staggered into a sprint back toward the library.

She leapt over fallen beams and chunks of stone, letting the Eye light her way, barely keeping her footing as she slipped on bones. The creature barreled after her, tearing through the obstacles as if they were no more than gossamer curtains. It stood like a man, but it wasn't a man—no, that face was something out of a nightmare. And its strength, to be able to shove aside those fallen beams as though they were stalks of wheat . . .

The iron doors had been there to keep this thing in.

And she had unlocked all of them.

She dashed up the short stairs and through the first doorway. As she veered left, it caught her by the back of her tunic. The cloth tore. Celaena slammed into the opposite wall, ducking as it lunged for her.

Damaris sang, and the creature roared, falling back. Black blood squirted from the wound across its abdomen. But she hadn't cut deep enough.

Surging to her feet, blood running down her back from where its claws had punctured, Celaena drew a dagger with her other hand.

The hood had fallen off the creature, revealing what looked like a man's face—looked like, but no longer was. His hair was sparse, hanging off his gleaming skull in clumpy strings, and his lips . . . there was such scarring around his mouth, as though someone had ripped it open and sewed it shut, then ripped it open again.

The creature pushed a gnarled hand against its abdomen, panting through those brown, broken teeth as it looked at her—*looked* at her with such hatred that she couldn't move. It was such a human expression . . .

"What *are* you?" She gasped, swinging Damaris as she took another step back.

But it suddenly began clawing at itself, tearing at the dark robes, pulling out its hair, pushing against its skull, as if it would reach in and rip something out. And the shrieks it made, the rage and despair—

The creature had been *in the castle hallway*.

Which meant . . .

This thing, this person—it knew how to use the Wyrdmarks, too. And with its unnatural strength, no mortal barrier would keep it contained.

The creature tipped its head back, and its animal eyes settled on her again. Fixating. A predator anticipating the taste of its prey.

Celaena turned and ran like hell.

Dorian had just passed through the third door when he heard the scream of something not human. A series of crashing noises filled the passage, and the bellowing was cut short with each slam.

"Celaena?" Dorian yelled in the direction of the commotion.

Another slam.

"Celaena!"

Then— *"Dorian, run!"*

The high-pitched shriek that followed Celaena's command shook the walls. The torches sputtered.

Dorian drew his rapier as Celaena came flying up the stairs, blood leaking from her face, and slammed the iron door shut behind her. She raced toward him, a sword in one hand, a dagger in the other. The amulet on her neck glowed blue, like the hottest fire.

Celaena was upon him in a second. The iron door burst open behind them, and—

The thing that came out was not of this earth—it couldn't be. It looked like something that used to be a man, but was twisted and dried and broken, with hunger and madness written on every protruding bone in its body. *Gods. Oh, gods.* What had she awoken?

They sprinted down the hall, and Dorian swore as he beheld the steps up to the next door. The time it would take for them to climb the stairs . . .

But Celaena was fast. And months of training had made her strong. To his eternal humiliation, as they hit the bottom of the stairs, she grasped him by the collar of his tunic, half-hauling him up the steps. She hurled him into the hallway beyond the threshold.

Behind them, the thing shrieked. Dorian turned in time to see its broken teeth glistening as it leapt up the stairs. Lightning swift, Celaena slammed the iron door shut in the creature's face.

Only one more door—he could picture the landing that led back to the first hallway, then that spiral staircase, then the second staircase, and—

What then, when they reached the main library? What could they do against this thing?

As Dorian saw the naked terror on Celaena's face, he knew she wondered the same.

~

Celaena threw Dorian into the hallway and then hurled herself backward, slamming into the last iron door that separated the thing's lair from the rest of the library. She put her weight into it and saw stars as the creature barreled into the other side. Gods, it was strong—strong and wild and unyielding . . .

For a moment, she stumbled away, and it tried to fling open the door. But Celaena lunged, throwing her back against it.

Its hand caught in the door and the creature bellowed, latching its claws into Celaena's shoulder as she pushed and pushed. Blood ran from her nose, mingling with the blood running down her shoulders. The claws dug in farther.

Dorian rushed to the door, bracing his back against it. He panted, gaping at her.

They had to seal the door. Even if this thing was intelligent enough to know the Wyrdmarks, they had to buy some time for themselves. She had to give Dorian enough time to get away. They would run out of strength soon, and the thing would break through and kill them and whoever else got in its path.

There had to be a lock somewhere, some way to shut it in, to slow it down just for a moment . . .

"*Push*," she breathed to Dorian. The creature gained an inch, but Celaena shoved hard, drawing on the strength of her legs. It roared again, so loudly that she thought blood would pour from her ears. Dorian swore viciously.

She glanced at him, not even feeling the pain of the talons embedded in her skin. Sweat ran down Dorian's brow as—as—

The metal began to heat along the edge of the door, glowing red, then fizzing—

Magic was here; magic was working right now, trying to seal the door against the creature. But it wasn't coming from her.

Dorian's eyes were scrunched in concentration, his face deathly pale.

She'd been right. Dorian *did* have magic. This was the information Yellowlegs had wanted to sell to the highest bidder, sell to the king himself. It was knowledge that could change *everything*. It could change the world.

Dorian had magic.

And if he didn't stop, he was going to burn himself out on the iron door.

⁓

The door suffocated Dorian. He was in a coffin, a coffin with no air. His magic couldn't breathe. *He* couldn't breathe.

Celaena swore as the creature gained ground. Dorian didn't even know what he was doing, only that he *needed* to seal this door. His magic had chosen the method. He pushed with his legs, pushed with his back, pushed his magic to the breaking point as he sought to weld the door. Spinning, heat, strangling . . .

The magic slipped from him.

The creature pushed hard, sending Dorian staggering forward. But Celaena threw herself harder against the door as he regained his balance.

Celaena's blade lay a few feet away, but what good was a sword?

They had no hope of escaping with their lives.

Celaena's eyes met with his, the question all too visible on her bloodied face:

What have I done?

Still gripped by the creature's talons, Celaena couldn't even move as Dorian made a sudden lunge for Damaris. The creature tried again to break free, and the prince swung, making direct contact with its wrist. Its shriek penetrated her bones, but the door slammed shut completely. Celaena stumbled, the beast's dismembered hand protruding from her shoulder, but she shoved back against the door as the creature again launched itself at it.

"What the hell is it?" Dorian barked, throwing his weight back against the iron.

"I don't know," Celaena breathed. Not having the luxury of a healer, she ripped the filthy hand from her shoulder, biting down on her scream. "It was down there," she panted. Another thud from behind the door. "You can't seal that door with magic. We need to—need to seal this another way." And find something that would outsmart whatever unlocking spells this creature knew—some way to keep it from getting out. She choked on the blood running from her nose into her mouth, and spat it onto the floor. "There is a book—*The Walking Dead*. It'll have the answer."

Their eyes met and held. A line stretched taut between them—a moment of trust, and a promise of answers from both of them.

"Where's the book?" Dorian asked.

"In the library. It'll find you. I can hold this for a few moments."

Not needing it to make sense, Dorian bolted upstairs. He ran through stack after stack, his fingers reading the titles, faster and faster, knowing each second drained her strength. He was about to bellow his frustration when he ran past a table and beheld a large black volume resting upon its surface.

The Walking Dead.

She had been right. Why was she always right, in her own odd way? He grabbed the book and hurtled to the secret chamber. She had shut her eyes, and her teeth were red with her own blood as she gritted them.

"Here," Dorian said. Without needing her to ask, he shoved himself into the door as she dropped to the floor and grabbed the book to her. Her hands trembled as she flipped a page, then another, and another. Her blood splattered onto the text.

"'To bind or to contain,'" she read aloud. Dorian peered down at the dozens of symbols on the page.

"This will work?" he asked.

"I hope so," she wheezed, already moving, clutching the open book in one hand. "Once the spell is cast, just passing over that threshold will hold it in place long enough to kill it." She dipped her fingers into the wounds on her chest, and he could only gape as she made the first mark, and then the second, turning her battered body into an inkwell as she drew mark after mark around the door.

"But for it to pass over the threshold," Dorian panted, "we'd have to—"

"Open the door," she finished for him, nodding.

He shifted so she could reach to draw above his head, their breath mingling.

Celaena let out a long breath as she made the last mark, and suddenly, they glowed a faint blue. He held himself against the door, even as he felt the iron go rigid.

"You can let go," she breathed, angling the sword. "Let go, and get the hell behind me."

At least she didn't insult him by telling him to flee.

With a final breath, he leapt away.

The creature slammed into the door, flinging it open.

And, just like she had said, it froze on the threshold, its animalistic eyes wild as its head jutted out into the hall. There was a pause then, a pause during which Dorian could have sworn that Celaena and the creature looked at each other—and its wildness calmed, just for a moment. Just for a moment, and then Celaena moved.

The sword flashed in the torchlight, and there was the squish of flesh and crunch of bone. The neck was too thick to sever in one blow, so before Dorian could draw another breath, she struck again.

The head hit the ground with a thud, black blood spraying from the severed neck—from the body that still stood paralyzed in the doorway.

"Shit," Dorian breathed. "Shit."

Celaena moved again, slamming her sword down onto the head, skewering it, as if she thought it could still bite.

Dorian was still spewing a steady stream of curses as Celaena reached out to the bloody marks around the door and swiped a finger through one of them.

The creature's headless body collapsed, the holding spell broken.

It had barely finished falling before Celaena made four strikes: three to sever the emaciated torso in two, and a fourth to stab through where its heart would be. His bile rose up again as she angled her blade a fifth time, prying open the chest cavity of the creature.

Whatever she saw made her face go even paler. Dorian didn't want to look.

With grim efficiency, she kicked the too-human head through the threshold, sending it knocking into the withered corpse of the creature. Then she shut the iron door and traced a few more marks over the threshold that glowed and then faded.

Celaena faced him, but Dorian looked at the door again, now sealed.

"How long does that—that *spell* hold?" He almost choked on the word.

"I don't know," she said, shaking her head. "Until I remove the marks, I think."

"I don't think we can let anyone else know about this," he said carefully.

She laughed, a bit wildly. Telling others, even Chaol, would mean answering difficult questions—questions that could earn them both a trip to the butchering block.

"So," Celaena said, spitting blood onto the stones, "do you want to explain yourself first, or should I?"

Celaena went first, because Dorian desperately needed to change his filthy tunic, and talking seemed like a good idea while he stripped naked in his dressing room. She sat on his bed, not looking much better herself—which was why they'd taken the dark servants' passages back to his tower.

"Beneath the library stretches an ancient dungeon, I think," Celaena said, trying to keep her voice as soft as possible. She caught a gleam of golden skin through the half-open door to his dressing room, and looked away. "I think . . . I think someone kept the creature in there until it broke out of its cell. It's been living under the library ever since."

No need to tell him that she was starting to believe the king had *created* it. The clock tower had been built by the king himself—so he had to know what it connected to. She knew that the creature had been made, because in its chest had been a human heart. Celaena was willing to bet that the king had used at least one Wyrdkey to make both tower and monster.

"What I don't understand," Dorian said from the dressing room, "is why this thing can now break through the iron doors when it couldn't before."

"Because I was an idiot and broke the spells on them when I walked through."

A lie—sort of. But she didn't want to explain, *couldn't* explain, why the creature had been able to break out before and had never hurt anyone until now. Why it had been in the hallway that night and disappeared, why the librarians were all alive and unhurt.

But perhaps the man that the creature had once been . . . Perhaps he hadn't been entirely lost. There were so many questions now, so many things left unanswered.

"And that last spell you did—on the door. It'll keep forever?" Dorian appeared in a new tunic and pants, still barefoot. The sight of his feet felt strangely intimate.

She shrugged, fighting the urge to wipe her bloody, filthy face. He'd offered her his private bath, but she'd refused. *That* felt too intimate, too.

"The book says it's a permanent binding spell, so I don't think anyone but us will be capable of getting through."

Unless the king wants to get in and uses one of the Wyrdkeys.

Dorian ran a hand through his hair, sitting down beside her on the bed. "Where did it come from?"

"I don't know," she lied. The king's ring flashed in her memory. That couldn't be the Wyrdkey, though; Yellowlegs had said they were slivers of black rock, not—not forged into shapes. But he could have made the ring using the key. She understood now why Archer and his society both coveted and sought to destroy it. If the king could use it to *make* creatures . . .

If he had made *more* . . .

There had been so many doors. Well over two hundred, all locked. And both Kaltain and Nehemia had mentioned wings—wings in their dreams, wings flapping through the Ferian Gap. What was the king brewing there?

"Tell me," Dorian pressed.

"I don't know," she lied again, hating herself for it. How could she make him understand a truth that might shatter everything he loved?

"That book," Dorian said. "How did you know it would help?"

"I found it one day in the library. It seemed to . . . trail me. Showed up in my rooms when I hadn't brought it there, reappeared in the library; it was full of those kinds of spells."

"But it's not magic," Dorian said, paling.

"Not the magic that you have. This is different. I didn't even know if that spell would work. Speaking of which," she said, meeting his eyes, "you have . . . magic."

He scanned her face, and she quelled the urge to fidget.

"What do you want me to say?"

"Tell me how you have magic," she breathed. "Tell me how *you* have it and the rest of the world doesn't. Tell me how you discovered it, and what manner of magic it is. Tell me everything." He started to shake his head, but she leaned forward. "You just saw me break at least a dozen of your father's laws. You think I'm going to turn you over to him when you could just as easily destroy me?"

Dorian sighed. After a moment, he said, "A few weeks ago, I . . . erupted. I got so mad at a council meeting that I stormed out and punched a wall. And somehow, the stone cracked, and then the window nearby shattered, too. Since then, I've been trying to figure out where it comes from, what kind of power it is, exactly. And how to control it. But it just . . . happens. Like—"

"Like when you used it to stop me from killing Chaol."

His neck bobbed as he swallowed hard.

She couldn't meet his stare as she said, "Thank you for that. If you hadn't stopped me, I . . ." No matter what had happened between her and Chaol, no matter what she now felt for him, if she had killed him that night, there would have been no coming back from it, no recovering. In some ways . . . in some ways, it might have made her into just another version of that thing in the library. It made her sick to even think about it. "No matter what your magic might be, it saved more lives than his that night."

Dorian shifted. "I still need to learn to control it—or else it might happen anywhere. In front of anyone. I've gotten lucky so far, but I don't think that luck will last."

"Does anyone else know? Chaol? Roland?"

"No. Chaol doesn't know, and Roland just left with Duke Perrington. They're going to Morath for a few months to . . . to oversee the situation in Eyllwe."

It all had to be tied together: the king, the magic, Dorian's power, the Wyrdmarks, even the creature. The prince went to his bed and hoisted up the mattress, pulling out a concealed book. Not the best hiding place, but a valiant effort. "I've been looking through the genealogy charts for Adarlan's noble families. We've hardly had any magic-users in the past few generations."

There were so many things she could tell him, but if she did, it would just result in too many questions. So Celaena merely studied the pages he displayed for her, flipping through one after another.

"Wait," she said. The puncture wounds in her shoulder gave a burst of pain when she lifted her hand to the book. She scanned the page he'd stopped on, her heart pounding as another clue about the king and his plans slipped into place. She let him continue on.

"See?" Dorian said, closing the book. "I'm not quite sure where it comes from."

He was still watching her, warily. She met his gaze and said quietly, "Ten years ago, many of the people I . . . people I loved were executed for having magic." Pain and guilt flickered in his eyes, but she went on. "So you'll understand when I say that I have no desire to see anyone else die for it, even the son of the man who ordered those deaths."

"I'm sorry," he said quietly. "So, what do we do now?"

"Eat a giant meal, see a healer, take a bath. In that order."

He snorted and playfully nudged her with a knee.

She leaned forward, clasping her hands between her legs. "We wait. We keep an eye on that door to make sure no one tries to go in, and . . . just take it day by day."

He took one of her hands in his own, staring toward the window. "Day by day."

CHAPTER
45

Celaena didn't get a meal, or take a bath, or see a healer for her shoulder.

Instead, she hurried to the dungeon, not even looking at the guards that she passed. Exhaustion ripped at her, but fear kept her moving, almost sprinting down the stairs.

They want to use me. They tricked me, Kaltain had said. And in Dorian's book of Adarlan's noble lineages, the Rompier family had been listed as one with a strong magical line, supposedly vanished two generations ago.

Sometimes I think they brought me here, Kaltain had said. *Not to marry Perrington, but for another purpose.*

Brought Kaltain here, the way Cain had been brought here. Cain, of the White Fang Mountains, where powerful shamans had long ruled the tribes.

Her mouth went dry as she strode down the dungeon hallway to Kaltain's cell. She stopped in front, staring through the bars.

It was empty.

All that was left inside was Celaena's cloak, discarded in the kicked-up hay. As if Kaltain had struggled against whoever had come to take her.

Celaena was at the guards' station a moment later, pointing down the hall. "Where is Kaltain?" Even as she said it, a memory began to clear, a memory hazed by days spent sedated in the dungeons.

The guards looked at each other, then at her torn and bloody clothes, before one said, "The duke took her—to Morath. To be his wife."

She stalked out of the dungeon, heading for her rooms.

Something is coming, Kaltain had whispered. *And I am to greet it.*

My headaches are worse every day, and full of all those flapping wings.

Celaena nearly stumbled on a step. *Roland has been suffering from awful headaches lately*, Dorian told her a few days ago. And now Roland, who shared Dorian's Havilliard blood, had gone to Morath, too.

Gone, or been taken?

Celaena touched her shoulder and felt the open, bloody wounds beneath. The creature had been clawing at its head, as though it were in pain. And when it had shoved through the door, for those last few seconds it had been frozen in place, she had seen something human in its warped eyes—something that looked so relieved, so grateful for the death she gave him.

"Who were you?" she whispered, recalling the human heart and manlike body of the creature under the library. "And what did he do to you?"

But Celaena had a feeling she already knew the answer.

Because that was the other thing the Wyrdkeys could do, the other power that the Wyrdmarks controlled: life.

They hear wings in the Ferian Gap, Nehemia had said. *Our scouts do not come back.*

The king was twisting far worse things than mortal men. Far, far worse things. But what did he plan to do with them—with the creatures, with the people like Roland and Kaltain?

She needed to learn how many of the Wyrdkeys he had found.

And where the others might be.

The next night, Celaena examined the door to the library catacombs, her ears straining for any hint of sound on the other side.

Nothing.

The bloody Wyrdmarks had turned flaky, but beneath the crust, as if welded onto the metal, was the dark outline of each mark.

From high, high above, the muffled bellow of the clock tower sounded. It was two in the morning. How did no one know that the tower sat atop an ancient dungeon that served as the king's own secret chamber?

Celaena glowered at the door in front of her. Because who would even *think* about that as a possibility?

She knew she should go to bed, but she'd been unable to sleep for weeks now and saw no point in even trying anymore. It was why she'd come down here: to do something while sorting through her jumbled thoughts.

She flipped the dagger in her right hand, angling it, and gave a light, tentative tug on the door.

It held. She paused, listening again for any signs of life, and yanked harder.

It didn't budge.

Celaena pulled a few more times, going so far as to brace a foot against the wall, but the door remained sealed. When she was at last convinced that *nothing* was getting through the door—in either direction—she loosed a long breath.

No one would believe her about this place—just like no one would believe her wild, highly unlikely story about the Wyrdkeys.

To find the Wyrdkeys, she'd first have to solve the riddle. And then convince the king to let her go for a few months. Years. It would take careful manipulation, especially since it seemed likely that he already had a key. But which one?

They hear wings . . .

Yellowlegs said that only combined could the three open the actual Wyrdgate, but alone each still wielded immense power. What other sorts of terrors could he create? If he ever got all three Wyrdkeys, what might he bring into Erilea to serve him? Things were already stirring on the continent; unrest was brewing. She had a feeling that he wouldn't tolerate it for long. No, it would only be a matter of time before he unleashed whatever he'd been creating upon them all, and crush all resistance forever.

Celaena looked at the sealed door, her stomach turning. A half-dried pool of blood lay at the base of the door, so dark it looked like oil. She crouched, swiping a finger through the puddle. She sniffed at it, almost gagged at the reek, and then rubbed her finger against the pad of her thumb. It felt as oily as it looked.

She got to her feet and reached into her pocket, looking for something to wipe off her fingers. She drew out a handful of papers. Scraps was more like it—bits of things that she'd carried around to study whenever she had a spare moment. Frowning, she shifted through them to sort out which one she could spare to use as a makeshift handkerchief.

One was just a receipt for a pair of shoes, which she must have accidentally tucked into her pocket that morning. And another . . . Celaena lifted that one closer. *Ah! Time's Rift!* had been written there. She'd scribbled it down when she'd been trying to solve the eye riddle. When everything in the tomb had felt like a great secret, one giant clue.

Some help that had been. Just another dead end. Cursing under her breath, she used it to wipe the grime off her fingers. The tomb still didn't make sense, though. What did the trees on the ceiling and the stars on the floor have to do with the riddle? The stars had led to the secret hole, but they could just as easily have been on the ceiling to do that. Why make everything backward?

Would Brannon have been so foolish as to put all the answers in one place?

She uncrumpled the scrap of paper, now stained with the creature's oily blood. *Ah! Time's Rift!*

There was no inscription at Gavin's feet—only Elena's. And the words made little sense.

. . . But what if they weren't meant to make sense? What if they were only just logical enough to imply one thing, but really mean another?

Everything in the tomb was backward, rearranged, the natural order in reverse. To hint that things were jumbled, misarranged. So the thing that should have been concealed was right in the open. But, like everything else, its meaning was warped.

And there was one person—one being—who could possibly tell her whether she was right.

CHAPTER 46

"It's an anagram," she panted as she reached the tomb.

Mort opened an eye. "Clever, wasn't it? To hide it right where everyone could see?"

Celaena eased open the door just wide enough to slip inside. The moonlight was strong, and her breath caught in her throat as she saw precisely where it fell. Trembling, she stopped at the foot of the sarcophagus and traced her fingers over the stone letters. "Tell me what it means."

He paused, long enough for her to take a breath to start yelling at him, but he then said, "I Am the First."

And that was all the confirmation she needed.

The first Wyrdkey of the three. Celaena moved around the stone body, her eyes on Elena's sleeping face. As she looked upon those fine features, she whispered the words.

In grief, he hid one in the crown
Of her he loved so well,

To keep with her where she lay down
Inside the starry cell.

She lifted shaking fingers to the blue jewel in the center of the crown. If this was indeed the Wyrdkey . . . what would she do with it? Would she be forced to destroy it? Where could she hide it so no one else would discover it? The questions swirled, threatening with all the difficulty they offered to send her running back to her rooms, but she steeled herself. She'd consider everything later. *I will not be afraid*, she told herself.

The gem in the crown glowed in the moonlight, and she gingerly pushed against one side of the jewel. It didn't move.

She pushed again, staying closer to the side, digging her nail into the slight crease between the gem and the stone rim. It shifted—and turned over to reveal a small compartment beneath. It was no larger than a coin, and no deeper than a knuckle's length.

Celaena peered in. The moonlight revealed only gray stone. She stuck a finger inside, scraping every surface.

There was nothing there. Not even a shard.

A shot of cold ran down her spine. "So he truly has it," she whispered. "He found the key before me. And he's been using its power for his own agenda."

"He was barely twenty when he found it," Mort said softly. "Strange, bellicose youth! Always poking about in forgotten places where he wasn't wanted, reading books no one his age— or any age—should read! Though," Mort added, "that does sound *awfully* like someone I know."

"And you somehow *forgot* to tell me until now?"

"I didn't know what it was then; I thought he merely took something. It wasn't until you read the riddle that I suspected."

It was a good thing he was made of bronze. Otherwise she'd have smashed his face in. "Do you have any suspicions about what he might have done with it?" She turned the gem back over as she fought her rising terror.

"How should I know? *He* never said anything to me, though I'll admit I didn't condescend to speak with him. He came back here once he was king, but he only poked around for a few minutes and then left. I suspect he was looking for the other two keys."

"How did he discover it was here?" she asked, stepping away from the marble figure.

"The same way you did, though far faster. I suppose that makes him cleverer than you."

"Do you think he has the other two?" she said, eyeing the treasure along the far wall, the stand where Damaris was displayed. Why hadn't he taken Damaris, one of the greatest heirlooms of his house?

"If he had the others, don't you think that our doom would have come upon us already?"

"You think he doesn't have all of the keys?" she asked, beginning to sweat despite the cold.

"Well, Brannon once told me that if you have all three keys, then you have control over the Wyrdgate. I think it's fair to assume the current king would have tried his hand at conquering another realm, or enslaved creatures to conquer the rest of ours, if he had all three."

"Wyrd save us if that happens."

"Wyrd?" Mort laughed. "You're pleading with the wrong force. If he controls the Wyrd, you're going to have to find another means of saving yourself. And don't you think it's too much of a coincidence that magic stopped as soon as he began his conquest?"

How magic stopped . . . "He used the Wyrdkeys to stifle magic. All magic," she added, "but his own."

And by extension, Dorian's.

She swore, then asked, "So you think he might also have the second Wyrdkey?"

"I don't think a person could *eliminate* magic with only one—though I might be wrong. No one really knows what they're capable of."

Celaena pressed the heels of her palms to her eyes. "Oh, gods. This was what Elena wanted me to learn. And now what am I supposed to do? Go hunt the third one down? Steal the other two from him?"

Nehemia—Nehemia, you had to have known. You must have had a plan. But what were you going to do?

The now-familiar abyss inside of her stretched wider. There was no end to it, that hollow ache. No end at all. If the gods had bothered to listen, she would have traded her life for Nehemia's. It would have been such an easy choice to make. Because the world didn't need an assassin with a coward's heart. It needed someone like Nehemia.

But there were no gods left to bargain with; no one to offer her soul to in exchange for another moment with Nehemia, just one more chance to talk to her, to hear her voice.

Yet . . . Maybe she didn't need the gods to talk to Nehemia.

Cain had summoned the ridderak, and he certainly hadn't possessed a Wyrdkey. No, Nehemia had said that there were spells to open a temporary portal, just long enough for something to slip through. If Cain could do that, and if Celaena could use the marks to freeze the catacombs creature in place and permanently seal a door, then couldn't marks open a portal to yet *another* realm?

Her chest tightened. If there were other realms—realms where the dead dwelled, in torment or in peace—who was to say that she couldn't speak to Nehemia? She could do it. No matter the cost, it would only be for a moment—just long enough to ask Nehemia where the king was keeping the keys, or how to find the third, and to find out what else Nehemia might have known.

She could do it.

There were other things she needed to tell Nehemia, too. Words she needed to say, truths she needed to confess. And that good-bye—that final good-bye that she hadn't been allowed to make.

Celaena took Damaris off its stand again. "Mort, how long do you think a portal can stay open?"

"Whatever you are thinking, whatever you are going to do right now, *stop it*."

But Celaena was already walking out of the tomb. He didn't understand—couldn't understand. She had lost and lost and lost, been denied countless good-byes. But not this time—not when she could change all of that, even for a few minutes. This time, it would be different.

She'd need *The Walking Dead*, another dagger or two, some candles, and space—more space than the tomb could offer. The drawings that Cain had made had taken up a fair amount of room. There was a large passage one level up in the secret tunnels, a long hallway and a set of doors she'd never dared open. The hallway was wide, its ceiling high: enough room to cast the spell.

For her to open a portal into an Otherworld.

⁓

Dorian knew he was dreaming. He was standing in an ancient stone chamber he'd never seen before, facing a tall, crowned warrior. The crown was familiar, somehow, but it was the man's eyes that stunned him into inaction. They were his own eyes—sapphire, blazing. The similarities ended there; the man had shoulder-length dark brown hair, an angular, almost cruel face, and was at least a hand taller than Dorian himself. And he carried himself like . . . a king.

"Prince," the man said, his golden crown gleaming. There was something feral in his eyes—as if the king was more accustomed to roaming the wilderness than walking these marble halls. "You must awaken."

"Why?" Dorian asked, not sounding very princely at all. Strange green symbols were glowing on the gray stones, similar to the symbols Celaena had made in the library. What was this place?

"Because a line that should never be crossed is about to be breached. It puts this entire castle in jeopardy—and the life of your friend." His voice wasn't harsh, but Dorian had a sense it could turn that way, if provoked. Which, judging by that ancient wildness, the arrogance and challenge in the king's eyes, seemed like a fairly easy thing to do.

Dorian said, "What are you talking about? Who are you?"

"Don't waste time with pointless questions." Yes, this king wasn't one to mince words at all. "You must go to her rooms. There is a door hidden behind a tapestry. Take the third passage on the right. Go *now*, Prince, or lose her forever."

And somehow, Dorian didn't think twice about the fact that Gavin, first King of Adarlan, had spoken to him as he awoke, yanked on his clothes, grabbed his sword belt, and sprinted from his tower.

CHAPTER 47

The cut on her arm throbbed, but Celaena kept her hand steady as she dipped her finger again into her blood and traced the Wyrdmark on the wall, copying the symbols in the book with perfect precision. They formed an archway—a door—and her blood gleamed in the light of the candles she had brought.

It had to be perfect—each symbol had to be flawless, or else it wouldn't work. She kept pressing on the wound to keep it from clotting. Not everyone could harness the marks; no, *The Walking Dead* said there had to be power in the blood to do it. Cain had clearly had some trace of power. That must be why the king had rounded up Kaltain and Roland, too. He'd used the Wyrdkeys to suppress magic, but he must have some way of harnessing the innate power in someone's blood—and the Wyrdmarks must be able to access that power, too.

She drew another symbol, nearly finished with the archway.

Their power could warp things. It had warped Cain. But it had also allowed him to summon the ridderak and gain even *more* power for himself.

Thank the Wyrd Cain was dead.

There was one mark left to draw, the one that would bring her the person she so desperately needed to see, if only for a moment. It was complex, a weave of loops and angles. She took out her chalk and practiced on the floor until she got it right, then etched it in blood on the wall. Nehemia's name in Wyrdmark form.

She examined the door she'd drawn and got to her feet, the book held in her clean hand.

She cleared her throat and began to read the words on the page.

She didn't know the language. Her throat burned and contracted, as if fighting the sounds, but she panted through it, the words making her teeth ache like she'd just come in from the cold and was drinking something hot.

And then the final words were out, her eyes watering.

No wonder this kind of power fell out of favor.

The symbols written in her blood began to glow green, one after another, until the whole archway was a line of light. The stones within its borders darkened, darkened, darkened, then disappeared.

The blackness within the green archway seemed to reach out for her.

It had worked. Holy gods, it had worked.

Was *that* what waited for her when she died? Nehemia had gone *here*?

"Nehemia?" she whispered, her throat raw from the spell.

There was nothing. Nothing there—just a void.

Celaena looked at the book, then to the wall and the symbols she'd drawn. She'd written it correctly. The spell was right. "Nehemia?" she whispered toward that endless dark.

There was no response.

Perhaps it needed time. The book hadn't specified how long it would take; maybe Nehemia had to travel through whatever this realm was.

So Celaena waited.

The longer she stared into that endless void, the more it seemed to stare back. It was just like that dream, the one where she was standing on the edge of that ravine.

You are nothing more than a coward.

"Please," Celaena whispered into the dark.

There was a sudden yelp from far, far above, and Celaena whirled toward the stairs at the end of the hall. Moments later, faster than should be possible, Fleetfoot bounded down the steps, racing for her.

Not for her, Celaena realized as she beheld the wagging tail, the panting, the yip of what could only be joy. Not for her, because—

Celaena looked toward the portal at the same moment Fleetfoot skidded to a halt.

And then everything stopped as she beheld the shimmering figure standing just on the other side of the portal.

Fleetfoot lay on the ground, tail still wagging, whining softly. The edges of Nehemia's body rippled and blurred, fracturing with some sort of inner light. But her face was clear—her face was . . . it was her face. Celaena sank to her knees.

She felt the warmth of her tears before she realized she was crying. "I'm sorry," was all she could say. "I'm so sorry."

But Nehemia remained on the other side of the portal. Fleetfoot whined again. "I may not cross this line," Nehemia said gently to the dog. "And neither may you." Her tone shifted, and Celaena knew Nehemia was now staring at her. "I thought you were smarter than this."

Celaena looked up. The light radiating off the princess didn't reach through the glowing portal, as if there truly were some sort of line— some final boundary.

"I'm sorry," Celaena whispered again. "I just wanted—"

"There is no time for you to tell me what you long to say. I came here because you need to be warned. *Do not* open this portal again. The next time you do, I will not be the one who answers your call. And you will not survive the encounter. *No one* has the right to open the door to this realm, no matter how fierce their grief."

She hadn't known, hadn't meant . . .

Fleetfoot pawed at the floor. "Good-bye, my dear friend," Nehemia said to the dog, and began walking into the blackness.

Celaena just stood there, unable to move or think. Her throat burned with those pent-up words, the words that now choked the life out of her.

"Elentiya." Nehemia paused to look back at her. The void seemed to be swirling, swallowing her up bit by bit. "You will not understand yet, but . . . I knew what my fate was to be, and I embraced it. I ran toward it. Because it was the only way for things to begin changing, for events to be set in motion. But no matter what I did, Elentiya, I want you to know that in the darkness of the past ten years, you were one of the bright lights for me. Do not let that light go out."

And before Celaena could reply, the princess was gone.

There was nothing in the dark. As though Nehemia had never been. As though she'd made it all up.

"Come back," she whispered. "Please—come back." But the darkness remained the same. And Nehemia was gone.

There was a scrape of footsteps—but not from the portal. Rather, it came from her left.

From Archer, who stood there gaping. "I don't believe it," he whispered.

CHAPTER 48

Celaena had Damaris drawn and leveled at Archer in a heartbeat. Fleetfoot growled at him, but kept back, a step behind Celaena.

"What are you *doing* here?" It was inconceivable that he'd be here. How had he gotten in?

"I've been tracking you for weeks," Archer said, eyeing the dog. "Nehemia told me about the passages, showed me the way in. I've been down here almost every night since she died."

Celaena glanced at the portal. If Nehemia had warned her not to open the portal, then she was certain her friend didn't want Archer seeing it, either. She moved to the wall, keeping well away from the blackness as she ran her hand over the glowing green marks, making to wipe them away.

"What are you doing?" Archer demanded.

Celaena pointed Damaris at him, furiously wiping at the marks. They didn't budge. Whatever this spell was, it was far more complex than the one that had sealed the library door—merely swiping away the marks wouldn't undo it. But Archer now stood between her and the book where she had the closing spell flagged. Celaena rubbed harder. It was all terribly wrong.

"Stop!" Archer lunged, getting past her guard with unnatural ease as he grasped her wrist. Fleetfoot barked a ferocious warning, but a sharp whistle from Celaena had the dog staying well away.

She whirled to Archer, already making to dislocate the arm that held her, but the green light of the portal illuminated the plane of his wrist, where the sleeve of his tunic had fallen back.

A black tattoo of some snakelike creature appeared there.

She'd seen that before. Seen it . . .

Celaena raised her eyes to his face.

Do not trust . . .

She had thought Nehemia's drawing had been of the Royal Seal—a slightly warped version of the wyvern. But it had actually been of this tattoo. Of *Archer's* tattoo.

Do not trust Archer, she'd been trying to tell her.

Celaena shoved back from him, drawing a dagger. She pointed both Damaris and the knife at him. How much had Nehemia hidden from Archer and his contacts? If she didn't trust them, then why had she told them all that she did?

"Tell me how you learned this," Archer whispered, his eyes going back to the portal and the darkness beyond. "Please. Did you find the Wyrdkeys? Is that how you did it?"

"What do you know of the Wyrdkeys?" she got out.

"Where are they? Where did you find them?"

"I don't have the keys."

"You found the riddle, though," Archer panted. "I let you find that riddle I hid in Davis's office. It took us five years to find that riddle— and you must have solved it. I knew you'd be the one to solve it. Nehemia knew, too."

Celaena was shaking her head. He didn't know that there had been a second riddle—a riddle with a map to the keys. "The king has at least one key. But where the other two are, I don't know."

Archer's eyes darkened. "We suspected as much. That was why she came here in the first place. To learn whether he'd actually stolen them, and if so, how many."

That was why Nehemia couldn't leave, she realized. Why she'd opted to stay here instead of returning to Eyllwe. To fight for the one thing that was more important than the fate of her country: the fate of the world. Of other worlds, too.

"I don't have to get on a ship tomorrow. We'll tell everyone," Archer breathed. "We'll tell everyone he has them, and—"

"*No*. If we reveal the truth, then the king will use the keys to do more damage than you can possibly imagine. We'll lose any chance of stealth we have to find the others."

He took a step closer to her. Fleetfoot let out another warning growl, but kept her distance. "Then we'll find where he's keeping the key. And the others. And then we'll use them to overthrow him. Then we'll create a world of our own making."

His voice was building into a frenzy, each word harsher than the next.

She shook her head. "I would sooner destroy them than use their power."

Archer chuckled. "She said the same thing. She said they should be destroyed—put back in the gate, if we could discover a way. But what is the point of finding them if we don't use them against him? Make *him* suffer?"

Her stomach turned. There was more he wasn't saying, more that he knew. So she sighed and shook her head, beginning to pace. Archer was silent as she walked—silent until she halted, as if suddenly understanding. She raised her voice. "He *should* suffer for as long as possible. And so should the people who destroyed us—who made us into what we are: Arobynn, Clarisse . . ." She chewed on her lip. "Nehemia could never understand that. She never tried to. You—you're right. They should be used."

He studied her warily enough that she came closer and tilted her head to the side—contemplating his words, contemplating *him*.

And Archer bought it. "That was why she left the movement. She left a week before she died. We knew it was a matter of time before she went to the king to expose us all—to use what she'd learned to grant clemency to Eyllwe, and to annihilate us with the same stroke. She said she'd rather have one all-powerful tyrant than a dozen of them."

Celaena said with deadly calm, "She would have ruined everything for you. She almost ruined everything for me, too. She told me to stay away from the Wyrdkeys. She tried to keep me from solving the riddle."

"Because she wanted to keep the knowledge to herself, for her own gain."

She smiled even as she felt the world shifting beneath her. And she couldn't explain why, or how she began to wonder, but if it was true, she had to get him to admit it. She found herself saying, "You and I worked for *everything* we have—we . . . we had everything taken away and used against us, too. Other people can't even begin to fathom the things we were forced to do. I think—I think that's why I was so infatuated with you when I was a girl. I knew, even then, that you understood. That you knew what it was like to be raised by people like Arobynn and Clarisse and then . . . *sold*. You understood me then." She willed her eyes to gleam, her mouth to tighten as if she were keeping it from wobbling. Blinking furiously, she murmured, "But I think I finally understand you now, too."

She reached out a hand as if to grab his, but lowered it—making her face tender and soft and bittersweet. "Why didn't you tell me sooner?

We could have been working toward this for weeks. We could have tried to solve the riddle together. If I'd known what Nehemia was going to do, how she could lie to me again and again . . . She betrayed me. In every possible way, Archer. She lied to my face, made me believe . . ." Her shoulders slumped. After a long moment, she took a step toward him. "Nehemia was no better than Arobynn or Clarisse in the end. Archer, you should have told me. About everything. I knew it wasn't Mullison—he wasn't smart enough. If you'd told me, I could have taken care of it." A risk—a leap of faith. "For you . . . For *us*, I would have taken care of it."

But Archer gave her a hesitant smile. "She spent so much time complaining about Councilman Mullison that I knew he'd be the easiest one to blame. And thanks to that competition, he already had a connection to Grave."

"Grave didn't recognize that you weren't Mullison?" she asked as calmly as she could.

"You'd be surprised how easily men see what they want to see. A cloak, a mask, and some fine clothes, and he didn't think twice."

Oh, gods. Gods.

"So the night at the warehouse," she went on, raising an eyebrow— an intrigued coconspirator. "Why did you really kidnap Chaol?"

"I had to get you away from Nehemia. And when I took that arrow for you, I knew you'd trust me, if only for that night. I apologize if my methods were . . . harsh. Trick of the trade, I'm afraid."

Trust him, lose Nehemia, and lose Chaol. He had isolated her from her friends—the same thing she'd suspected Roland had wanted to do with Dorian.

"And that threat the king received before Nehemia's death—the threat on her life," Celaena said, her lips curling upward. "You planted that threat, didn't you? To show me who my real friends are—who I can really trust."

"It was a gamble. Just as I'm gambling now. I didn't know whether or not the captain would warn you. Seems I was right."

"Why me? I'm flattered, of course, but—you're clever. Why couldn't you have figured the riddle out on your own?"

Archer bowed his head. "Because I know what you are, Celaena. Arobynn told me one night, after you went to Endovier." She shoved the twinge of genuine pain and betrayal down until it couldn't distract her. "And for our cause to succeed, we *need* you. *I* need you. Some members of the movement are already starting to fight me, to question my leadership. They think my methods are too rough." That explained the fight she'd seen with that young man. He took a step toward her. "But you . . . Gods, from the moment I saw you outside the Willows, I've known how good we'd be together. The things we'll accomplish . . ."

"I know," she said, looking into those green eyes, so bright in the matching lights of the portal. "Archer, I know."

He didn't see the dagger coming until she'd shoved it into him.

But he was fast—too fast—and turned just in time to have it pierce his shoulder instead of his heart.

He staggered back with dazzling speed, wrenching her dagger so swiftly that she lost her grip on the blade and had to brace a hand on the arch of the portal to keep from stumbling. Her bloodied palm slapped against the stones, and a greenish light flared beneath her fingers. A Wyrdmark burned, then faded.

Not giving herself time to look at what she'd done, she leapt for him with a roar, dropping Damaris to grab two more daggers. He had his own blade up in a moment, dancing away lightly as she sliced for him.

"I'm going to tear you apart piece by piece," she hissed, circling him.

But then a shudder ran through the floor, and something in the void made a sound. A guttural growl.

Fleetfoot let out a low warning whine. She rushed toward Celaena, pushing against her shins, herding her toward the stairs.

The void shifted, mist now swirling inside, parting long enough to reveal rocky, ashen ground. And then a figure emerged through the mist.

"Nehemia?" she whispered. She'd come back—come back to help, to explain everything.

But it was not Nehemia who stepped through the portal.

Chaol couldn't sleep. He stared up at the canopy of his bed, the will he'd seen on Celaena's desk glaring in his mind. He couldn't stop thinking about it. He'd just let her kick him out of her rooms without telling her what the will meant to him. And maybe he deserved her hate, but—but she *had* to know that he didn't want her money.

He had to see her. Just long enough to explain.

He ran a finger along the scab down his cheek.

Rushing footsteps sounded down the hall, and Chaol was already out of bed and half-dressed by the time someone began pounding on his door. The person on the other side got all of one knock in before Chaol flung open the door, a dagger concealed behind his back.

He lowered the blade the second he beheld Dorian's face, shining with sweat, but he didn't sheath it. Not when he saw the raw panic in Dorian's eyes, the sword belt and scabbard dangling from the prince's clenched fingers.

Chaol believed in trusting his instinct. He didn't think humans had survived for so long without developing some ability to tell when things were wrong. It wasn't magic—it was just . . . gut feeling.

And it was Chaol's instinct that told him who this was about before Dorian opened his mouth.

"Where?" was all Chaol asked.

"Her bedroom," Dorian said.

"Tell me everything," Chaol ordered, hurrying back into his room.

"I don't know, I—I think she's in trouble."

Chaol was already shrugging on a shirt and tunic; then he stomped his feet into his boots before grabbing his sword. "What kind of trouble?"

"The kind that had me coming to get you, instead of the other guards."

That could mean anything; but Chaol knew Dorian was too smart, too aware of how easily words could be overheard in this castle. He sensed the tightening in Dorian's body a heartbeat before the prince launched into a run, and grabbed him by the back of his tunic. "Running," Chaol said under his breath, "will attract attention."

"I already wasted too much time coming to get you," Dorian retorted, but he matched Chaol's brisk but calm pace. It would take five minutes to get to her rooms if they kept this speed. If there were no distractions.

"Is anyone hurt?" Chaol said quietly, trying to keep his breathing even, keep his focus.

"I don't know," Dorian said.

"You have to give me more than that," Chaol snapped. The leash on his temper strained with each step.

"I had a dream," Dorian said, so soft only he could hear. "I was warned that she was in danger—that she was a danger to herself."

Chaol almost stopped, but Dorian had said it with such conviction.

"You think I wanted to come get you?" Dorian said, not looking at him.

Chaol didn't reply but hurried his steps as much as he could without attracting undue attention from the servants and guards still on duty. He could feel his heart hammering through every inch of his body by the time they got to her suite doors. Chaol didn't bother knocking and nearly took the front door off its hinges as he burst through, Dorian on his heels.

He was at her bedroom door in an instant, and didn't bother knocking on it, either. But the handle didn't move. The door was locked. He shoved into it again.

"Celaena?" Her name was more of a growl that rippled out of him. No answer. He fought his rising panic, even as he drew a dagger, even as he listened for any signs of trouble. *"Celaena."*

Nothing.

Chaol waited all of a second before he slammed his shoulder into the door. Once. Twice. The lock snapped. The door burst open, revealing her empty bedroom.

"Holy gods," Dorian whispered.

The tapestry on the wall had been folded back to reveal an open door—a secret, stone door that opened into a dark passage.

It was how she'd gotten out to kill Grave.

Dorian drew his sword from the scabbard. "In my dream, I was told I would find this door."

The prince stepped forward, but Chaol stopped him with an arm. He'd think about Dorian and his clairvoyant dreams later—much later. "You're not going down there."

Dorian's eyes flashed. "Like hell I'm not."

As if in answer, a guttural, bone-grinding growl sounded from within. And then a scream—a human scream, followed by a high-pitched bark.

Chaol was running for the passage before he could think.

It was pitch-black, and Chaol almost tumbled down the stairs, but Dorian, close behind, grabbed a candle.

"Stay upstairs!" Chaol ordered, still charging down. If he'd had time, he would have locked Dorian in the closet rather than risk bringing the Crown Prince into danger, but . . . What the hell had that

growl been? The bark he knew—the bark was Fleetfoot. And if Fleet-foot was down there . . .

Dorian kept following him. "I was sent here," he said. Chaol took the stairs by twos and threes, hardly hearing the prince's words. Had that scream been hers? It had sounded male. But who else could be down here with her?

Blue light flashed from the bottom of the stairs. What was *that*?

A roar shook the ancient stones. *That* was not human, nor was it Fleetfoot. But what—

They had never found the creature that had been killing the champions. The murders had just stopped. But the damage he'd seen to those corpses . . . No, Celaena had to be alive.

Please, he begged any gods who would listen.

Chaol leapt onto the landing and found three doorways. The blue light had flashed from the right. They ran.

How had such a massive cavern of chambers been forgotten? And how long had she known about them?

He flew down a spiral staircase. And then a new, greenish light began shining steadily, and he turned onto a landing to see—

He didn't know where to look first—at the long hallway, where one wall glowed with an arch of green symbols, or at the . . . the *world* that showed through the arch, depicting a land of mist and rock.

At Archer, cowering against the opposite wall, chanting strange words from a book held in his hands.

At Celaena, prostrate on the floor.

Or at the monster: a tall, sinewy thing, but definitely not human. Not with those unnaturally long fingers tipped with claws, white skin that looked like crumpled paper, a distended jaw that revealed fish-like teeth, and those eyes—milky and tinged with blue.

And there was Fleetfoot, hackles raised and fangs bared, refusing to let the demon anywhere near Celaena, even as the half-grown pup limped, even as the blood pooled from the wound in her right hind leg.

Chaol had all of two heartbeats to size up the monster, to take in every detail, to mark his surroundings. "*Go,*" he snarled at Dorian before launching himself at the creature.

CHAPTER 49

She didn't remember anything after the first two swings of her sword, only that she'd suddenly seen Fleetfoot come flying at the creature. The sight had distracted her enough for the demon to get past her guard, its long, white fingers grabbing her by the hair and slamming her head into the wall.

Then darkness.

She wondered whether she'd died and awoken in hell as she opened her eyes to a pulsing headache—and the sight of Chaol, circling the pale demon, blood dripping from both of them. And then there were cool hands on her head, on her neck, and Dorian crouching in front of her as he said, "Celaena."

She struggled to her feet, her head aching even more. She had to help Chaol. Had to—

She heard a rip of clothing and a yelp of pain, and she looked at Chaol in time to see him grasp the cut on his shoulder, inflicted by those filthy, jagged nails. The creature roared, its overlong jaw gleaming with saliva, and it lunged again for the captain.

Celaena tried to move, but she wasn't fast enough.

But Dorian was.

Something invisible slammed into the creature, sending it flying into the wall with a crunch. *Gods.* Dorian didn't just have magic—he had *raw* magic. The rarest, and deadliest, kind. Sheer undiluted power, capable of being shaped into whatever form the wielder desired.

The creature crumpled but instantly got up, whirling toward her and Dorian. The prince just stood there, hand outstretched.

The milky-blue eyes were ravenous now.

Through the portal Celaena heard the rocky earth crunching beneath more pairs of bare, pale feet. Archer's chanting grew louder.

Chaol attacked the thing again. It surged toward him just before his sword struck, swiping with those long fingers, forcing the captain to dart back.

She grabbed Dorian. "We have to close it. The portal should close on its own eventually, but—but the longer it's open, the greater the threat of more coming through before it does."

"How?"

"I—I don't know, I . . ." Her head spun so badly her knees wobbled. But she turned to Archer, who stood across the hall, separated from them by the pacing creature. "Give me the book."

Chaol wounded the demon across its abdomen with a sure, deft stroke, but it didn't slow down. Even from a few feet away, the tang of the dark blood reached her nose.

Celaena watched Archer take it all in, his eyes wide, panicked beyond reason. And then he sprinted down the hall, taking with him the book—and any hope of shutting the portal.

Dorian couldn't move fast enough to stop the handsome man from fleeing with the book in his hands, and didn't dare, with that demon between them. Celaena, her forehead bleeding, made a lunge for him, but the man was too fast. Her eyes kept darting to Chaol, who was keeping the *thing* distracted. Dorian knew without being told that she didn't want to leave the captain.

"I'll go—" Dorian began.

"No. He's dangerous, and these tunnels are a labyrinth," she panted. Chaol and the creature circled each other, the thing slowly backing toward the portal entrance. "I can't close it without that book," she moaned. "There are more books upstairs, but I—"

"Then we flee," Dorian breathed, grabbing her by the elbow. "We flee and try to get to those books."

He dragged her with him, not daring to take his eyes off Chaol or the creature. She swayed in his grasp. The wound to her head must be as bad as it looked. Something was glowing at her throat: the amulet she'd told him was just a "cheap replica," shining like a tiny blue star.

"Go," Chaol told them, staring down the thing in front of him. "*Now.*"

She stumbled, tugging toward Chaol, but Dorian pulled her back.

"*No,*" she got out, but the wound to her head made her sag in Dorian's grip. As if realizing that she'd be a hindrance to Chaol, she stopped fighting Dorian as he hauled her toward the stairs.

Chaol knew he couldn't win this fight. His best option was to flee with them, to guard the way until they could get to that stone door far, far above and lock the creature down here. But he wasn't sure he'd even make it to the stairs. The creature thwarted his attacks so easily it seemed to have an uncanny intelligence.

At least Celaena and Dorian had reached the stairs. He could accept his end if it meant they could escape. He could embrace the darkness when it came.

The creature paused just long enough for Chaol to gain a few more feet of distance. He backed toward the bottom step.

But then she started shouting—the same word again and again as Dorian tried to keep dragging her up the stairs.

Fleetfoot.

Chaol looked. In a dark shadow by the wall, Fleetfoot had been left behind, her leg too injured to run.

The creature looked, too.

And there was nothing he could do, absolutely nothing, as the creature whirled, grabbed Fleetfoot by her injured hind leg, and dragged her through the portal with it.

There was nothing he could do, he realized, except run.

Celaena's scream was still echoing through the passageway as Chaol leapt off the stairs and hurtled through the misty portal after Fleetfoot.

If she had thought she'd known fear and pain before, it was nothing compared to what went through her when Chaol ran through the portal after Fleetfoot.

Dorian didn't see her coming as she whirled, slamming his head into the stone wall hard enough that he crumpled to the steps, freeing her from his grip.

But she didn't care about Dorian, didn't care about anything except Fleetfoot and Chaol as she sprinted down those few stairs and across the hall. She had to get them out, get them back before the portal shut forever.

She was through in a heartbeat.

And when she saw Chaol shielding Fleetfoot with nothing but his bare hands, his discarded sword snapped in two by the demon who hovered over them, she didn't think twice before she unleashed the monster inside herself.

From the corner of his eye, Chaol saw her coming, the ancient sword in her hands and her face set with feral rage.

The moment she burst through the portal, something changed. It was like a fog vanished from her face, her features sharpening, her steps becoming longer and more graceful. And then her ears—her ears shifted into delicate points.

The creature, sensing it was about to lose its prey, made a final lunge for Chaol.

It was blasted away by a wall of blue flame.

The fire vanished to reveal the creature slamming into the ground, flipping again and again. It was on its feet before it finished rolling, whirling toward Celaena in the same move.

She was between them now, sword raised. She roared, revealing elongated canines, and the sound was unlike anything he'd ever heard. There was nothing human in it.

Because she wasn't human, Chaol realized, gaping up at her from where he still crouched over Fleetfoot.

No—she wasn't human at all.

Celaena was Fae.

CHAPTER 50

She knew the shift had happened, because it hurt like hell. A flash of blinding pain as her features ripped free of the hold that hid them. The demon lunged, and she plummeted into the well of power that was suddenly overflowing inside of her.

Magic, savage and unforgiving, erupted out of her, punching into the creature and sending it flying. Flame—years ago, her power had always manifested as some form of fire.

She could smell everything, see everything. Her heightened senses pulled her attention every which way, telling her that this world was *wrong*, and she needed to get out *now*.

But she wouldn't get out, not until Chaol and Fleetfoot made it to safety.

The creature stopped rolling, on its feet in an instant, and Celaena put herself between it and Chaol. The demon sniffed at her, sinking onto its haunches.

She lifted Damaris and bellowed her challenge.

From far off in the mist, roars answered. One of them came from the thing in front of her.

She looked at Chaol, still crouched over Fleetfoot, and bared her teeth, canines glistening in the gray light.

Chaol was staring up at her. She could smell his terror and his awe. Smell his blood, so human and ordinary. The magic welled up more and more and more, uncontrollable and ancient and burning.

"*Run*," she snarled, more a plea than a command, because the magic was a living thing, and it wanted *out*, and she was just as likely to hurt him as she was to hurt the creature. Because that portal might close at any moment and seal them here forever.

She didn't wait to see what Chaol did. The creature rushed for her, a blur of withered white flesh. She ran toward it, flinging her immortal power like a phantom punch. It shot out in a blue burst of wildfire, but the creature dodged it, and the next blow and the next.

Celaena swung Damaris, and the creature ducked before jumping back a few paces. The roars in the distance were getting closer.

Crunching rock sounded behind her, and she knew Chaol was making for the portal.

The demon began pacing. Then the crunching stopped. That meant Chaol was in the passageway again; he must have carried Fleetfoot with him. He was safe. Safe.

This thing was too smart, too fast—and too strong, despite its gangly limbs.

And if others were coming—if more got through the portal before it closed . . .

Her magic was building again, the spring deeper now. Celaena gauged the distance between them as she backed toward the portal.

She had little control over the power, but she did have a sword—a sacred sword made by the Fae, capable of withstanding magic. A conduit.

Not giving herself time to think it through, she threw all her raw power into the golden sword. Its blade glowed red-hot, its edges crackling with lightning.

The creature tensed, as if sensing what she was about to do as she lifted the sword over her head. With a battle cry that shattered through the mists, Celaena plunged Damaris into the earth.

The ground cracked toward the demon, a burning web of lines and fissures.

And then the ground between them began to collapse, foot by foot, until the creature was sprinting away. Soon there was just a small lip of land surrounding Celaena, backed by the open portal, and an ever-growing chasm before her.

She wrenched Damaris from the broken earth. She knew she had to get out—*now*. But before she could move, before she could get to the portal, the magic rippled, so violently that she sagged to her knees. Pain flashed, and she shifted back into her clumsy, frail mortal body.

And then there were strong hands under her shoulders, hands she knew so well, dragging her back through the portal and into Erilea, where her magic was snuffed out like a candle.

⁓

Dorian came to just in time to see Chaol hauling Celaena back through the portal. She was conscious, but was a dead weight in the captain's arms as he dragged her across the ground. Once they were over the border, he dropped her as though she were made of flame, and Celaena lay panting on the stones.

What had happened? There had been a land of rock beyond the portal, and now . . . now there was nothing but a small ledge and a massive crater. The pale creature was gone.

Celaena pushed herself up onto her elbows, her limbs wobbling. Dorian's head ached, but he managed to walk to them. He'd been dragging her one moment, and then—then she'd knocked him out. Why?

"Close it," Chaol was saying to her, his face so white that the blood splattered on it stood out even more starkly. *"Close it."*

"I can't," Celaena breathed. Dorian gripped the wall to keep himself from falling to his knees from the ache in his head. He made it to where they were positioned in front of the portal, Fleetfoot nuzzling Celaena.

"They're going to keep coming through," Chaol panted. Something was wrong, Dorian realized—something was wrong between them. Chaol wasn't touching her, wasn't helping her up.

Beyond the crater inside the portal, the roaring was growing louder. No doubt those things would find some way to get through.

"I'm drained; I don't have anything left to close this gate . . ." Celaena winced, then lifted her eyes to Dorian's. "But you do."

From the corner of her eye, Celaena saw Chaol whirl to face Dorian. She staggered to her feet. Fleetfoot had again put herself between Celaena and the portal, snarling softly. "Help me," she whispered to the prince, some semblance of energy returning.

Dorian didn't look at Chaol. He stepped forward. "What must I do?"

"I need your blood. The rest I can do. At least, I hope I can." Chaol started to object, and Celaena gave him a faint, bitter smile. "Don't worry. Only a cut on the arm."

Sheathing his sword, Dorian rolled up the sleeve of his shirt and drew a dagger. Blood welled from the cut, quick and bright.

Chaol growled, "How did you learn to open a portal?"

"I found a book," she said. It was the truth. "I wanted to speak to Nehemia."

Silence fell—pitying, horrifying silence.

But then she added, "I—I think I accidentally changed a symbol." She pointed to the Wyrdmark she'd smeared, the one that had rearranged itself. "It went to the wrong place. But this might close the door—if we're lucky."

What she didn't tell them was that there was a good chance it wouldn't work. But because there were no other books in her rooms, and because Archer had taken *The Walking Dead* with him, all she had left was that sealing spell she'd used on the door in the library. And there was no way—no way in hell—she was going to abandon this open portal, or leave one of them to guard it. The portal would eventually close on its own, but she didn't know when. More of those things could creep through at any time. So she'd try this, because it was her only option. She'd figure out something else if it didn't work.

It will *work*, she told herself.

Dorian put a warm, reassuring hand on her back as she dipped her fingers into his blood. She hadn't realized how freezing her hands were until the heat of his blood warmed her fingertips. One by one, she drew the sealing marks over the green-glowing symbols. Dorian never let go of her—only stepped even closer when she swayed. Chaol said nothing.

Her knees buckled, but she finished covering the symbols with Dorian's blood. A lingering roar echoed through the damned world as the final symbol flared, the mists and rock and ravine fading into black, then into familiar stone.

Celaena kept her breathing steady, throwing all her focus into that. If she could keep breathing, she wouldn't fall apart.

Dorian lowered his arm and loosed a sigh, finally letting go of her.

"Let's go," Chaol ordered, scooping up Fleetfoot, who whined in pain and gave him a warning growl.

"I think we all need a drink," Dorian said quietly. "And an explanation."

But Celaena looked down the hall, to the stairwell where Archer had fled. Had it only been minutes ago? It had felt like a lifetime.

But if it had only been minutes . . . Her breathing stumbled. She had discovered only one way out of the castle, and she was certain that was where Archer had gone. After what he'd done to Nehemia, after taking the book and abandoning them to that creature . . . Exhaustion was replaced by familiar anger—anger that burned through everything, just as Archer had destroyed what she loved.

Chaol stepped into her path. "Don't you even think—"

Panting, she sheathed Damaris. *"He's mine."*

Before Chaol could grab her, she hurtled down the stairs.

CHAPTER
51

Though Celaena's Fae senses were extinguished, she could swear she still smelled Archer's cologne as she moved toward the sewer tunnel, still smelled the blood on him.

He had destroyed *everything*. He'd had Nehemia assassinated, had manipulated them both, had used Nehemia's death to drive a wedge between her and Chaol, all in the name of power and revenge . . .

She would take him apart. Slowly.

I know what you are, he'd said. She didn't know what Arobynn had told him about her heritage, but Archer had no idea what sort of darkness lurked inside her, or what sort of monster she was willing to become in order to make things right.

Ahead of her, she could hear muffled curses and banging against metal. By the time she reached the sewer tunnel, she knew what had happened. The grate had slid shut, and none of Archer's attempts to open it had worked. Perhaps the gods did listen sometimes. Celaena smiled, drawing both of her daggers.

She walked through the archway, but the passage was empty on either side of the small river. She stepped farther onto the walkway, peering into the water, wondering if he'd tried to swim deep enough to go under the grate.

She sensed him a heartbeat before he attacked from behind.

She met his sword with both her daggers raised over her head, darting back to give herself enough time to assess. Archer had trained with the assassins—and from the way he wielded his blade, coming after her again and again, she knew he'd kept up those lessons.

She was exhausted. Archer was at full strength, and his blows made her arms quake.

He swiped for her throat, but she ducked, slicing for his side. Swift as lightning, he leapt to avoid her gutting him.

"I killed her for *our* sake," Archer panted as she scanned for any weakness, any opening. "She would have ruined us. And now that you can open portals without the keys, think of what we could do. *Think*, Celaena. Her death was a worthy sacrifice to keep her from destroying the cause. We *must* rise up against the king."

She lunged, feinting left, but he caught the attack. She growled, "I would rather live in his shadow than in a world where men like you rule. And when I'm done with you, I'm going to find all your friends and return the favor."

"They don't know anything. They don't know what I know," he said, dancing past all her attacks with maddening ease. "Nehemia was hiding something else about you. She didn't want you involved, and I thought it was just because she didn't want to share you with us. But now I wonder *why*, exactly. What more did she know?"

Celaena laughed softly. "You're a fool if you think I'll help you."

"Oh, once my men start working on you, you'll soon change your mind. Rourke Farran was a client of mine—before he was killed, that is. You remember Farran, don't you? He had a special love for pain. He told me that torturing Sam Cortland was the most fun he ever had."

She could hardly see through the bloodlust that seized her in that moment, hardly remember her own name.

Archer feinted toward the river to get her to return to the wall—where she would impale herself on his blade. But Celaena knew that move, too—knew it because she herself had taught it to him all those years ago. So as he struck, she ducked past his guard and rammed the pommel of her dagger up into his jaw.

He dropped like a stone, sword clattering, and she was upon him before he'd finished falling, her dagger at his throat.

"Please," he whispered hoarsely.

She pushed the edge of the blade into his skin, wondering how she could make this last without killing him too quickly.

"*Please,*" he begged, chest heaving. "I'm doing it for our freedom. Our *freedom.* We're on the same side in the end."

One flick of the wrist, and she could slit his throat. Or she could disable him the way she'd disabled Grave. She could give him the injuries Grave had given Nehemia. She smiled.

"You're not a murderer," he whispered.

"Oh, I am," she purred, torchlight dancing on the dagger as she considered what to do with him.

"Nehemia wouldn't want this. She wouldn't want you to do this."

And though she knew she shouldn't listen, the words struck home.

Don't let that light go out.

The darkness that thrived in her soul had no light left. No light—save for a kernel, a faint flicker that grew smaller by the day. Wherever she was now, Nehemia knew how small the flame had become.

Don't let that light go out.

Celaena felt the tension go out of her body, but she kept her dagger on Archer's throat until she was on her feet.

"You're leaving Rifthold tonight," she told him. "You and all of your friends."

"Thank you," Archer breathed, standing.

"If I find out you're still in the city at dawn," she said, putting her back to him as she stalked toward the tunnel stairs, "I'll kill you." Enough. It was enough.

"Thank you," Archer said again.

She kept walking, listening for any sign of him moving to attack her back.

"I knew you were a good woman," he said.

Celaena halted. Turned.

There was a hint of triumph in his eyes. He thought he'd won. Manipulated her again. One foot after another, she walked back toward him with predatory calmness.

She stopped, close enough to kiss him. He gave her a wary smile.

"No, I'm not," she said. Then she moved, too fast for him to stand a chance.

Archer's eyes went wide as she slid the dagger home, jamming it up into his heart.

He sagged in her arms. She brought her mouth to his ear, holding him upright with one hand and twisting the dagger with the other as she whispered, "But Nehemia was."

CHAPTER 52

Chaol watched blood bubble out of Archer's lips as Celaena let him slump to the stone floor. She stared down at the body, her final words to him hovering in the air, running claws over Chaol's already chilled skin. She closed her eyes, tilting her head back as she took a long breath—as if she were embracing the death before her, and the stain it left as payment for her vengeance.

He had arrived in time to hear Archer beg for his life—and utter the words that had been his last mistake. Chaol shifted his boot against the step to warn her that he was there. How much of her Fae senses did she retain when she looked like a human?

Archer's blood spread across the dark stones, and Celaena opened her eyes as she slowly turned to Chaol. The blood had soaked the ends of her hair, turning them a brilliant red. And her eyes . . . There was nothing there, as though she'd been hollowed out. For a heartbeat, he wondered if she would kill him, too—just for being there, for seeing the dark truth of her.

She blinked, and the killing calm in her eyes vanished, replaced only by bone-deep weariness and sorrow. An invisible burden that he couldn't begin to imagine made her shoulders slump. She picked up the black book that Archer had dropped on the damp stones, but let it dangle from her fingers as if it were a piece of dirty clothing.

"I owe you an explanation," was all she said.

Celaena refused to let the healer look at her until Fleetfoot's leg had been fixed. It was only a long scratch, but it was deep. Celaena had held Fleetfoot's head in her arms as the thrashing dog was forced to swallow water laced with a sedative. Dorian helped as best he could while the healer worked on the dog lying unconscious on Celaena's dining-room table. Chaol leaned against the wall of the room, arms crossed over his chest. He'd said nothing to Dorian since they'd gone down into the passageway.

The young, brown-haired healer didn't ask any questions, either. Once Fleetfoot was patched up and moved to Celaena's bed, Dorian insisted Celaena get her head looked at. But Celaena waved him off and told the healer that if she didn't inspect the Crown Prince first, she'd report her to the king. Scowling, Dorian let the young woman clean the small wound on his temple, received when Celaena had knocked him out cold. Considering how bloody Celaena and Chaol were, he felt utterly ridiculous, even if his head still pounded.

The healer finished with him, giving him a timid, slightly concerned smile. And when it was time to decide who should be looked at next, the glaring contest between Chaol and Celaena was one for the ages.

At last, Chaol just shook his head and slumped into the seat that Dorian had recently vacated. He had blood everywhere, and ended up peeling off his tunic and shirt so the healer could cleanse his minor wounds. Despite the scratches and cuts, the abrasions on his hands and knees, the healer still asked no questions, her pretty face an unreadable, professional mask.

Celaena turned to Dorian, her voice quiet. "I'll come to your rooms when I'm done here."

From the corner of his eye, he sensed Chaol stiffening, and Dorian bit down on his surge of jealousy as he realized he was being dismissed. The captain was making a good show of not looking at them. What had happened during the time he'd blacked out? And what had happened when she'd gone to kill Archer?

"Fine," Dorian said, and thanked the healer for her help.

At least he had time now to piece himself together, to sort through all that had happened in the last few hours. And to plan how to explain his magic to Chaol.

But even as he walked out of the dining room, part of him realized that his magic—that *he*—was the least of their concerns. Because even from that first day in Endovier, this had always been about *them*.

Celaena didn't need a healer to look at her head. When the magic had taken her over, it had somehow healed everything. All that was left of her wounds now were bloodstains and torn clothing. And exhaustion—utter exhaustion.

"I'm taking a bath," she told Chaol, who still sat shirtless under the healer's ministrations.

She needed to wash Archer's blood off her.

She shucked off her clothing and bathed, scrubbing herself until her skin hurt, washing her hair twice. When she emerged, she slipped into a clean tunic and pants, and just as she finished combing out her dripping hair, Chaol walked into her bedroom and sat at the chair before her desk. The healer gone, he'd put his shirt back on, and she could see the white bandages peeking through the rips in the dark cloth.

Celaena checked on Fleetfoot, who was still unconscious on the bed, and then walked to the balcony doors. She studied the night sky for a long moment, seeking out a familiar constellation—the Stag, the Lord of the North. She took a long breath.

"My great-grandmother was Fae," she said. "And even though my mother couldn't switch into an animal form the way the Fae can, I somehow inherited the ability to shift. Between my Fae form and my human form."

"And you can't shift anymore?"

She looked over her shoulder at him. "When magic stopped ten years ago, I lost my ability. It's what saved my life, I think. As a child, when I was scared or upset or had tantrums, I couldn't control the shift. I was learning to master it, but I would have given myself away at some point."

"But in that—that other world, you could . . ."

She turned to face him, seeing the haunted gleam in his eyes. "Yes. In that world, magic, or something like it, still exists. And it is just as awful and overwhelming as I remembered." She eased onto the edge of her bed, the distance between them feeling like leagues. "I had no control over it—over the shift, or the magic, or myself. I was as likely to hurt you as I was to hurt that creature." She closed her eyes, her hands shaking a bit.

"So you *did* open a portal to another world. How?"

"All those books I've been reading on the Wyrdmarks—they had spells to open temporary portals." And then she explained about finding the passage on Samhuinn, and the tomb and Elena's command to become the Champion, and what Cain had been doing and how she had killed the ridderak, and how tonight she had wanted to open a portal to see Nehemia. She left out the Wyrdkeys, the king, and what she suspected he might be doing with Kaltain and Roland.

When she finished, Chaol said, "I would say you're insane, except I have the blood of that creature on me, and went into that world myself."

"If anyone knew—not just about the spells to open portals, but about what I am," she said wearily, "you understand that I would be executed."

His eyes flashed. "I'm not going to tell anyone. I swear it."

She bit her lip, nodding, and walked back to the window. "Archer told me that he was the one who had Nehemia assassinated, because she was a threat to his control over the group. He posed as Councilman Mullison and hired Grave. He kidnapped you to lure me away. He planted that anonymous threat against her life, too. Because he wanted me to blame you for her death."

Chaol swore, but she kept gazing out the window, kept looking at that constellation.

"But even though I know you're not responsible," she said softly, "I still . . ." She found his face full of anguish.

"You still can't trust me," he finished.

She nodded. In this, she knew Archer had won, and hated him for it. "When I look at you," she whispered, "all I want to do is touch you. But what happened that night . . . I don't know if I can ever forget it." The deepest cut on his cheek had scabbed, and she knew it would scar. "For my part, I am sorry for what I did to you."

He stood, wincing at his wounds, and walked over to her. "We both made mistakes," he said in that voice that made her heart stumble.

She found the nerve to turn to him, gazing up into his face. "How can you still look at me like that when you know what I truly am?"

His fingers grazed her cheeks, warming her chilled skin. "Fae, assassin—no matter what you are, I—"

"Don't." She stepped back. "Don't say it."

She couldn't give him everything again—not now. It wouldn't be fair to either of them. Even if she ever learned to forgive him for picking the king over Nehemia, her journey to find the Wyrdkeys would require her to go far away, to a place where she would never ask him to follow.

"I need to prepare Archer's body to present to the king," she got out. Before he could say anything else, she picked up Damaris from where she'd dropped it by the door and vanished into the passage.

She waited until she was deep inside before she let the tears start flowing.

⌒

Chaol stared at where she had gone and wondered if he should follow her into that ancient darkness. But he thought of all that she'd told him, all the secrets she'd revealed, and knew he needed time to comprehend it all.

He could tell that she had left out information. She'd told him only the vaguest details; and then there was the matter of her Fae heritage. He'd never heard of anyone inheriting their powers in such a throwback way, but then again, no one spoke of the Fae nowadays. It explained how she knew the ancient dirges.

With a gentle pat on Fleetfoot's head, he left the room. The halls were empty and silent.

And Dorian—she had acted like Dorian had some power, too. There had been the moment when the creature was blasted away by an invisible wall . . . But it was impossible for Dorian to have power. How could he, when Celaena's own—own *magic* had disappeared as soon as she returned to this world?

Celaena was Fae, and heir to a power she couldn't control. Even if she couldn't shift, if anyone ever discovered what she was . . .

It explained why she was so terrified of the king, why she never said anything about where she'd come from, or what she'd been through. And living *here* . . . this was the most dangerous place for her—or any Fae—to be.

If someone found out what she was, they could use that information against her, or have her killed. And there would be nothing he could do to save her. No lie he could tell, no strings he could pull. How long before someone else went digging into her past? How long before someone decided to go right to Arobynn Hamel and torture him for the truth?

Chaol's feet knew where he was going long before he'd made the choice, formed the plan. Minutes later, he found himself knocking on a wooden door.

His father's eyes were bleary with sleep, and they narrowed as they saw him. "Do you know what time it is?"

He didn't, and he didn't care. Chaol shouldered his way into the room and shut the door, scanning the dimness for any other people. "I have a favor to ask you, but before I do, promise you won't ask any questions."

His father gave him a slightly bemused look, then crossed his arms. "No questions. Make your request."

Beyond the window, the sky was beginning to lighten into a softer shade of black. "I think that we should send the King's Champion to Wendlyn to dispatch the royal family."

His father's brows rose. Chaol went on. "We've been at war with them for two years, and have yet to break past their naval defenses. But if the king and his son are eliminated, we might stand a chance of getting through in the ensuing chaos. Especially if the King's Champion also gets her hands on their naval defense plans." He took a breath, keeping his voice disinterested. "I want to present the idea to the king this morning. And I want you to support me."

Because Dorian would never agree to it, not without knowing what Celaena was. And Chaol would never tell anyone, Dorian included. But with an idea this drastic, he'd need as much political muscle as he could get.

"An ambitious, ruthless plan." His father smiled. "And if I support this idea and convince my allies on the council to support it, too, then what can I expect in return?" From the way his eyes gleamed, his father already knew the answer.

"Then I will go back to Anielle with you," Chaol said. "I will leave my position as Captain and . . . return home."

It wasn't his home, not anymore, but if it meant getting Celaena out of the country . . . Wendlyn was the last stronghold of the Fae, and the one place in Erilea where she'd be truly safe.

Whatever shred of hope he'd had for a future with her was gone. She still felt something for him, she'd admitted, but she would never trust him. She would always hate him for what he'd done.

But he could do this for her. Even if he never saw her again, even if she abandoned her duties as King's Champion and stayed with the Fae in Wendlyn forever—as long as he knew that she was safe, that no one could hurt her . . . He'd sell his soul again and again for that.

His father's eyes gleamed with triumph. "Consider it done."

CHAPTER 53

When Celaena finished telling Dorian the story she'd told Chaol—albeit a much more limited version—he let out a long sigh and fell back onto his bed. "It sounds like something out of a book," he said, staring at the ceiling. She sat down on the other side of the bed.

"Believe me, I thought I was going mad for a while."

"So you actually opened a portal to another world? Using these Wyrdmarks?"

She nodded. "*You* also knocked that creature aside like it was a leaf caught in a wind." Oh, she hadn't forgotten about that. Not for one moment had she forgotten what it meant for him to have such raw power.

"That was dumb luck." She watched him, this kind, clever prince of hers. "I still can't control it."

"In the tomb," she said, "there is someone who might . . . offer you some advice on how to control it. Who might have some information about the kind of power you've inherited." Right then, though, she didn't exactly know how to explain Mort to him, so she just said, "Someday soon, you and I could go down there and meet him."

"Is he—"

"You'll see when we get there. *If* he deigns to speak to you. It might take a while for him to decide he likes you."

After a moment, Dorian reached over and took her hand, bringing it to his lips for a swift kiss. Nothing romantic—a gesture of thanks. "Even though things are different between us now, I meant what I said after the duel with Cain. I will always be grateful that you came into my life."

Her throat tightened, and she squeezed his hand.

Nehemia had dreamed of a court that could change the world, a court where loyalty and honor were more valued than blind obedience and power. The day Nehemia had died, Celaena had thought the dream of that court forever vanished.

But looking at Dorian as he smiled at her, this prince who was smart and thoughtful and kind, who inspired good men like Chaol to serve him . . .

Celaena wondered if Nehemia's impossible, desperate dream of that court might yet come to pass.

The real question now was whether his father knew what a threat his son posed.

The King of Adarlan had to give the captain credit; the plan was ruthless and bold, and would send a message not just to Wendlyn, but to all their enemies. With the embargo between their countries, Wendlyn refused to let Adarlanian men into its borders. But women and children seeking refuge could still enter. It made sending anyone else impossible, but his Champion . . .

The king looked down his council table, where the captain was waiting for his decision. Westfall's father and four others had immediately supported the idea. Another bit of unexpected cunning from the captain. He'd brought allies to this meeting.

Dorian, however, was watching the captain with barely concealed surprise. Clearly, Westfall hadn't thought Dorian would support his decision. If only Westfall had been his heir instead; his warrior's mind was sharp, and he didn't balk from doing what needed to be done. The prince had yet to learn that kind of ruthlessness.

Getting the assassin away from his son would be an unexpected benefit. He trusted the girl to do his dirty work—but he didn't want her around Dorian.

She'd brought Archer Finn's head to him this morning, not a day later than she'd promised him, and explained what she'd discovered: that Archer had been responsible for Nehemia's assassination due to their mutual involvement in that traitorous society. He wasn't surprised that Nehemia was involved.

But what would the assassin have to say about this journey?

"Summon my Champion," he said. In the ensuing silence, the council members murmured to each other, and his son tried to catch Westfall's eye. But the captain avoided looking at the prince.

The king smiled slightly, twisting the black ring on his finger. A pity Perrington wasn't here to see this. He was off dealing with the slave uprising in Calaculla—news of which had been kept so secret that even the messengers had forfeited their lives. The duke would have been greatly amused by today's turn of events. But he wished Perrington here for more important reasons, too—to help him find out who had opened a portal last night.

He'd sensed it in his sleep—a sudden shift in the world. It was open for only a few minutes before someone closed it again. Cain was gone; who else in this castle possessed that kind of knowledge, or that power in the blood? Was it the same person who had killed Baba Yellowlegs?

He put a hand on Nothung, his sword.

There had been no body—but he didn't think for one moment that Yellowlegs had just disappeared. The morning after she'd vanished, he'd gone to the carnival himself to look at the ruined wagon. He'd seen the flecks of dark blood staining the wooden floor.

Yellowlegs had been a queen among her people, one of the three brutal factions that had destroyed the Crochan family five hundred years ago. They'd relished erasing much of the wisdom of the Crochan women who had ruled justly for a thousand years. He'd invited the carnival here to meet with her—to purchase a few of her mirrors, and learn what remained of the Ironteeth Alliance that had once been strong enough to rip apart the Witch Kingdom.

But before she had yielded any decent information, she had died. And it frustrated him not to know why. Her blood had been spilled at his castle; others might come to demand answers and retribution. If they came, he would be ready.

Because in the shadows of the Ferian Gap, he'd been breeding new mounts for his gathering armies. And his wyverns still needed riders.

The doors to the council room opened. The assassin walked in, shoulders thrown back in that insufferable way of hers. She coolly took in the details of the room before stopping a few feet away from the table and bowing low. "Your Majesty summoned me?"

She kept her eyes averted, as she usually did. Except for that delightful day when she'd come in and practically flayed Mullison alive. Part of him wished he didn't now have to free the sniveling councilman from the dungeons.

"Your companion, Captain Westfall, has come up with a rather . . . unusual idea," the king said, and waved a hand at Chaol. "Why don't you explain, Captain?"

The Captain twisted in his chair, then rose to his feet to face her. "I have suggested that we send you to Wendlyn to dispatch the king and his heir. While you are there, you will also seize their naval and military defense plans—so that once the country is in chaos, we will be able to navigate their impenetrable barrier reefs and take the country for ourselves."

The assassin looked at him for a long moment, and the king noticed that his son had gone very, very still. Then she smiled, a cruel, twisted thing. "It would be an honor to serve the crown in such a way."

He had never learned anything about the mark that had glowed on her head during the duel. The Wyrdmark was impossible to decipher. It either meant "nameless" or "unnamed," or something akin to "anonymous." But gods-blessed or not, from the wicked grin on her face, the king knew she'd enjoy this task.

"Perhaps we'll have some fun with it," the king mused. "Wendlyn is having their Solstice ball in a few months. What a message it would send if the king and his son were to meet their end right under the noses of their own court, on their day of triumph."

Though the captain shifted on his feet at the sudden change of plans, the assassin smiled at him again, dark glee written all over her. What hellhole had she come from, to find delight in such things? "A brilliant idea, Your Majesty."

"It's done, then," the king said, and they all looked at him. "You'll leave tomorrow."

"But," his son interrupted, "surely she needs some time to study Wendlyn, to learn its ways and—"

"It's a two-week journey by sea," he said. "And then she'll need time to infiltrate the castle in time for the ball. She can take whatever materials she needs and study them onboard."

Her brows had lifted slightly, but she just bowed her head. The captain was still standing, stiffer than usual. And his son was glaring—glaring at him and at the captain, so angry that he wondered whether he'd snap.

But the king wasn't particularly interested in their petty dramas, not when this brilliant plan had arisen. He'd have to send riders immediately to the Ferian Gap and the Dead Islands, and have General Narrok ready his legion. He didn't mean to make mistakes with this one chance in Wendlyn.

And it would be the perfect opportunity to test a few of the weapons he'd been forging in secret all these years.

Tomorrow.

She was leaving *tomorrow*.

And *Chaol* had come up with the idea? But why? She wanted to demand answers, wanted to know what he was thinking when he'd come up with this plan. She'd never told him the truth about the king's threats—that he would execute Chaol if she didn't return from a mission, if she failed. And she could fake the deaths of petty lords and merchants, but not the King and Crown Prince of Wendlyn. Not in a thousand lifetimes could she find a way out of it.

She paced and paced, knowing Chaol wouldn't be back in his rooms yet, and wound up going down to the tomb, if only to give herself something to do.

She expected Mort to lecture her about the portal—which he did, thoroughly—but she *didn't* expect to find Elena waiting for her inside the tomb. "You have enough power to appear to me *now*, but you couldn't help close the portal last night?"

She took one look at the queen's frown and began pacing again.

"I could not," Elena said. "Even now, this visit is draining me faster than it should."

Celaena scowled at her. "I can't go to Wendlyn. I—I *can't* go.

Chaol *knows* what I'm doing for you—so why would he make me go there?"

"Take a breath," Elena said softly.

Celaena glared at her. "This ruins *your* plans, too. If I'm in Wendlyn, then I can't deal with the Wyrdkeys and the king. And even if I pretended to go and instead went questing across this continent, it wouldn't take long for the king to realize I'm not where I'm supposed to be."

Elena crossed her arms. "If you are in Wendlyn, then you will be near Doranelle. I think that's why the captain wants you to go."

Celaena barked a laugh. Oh, what a tangled mess he'd gotten her into! "He wants me to go hide with the Fae and never come back to Adarlan? That's not going to happen. Not only will he be *killed*, but the Wyrdkeys—"

"You will sail to Wendlyn tomorrow." Elena's eyes glowed bright. "Leave the Wyrdkeys and the king for now. Go to Wendlyn, and do what needs to be done."

"Did you plant this idea in his head somehow?"

"No. The captain is trying to save you the only way he knows how."

Celaena shook her head, looking at the sunlight pouring into the tomb from the shaft above. "Will you ever stop giving me commands?"

Elena let out a soft laugh. "When you stop running from your past, I will."

Celaena rolled her eyes, then let her shoulders droop. A shard of memory sliced through her. "When I spoke to Nehemia, she mentioned . . . mentioned that she knew her own fate. That she had embraced it. That it would set things in motion. Do you think she somehow manipulated Archer into . . ." But she couldn't finish saying it, couldn't let herself voice what the horrible truth might be: that Nehemia had engineered her own death, knowing that she might change the world—change *Celaena*—more through dying than living.

A cold, slender hand grasped hers. "Cast that thought into the far reaches of your mind. Knowing the truth, whatever it may be, will not change what you must do tomorrow—where you must go."

And even though Celaena knew the truth in that moment, knew it just from Elena's refusal to answer at all, she did as the queen commanded. There would be other moments, other times to take out that truth to examine every dark and unforgiving facet. But right now—right now . . .

Celaena studied the light pouring into the tomb. Such a little light, holding the darkness at bay. "Wendlyn, then."

Elena smiled grimly and squeezed her hand. "Wendlyn, then."

CHAPTER 54

When the council meeting was over, Chaol did his best not to look at his father, who had been watching him so carefully while he'd announced his plans to the king, or at Dorian, whose sense of betrayal rippled off of him as the meeting went on. He tried to hurry back to the barracks, but he wasn't all that surprised when a hand clapped on his shoulder and turned him around.

"*Wendlyn?*" Dorian snarled.

Chaol kept his face blank. "If she's capable of opening a portal like she did last night, then I think she needs to get out of the castle for a while. For all of our sakes." Dorian couldn't know the truth.

"She'll never forgive you for having her shipped off like that, to take down a whole *country*. And in such a public way—making a spectacle out of it. Are you mad?"

"I don't need her forgiveness. And I don't want to worry about her letting in a horde of otherworldly creatures just because she's missing her friend."

He hated each lie that came out of his mouth, but Dorian drank them up, his eyes seeming to glow with rage. This was the other sacrifice he'd have to make; because if Dorian didn't hate him, if he didn't *want* Chaol gone, then leaving for Anielle would be that much more difficult.

"If anything happens to her in Wendlyn," Dorian growled, refusing to back down, "I'll make you regret the day you were born."

If anything happened to her, Chaol was fairly certain he'd forever regret that day, too.

But he just said, "One of us has to start leading, Dorian," and stalked off.

Dorian didn't follow him.

Dawn was just breaking as Celaena arrived at Nehemia's grave. The last of the winter snows had melted, leaving the world barren and brown, waiting for spring.

In a few hours, she'd set sail across the ocean.

Celaena dropped to her knees on the damp ground and bowed her head before the grave.

Then she said the words she'd wanted to say to Nehemia last night. The words that she should have said from the beginning. Words that wouldn't change, no matter what she learned about Nehemia's death.

"I want you to know," she whispered to the wind, to the earth, to the body far beneath her, "that you were right. You were right. I am a coward. And I have been running for so long that I've forgotten what it is to stand and fight."

She bowed deeper, putting her forehead against the dirt.

"But I promise," she breathed into the soil, "I promise that I will stop him. I promise that I will never forgive, never forget what they did to you. I promise that I will free Eyllwe. I promise that I will see your father's crown restored to his head."

She raised herself, drawing a dagger from her pocket, and sliced a line across her left palm. Blood welled, ruby-bright against the golden dawn, sliding down the side of her hand before she pressed her palm to the earth.

"I promise," she whispered again. "On my name, on my life, even if it takes until my last breath, I promise I will see Eyllwe freed."

She let her blood soak into the ground, willing it to carry the words of her oath to the Otherworld where Nehemia was safe at last. From now on, there would be no other oaths but this, no other contracts, no other obligations. *Never forgive, never forget.*

And she didn't know how she would do it, or how long it would take, but she would see it through. Because Nehemia couldn't.

Because it was time.

CHAPTER 55

The shattered lock on Celaena's bedroom door still wasn't fixed by the time Dorian appeared after breakfast, a stack of books in his arms. She stood before her bed, stuffing clothing into a large leather satchel. Fleetfoot was the first to acknowledge him, though he had no doubt Celaena heard him coming from the hallway.

The dog limped to him, tail wagging, and Dorian set the books on the desk before kneeling on the plush rug. He ran his hands over Fleetfoot's head, letting her lick him a few times.

"The healer said her leg is going to be fine," Celaena said, still focused on her satchel. Her left hand was bandaged—a wound he hadn't noticed last night. "She just left a few minutes ago."

"Good," Dorian said, rising to his feet. She was wearing a heavy tunic and pants and a thick cloak. Her brown boots were sturdy and sensible, far more subdued than her usual attire. Traveling clothes. "Were you going to leave without saying good-bye?"

"I thought it would be easier this way," she said. In two hours, she would sail to Wendlyn, that land of myths and monsters, a kingdom of dreams and nightmares made flesh.

Dorian approached her. "This plan is madness. You don't have to go. We can convince my father to do something else. If they catch you in Wendlyn—"

"They won't catch me."

"There will be no help for you," Dorian said, putting a hand on the satchel. "If you are captured, if you are hurt, you are beyond our reach. You will be entirely on your own."

"I'll be fine."

"But *I* won't be. Every day that you're there, I will wonder what has become of you. I won't . . . I won't forget you. Not for one hour."

Her throat bobbed, the only sign of emotion she allowed to show, and she looked toward her dog, watching them from the rug. "Will you . . ." He watched her swallow again before meeting his gaze. The gold in her eyes glowed in the morning sun. "Will you look after her while I'm gone?"

He took her hand, squeezing. "As if she's one of my own. I'll even let her sleep in the bed."

She gave him a small smile, and he had a feeling that any greater sign of emotion would shatter her self-control. He waved a hand to the books he'd brought. "I hope you don't mind, but I need a place to store these, and your rooms might be . . . safer than mine."

She glanced at the desk but, to his relief, didn't go to it. The books he'd brought would only lead to more questions. Geneaologies, royal chronicles, anything on how and why he might have magic. "Of course," was all she said. "I think *The Walking Dead* is still floating around in here, anyway. Maybe it'll be glad to have company."

He might have smiled had it not been eerily true. "I'll leave you to your packing. I have a council meeting at the same time your ship departs," he said, fighting the ache in his chest. It was a lie—and a bad one. But he didn't want to be at the docks, not when he knew someone else would be there to see her off. "So . . . I suppose this is good-bye." He didn't know whether he was allowed to embrace her anymore, so he stuffed his hands into his pockets and gave her a smile. "Take care of yourself."

A faint nod.

They were friends now, and he knew that the physical boundaries between them had been altered, but . . . He turned away rather than let her see the disappointment he knew was all too clear on his face.

He took all of two steps toward the door before she spoke, the words soft and strained. "Thank you for all that you have done for me, Dorian. Thank you for being my friend. For not being like the others."

He paused, turning to face her. She kept her chin high, but her eyes were gleaming.

"I'll come back," she said quietly. "I'll come back for you." And he knew that there was more that she wasn't saying, some bigger meaning behind those words.

But Dorian still believed her.

The docks were crowded with sailors and slaves and workers loading and unloading cargo. The day was warm and breezy, the first hint of spring in the air, and the sky was cloudless. A good day for sailing.

Celaena stood before the ship that would carry her through the first leg of the journey. It would sail to a prearranged location where a ship from Wendlyn would meet it to take aboard refugees fleeing the shadow of Adarlan's empire. Most of the women traveling on her ship were already belowdecks. She shifted the fingers of her bandaged left hand, wincing at the dull pain radiating outward from her palm.

She had hardly slept that night, holding Fleetfoot close to her instead. Saying good-bye an hour ago had been like ripping out a piece of her heart, but the dog's leg was still too injured for her to risk the journey to Wendlyn.

She hadn't wanted to see Chaol, hadn't bothered saying good-bye, because she had so many questions for him that it was easier not to ask at all. Hadn't he known what an impossible trap he was setting for her now?

The ship captain bellowed a five-minute departure warning. The sailors started scrambling, doubling their efforts to prepare to leave the harbor and set out down the Avery, and then into the Great Ocean itself.

To Wendlyn.

She swallowed hard. *Do what needs to be done*, Elena had told her. Did that mean actually killing the royal family of Wendlyn, or something else?

A salty breeze ruffled her hair, and she stepped forward.

But someone emerged from the shadows of the buildings lining the docks.

"Wait," Chaol said.

Celaena froze as he walked to her, and didn't move even when she found herself looking up into his face.

"Do you understand why I did this?" he asked softly.

She nodded, but said, "I have to return here."

"*No*," he said, his eyes flashing. "You—"

"*Listen.*"

She had five minutes. She couldn't explain it to him now—couldn't explain that the king would kill him if she didn't return. That knowledge could be fatal to him. And even if he ran away, the king had threatened Nehemia's family, too.

But she knew that Chaol was trying to protect her. And she couldn't leave him wholly ignorant. Because if she did die in Wendlyn, if something happened to her . . .

"Listen carefully to what I am about to tell you."

His brows rose. But she didn't give herself a moment to reconsider, to second-guess her decision.

As succinctly as she could, she told him about the Wyrdkeys. She told him about the Wyrdgates, and about Baba Yellowlegs. She told him about the papers she'd stashed down in the tomb—the riddle with the locations of the three Wyrdkeys. And then she told him that she knew the king had at least one. And that there was a dead creature sealed beneath the library. And that he should never open the door to the catacombs—*never.* And that Roland and Kaltain might be part of some bigger, deadlier plan.

And when that horrible truth had been revealed, she unfastened the Eye of Elena from her neck and folded it into his palm. "Never take it off. It will protect you from harm."

He was shaking his head, his face deathly pale. "Celaena, I can't—"

"I don't care if you go looking for the keys, but *someone* has to know about them. Someone other than me. All the proof is in the tomb."

Chaol grabbed her hand with his free one. "Celaena—"

"*Listen,*" she repeated. "If you hadn't convinced the king to send me away, we could have . . . figured them out together. But now . . ."

Two minutes, the sea captain shouted. Chaol was just staring at her, such grief and fear in his eyes that speech failed her.

And then she did the most reckless thing she'd ever done in her life. She stood on her toes and whispered the words into his ear.

The words that would make him understand, understand why it was so important to her, and what it meant when she said she would return. And he would hate her forever for it, once he understood.

"What does that mean?" he demanded.

She smiled sadly. "You'll figure it out. And when you do . . ." She shook her head, knowing she shouldn't say it, but doing it anyway. "When you do, I want you to remember that it wouldn't have made any difference to me. It's never made any difference to me when it came to you. I'd still pick you. I'll always pick you."

"Please—please, just tell me what that means."

But there was no time, so she shook her head and stepped back.

Chaol took one step toward her, though. One step, then he said, "I love you."

She strangled the sob that built in her throat. "I'm sorry," she said, hoping he would remember those words later—later, when he knew everything.

Her legs found the strength to move. She took a breath. And with a final look at Chaol, she strode up the gangplank. Taking no notice of those onboard, she set down her sack and took up a place by the railing. She looked down at the dock to find Chaol still standing by the walkway as it was lifted.

The ship's captain called for them to cast off. Sailors scurried, ropes were untied, tossed, and tied again, and the ship lurched. Her hands clasped the railing so hard they hurt.

The ship began moving. And Chaol—the man she hated and loved so much that she could hardly think around him—just stood there, watching her go.

The current grabbed the ship, and the city began to diminish. The ocean breeze soon caressed her neck, but she never stopped staring at Chaol. She stared toward him until the glass castle was a sparkling speck in the distance. She stared toward him until there was only gleaming ocean around her. She stared toward him until the sun dropped beyond the horizon and a smattering of stars hung overhead.

It was only when her eyelids drooped and she swayed on her feet that Celaena stopped staring toward Chaol.

The smell of salt filled her nostrils, so different from the salt of Endovier, and a spirited wind whipped through her hair.

With a hiss through her teeth, Celaena Sardothien turned her back on Adarlan and sailed toward Wendlyn.

CHAPTER
56

Chaol didn't understand what she'd told him, the words she'd whispered in his ear. It was a date. Not even a year attached to it. A month and a day—a date that had passed weeks and weeks ago. It was the day that Celaena had left the city. The day she had snapped at Endovier a year before. The day her parents had died.

He stayed on the docks long after the ship was out of the harbor, watching its sails become smaller and smaller as he mulled over the date again and again. Why had she told him everything about those—those Wyrdkeys, but made this hint so obscure? What could possibly be more important than the horrible truth about the king he served?

The Wyrdkeys, while they terrified him, made sense. They explained so much. The king's great power, his journeys that ended with the whole party mysteriously dying, how Cain had become so strong. Even that time Chaol had looked at Perrington and seen his eyes darken so strangely. But when she'd told him, had she known what kind of choice she'd left him? And what could he possibly do about it from Anielle?

Unless he could find a way out of the vow he'd made. He'd never said *when* he would go to Anielle. He could think about that tomorrow. For now . . .

When Chaol returned to the castle, he went to her rooms, sorting through the contents of her desk. But there was nothing about that date. He checked the will she'd written, but that had been signed several days after. The silence and emptiness of her chambers threatened to swallow him whole, and he was about to leave when he spotted the stack of books half hidden in the shadows of her desk.

Geneaologies and countless royal chronicles. When had she brought these books here? He hadn't seen them the other night. Was it somehow another clue? Standing before the desk, he pulled out the royal chronicles—all from the past eighteen years—and started back, one by one. Nothing.

Then came the chronicle from ten years ago. It was thicker than all the rest—as it should be, given the events that had happened that year. But when he saw what was written about the date she had given, everything froze.

This morning, King Orlon Galathynius, his nephew and heir, Rhoe Galathynius, and Rhoe's wife, Evalin, were found assassinated. Orlon was murdered in his bed at the royal palace in Orynth, and Rhoe and Evalin were found dead in their beds at their country estate along the River Florine. There is no word yet about the fate of Rhoe and Evalin's daughter, Aelin.

Chaol grabbed for the first geneaology book, the one on the bloodlines of the royal houses of Adarlan and Terrasen. Was Celaena trying to tell him she knew the truth about what had happened that night—that she might know where the lost princess Aelin was hiding? That she had been there when this all happened?

He flipped through the pages, scanning the genealogies he had already read. But then he remembered something about the name Evalin Ashryver. *Ashryver.*

Evalin had come from Wendlyn, had been a princess of the king's court. Hands shaking, he yanked out a book containing Wendlyn's royal family tree.

On the last page, Aelin Ashryver Galathynius's name was written at the bottom, and above it, her mother, Evalin's. But the family tree traced only the female line. The female, not the male, because—

Two spots above Evalin's name was written Mab. Aelin's great-grandmother. She was one of the three Fae Sister-Queens: Maeve, Mora, and Mab. Mab, the youngest, the fairest, who, when she died, had been made into a goddess, known to them now as Deanna, Lady of the Hunt.

The memory hit him like a brick to the face. That Yulemas morning, when Celaena had looked so uncomfortable to be receiving the golden arrow of Deanna—the arrow of Mab.

And Chaol counted down the family tree, one after one, until—

My great-grandmother was Fae.

Chaol had to brace a hand against the desk. No, it couldn't be. He turned back to the chronicle still lying open, and turned to the next day.

Aelin Galathynius, heir to the throne of Terrasen, died today, or sometime in the night. Before help could reach her deceased parents' estate, the assassin who had missed her the night before returned. Her body has still not been found, though some believe it was thrown into the river behind her parents' house.

She'd once said that Arobynn had . . . had *found* her. Found her half-dead and frozen. On a riverbank.

He was just jumping to conclusions. Maybe she merely wanted him to know that she still cared about Terrasen, or—

There was a poem scribbled at the top of the Ashryver family tree, as though some student had dashed it down as a reminder while studying.

Ashryver Eyes
The fairest eyes, from legends old
Of brightest blue, ringed with gold.

Bright blue eyes, ringed with gold. A strangled cry came out of him. How many times had he looked into those eyes? How many times had he seen her avert her gaze, that one bit of proof she couldn't hide, from the king?

Celaena Sardothien wasn't in league with Aelin Ashryver Galathynius.

Celaena Sardothien *was* Aelin Ashryver Galathynius, heir to the throne and rightful Queen of Terrasen.

Celaena was Aelin Galathynius, the greatest living threat to Adarlan, the one person who could raise an army capable of standing against the king. Now, she was also the one person who knew the secret source of the king's power—and who sought a way to destroy it.

And he had just sent her into the arms of her strongest potential allies: to the homeland of her mother, the kingdom of her cousin, and the domain of her aunt, Queen Maeve of the Fae.

Celaena was the lost Queen of Terrasen.

Chaol sank to his knees.

ACKNOWLEDGMENTS

More than anyone, this novel belongs to Susan Dennard. For being the kind of friend that usually exists only in books. For being a friend worth waiting for. For being my *anam cara*. Thank you for the (mis)adventures, for laughing until our stomachs hurt, and for all the joy you've brought into my world. Love you.

Endless gratitude to my A Team: my incredible agent, Tamar Rydzinski; my stellar editor, Margaret Miller; and the incomparable Michelle Nagler. I'm tremendously blessed to have you in my corner. Thank you for everything you've done for me.

To my good friend and critique partner, Alex Bracken, who never fails to offer sage advice and brilliant ideas, and who has talked me off many, many ledges. Thank you for being one of the bright lights on this journey. To Erin "Ders" Bowman, for the Friday chats, shenanigans in "Wilderness," and being a fellow survivor of the brutal 2012 crawfish attack in Lake Glenville, North Carolina. I'm so glad I e-mailed you.

Thanks are also due to Amie Kaufman, Kat Zhang, and Jane Zhao, who have been everything from sounding boards to critique partners to cheerleaders, but always wonderful friends. To the ridiculously clever Biljana Likic, for helping with the riddle all those years ago. To Dan "DKroks" Krokos, for being a true friend and partner in crime. To the legendary Robin Hobb, for taking two debut authors to dinner in Decatur, Georgia—thank you for the wisdom and kindness you showed me and Susan.

There are so many people who work so tirelessly to make my books a reality and get them into readers' hands. Thank you from the bottom of my heart to Erica Barmash, Emma Bradshaw, Susannah Curran, Beth Eller, Alona Fryman, Shannon Godwin, Natalie Hamilton, Bridget Hartzler, Katy Hershberger, Melissa Kavonic, Linette Kim, Ian Lamb, Cindy Loh, Donna Mark, Patricia McHugh, Rebecca McNally, Regina Roff Flath, Rachel Stark, and Brett Wright. And a huge thank-you to the entire worldwide team at Bloomsbury—it's an honor to work with you all.

A giant hug for my parents, family, and friends—thank you for the unwavering support. And to my amazing husband, Josh: there aren't enough words in any language to describe how much I love you.

Thank you to Janet Cadsawan, who makes the world of Throne of Glass come alive with her stunning jewelry. And thank you to Kelly de Groot for the map, the enthusiasm, and just for being awesome.

To my readers: thank you for making this journey such a fairy tale; thank you for the letters and art and for coming to my events; thank you for spreading the word about this series; thank you for letting Celaena into your hearts. You make the long hours and hard work absolutely worth it.

And lastly, I'd like to thank my FictionPress readers, who have been with me for so many years, and to whom I owe a debt I can never repay. No matter where this road takes me, I'll be forever grateful that it brought you into my life. Thank you, thank you, thank you.

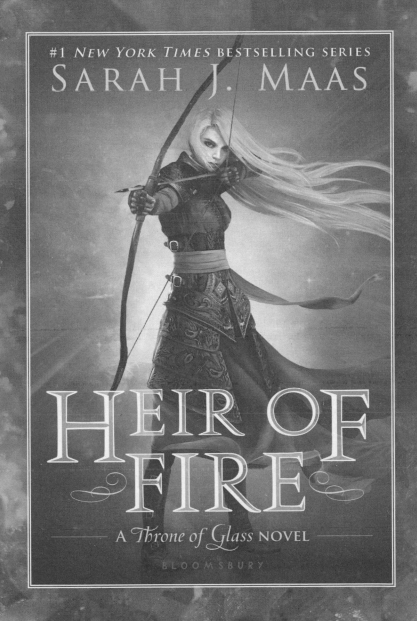

Gods, it was boiling in this useless excuse for a kingdom.

Or maybe it felt that way because Celaena Sardothien had been lounging on the lip of the terra-cotta roof since midmorning, an arm flung over her eyes, slowly baking in the sun like the loaves of flatbread the city's poorest citizens left on their windowsills because they couldn't afford brick ovens.

And gods, she was sick of flatbread—*teggya*, they called it. Sick of the crunchy, oniony taste of it that even mouthfuls of water couldn't wash away. If she never ate another bite of teggya again, it would be too soon.

Mostly because it was all she'd been able to afford when she landed in Wendlyn two weeks ago and made her way to the capital city, Varese, just as she'd been ordered by his Grand Imperial Majesty and Master of the Earth, the King of Adarlan.

She'd resorted to swiping teggya and wine off vendors' carts since her money ran out, not long after she'd taken one look at the heavily fortified limestone castle, at the elite guards, at the cobalt banners flapping so proudly in the dry, hot wind and decided *not* to kill her assigned targets.

So it had been stolen teggya . . . and wine. The sour red wine from the vineyards lining the rolling hills around the walled capital—a taste she'd initially spat out but now very, very much enjoyed. Especially since the day when she decided that she didn't particularly care about anything at all.

She reached for the terra-cotta tiles sloping behind her, groping for the clay jug of wine she'd hauled onto the roof that morning. Patting, feeling for it, and then—

She swore. Where in hell was the wine?

The world tilted and went blindingly bright as she hoisted herself onto her elbows. Birds circled above, keeping well away from the white-tailed hawk that had been perched atop a nearby chimney all morning, waiting to snatch up its next meal. Below, the market street was a brilliant loom of color and sound, full of braying donkeys, merchants waving their wares, clothes both foreign and familiar, and the clacking of wheels against pale cobblestones. But where in hell was the—

Ah. There. Tucked beneath one of the heavy red tiles to keep cool. Just where she'd stashed it hours before, when she'd climbed onto the roof of the massive indoor market to survey the perimeter of the castle walls two blocks away. Or whatever she'd thought sounded official and useful before she'd realized that she'd rather sprawl in the shadows. Shadows that had long since been burned away by that relentless Wendlyn sun.

Celaena swigged from the jug of wine—or tried to. It was empty, which she supposed was a blessing, because *gods* her head was spinning. She needed water, and more teggya. And perhaps something for the gloriously painful split lip and scraped cheekbone she'd earned last night in one of the city's *tabernas*.

Groaning, Celaena rolled onto her belly and surveyed the street forty feet below. She knew the guards patrolling it by now—had marked their faces and weapons, just as she had with the guards atop the high castle walls. She'd memorized their rotations, and how they opened the three massive gates that led into the castle. It seemed that the Ashryvers and their ancestors took safety very, very seriously.

It had been ten days since she'd arrived in Varese itself, after hauling ass from the coast. Not because she was particularly eager to kill her targets, but because the city was so damn large that it seemed her best chance of dodging the immigration officials, whom she'd given the slip instead of registering with their oh-so-benevolent work program. Hurrying to the capital had also provided welcome activity after weeks at sea, where she hadn't really felt like doing anything other than lying on the narrow bed in her cramped cabin or sharpening her weapons with a near-religious zeal.

You're nothing but a coward, Nehemia had said to her.

Every slice of the whetting stone had echoed it. *Coward, coward, coward.* The word had trailed her each league across the ocean.

She had made a vow—a vow to free Eyllwe. So in between moments of despair and rage and grief, in between thoughts of Chaol and the Wyrdkeys and all she'd left behind and lost, Celaena had decided on one plan to follow when she reached these shores. One plan, however insane and unlikely, to free the enslaved kingdom: find and obliterate the Wyrdkeys the King of Adarlan had used to build his terrible empire. She'd gladly destroy herself to carry it out.

Just her, just him. Just as it should be; no loss of life beyond their own, no soul stained but hers. It would take a monster to destroy a monster.

If she had to be here thanks to Chaol's misplaced good intentions, then at least she'd receive the answers she needed. There was one person in Erilea who had been present when the Wyrdkeys were wielded by a conquering demon race that had warped them into three tools of such mighty power that they'd been hidden for thousands of years and nearly wiped from memory. Queen Maeve of the Fae. Maeve knew everything—as was expected when you were older than dirt.

So the first step of her stupid, foolish plan had been simple: seek out Maeve, get answers about how to destroy the Wyrdkeys, and then return to Adarlan.

It was the least she could do. For Nehemia—for . . . a lot of other people. There was nothing left in her, not really. Only ash and an abyss and the unbreakable vow she'd carved into her flesh, to the friend who had seen her for what she truly was.

When they had docked at the largest port city in Wendlyn, she couldn't help but admire the caution the ship took while coming to shore—waiting until a moonless night, then stuffing Celaena and the other refugee women from Adarlan in the galley while navigating the secret channels through the barrier reef. It was understandable: the reef was the main defense keeping Adarlan's legions from these shores. It was also part of her mission here as the King's Champion.

That was the other task lingering in the back of her mind: to find a way to keep the king from executing Chaol or Nehemia's family. He'd promised to do it should she fail in her mission to retrieve Wendlyn's naval defense plans and assassinate its king and prince at their annual midsummer ball. But she'd shoved all those thoughts aside when they'd docked and the refugee women had been herded ashore for processing by the port's officials.

Many of the women were scarred inside and out, their eyes gleaming with echoes of whatever horrors had befallen them in Adarlan. So even after she'd vanished from the ship during the chaos of docking, she'd lingered on a nearby rooftop while the women were escorted into a building—to find homes and employment. Yet Wendlyn's officials could later bring them to a quiet part of the city and do whatever they wanted. Sell them. Hurt them. They were refugees: unwanted and without any rights. Without any voice.

But she hadn't lingered merely from paranoia. No—Nehemia would have remained to ensure they were safe. Realizing that, Celaena had wound up on the road to the capital as soon as she was certain the women were all right. Learning how to infiltrate the castle was merely something to occupy her time while she decided how to execute the first steps of her plan. While she tried to stop thinking about Nehemia.

It had all been fine—fine and easy. Hiding in the little woods and barns along the way, she passed like a shadow through the countryside.

Wendlyn. A land of myths and monsters—of legends and nightmares made flesh.

The kingdom itself was a spread of warm, rocky sand and thick forest, growing ever greener as hills rolled inland and sharpened into towering peaks. The coast and the land around the capital were dry, as if the sun had baked all but the hardiest vegetation. Vastly different from the soggy, frozen empire she'd left behind.

A land of plenty, of opportunity, where men didn't just take what they wanted, where no doors were locked and people smiled at you in the streets. But she didn't particularly care if someone did or didn't smile at her—no, as the days wore on, she found it suddenly very difficult to bring herself to care about anything at all. Whatever determination, whatever rage, whatever *anything* she'd felt upon leaving Adarlan had ebbed away, devoured by the nothingness that now gnawed at her.

It was four days before Celaena spotted the massive capital city built across the foothills. Varese, the city where her mother had been born; the vibrant heart of the kingdom.

While Varese was cleaner than Rifthold and had plenty of wealth spread between the upper and lower classes, it was a capital city all the same, with slums and back alleys, whores and gamblers—and it hadn't taken too long to find its underbelly.

On the street below, three of the market guards paused to chat, and Celaena rested her chin on her hands. Like every guard in this kingdom, each was clad in light armor and bore a good number of weapons.

Rumor claimed the Wendlynite soldiers were trained by the Fae to be ruthless and cunning and swift. And she didn't want to know if that was true, for about a dozen different reasons. They certainly seemed a good deal more observant than the average Rifthold sentry—even if they hadn't yet noticed the assassin in their midst. But these days, Celaena knew the only threat she posed was to herself.

Even baking in the sun each day, even washing up whenever she could in one of the city's many fountain-squares, she could still feel Archer Finn's blood soaking her skin, into her hair. Even with the constant noise and rhythm of Varese, she could still hear Archer's groan as she gutted him in that tunnel beneath the castle. And even with the wine and heat, she could still see Chaol, horror contorting his face at what he'd learned about her Fae heritage and the monstrous power that could easily destroy her, about how hollow and dark she was inside.

She often wondered whether he'd figured out the riddle she'd told him on the docks of Rifthold. And if he had discovered the truth . . . Celaena never let herself get that far. Now wasn't the time for thinking about Chaol, or the truth, or any of the things that had left her soul so limp and weary.

Celaena tenderly prodded her split lip and frowned at the market guards, the movement making her mouth hurt even more. She'd deserved that particular blow in the brawl she'd provoked in last night's taberna—she'd kicked a man's balls into his throat, and when he'd caught his breath, he'd been enraged, to say the least. Lowering her hand from her mouth, she observed the guards for a few moments. They didn't take bribes from the merchants, or bully or threaten with fines like the guards and officials in Rifthold. Every official and soldier she'd seen so far had been similarly . . . good.

The same way Galan Ashryver, Crown Prince of Wendlyn, was good.

Dredging up some semblance of annoyance, Celaena stuck out her tongue. At the guards, at the market, at the hawk on the nearby chimney, at the castle and the prince who lived inside it. She wished that she had not run out of wine so early in the day.

It had been a week since she'd figured out how to infiltrate the castle, three days after arriving in Varese itself. A week since that horrible day when all her plans crumbled around her.

A cooling breeze pushed past, bringing with it the spices from the vendors lining the nearby street—nutmeg, thyme, cumin, lemon verbena. She inhaled deeply, letting the scents clear her sun-and-wine-addled head. The pealing of bells floated down from one of the neighboring mountain towns, and in some square of the city, a minstrel band struck up a merry midday tune. Nehemia would have loved this place.

That fast, the world slipped, swallowed up by the abyss that now lived within her. Nehemia would never see Wendlyn. Never wander through the spice market or hear the mountain bells. A dead weight pressed on Celaena's chest.

It had seemed like such a perfect plan when she'd arrived in Varese. In the hours she'd spent figuring out the royal castle's defenses, she'd debated how she'd find Maeve to learn about the keys. It had all been going smoothly, flawlessly, until . . .

Until that gods-damned day when she'd noted how the guards left a hole in their defense in the southern wall every afternoon at two o'clock, and grasped how the gate mechanism operated. Until Galan Ashryver had come riding out through those gates, in full view of where she'd been perched on the roof of a nobleman's house.

It hadn't been the sight of him, with his olive skin and dark hair, that had stopped her dead. It hadn't been the fact that, even from a distance, she could see his turquoise eyes—*her* eyes, the reason she usually wore a hood in the streets.

No. It had been the way people cheered.

Cheered for him, their prince. Adored him, with his dashing smile and his light armor gleaming in the endless sun, as he and the soldiers behind him rode toward the north coast to continue blockade running. *Blockade running.* The prince—her target—was a gods-damned blockade runner against Adarlan, and his people *loved* him for it.

She'd trailed the prince and his men through the city, leaping from rooftop to rooftop, and all it would have taken was one arrow through those turquoise eyes and he would have been dead. But she followed him all the way to the city walls, the cheers growing louder, people tossing flowers, everyone beaming with pride for their perfect, perfect prince.

She'd reached the city gates just as they opened to let him through. And when Galan Ashryver rode off into the sunset, off to war and glory and to fight for good and freedom, she lingered on that roof until he was a speck in the distance.

Then she had walked into the nearest taberna and gotten into the bloodiest, most brutal brawl she'd ever provoked, until the city guard was called in and she vanished moments before everyone was tossed into the stocks. And then she had decided, as her nose bled down the front of her shirt and she spat blood onto the cobblestones, that she wasn't going to do *anything*.

There was no point to her plans. Nehemia and Galan would have led the world to freedom, and Nehemia should have been breathing. Together the prince and princess could have defeated the King of Adarlan. But Nehemia was dead, and Celaena's vow—her stupid, pitiful vow—was worth as much as mud when there were beloved heirs like Galan who could do so much more. She'd been a fool to make that vow.

Even Galan—Galan was barely making a dent against Adarlan, and he had an entire armada at his disposal. She was one person, one complete waste of life. If Nehemia hadn't been able to stop the king . . . then that plan, to find a way to contact Maeve . . . that plan was absolutely useless.

Mercifully, she still hadn't seen one of the Fae—not a single damn one—or the faeries, or even a lick of magic. She'd done her best to avoid it. Even before she'd spotted Galan, she'd kept away from the market stalls that offered everything from healing to trinkets to potions, areas that were usually also full of street performers or mercenaries trading their gifts to earn a living. She'd learned which tabernas the magic-wielders liked to frequent and never went near them. Because sometimes she felt a trickling, writhing *thing* awaken in her gut if she caught a crackle of its energy.

It had been a week since she'd given up her plan and abandoned any attempt to care at all. And she suspected it'd be many weeks more before she decided she was truly sick of teggya, or brawling every night just to feel something, or guzzling sour wine as she lay on rooftops all day.

But her throat was parched and her stomach was grumbling, so Celaena slowly peeled herself off the edge of the roof. Slowly, not because of those vigilant guards, but rather because her head was well and truly spinning. She didn't trust herself to care enough to prevent a tumble.

She glared at the thin scar stretching across her palm as she shimmied down the drainpipe and into the alley off the market street. It was now nothing more than a reminder of the pathetic promise she'd made at Nehemia's half-frozen grave over a month ago, and of everything and everyone else she'd failed. Just like her amethyst ring, which she gambled away every night and won back before sunrise.

Despite all that had happened, and Chaol's role in Nehemia's death, even after she'd destroyed what was between them, she hadn't been able to forfeit his ring. She'd lost it thrice now in card games, only to get it back—by whatever means necessary. A dagger poised to slip between the ribs usually did a good deal more convincing than actual words.

Celaena supposed it was a miracle she made it down to the alley, where the shadows momentarily blinded her. She braced a hand on the cool stone wall, letting her eyes adjust, willing her head to stop spinning. A mess—she was a gods-damned mess. She wondered when she'd bother to stop being one.

The tang and reek of the woman hit Celaena before she saw her. Then wide, yellowed eyes were in her face, and a pair of withered, cracked lips parted to hiss, "Slattern! Don't let me catch you in front of my door again!"

Celaena pulled back, blinking at the vagrant woman—and at her door, which . . . was just an alcove in the wall, crammed with rubbish and what had to be sacks of the woman's belongings. The woman herself was hunched, her hair unwashed and teeth a ruin of stumps. Celaena blinked again, the woman's face coming into focus. Furious, half-mad, and filthy.

Celaena held up her hands, backing away a step, then another. "Sorry."

The woman spat a wad of phlegm onto the cobblestones an inch from Celaena's dusty boots. Failing to muster the energy to be disgusted or furious, Celaena would have walked away had she not glimpsed herself as she raised her dull gaze from the glob.

Dirty clothes—stained and dusty and torn. Not to mention, she smelled *atrocious*, and this vagrant woman had mistaken her for . . . for a fellow vagrant, competing for space on the streets.

Well. Wasn't that just *wonderful*. An all-time low, even for her. Perhaps it'd be funny one day, if she bothered to remember it. She couldn't recall the last time she'd laughed.

At least she could take some comfort in knowing that it couldn't get worse.

But then a deep male voice chuckled from the shadows behind her.

The man—male—down the alley was Fae.

After ten years, after all the executions and burnings, a Fae male was prowling toward her. Pure, solid Fae. There was no escaping him as he emerged from the shadows yards away. The vagrant in the alcove and the others along the alley fell so quiet Celaena could again hear those bells ringing in the distant mountains.

Tall, broad-shouldered, every inch of him seemingly corded with muscle, he was a male blooded with power. He paused in a dusty shaft of sunlight, his silver hair gleaming.

As if his delicately pointed ears and slightly elongated canines weren't enough to scare the living shit out of everyone in that alley, including the now-whimpering madwoman behind Celaena, a wicked-looking tattoo was etched down the left side of his harsh face, the whorls of black ink stark against his sun-kissed skin.

The markings could easily have been decorative, but she still remembered enough of the Fae language to recognize them as words, even in such an artistic rendering. Starting at his temple, the tattoo flowed over his jaw and down his neck, where it disappeared beneath the pale surcoat and cloak he wore. She had a feeling the markings continued down the rest of him, too, concealed along with at least half a dozen weapons. As she reached into her cloak for her own hidden dagger, she realized he might have been handsome were it not for the promise of violence in his pine-green eyes.

It would have been a mistake to call him young—just as it would have been a mistake to call him anything but a warrior, even without the sword strapped across his back and the vicious knives at his sides. He moved with lethal grace and surety, scanning the alley as if he were walking onto a killing field.

The hilt of the dagger was warm in her hand, and Celaena adjusted her stance, surprised to be feeling—fear. And enough of it that it cleared the heavy fog that had been clouding her senses these past few weeks.

The Fae warrior stalked down the alley, his knee-high leather boots silent on the cobblestones. Some of the loiterers shrank back; some bolted for the sunny street, to random doorways, anywhere to escape his challenging stare.

Celaena knew before his sharp eyes met hers that he was here for her, and who had sent him.

She reached for her Eye amulet, startled to find it was no longer around her neck. She'd given it to Chaol—the only bit of protection she could grant him upon leaving. He'd probably thrown it away as soon as he figured out the truth. Then he could go back to the haven of being her enemy. Maybe he'd tell Dorian, too, and the pair of them would both be safe.

Before she could give in to the instinct to scuttle back up the drainpipe and onto the roof, she considered the plan she'd abandoned. Had some god remembered she existed and decided to throw her a bone? She'd needed to see Maeve.

Well, here was one of Maeve's elite warriors. Ready. Waiting.

And from the vicious temper emanating from him, not entirely happy about it.

The alley remained as still as a graveyard while the Fae warrior surveyed her. His nostrils flared delicately, as if he were—

He was getting a whiff of her scent.

She took some small satisfaction in knowing she smelled horrific, but it wasn't that smell he was reading. No, it was the scent that marked her as *her*—the smell of her lineage and blood and what and who she was. And if he said her name in front of these people . . . then she knew that Galan Ashryver would come running home. The guards would be on high alert, and *that* was not part of her plan at all.

The bastard looked likely to do such a thing, just to prove who was in charge. So she summoned her energy as best she could and sauntered over to him, trying to remember what she might have done months ago, before the world had gone to hell. "Well met, my friend," she purred. "Well met, indeed."

She ignored the shocked faces around them, focusing solely on sizing him up. He stood with a stillness that only an immortal could achieve. She willed her heartbeat and breathing to calm. He could probably hear them, could probably smell every emotion raging through her. There'd be no fooling him with bravado, not in a thousand years. He'd probably lived that long already. Perhaps there'd be no beating him, either. She was Celaena Sardothien, but he was a Fae warrior and had likely been one for a great while.

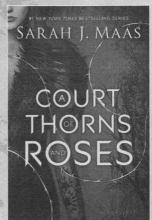

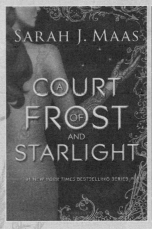

Josh Wasserman

SARAH J. MAAS is the #1 *New York Times* and internationally bestselling author of the young adult series Throne of Glass and A Court of Thorns and Roses, as well as her upcoming adult series, Crescent City. Her books are published in over thirty-six languages. A New York native, Sarah lives near Philadelphia with her husband, son, and dog.

www.sarahjmaas.com
facebook.com/worldofsarahjmaas
instagram.com/therealsjmaas